Nothing Has Ever Felt Like This

Also by Mary B. Morrison

Somebody's Gotta Be On Top

He's Just a Friend

Never Again Once More

Soul Mates Dissipate

Who's Making Love

Justice, Just Us Just Me

Nothing Has Ever Felt Like This

MARY B. MORRISON

KENSINGTON PUBLISHING CORP.
http://www.kensingtonbooks.com

DAFINA BOOKS are published by

Kensington Publishing Corp.
850 Third Avenue
New York, NY 10022

ISBN 0-7582-0728-X

First Hardcover Printing: August 2005
First Trade Paperback Printing: July 2006
10 9 8 7 6 5 4 3 2 1

Printed in the United States of America

Dedicated to three women of distinction.

Karen Thomas, my editor,

Joan Schulhafer, my publicist,

Claudia Menza, my agent.

PREFACE

Soul Mates Dissipate, Never Again Once More, He's Just a Friend, Somebody's Gotta Be On Top, Nothing Has Ever Felt like This, and my next two novels, *When Somebody Loves You Back* and *Our Little Secret* are intertwined. I recommend, if possible, reading the series in the order listed above. Hopefully the brief background below will help the reader better understand the characters' connections. To preview an excerpt of each novel, visit www.marymorrison.com.

Soul Mates Dissipate is, for now, the beginning. This page-turning drama takes you on a journey with Jada Diamond Tanner and Wellington Jones, aka . . . soul mates. Wellington's mother, Cynthia Jones—who has a history of her own with her sister Katherine, friend Susan, and ex-lover Keith—secretly despises Jada. Cynthia invites a sexy, single woman, Melanie Marie Thompson, to live with Wellington, with the hopes of sabotaging Wellington's engagement to Jada.

Never Again Once More, the sequel to *Soul Mates Dissipate,* spans twenty years into the lives of Jada and Wellington. Darius Jones, Jada's son, is born and matures to twenty years of age. Before the end of this story, Jada appoints Darius as executive vice president of her company. Immediately Darius takes advantage of the fringe benefit by having sex with four of his mother's top-level directors.

In *He's Just a Friend*, Fancy Taylor is a beautiful but not so brilliant woman on the move to conquer a rich husband by any means necessary. Along her journey she'll meet several male friends, some of whom become foes, and eventually Fancy meets Jada's son, Darius Jones.

In *Somebody's Gotta Be On Top*, regardless of the situation, Darius Jones is always on top. His motto, "If it doesn't make money, it doesn't make sense," includes the women in his life. That is, until he meets Fancy Taylor.

In *Nothing Has Ever Felt Like This*, will Fancy Taylor outsmart Darius Jones for his money? Or will Fancy fall in love with Darius? What happens when two people love so deeply, they're willing to die for, with, and because of one another? By the end of their story, Darius and Fancy will learn the true meaning of love.

In *When Somebody Loves You Back*, death has a way of making people appreciate life. Which one of your favorite characters will die? Will Jada take Wellington back? Or does Jada sign divorce papers? Why did Melanie mysteriously disappear? Who humbles Darius? Will Fancy marry Darius or Desmond? Will Darius marry Fancy or Ashlee? Can Tyronne remain faithful to SaVoy? Or does marriage bore Tyronne after SaVoy helps him establish a successful business? Now that Candice has earned millions writing and selling screenplays based on her friends' lives, spiced up her lifestyle, and thrown away all of her conservative clothing, will Terrell ask for a divorce and half of Candice's empire? Will Darius kill Candice for publicizing his personal life on the big screen? Or does Candice's movie production catapult Darius's celebrity status to a higher level? This novel gives closure to all the main characters in the series, except Cynthia Elaine Jones.

In *Our Little Secret,* if you've read each novel, as I mentioned before, Cynthia Jones has a history so moving, trust me, her story will be worth the wait. Cynthia's story creates the beginning and concludes the end of the seven-book series.

After Cynthia's novel, *Our Little Secret,* I know I promised not to keep you waiting for *Kiss Me: Now Tell Me You Love Me,* a chilling drama about Harrison and Angela Gray, but my new characters Destiny, Brenda, Shay, Trevor, Malcolm, and Larry have spoken to me and claimed my next series entitled: *Dicktation.* The Dicktation series, set in my hometown of New Orleans—known as the city that care forgot—explores the wildest sexual fantasies imaginable while conquering some of the most difficult relationship challenges. Ladies, if you thought you wanted a southern man, wait until you read this series. Men, if you've ever wondered if southern women practice voodoo, you'll find out. Here's a tip: Never kiss before you smell.

ACKNOWLEDGMENTS

There is interconnectedness amongst people. Everybody needs somebody and everyone should have a personal relationship with his or her God. No one person becomes successful without the assistance of family, friends, and others whom are often unknown contributors.

When I order food at a drive-through or dine at restaurants, I'm thankful that someone prepares and delivers the meal. Wherever I use a public rest room, I'm pleased when it's clean. I appreciate the support and dedication exhibited by booksellers, readers, writers, editors, publicists, agents, parents, coaches, students, airline personnel, bankers, brokers, teachers, janitors, sanitation engineers, policemen, firemen, war veterans, military enlistees, doctors, lawyers, entrepreneurs, et cetera. To each of you I say "thanks" for your contributions to our society and, "Please use your skills, talents, and education for the betterment of mankind, for we all shall perish but let's cherish one another while we exist on this planet called earth."

I've never written a book without expressing gratitude for my family and I never will. In loving memory of my biological parents, Joseph Henry Morrison and Elester Noel. To my deceased great aunt and uncle, who reared me, Willie Frinkle and Ella Beatrice Turner, I love you.

To my loving son, Jesse Byrd, Jr., I love you, and remember, now that you're living on your own in college, there are times to practice, study, and make sacrifices for your future, and there are opportunities to chill, date, and simply have fun. Remain a wise man and never confuse the two or you will fall short of maximizing your potential. I'm proud of you, sweetie. You are truly a wonderful young man with great character and you are Mommy's most cherished gift from God.

To my siblings, I love you guys immensely: Wayne, Derrick, Andrea, and Regina Morrison, Margie Rickerson, and Debra Noel. A special thanks to Angela Dionne Davis, my niece who faithfully reads each of my novels and blesses me with sharing her candid thoughts. Each of my siblings has wonderful spouses whom have also supported me over the years. Thanks to Angela Lewis-Morrison, John Ferguson, Dannette Morrison, Roland Johnson, and Desi Rickerson.

Shannette Slaughter, Barbara Cooper, Carmen Polk, Gloria Mallette, E. Lynn Harris, Mary Monroe, Carl Weber, Victoria Christopher Murray, Kim Roby, Ruth and Howard Kees, Vanessa Ibanitoru, Brenda and Aaron, Lillie Zinnerman, Erma Harris, Geri Henson, Daisy Davis, and my McDonogh No. 35 Roneagles family, thanks for your continued support.

To my entire Kensington family: Joan, Karen, Jessica, Mary, Maureen, Nicole, Steven Zacharius, and Barbara Bennett, I am grateful for all you do.

Felicia Polk, you are my friend and the world's greatest publicist, thanks for believing in me. Much love to my man Curtis Webster. I have so many more people to acknowledge but I also have other books to write, so if I didn't mention you this time, forgive me now, remind me later.

Who Do You Love

How do you know when you're in love

Is it the butterflies
Or when you ask yourself why
Why do you settle
Why won't you leave

When your lover pushes you away
You beg to stay
Life without your partner
You don't want to breathe
Or live
Or give
Some stranger a chance
To recycle your heart
You know
The part
You've already given to someone else

Is that love

Your heart beats to the rhythm of your lover's drum
Suddenly there is silence
Echoing in your mind
But who stopped drumming

How do you know when you're in love

When you are not
But you want to be
But infidelity
Then you don't care for me
Like you used to
Because you don't do . . .
You know
The things I do
To show you care
Or is it the way you feel
When the other one is not there

I miss you

Or is love an illusion in your mind
Created to share
The emotions you bare
But how do know when you're in love
Is it simply because you say you care

I love you too

Is it the way you speak
Or the way you stroke
A piece
Of your mate's anatomy
Evoking pleasure
Beyond measure

Is that love
Or lust
That cums through the guts
And explodes from the nuts
Showering seeds of life
The way you like
Making you feel real good

Like when Stephanie Mills melodically sings
"Baby, I feel good all over"

But do you discharge
Or discard
Then disregard
The lifeline that connects
The two
When the shower is neither
For nor from you

Or do you forgive
Forget
Or move on to the next ex
With your heart not your head
Anyone can share a bed
But can you sleep in the one you've made
Or do you simply change the sheets
And wait for the next pair of feet
To walk its way into your heart

Suddenly the beat of the drum stops again
You gasp for air
From someone who truly cares
For you

How do know when you're in love

How do you show the intangible
Master of faith
Which masturbates
In the mind, heart, and soul

Do you hold
Your lover accountable
Insurmountable

To your standards
And measures
Of love
Or do you surrender
To the contender
Or are you a pretender

How do you know when you're in love

You don't
You see love is but a vision
Of what one desires to have
To hold
And sometimes to be

Love unfolds
In time
First within the heart
Then within your mind
Because you cannot separate
The ying from the yang

Ain't that some shit
You're called a bastard or a bitch
Then hit with an invisible fist
Filled with anger, hate, and envy
But here's the trick
Where is the click
Or flip of the switch
Or changing of the script
It's kinda sad when
Your heart doesn't even know when to quit
Or how to sit
And simply be quiet

How do you know when you're in love

It's not when you set someone free
Excuse me your majesty
But you cannot possess
That which does not belong to thee
You see lovers are not property

So what if you've tied the knots
Of forget me nots
To have and to hold
Until death do you part
Well that sounds smart
Or clever
Whateva
But love does not require a signature
Or license
Or a spoken word
No nouns
No people
No actions
No verbs

How do you know when you are in love

It's simple
When you're willing to give
The life you live
The ultimate price
Sacrifice
Love does not lie
True love is when you are willing to die
In order to let someone else live

Who do you love

GET REAL WITH THE SPIRIT WITHIN YOU

Do you believe in magic? The power of the spirit? Do you have faith? Or do you believe in your God? Intangible things that you cannot see, do they exist? Love. Truth. Respect. If so, where? How about the presence of a deceased loved one? Does he or she speak to you? If you believe in any of the above then my next question is, "Do you believe in yourself?"

Before you answer, respond to these questions. Do you suppress the spirit within you? Do you allow others to use you? Abuse you? Disrespect you? Are you oblivious to your self-worth? How much are you worth? Seriously. Are you afraid to take a risk? Live your dreams? Fall in love? Show someone you care? Are you unhappy more than you're happy?

If you've answered yes to any of the questions in the aforementioned paragraph, I want you to do this. Every day for the rest of your life, look into your soul. If you have the gift of sight—it is genuinely a gift—stare into your eyes in a mirror until you can see yourself beyond the physical. If you are blind, and many people with vision cannot see, allow your spirit to search your soul.

Say aloud to yourself, "I love me more than I love anyone else." Repeat these words until you believe them. Why? Because people who truly love themselves do not allow others to use, mistreat, or abuse them. I'm not suggesting that you won't be hurt mentally, physically, spiritually, or emotionally. What I am saying is that you will begin to recognize the early warning signs of negative people who consciously and sometimes unconsciously inflect pain upon you. You will determine the individuals who remain an intimate part of your life and those you need to sever ties with and move on.

Then you must stand in your own truth. Not denial, but truth. Get real with the spirit within you. The simplest way to express yourself to those who attempt to hurt you is to gently respond with these kind words, "I love me more than I love you. Therefore, I will not create, perpetuate, nor allow your unacceptable behavior. I'm not saying I don't love you because I do. But if you love me, too, then I need for you to respect and hear me."

Your partner should be your lover, your friend, and your confidant. Your friends should simply be your friends. Not your boss, or your dictator, or your oppressor. Be careful that you are not the culprit of your demise. More often than not people initiate their own problems through cultivating bad habits and/or accepting adverse behavior.

You may have to speak the above words or something similar several times before the person understands you. Change takes time but your actions must reflect your words. Whether you are on your job or in your home, speak calmly in your moments of frustration and despair. Remember, anger generates hostility. Be at peace and become one with the love inside of you. For only you can make manifest your destiny.

If you don't remember anything else I've said, do not forget these words sung best by the late, great Aaliyah, "At your best you are love." Know that those words apply to your spirit within. It is true. At your best you are love. Don't give away your power. You don't need approval to know you are wonderful. If a positive change in your life is to come, personal growth has to come not from you but through you.

And so it is

CHAPTER 1

A woman didn't have to stand on the corner to become a prostitute. All women at some point in their lives have exchanged pussy for goods and services. The best tricksters could barter for homes, cars, diamonds, furs, and enough cash to maintain a five-figure bank account. The unsophisticated females, oblivious to how much men would pay to bust a nut or have their dicks sucked, were happy with a movie, a meal, and a few lies about how much the man loved her. The naïve chicken-heads came out of their pockets with top dollars, leasing their showcase men, not realizing that gigolos were always on auction awaiting the next highest bidder. No matter what the circumstances or consequences were: Men needed to get laid. Women wanted to get paid.

"Females! Fuck!" Darius yelled, thrusting his fist, parting the gushing water with the force of his hand. Starting the new year masturbating in the shower wasn't his idea of pleasurable sex but it was safe. At least he didn't have to worry about allegedly getting another feline pregnant. Tricksters spelled financial security *b-a-b-y*.

"The next female kickin' it with me better not have the word *baby* in her vocabulary," Darius said aloud to himself, massaging his dick under the water. "Darius, please, baby, just put it in one more time. Baby, don't leave, I'm not finished cumming yet. Oh, baby, your dick is so good," Darius mimicked. "Please, baby, please my ass." Stroking his dick with each syllable, Darius said, "I'll beat my shit every day befo' I get suckered in by another leeching-ass woman."

Warm streams of water, pounding against Darius's muscular neck and shoulders, drenched his locks. Darius admired his caramel reflection illuminated by candlelight, dancing on the glass shower door. Massaging the creamy body wash into his well-defined chest, Darius's hand slid along the crevices in his abdomen, over his inward navel, then teased his curly dark chocolate pubic hairs. Cupping his balls, Darius squeezed his nuts, watching his dick grow longer.

"Damn! Women are straight up scandalous."

Didn't matter if the fe-fe was a VP, VIP, stay-at-home wife, his wife, his sister, a lover, an employee, an associate, a groupie, a counterpart, smart, fine, dumb, ugly, dumb and ugly, a model, a hooker, a Christian, his best friend, or his mother. The one thing Darius knew women shared in common was placing an invisible price tag on their pussies.

"If I give you some, what you gon' do for me?" Undercover prostitutes in denial, like he owed them something. If anyone was getting paid, it should've been him. Hell, Darius did most of the work most of the time. Darius didn't mind working for his, but the lazy females were history. The next woman he met had to be physically fit, no exceptions. Females unable to ride Slugger for five minutes straight without falling off or holding on had to get up off of his dick and out of his bed. Surely he'd cum within five minutes, and if she didn't get hers, oh well, she could work for it or take her lazy ass to a gym and learn how to work it out.

Women were simple and Darius didn't mean in a basic kinda way. Ignorant. Shysters. Dick-headhunters. The sweeter the pussy, the higher the ransom: Husband Wanted, Medical Benefits Needed, Rent Overdue, Children Gotta Eat, Desire a Trip to Paris, Pussy Needs Recreational Lickin' and Stickin' While Man Is Away.

And the tag lines were consistent: "Here's my number, Darius, call me on my cell. Hit me on e-mail, Daddy. Oh, what the hell, you can come on over to my place." On the first date? Damn! But if all he wanted to do was hit it, Darius was down for banging a female's cranium against the headboard so hard that he cared less about re-membering her first, last, or nickname, never taking her public, and never seeing or calling her again. The easier the woman, the cheaper the pussy. Cheap pussy was not on his list of chicks to do. Some females—just because he was rich—were so dumb, they'd do anything to lay with him. Those were the ones who got nada, noth-ing, zilch.

Darius's large thick fingers and manicured nails wrapped snug-gly around his slippery shaft as his dick penetrated an imaginary womb. "Aw, yes. Make your pussy suck this dick, gurl," Darius moaned, daydreaming about the one woman he was in love with. Ashlee.

With numerous hidden agendas, women, including Ashlee, re-fused to have sex when they were mad, teased him with sex if they were interested, and gladly fucked him unconscious whenever he surrendered his money or his time. But when Darius treated a woman like a whore, even if she was a ho, that was when her ass transformed into a black widow—fucking, devouring, then killing him—defacing his personal property, determined to strip him of his dignity, cash, or whatever else she could sap out of him, all in exchange for pussy and sometimes bad pussy. Like his wife, Ciara.

"*Huuhhh,*" Darius exhaled, releasing his grip. "I'm not wasting an orgasm on feline frustrations. I'll probably fuck around and im-pregnate some sewer animal."

Layering his wet skin with baby oil then toweling dry, Darius cov-ered his locks with a terrycloth silk-lined cap, sprawled his naked flesh atop his oversized king comforter, then clamped his hands behind his head, gazing in the mirrored ceiling and admiring his sexy body.

"Damn, you look good, boy-ie."

Darius's sexy physique and manly facial features were a blessing and a curse. It wasn't Darius's fault women couldn't resist surren-dering their pussies to him, but unfortunately their troubles had become his. Today was one of those rare days Darius didn't feel like doing a goddamn thing. Seeing anybody. Talking to no damn body on the phone. Not even his mother. Especially, not his mom.

After all he'd been through last year, almost losing his life in a fire that destroyed his business, and supposedly getting three women pregnant, his mom had the audacity to exacerbate his problems and side with his stepfather, insisting he, Darius Jones, the only child of a self-made millionaire woman, Jada Diamond Tanner, sole owner of Black Diamonds, get a job? What a joke.

Taking in the entire view of his lean six-foot-seven, two hundred twenty pounds stretched atop the royal blue and gold suede comforter—the colors that represented his future college, UCLA—Darius closed his eyes and prayed.

"Dear God, I know I don't deserve Your mercy, but as Your child, I have Your permission to ask. Right? Please, Lord, please send me a sign that those unborn children aren't mine. I'm still a kid at heart myself and, well, Lord, honestly I'm not ready to be a father. Yes, I know You spared me from contracting HIV from my ex-fiancée, Maxine. And yes, You did deliver me from almost committing suicide when I thought I had HIV. And I'm so grateful you've given me an opportunity to play professional basketball. Well, almost. So You can see with so many positive things in my future, there's no way I can deal with any negativity. Thank you, Jesus, for listening. But as I lie here today, needing You again, Lord, I beg You to deliver me once more, from having to get a job, deliver me from being broke, and please Lord, please deliver me from being a father. Amen."

Darius's grandma, Ma Dear, had taught him how to pray for what he wanted. That God answered prayers. Well, right now, lying in the midst of loneliness, Darius certainly hoped Ma Dear was right when she'd said, "No matter how down you get, pray. And don't forget to pray when God blesses you with good fortune, my child, because just like the Lord giveth, the Lord also taketh away. God is forgiving. But you can't outsmart Him." Yeah, Pastor Tellings had spoken those same words New Year's Eve while Darius sat in church on the back pew next to a fine woman.

Tears escaped Darius's closed eyelids, rolled down his temples and into his ears. The only woman Darius respected was dead. Ma Dear, no matter how upsetting, always kept things real by telling him the truth. So why didn't Ma Dear tell him that Wellington wasn't his biological dad? But Ma Dear had never said that Wellington was his father. Cupping his hands over his face, Darius wished his grandmother was alive. "Oh, shit." The side of the bed beside him moved slightly. Lifting his head, Darius saw an imprint in his mattress next to his torso.

"Couldn't be," Darius thought, laying his head on the pillow. "Chill out man. Stop trippin'. It's all good. Ma Dear, if you're here, I need you."

Ma Dear had also told him, "Never kick a man while he's down." Darius wished those words would've held true for him last year when he was hospitalized.

Through watery eyes, Darius gazed at his ceiling, vividly recalling the night he was incapacitated—the night his life changed for the worse—when his stepdad Wellington stood over his hospital bed preaching, "Son, lie back down. The only thing you're going to do right now is listen to us. We've decided that the money we loaned you must be repaid by the end of the year. And since we already know you can't afford to repay us, we're taking over your company. And you can't work for us, son. You're going to have to get a job. Working for someone else."

Wellington was twisted. Confused. Who in hell did Wellington think he was talking down to. Instantly Darius had rebelled and said, "Oh, hell no!" then pleaded with his mother, "Ma! You can't let him do this!"

What a joke. Standing in his hospital room, Moms didn't say a word that night, so Wellington had continued his soliloquy, "Son, you don't respect your mother. You don't respect me. You don't respect your wife. You don't even respect yourself. So why should we contribute to you using other people? We won't. Never again. And if you don't get a job, we're taking your name out of our will. You'll inherit nothing."

What made Wellington a sanctified authority on Darius's behavior? Judging Darius when Wellington should've been confessing the affair he was having to Darius's mother. But Moms wasn't any better than Wellington. They deserved one another. That same night at the hospital Wellington couldn't leave the conversation alone. No, seemed like he was just getting warmed up.

Wellington had insisted, "Darius, you owe Lawrence an apology for misleading Ashlee."

Misleading Ashlee? Darius had thought, lying in that hospital bed and glancing over at Ashlee, who was lying in the hospital bed across from him. Ashlee's second-degree face wound was wrapped in bandages. Darius felt sorry for her wounds but he'd risked his life to save Ashlee. Seems as though he was one who deserved a thank you.

Besides, Ashlee wasn't a kid. She'd made her own decisions. At first Ashlee didn't want to have sex with Darius because his mom had married Ashlee's dad, Lawrence. But, to Darius, their parents' commitment could never make Ashlee his biological sister, so Darius explained to Ashlee, after they'd made love, that there was no incest.

Since Wellington wouldn't back the fuck up, Darius caved Wellington's chest in with backlash and replied, "Maybe your wife owes Lawrence an apology for aborting his baby."

Darius's mom stood there like she was the one shocked. But having aborted her ex-husband's baby when Lawrence never knew she was pregnant was wrong. Hell, just like his mom had waited over twenty years to disclose that Wellington wasn't his biological father, maybe Darius's mother wasn't pregnant for Lawrence. Maybe she'd aborted Wellington's child. Darius's mother wasn't perfect, but she seemed innocent, so no one had ever questioned her motives, actions, or whereabouts. But Darius knew his mom never stopped fucking Wellington, even while she was married to Lawrence. Darius knew a lot of secrets his parents assumed he had no knowledge of. As screwed up as his life was at times, Darius didn't hate on other people, but if Wellington didn't stop trying to control him, Darius would tell his mother about Wellington's other woman. What a fucked-up world to live in when Darius couldn't trust anyone but himself.

As he picked up the remote and pressed a few buttons, Darius's circular bed elevated three feet above the hardwood floor then rotated one hundred and eighty degrees clockwise. He started to see if the indent in his bed was still adjacent to his side when unexpectedly, a damn near foot-long erection distracted him, so he blocked Ma Dear from his mind and began stroking his dick.

Darius didn't have a problem working for his mom again, holding down her executive VP position, or working for himself at the company his mother had given him, Somebody's Gotta Be on Top Enterprises. But Darius should've known his company was subject to takeover by his parents when they insisted on holding sixty-six and two-thirds percent ownership.

Now instead of organizing, funding, and producing film projects in Los Angeles, Darius was home alone in his Oakland mansion jacking off his frustrations. On the verge of cumming, Darius said, "Fuck this bullshit," pissed that his parents were jocking him to sign over the multi-million-dollar insurance claim check from when his office building burned to ashes.

Wellington already had plans to keep *all* of Darius's settlement money, expanding Wellington Jones and Associates' two office locations—Los Angeles and San Francisco—to include Somebody's Gotta Be on Top's two offices. While Darius was hospitalized, Wellington had secured three new film options for *Never Again Once More, He's Just a Friend,* and *Player Haters.* And Wellington had planned to take credit at the premiere for the release of Darius's first film, *Soul Mates Dissipate,* and stated, "If you find yourself a job, I might invite you to the premiere."

"Fuck him!" Darius yelled. "This is bullshit!" What a trip. What a goddamn trip.

Damn, Darius's dick was functioning independent of his brain. His dick was hot from the friction and hard as steel, ready to explode in his hand. Pumping Slugger several times, Darius slowed his pace to prolong his ejaculation.

"Fuck 'em! Treating me like some orphan and shit! I'd starve before kissing their asses or working for 'the man.' That's not how Darius Jones gets down. I'm a man. The man."

And that fine sistah Darius had met at church on New Year's Eve, what was her name, Fancy, yeah, Fancy Tyler or Taylor, or somethin' like that, she was all woman. Picturing sliding his dick between Fancy's nice, large, perky breasts with firm nipples beckoning him to suck 'em, Darius stroked faster.

Sexy, teasing cocoa complexion. Beautiful brown eyes. Immaculate physique. From her pedicure to the top of her head, Fancy was without question the most beautiful woman Darius had met. They'd make a great-looking couple. Darius had wanted to hit that pussy for almost a year, and he would be straight lyin' if he said he cared that Fancy was dating his boy Byron. She'd mentioned something about being single when they'd met so maybe she was no longer dating Byron. Either way, Darius wasn't trying to take Fancy from Byron, be her man, be her sponsor, marry her, or any ig'nant shit like that. Why did females take him seriously? He just wanted to bang her a time or two 'til the backed-up cum inside his balls rumbled through his big-ass nuts and blasted inside his jimmie, then he'd move on to the next female.

"Whoa!" Darius watched his thick white cum squirt in the air like a fountain, landing in the crevices of his stomach. "Wheew. Oh my gosh. Damn, that shit felt good." Massaging the semen into his balls, Darius's erection wouldn't subside, so he continued stroking his shaft. Forget Fancy, today wasn't a good day for anything except putting his life in order.

Three expecting women were liable for Darius's fucked-up mood: Ciara, Ashlee, and Desire. Ciara had it coming. Any woman who tried to date like a man could only blame herself for getting caught up in the game.

If Darius was lucky . . . Luck did have a way of protecting his ass from the dumb shit he'd done, but Darius hadn't been as fortunate since Ma Dear had died. Ma Dear was his foundation. His salvation. The edge of his bed moved again. Cool air swept his feet. Darius lifted his head to witness a different indentation only this time the imprint was at the edge of his bed, closer, seemingly holding his feet. Darius smiled.

Every man needed a woman that he cherished. If Ma Dear were alive instead of visiting him by spirit, Darius was positive she'd convince his mother to give him back his business. Death was inevitable and having his grandmother was impossible. Or so he'd thought until now. He knew she was there with him. Darius was a survivor but hopefully his mom wouldn't let him suffer much longer.

With a measly quarter of a million dollars in his combined accounts, Darius could sponge off of that until he started college at UCLA in the fall, about seven months from now. Around the same time all of those money-consuming brats were due to arrive, crying, eating, shitting, and sleeping all day long. Fortunately child-rearing was a woman's job. The only dependent Darius wanted to treasure was Ashlee.

Ashlee. Darius thought he could trust his stepsister. They shared everything from childhood memories to walking down the aisle in their parent's wedding, to a hospital room after they were injured, when Darius rescued Ashlee from the fire that Ciara had set in his office building. But when Ashlee's nurse handed Darius that small brown paper bag with a bottle of prenatal vitamins inside, prescribed for Ashlee Anderson, Darius had discovered Ashlee was carrying his child. Ashlee was the one woman who wouldn't fuck around on him.

"Huuhhh." Sighing heavily, Darius couldn't imagine another guy nibbling on Ashlee's pink nipples, gently kissing her small clit, or bringing Ashlee to a sweet, savory release of vaginal fluids that he'd grown to enjoy tasting. Narrowing his eyes, Darius couldn't envision another man's dick roaming inside Ashlee, spitting seeds inside his woman. No man could love a woman better than Darius. Leaning on his side, Darius held his dick at the base of his shaft, smiling. Slugger was nine and three-quarters of an inch long, four inches thick, skilled in pussy satisfaction, and certified triple platinum. A dick made to share.

Thinking of dicks, the corners of Darius's mouth retracted as he rolled onto his back. If his half brother Kevin hadn't stolen over a million dollars from his company . . . Well, the company wasn't his anymore, but that nigga had done righteous to get out of town overnight. Kevin wasn't slick. But Darius blamed himself for going against his main principle, to never trust anyone except himself. After Darius announced Kevin as his executive vice president at

Somebody's Gotta Be On Top, Kevin had gotten closer to Ashlee, and Darius had foolishly appointed Ashlee as his finance director. No woman would ever manage his money again. Kevin was clever enough not to steal any checks. Instead, he had copied one check then ordered duplicates.

Kevin had probably flown the red-eye back to Harlem to beg for that old janitorial position he'd had before working for Darius. Lots of shit fell apart last year, all in one day. That same night Kevin left L.A., Ashlee's father picked her up from the hospital in Los Angeles and flew her back with him to live in Dallas, like he was her knight in shining armor and shit. Darius hadn't seen nor spoken with Ashlee since that night because Lawrence kept answering her got damn phone. When would Lawrence realize he couldn't protect his grown-ass daughter from Slugger? No man could. With or without Lawrence's blessings, Darius would fulfill his desires of divorcing Ciara and marrying Ashlee.

Desire. Now that was a bitch who had a slither of faith so shallow it could effortlessly slide underneath the belly of a dead snake without touching a thing. Darius had been too drunk to remember to put on a condom and Desire had been too eager to claim her baby was from a twenty-two-year-old multimillionaire. Trickster. That's why she'd raced back to London, so Darius wouldn't confront her and make her have an abortion. Desire's baby probably wasn't his anyway. A one-night stand and a passion for hardcore sex was all they'd shared in common.

The way Desire circled the outside of Darius's asshole with her tongue, then tea-bagged his balls into her mouth before squatting down onto his thick chocolate bar as she wrapped her pussy muscles around his shaft, suctioning the cum from his nuts, made Darius yell her name twice, and that was a first. If he could remember all that shit, why couldn't he remember to wrap up Slugger?

Wait a minute. Sitting up in his bed, Darius suddenly recalled he had put on a condom. But it was nowhere in sight the next morning. "That trickster pulled my protection off." Otherwise how could she possibly be pregnant with his baby?

The hell with females. Darius decided to chill at his Oakland residence—his home away from his Los Angeles home—for a few more days until after his half brother's funeral. Darius didn't mean to sound as though he didn't give a damn about Darryl Junior, but oo-whee, Darius was relieved like a muthafucka when Kevin clarified that the Darryl who was shot and killed New Year's Eve wasn't their father.

Answering his phone New Year's Day, Darius had been ready to hang up as soon as he'd recognized Kevin's voice, then Kevin yelled, "Darryl's dead!"

Immediately Darius thought it was Darryl Senior, his father. The dad he'd never known. The dad who'd finally accepted responsibility for being his father. Darius was speechless.

"Man, you still there?" Kevin had asked.

Darius recalled whispering, "What happened?"

"On that corner, mein. Wrong place. Wrong time," Kevin had said, pronouncing man like he was ordering Chinese food.

"You mean D.J.? Not dad?"

"Yes, brother. Our brother. D.J."

Inhaling through his nostrils for what seemed to be a full sixty seconds, Darius's lungs had inflated. Slowly the warm air escaped his mouth. "Where are you?"

"Don't worry about me, mein. I gotta run. I'll see you at the funeral."

Darius was relieved because his biological dad, a former NBA All-Star, had become more of a friend than a father, and Darius was so happy to have Darryl Senior acknowledge him as his son.

Irrespective of age, every man needed his father just as much as his mother, if not more. And hearing his real dad say, "I love you, Son," allowed Darius to shed tears of forgiveness for Darryl Senior not being a part of his childhood. Now that Darius's funds were dwindling, and his mom and Wellington were trippin', Darius desperately needed Darryl's continued help. Darryl Senior had single-handedly gotten Darius the full basketball scholarship to UCLA with the promise of Darius entering the NBA draft within a year or two.

The lubricant had dried to a crust but Darius's dick was still swollen. He hadn't had sex in over a week. That was ridiculous.

"Let me call Fancy. I know we just met a few days ago but I need to bust this second nut before my balls erupt. All I really need is a warm, pulsating pussy. And since I'm in Oakland, based on proximity, Fancy happens to be option number one."

Lowering his bed, Darius retrieved Fancy's business card, which only contained her first name, e-mail address, and phone number, from his nightstand.

Fancy answered on the first ring. "Hello."

"Hey, Ladycat. What's up?"

"Who's this?" Fancy replied.

Yeah, right. Women. Like she didn't have caller ID. "Darius. You wanna hang for a minute?"

Fancy snapped, "I don't just hang. You need a destination. Call me back in five."

"Whateva nigga you talkin' to on the other line can wait. You've got a real man now."

"Apparently not, because a real man would respect my choice to call him back. Hold on."

"Yeah, she's no fool," Darius mumbled, waiting for Fancy to click back over.

"Hey, I apologize. I've had a pretty hectic day. I was just finishing up scheduling an interview for a job, and earlier I was surfing the employment section."

"Okay. That's cool, I guess," Darius said, pretending to be interested. "So when do you start work?"

"Who knows? You know how bad this job market is. I would've started at this property management company today if they'd offered a managerial position. Hey, maybe you can give me a job with your company. I've got great skills."

"Well, let me invite you over for a private screening. Who knows? Maybe I'll cast you in one of my films."

"Thanks, but I'm not that easy. I don't do bedside interviews. Besides, I already have plans. In fact, I need to start getting ready for my date, but if you'd like you can take me out this Saturday night and we can talk. Call me tomorrow. 'Bye, Darius."

"Talk?" Darius shook his head. "'Bye, Ladycat."

"By the way, I like that nickname. I'll keep it. Good-bye."

Ladycat was just like all the rest of the women except Darius knew Fancy wasn't independent. But she was a fool if she thought Darius would pay her bills and give her money like Byron. Kimberly Stokes was the only pussy Darius ever had paid or would pay for. Women. As he thought of tricksters, still holding the cordless in his hand, Darius's mom's name popped up on the caller ID.

Reluctantly, Darius answered. "Hi, Mom."

"Hi, sweetheart. How are you?"

"Depressed," Darius lied. "Can't believe my brother is actually dead. But," Darius sniffled, "I'll be okay. Eventually. I guess."

"Oh, honey, I know it's so sad. When are you coming back to L.A.? Your father and I need to sit and talk with you about finding a job. And you still need to sign off on this check."

Forcing tears, Darius cried, "I just said I was depressed. I can't think about anything right now. I need time to myself."

"Okay, honey. Don't cry. But Wellington is threatening to—

Darius cried louder.

"Never mind. It can wait. I'll deal with Wellington. Just let me know when you can make it back to L.A. Sometime this week or at least before the end of January would be good."

Sniffling, Darius replied, "Sure, Mom. Whateva you want."

"Okay, sweetheart. I know you're sad but you really didn't know Darryl that well."

"What?!" Darius yelled. "I don't believe you! I'm suffering and as usual you're being selfish."

"You'll be all right. I've got to go. I love you, sweetie. Call me tomorrow."

"You sure don't act like you love me. 'Bye." Darius laid the phone beside his thigh. The person his mom truly loved was her husband, and anything Wellington said went, even if it was about her only child.

"Fuck 'em!" Darius didn't need his mom. Or Wellington.

Looking up in the mirror, Darius's dick stood alone, lonely with no playmates, pointing toward the ceiling. Darius had to release his frustration so he picked up the cordless and dialed option number two, Kimberly Stokes.

Darius felt his bed move again. This time the imprint had vanished. Ma Dear was gone. Hopefully his grandmother hadn't given up on him. Dead or alive, Ma Dear was still the only woman he could trust.

CHAPTER 2

"Men just don't fuckin' get it."

Cursing wasn't attractive, but Byron's constant nagging provoked Fancy. Holding the cordless phone two feet away from her ear, staring into the receiver, Fancy slid her patio door open barely enough to turn sideways and step outside onto her balcony. Overlooking Lake Merritt, the crisp winter morning air complemented the sun rays helping to soothe the migraine headache Byron had created. Why did he have to make simple things complicated?

Fancy focused on the seagulls, ducks, and geese peacefully drifting on the man-made sanctuary, a haven for migrating and native birds. In the distance, a breathtaking backdrop of haze settled over the Oakland Hills. Inhaling the fresh air, Fancy reluctantly placed the phone up to her ear, knowing she hadn't missed a thing she hadn't heard before.

"You know I love you," Byron professed, pleading, "Please give me another chance to—"

Balancing her body with one hand, Fancy jumped, sat on the brass rail, and then interrupted Byron. "To what? Choke the life out of me? Leave me stranded on the top of a mountain in the middle of the night? What, Byron, what?" Fancy refused to allow Byron to forget how he'd mistreated her. "I've seen a side of you that's totally unpredictable. And the worst part is you won't even admit what you did was wrong." Across the street, joggers and walkers, some young, a few old, exercised along the paved trail.

Last year, if Desmond hadn't snatched Fancy by the waist, she would've committed suicide by throwing her body over the rail she now sat on, seventeen stories above the cemented sidewalk below. Briefly Fancy thought about the day she was raped and the day she'd aborted her baby. Solely fascinated with her outer beauty, men were so asinine and egotistical they didn't care about her feelings.

Byron replied, "What about you? If you hadn't called the cops and had me arrested for taking back my own car, we wouldn't be having this conversation. Besides, I was generous enough to give you back the Benz. That's because I care about you, baby. You're too attractive to stand on a corner waiting for a bus. Plus, I'm the one who made sure my accountant resent your paychecks to the correct address. Don't I get some credit for trying to do the right things?"

No. Fancy had been in love and for the first time she'd tried to do the right thing by being loyal to one man. What a joke. Why hadn't Fancy taken more of Byron's wealthy clients' contact information when she worked for him? Why couldn't one man satisfy all of her needs? Easing off the rail, Fancy walked inside then closed the sliding glass door.

"As far as my checks are concerned, you should've compensated me interest for paying me almost a year late. And the Benz is still in your name so do you care enough about me to take it back again? Huh? What's next?"

"Baby, please. Don't—" Byron insisted.

Priding herself on not being the same fool twice, Fancy interrupted again, "Give me one reason why I should take you back. And make it a damn good one."

"Um, you know, baby. Because no man can ever sex you the way I do. That, and the fact that"—Byron paused—"you love me."

Love? Right. Whateva. Fancy looked at the huge circular clock hanging in her kitchen above the stove she'd never used. The small hand was on the nine and the big hand moved directly onto the eight, reminding Fancy how long Byron's dick was. Before she got caught up thinking about Byron's gorgeous, gigantic, melt-in-your-mouth circumcised dick that fit so snug inside her pussy, Fancy quickly said, "Byron, I gotta go before I'm late. Call me tonight." Shit, talking to Byron at night when her pussy was its wettest wasn't a wise idea, especially since Fancy hadn't had sex in over a week.

"Gotta go where?" Byron questioned.

Click.

Byron called right back. Throwing the phone onto her bed, Fancy quickly put on her pink leather boots, picked up her Coach bag, and tossed her white mink coat over her forearm, hurrying to her car. Driving forty-five in a thirty mile per hour zone along Harrison Street, Fancy shook her head thinking about her conversations, yesterday with Darius and a few minutes ago with Byron.

Why did men feel as though their desires were the only ones that mattered? Darius needed a reality check on his ego and Byron, well, Byron simply needed to move on and find another woman who could love him. Exiting University Avenue off of Interstate 80, with five minutes remaining, Fancy continued exceeding the speed limit until she reached her destination.

"Oh, great, she's moving her car." Beep-beep. Fancy fanned her hand, signaling, then mouthed, "Move. Come on, lady." All that unnecessary adjustment to her mirrors was wasting Fancy's time.

After parking her car and grabbing her belongings, Fancy remotely locked her car and stood on the sidewalk in front of a homeless woman seated on a bench, then proceeded to tie an Albertson's bag over the flashing meter.

"Merry Christmas." The homeless woman greeted Fancy with a quizzical smile, rocking a loaf of French bread like an infant.

There was no time to respond to a crazy lady who didn't realize Christmas had passed almost two weeks ago. Disregarding the woman, Fancy raced across the street and dashed into Mandy's office.

"Happy New Year, Fancy," the receptionist said. "You can go in. Mandy's waiting for you."

Opening Mandy's door, Fancy replied, "Thanks, and merry—I mean, happy New Year to you, too."

Routinely, Fancy placed her coat on a hanger then hung it on the cedar rack adjacent to Mandy's door. On the other gold hook, she secured her purse, and then sat on the cold blue leather sofa.

"Happy New Year, Fancy. You're looking marvelous, as usual," Mandy commented, sifting through Fancy's file.

"Yeah, thanks." A contrived smile decorated Fancy's face. "I hope this New Year brings me lots of happiness."

Immediately, Mandy inquired, "What are your resolutions for this year? Prioritize them for me, Fancy."

When in the hell was Mandy going to develop a new list of questions? The first session of every year was rehearsed. Each session for the past five years had started the same. Not this time. Fancy's chaotic life warranted comprehension, not structure.

Hunching her shoulders, Fancy emphatically replied, "None. I have no resolutions this year. I have a hard enough time living each day. I don't need to add self-imposed expectations to my growing list of disappointments. Especially those I know I won't keep anyway." Like the promise Fancy had made last year to call Caroline once a week. "Can we discuss something else?"

"Okay." Setting the legal-sized pad on her desk, Mandy intensely stared at Fancy, then asked, "Who do you love?"

"Huuuhhh." Exhaling through her mouth, Fancy sat on the edge of the couch matching Mandy's intensity. Fancy wondered if her time spent with Mandy was therapeutic or habit, but what did love have to do with Fancy's issues? Mandy should've queried the men in Fancy's life for that response.

Long ago, Fancy concluded that love was an illusion and people in love were disillusioned. Fancy had observed her mother, her friends, and people at her job. That was before she'd quit working for Harry and Associates. One day they loved one another to death, and the next day they wished their lover were dead or, at a minimum, no longer a part of their lives.

Like Fancy's ex-lover and ex-boss, Harry, who'd raped her in his office after she refused to fuck him. The scar on Harry's forehead where Fancy bashed his face with the first blunt object she'd placed her hand on would make Harry think twice before raping another woman. If Fancy could've killed that old dirty bastard without going to jail, she'd have no remorse. The same way Fancy harbored no regrets for sending Harry's wife a bleeding heart that read, "R.I.P. Henrietta Washington."

Men. Married men always tried to protect their precious households while using other women on the side. Single men, the rich ones that Fancy wanted, were the same as the married ones, dating multiple women. Fancy hadn't caught Byron with anyone else, but she knew she wasn't his only one. God should've given women dicks and men pussies. Naw, humans would become extinct because women would rule the world, fuck other women, and say, "The hell with thoughtless-ass men." Wasn't that the way the secret male bisexual community operated against women?

Mandy leaned back against her mustard-colored chair. Calm. Reserved. Patiently waiting for an answer.

Fancy despised Mandy. Why? Fancy wasn't sure. Maybe subconsciously Fancy admired Mandy and hated herself. Fancy's eyes bulged as the sadness in her corneas swept her inside lids, from corner to corner, regretting she'd kept the damn appointment and doubting she'd ever find a man she loved.

"Huuuhhh." Opening her eyes, Fancy concealed her envy while imagining what issues Mandy hid underneath her short tapered auburn hair; her ass wasn't perfect. Maybe that was the reason Fancy felt inferior. Mandy seemed flawless. But that was probably a façade. Just because Mandy held a Ph.D. in psychology didn't make her a qualified judge of Fancy's character. One of these days Fancy would have her own business like Mandy. But the remaining half hour of their meeting wasn't about Mandy so Fancy shifted her focus and thought about Mandy's question for a moment.

Both six-shelved redwood bookcases behind Mandy's desk were filled with psych books and African-American literature. Aimlessly, Fancy's eyes roamed pausing on an intriguing title, *A Woman's Worth* by Tracy Price-Thompson.

Shifting in her seat, Mandy's pivotal movement interrupted Fancy's thoughts.

Love. Love. Right. "I love myself," or so Fancy thought but had begun to wonder. What was a woman worth? What was she worth? To herself? Society?

A little girl who'd grown up poor. Fancy was overweight. Misunderstood. Rejected by her classmates and abandoned by a drunken mom whom Fancy seldom called mother and never addressed as Mommy, Fancy had grown up alone and lonely. Caroline wasn't an alcoholic but her intoxicated selection of men influenced Fancy's decision to love the money not the man, and with time, Fancy's preferred men were Benjamin, Grant, Jackson, and occasionally Hamilton but never Washington. Sniffling, briefly holding her breath, Fancy refused to cry. No more tears. The next tears Fancy would shed for Caroline would be on Caroline's grave. Maybe.

After she retrieved a tissue from the decorated box on the glass end table, Fancy's lips parted again, but before she continued speaking Mandy deliberately articulated, "If you love yourself, Fancy, then why do you keep hurting yourself? Disappointing yourself? Rejecting yourself? Disrespecting yourself?"

That's enough! Fancy's sniffling escalated. *Not this again, Miss Goodie "I got my own money don't need a man" Two-Shoes, you need to back the fuck up!*

Truth was, Fancy detested being vulnerable and Mandy was probing into a part of her heart that Fancy had sealed since childhood. Sad, but no one ever taught Fancy or showed her, so she didn't know how to love. Not even herself.

Mandy paused then added, "Neglecting yourself? Depriving yourself? Fancy, you've been coming to me for therapy since your senior year of high school, almost five years, and you still have the same unresolved issues you had during our very first session. If you don't show improvement by the end of this year, I'm going to have to refer you to someone else because we can't continue on like this."

The chill of Mandy's words traveled down Fancy's spine and underneath her thighs. The leather was warm but suddenly Fancy felt cold again. Numb. Trembling, staring at the floral wallpaper, Fancy focused on the usual unaligned row of gardenias. When was

Mandy going to redecorate her office? When would Fancy get her life together?

"Huuuhhh." Exhaling, Fancy said, "I don't hurt myself," then shouted in defense, "Others hurt me! Byron! Harry! Adam!" The only man that had never harmed Fancy was her best friend Desmond. *The nerve of this never-had-to-pay-a-dime-for-college shrink ditching me. I don't need her validation. I pay Mandy; Mandy doesn't pay me.*

Interrupting Fancy's mental monologue, Mandy countered, "Same difference."

Bucking her eyes, Fancy's eyebrows moved closer together. "Same difference?" Fancy repeated hugging her chill bumps, and then said, "Whoa. You act as though I'm responsible for controlling other people's actions." Fancy's French manicured nails meandered from her elbows to her shoulders then curled under her biceps. The hairs on her forearms penetrated her sweater, causing her arms to itch.

Quietly Mandy retrieved her pad then scribbled before calmly responding, "Not at all. But what you do control, Fancy, are your reactions. So why do you allow others to continuously hurt you?"

"I don't!" was all Fancy thought of and said, while her brain searched for a more intelligent response. The pupils of her eyes vanished, hiding behind insecure eyelids and false eyelashes concealing Fancy's tears. Smothering her fears. Fancy's lips quivered then tightened. Between sniffles, oxygen and carbon monoxide rapidly exchanged places inside her lungs, causing her breasts to rise and fall under her pink cotton-candy lace bra.

Just because Fancy didn't know which of the four men she'd slept with had fathered her aborted baby didn't make her the whore that her girlfriend's fiancé Tyronne had labeled her. Fancy selected her rich sponsors very carefully. Eventually SaVoy would realize Tyronne didn't love her as much as he wanted to use SaVoy's father's commercial space to start his business. Clearly SaVoy was perfect for Tyronne but was Tyronne good for SaVoy? Time would tell. Fancy's session wasn't about Tyronne or SaVoy so Fancy took a deep breath and refocused again. And who cared that Fancy's mother had never, not even once, told Fancy, "I love you"? Fancy wasn't an insensitive person incapable of showing her true feelings.

Quickly Fancy asked, "What's your definition of love?"

Mandy sat up straighter, watched Fancy, and then silently peeped over the top rim of her gold-framed eyeglasses. Why did Mandy bother wearing those stupid glasses if she only periodically glimpsed through the lenses? Mandy's reddish bronze lipstick surrounded her perfect white teeth. Crossing her short legs, Mandy's coffee-colored boot immaculately shone against her wool taupe pants. Why Fancy zeroed in on one shoe she didn't know. Perhaps she continued staring toward the floor to avoid contact with Mandy's piercing brown eyes.

Uncrossing her legs, Mandy took a few steps then sat on the sofa next to Fancy. With Mandy's thigh grazing Fancy's, the warmth of Mandy's palms caressed Fancy's hands. Fancy gazed at Mandy's degree hanging on the wall between her bookcases.

"Look at me, Fancy. Love is defined for self. I cannot give you a description or write you a script or prescription for love. Some people have a passion for material things like the expensive designer clothes you always wear and the Mercedes you drive. My gosh, look at you. Pink leather low-rise pants. Matching boots. A snow white cashmere sweater. You're the most physically fit person I know. A top-notch flowing hair weave. Magnificent lashes. Radiant skin. Impeccable facial features. Five-carat princess-cut diamonds in your navel and in each ear."

Mandy fingered Fancy's earlobes lightly, holding her face in her palms. Normally, Fancy wouldn't permit anyone to touch her face unless she knew they'd recently showered or washed their hands but Fancy's body was motionless. Lifeless. Hopelessly, Fancy attempted to avoid Mandy's intrusive eyes.

"Other people value beliefs or causes like justice and equality. Fancy, you are so gorgeous. On the outside. If a positive change in your life is to come, personal growth has to come not from you but through you. Let your inner beauty outshine your physical attributes because faith and determination will carry you during your hardest times. And heaven forbid if you become disfigured. Listen, if you don't know where to begin your definition of love, think about this: who or what are you willing to die for?"

"That's it!" Leaping up on her five-inch spiked heels, Fancy grabbed her mink, her purse, and screamed, "You are crazy! Why I continue to pay you is beyond me. I think you need to see a shrink your damn self." Fancy pointed toward Mandy's pale, turning feverish red, forehead. "Fancy Taylor is not willing to die for anyone or anything!"

Honestly, Mandy was too close to Fancy physically and emotionally. Once more, Fancy was afraid to examine her true feelings. When Fancy swallowed, the lump of sadness in her throat choked her vocal chords. Fancy's eyelids fluttered, washing away the saline tears threatening to detach the glue securing her fifty-dollar lashes.

Mandy politely whispered, "That's because you've never truly found love. This is our last session. Good-bye, Fancy."

"Bitch!" Snatching the round brass knob, Mandy's door flung back with equal intensity, ripping a hole in Fancy's new sweater. Covering her bra with her hand, Fancy yelled, "You're not better than me! You're not! You're not! You are not!" Leaving Mandy's office, she stumped and stumbled down two flights of gray cement stairs in the damp, dimly lit hallway. Opening the heavy metal door, Fancy exited onto University Avenue. Bending, hugging her stomach, Fancy gasped gobs of fresh air. Jaywalking with her heels clicking atop the black asphalt, Fancy ignored the red flashing "don't walk" sign, crossed University, and remotely unlocked her car.

"Merry Christmas," said the homeless woman, still perched on a bench outside a café.

Opening her car door, Fancy yelled, "Shut up! Crazy lady!"

Why was she now brushing a matted wig when she already had a cheap uncombed synthetic hairpiece propped lopsided on her tilted head? Fancy sat in her car angrily starring at the homeless woman. Tears poured, ruining her mascara and clothes. Fancy didn't care. About her clothes. Herself. Or the homeless woman who stared back while constantly grooming her wig. Gradually her tattered image, draped in a frail, dingy gray cardigan sweater that should've been white, vanished between the layers of fog invading Fancy's windows.

Maybe this time Fancy should really check out of life so her unhappiness would end. What was her purpose in life anyway? Fancy had no siblings, a horrible mother, and no idea who her father was. Caroline's parents were deceased. Who'd miss Fancy? Who'd care? The salty drops flowed faster, racing into her mouth.

Tap. Tap. Tap.

Squinting, dabbing underneath her eyes with her sleeve, Fancy couldn't recognize the face through her cloudy windows. "Whatever it is, I'm not interested. Go away."

Tap. Tap. Tap.

"Fancy, you okay? Let down the window."

Moving in slow motion, Fancy's palm smeared a circle. She pressed the automatic button to lower the window. Her guardian angel, Desmond Brown. Her only true male friend. Desmond must've been a sign from God that Fancy's time to die wasn't today because, otherwise, why was Desmond here in another moment of her despair?

"You okay. We still going out tonight?" Desmond asked, flashing his white teeth between full chocolate lips.

Fancy whispered, "No, I'm not okay. What kind of question is that? And I don't know if I want to go anywhere tonight. I need to be alone."

Playfully, Desmond stuck his untamed afro inside Fancy's window. "Oh, damn." His smile faded. "You're crying. I'm sorry. Unlock the door and let me in."

Desmond must've recently left his barber at Lazarus Hair Studio over on Martin Luther King, Jr. Way because Desmond's hair lining and shapely goatee was freshly trimmed. Whenever Desmond's stylist washed his hair he massaged from the scalp then teased the edges to create an uncombed image.

Hurrying to the passenger side, Desmond sat quietly. Fancy turned on the defroster as Desmond squeezed then held her hand. Desmond's touch wasn't at all like Mandy's. Fancy felt comfortable with Desmond. His cold masculine fingers stroked her cheeks. Drying her tears, Desmond avoided touching Fancy's lashes.

"What's wrong, baby? Please stop crying." Desmond tried closing the torn gap in Fancy's sweater, touching her breast several times.

Covering his hand Fancy said, "It's okay, it's ruined just like me." Fancy sobbed. "You're leaving me here in Oakland to go to law school in Atlanta. My shrink just fired me. I'm broke. I have no job. This is a fucked-up way to start a New Year. I try so hard, Dez, to be happy. I really do." Salty tears saturated her drying mascara once more, this time creating new stains. "I don't want to go back to Byron but Byron will pay my bills if I do. And the new guy I met New Year's Eve, Darius, you remember?" Fancy reminisced about how she'd meet Darius at church and how that same night Darius had begged her to stay with him, then continued, "Oh, um, the one who gave me a ride home in his limo when I gave you the keys to that broken-down ride you'd given me. Anyway, I don't know Darius well enough to have him sponsor me."

Clenching the corner of his bottom lip between his teeth, Desmond patted Fancy's shoulder, then said, "Fancy, you've broken my heart countless times, including right now. You always overlook me. Degrade me. I'm a man but I have feelings, too. You know I'll always care for you. Your quest for material things is what makes you unhappy. Why can't you love me for me? You should be moving to Atlanta with me as my wife. It's my last night in town, and I'm spending it with you, not my woman, Carlita. She's taking me to the airport tomorrow but the woman I love is you. I've never felt good enough nor rich enough to be your man. I don't have expensive things to offer you. At least not yet. But, Fancy, you don't need a man to take care of you. You're beautiful and you're smart. You can support yourself. Besides, what happened to all that money Byron gave you?"

Desmond acknowledged what Fancy already knew and had recently heard from Mandy about her good looks. Fancy's forehead wrinkled. "Paid me, thank you. For the work I'd done for his company, thank you. I'm telling you, Dez, I have bad luck. The same week those checks cleared my account, the IRS and the state stole all except five thousand dollars."

Laughing, Desmond shook his head, and said, "Well, did you pay your taxes?"

"No, but that's not my point. How am I supposed to maintain

my lifestyle off of a few grand when I spend that kind of money in one shopping spree?"

"What happened to those real estate classes you charged to Harry's credit card before he fired you?"

Although Fancy realized Desmond's intentions were to help, Desmond had seriously agitated her. "I wasn't fired. I quit."

"Quit. Fired. That's not my point. You already have your salesperson's license. Can you still take the broker classes? Start your own firm."

Turning the key in her ignition to off, Fancy had hoped the windows would fog again so that vagabond woman would stop staring into the car. "I don't know. Besides, I can't start a business with no money. "

"Take one step at a time. Let's go find out about the classes. I'll drive."

Any reason was a good one to leave. Post-holiday shoppers roamed Shattuck Avenue with shopping bags in tow. Desmond held Fancy's hand with one hand and the steering wheel with the other.

"Everything's gonna be all right. I'll do my best to make sure of it before I leave and if you need me, I'll come back. Even after I graduate law school." Gazing at Fancy, Desmond said, "I don't know if you're going to move to Atlanta or me back to Oakland, but mark my words, Fancy, you are going to be my wife."

Fancy hadn't forgotten about Desmond's high school sweetheart anxiously awaiting his arrival in Georgia. "What about Trina? You told me she's still single with no kids."

Exiting Hegenberger Road toward the Oakland Airport, Desmond said, "Let me handle Trina. I know where my heart is."

Desmond parked in the lot on Edgewater Drive in front of Anthony's School of Real Estate, wiped Fancy's face, kissed her lips, and then said, "You're beautiful. You can do this. This is the beginning of your independence. You said the next person you worked for would be yourself. Now prove it."

Desmond was right. Fancy was the only person in control of her destiny. Cracking a half smile, Fancy whispered, "Thanks."

Holding Desmond's hand, Fancy marched into the lobby with a

torn sweater and jacked-up makeup. The young man behind the counter frowned and then greeted them. "How may I help you?"

Fancy's California ID was one of the most flattering pictures she'd taken. Proudly Fancy handed her driver's license to the guy, who looked barely twenty-one. "I'm here to confirm my registration for the Real Estate Practice course."

Reading her name, the long, lanky guy said, "Fancy Taylor," and as his fingers clicked against the keyboard, he began to smile. "We were wondering what happened to you. You paid for Legal Aspects, Appraisal, Economics, Finance, Escrow, Loan Brokering and Lending, Property Management, and all of the rest of the electives last year. You do know you only need three electives?"

"That's right," Fancy lied. "I'd like to start today and continue until I get my broker's license."

"The next broker's session for Finance starts tomorrow night. Do you have a college degree?" he asked constantly tapping on keys.

Frowning, Fancy replied, "Why, do I need one?"

"No, it's just that if you'd already taken the required or elective courses, you'd receive credit. But that's okay. I'll get you signed up for tomorrow."

Sucking her teeth, Fancy said, "Damn, really? Well, since that's not an option, I'll definitely see you tomorrow night."

"And since you've held your salesperson's license for nine months, if you complete the course requirements, you can have a broker's license nine months from now."

"This feels so good. I was meant to be here," Fancy said, nodding and smiling at Desmond.

Thankfully Harry's credit card charges hadn't been reversed. That was the least that low-down scoundrel should've done. After raping her, Harry agreed to pay Fancy a lump sum not to press charges. That bastard deducted the fees for all of her classes and everything else he'd given Fancy, claiming that after all expenses, she owed him money. Yeah, right. So Fancy had assumed, to recoup his deficit, Harry would reverse the charges for her classes.

Why hadn't Fancy taken more classes sooner? She could've been working on her broker's license months ago. Probably because the only thing Fancy had mastered was spending other people's money. She'd never had a real marketable skill, let alone her own business. At one time, Fancy dreaded failure as much as she feared success. What would happen if for once in her life, the real Fancy Taylor lived her dreams? Beginning today, Fancy Taylor was getting paid for working men out of bed instead of under the sheets, starting with Mr. Darius "Wanna Be a Player" Jones. With his millions of dollars, Darius wouldn't taste Fancy's pussy until she sold him a mansion. Maybe two.

The ride back to University Avenue was a blur. Desmond doubled-parked next to his car, kissed Fancy's lips, and said, "I'll pick you up at eight."

Before Desmond exited Fancy's car, Fancy tightly wrapped her arms around his strong shoulders and whispered, "Thanks, Dez. For being my true friend. I love you." She thought.

Driving home, Fancy reflected on her session with Mandy. Mandy's good-bye seemed so definite, as though she felt sorry for Fancy—the way Fancy had felt pity for that homeless woman—like Fancy was incapable of loving someone so deeply that she'd willingly give her life.

Fancy hated to admit that Mandy was right. As Fancy sat behind the steering wheel of her luxury car, she realized that she wouldn't voluntarily die for anything or anyone. Including her mother. Especially her mother. Because of all the things in the world that Fancy believed she could accomplish, the one thing she couldn't do was make her mother love her.

CHAPTER 3

Women had been his weakness since he was a toddler peeping up at them from underneath the bathroom stalls. Most women thought he was cute and smiled back at him when he grinned, glaring between their legs, intrigued with the hairy monster, as he called it then, that shot pee-pee into the toilet. Not much had changed over the years. Only now Darius craved fucking and sucking those hairy monsters every single day.

No finer female in all of California existed than Kimberly Stokes. When Darius phoned Kimberly last night, she'd pleasantly agreed to take a morning flight into Oakland. While his preference was sistahs, Darius also enjoyed fucking Latinas, Puerto Ricans, Jews, Asians, Caucasians, Brazilians, French, Swedish, and German women, and he'd had them all. As long as a woman was a lady, intelligent, well-versed, didn't speak loudly, and had something to lose—like a celebrity reputation, a high-profile career, a business, or lots of money—her nationality was insignificant. Hustlers with no bank accounts, no job, or unskilled occupations were worthy of a "Hell, no," not a "Hel-lo."

The harder Darius tried not to think with his dick, the more he thought about sex. How many women had he slept with? One hundred. Two. More. Was he a sex addict and didn't realize it? Bump that thought. Darius was a young man, and like most youngsters, his sex drive revved out of control. While attending high school in Los Angeles and during his freshman and sophomore years at Georgetown, Darius had so many females he was convinced he'd break Wilt Chamberlain's record of having fucked over ten thousand women.

Darius quickly learned that every woman who opened her legs welcomed more than a stiff dick. If Darius could have his company back, he'd occupy the majority of his time producing and financing films in Hollywood instead of lounging around weightlifting and reproducing sperm for his next orgasms.

Thinking of Hollywood, Darius glanced at the caller ID on his nightstand. How many times in one day was his mother going to call him?

Already annoyed, anticipating the repetitive tone of her voice, Darius picked up the handset, closed his eyes, exhaled heavily, then answered, "Yes, Mom."

"Hi, sweetheart," she said, sounding chipper. "Are you busy?"

No busier than he was thirty minutes ago. Somberly Darius replied, "Kinda. At least I will be"—knee-deep in some pussy—"in a minute. What's up?"

"Darius, you can't keep avoiding your father." His mom's voice became predictably stern.

Can and will. "He's not my father. And I'm not sure who my mother is, either."

"Honey, you're making this more complicated than it has to be. If you make Wellington upset, he's going to cut you off before you find a job."

News flash! He's already done that, Mom. "Then forget him! Let him do what the fuck he wants!" Hopefully after this call his mother wouldn't call back.

"Darius, have you lost your mind?! Don't speak to me like that!"

"Sorry, Mom. Look, I'll make it to L.A. next week. Since I'm no longer your priority, Wellington can have whatever the F he wants. And I'll just stay out of y'all's way. How's that?"

"Wellington said you would try to make me feel guilty. I'm not going to let you do that to me this time. I'll see you next week, sweetheart. I love you."

Love. Right. Whateva. "You don't love me. 'Bye, Mom."

Hanging up the phone, Darius walked to his front door and strolled outside. His five-bedroom house in the Oakland Hills was courtesy of his mother. Standing tall next to one of the six giant white pillars which separated the driveway from the house, Darius folded his arms across his chest then spread his legs, granting space to the erection invading his pecan-colored slacks. He was blessed to have such a nice mom but Wellington had poisoned Darius's mother's loving ways, making her cold and callous. Darius hoped she'd used that same heartless attitude toward Wellington one day.

Shifting his thoughts, Darius said, "Just say no, dawg," trying to convince himself not to fuck his dime piece. "Send her back to Los Angeles. Go inside and work on something constructive like a business plan to regain your corporation." After all the money Darius had spent to fly Kimberly to Oakland, there was no way he'd send her back to L.A. without getting a return on his investment.

"Aw, yeah. Here she comes." Smiling, Darius watched the limousine driver cruise into the circular driveway of his mansion. Black. Long. Trimmed in gold with tinted windows so dark he couldn't see anyone inside. When the chauffeur opened the back door, a bare set of glowing cinnamon legs extended into view. Rhinestone straps buckled at the ankles were connected to clear pointed heels that greeted the black asphalt. Kimberly's lips curved wide as Darius watched the driver extend his hand, assisting Kimberly out of the car.

Slowly parting the collar of her mink, Kimberly's bare breasts, plump and firm, were exposed. Licking his lips, Darius lustfully watched her flat stomach, ruby belly stone, and shiny pubic hairs glisten into view. Seductively Kimberly released the black sable which trickled over her smooth shoulders, down her back, over her hips, and wrinkled into a fluffy puddle covering her stilettos.

Fumbling in his trunk, the driver removed Kimberly's carry-on, then quietly placed the suitcase inside Darius's doorway. Staring in his rearview mirror, the limo driver shook his head as he cruised then exited the double gates that automatically closed behind him.

"Yeah, now that's what I'm talkin' 'bout," Darius said, nodding. His dick sprang forward, pleased that all Kimberly had worn underneath her coat were thin strands of elegant freshwater pearls—black and white—draped around her waist.

"Don't move. Stay right there," Darius instructed, approaching Kimberly. Whispering in her ear, Darius said, "Thanks for flying in on such short notice." Holding Kimberly's hand high above her flowing hairweave, Darius coaxed her to twirl. Scanning her sculpted body, five feet seven inches, slender waist, bodacious booty, and bulging calves, the morning breeze joined him in saluting Kimberly's protruding nipples. The platinum barbell piercing Kimberly's warm tongue flicked inside his ear. His dick jumped. Damn, he enjoyed a woman's tongue inside his ear. That shit turned him on. "Yes, gurl. Do your thang."

"Well, with two drivers," Kimberly moaned, kissing Darius's strong neck, his hot spot, right below and slightly behind his ear. "Um, you taste so delicious. One in L.A. and that poor guy who sat in the driveway longer than he should've, watching my naked body that I spent all day preparing just for you, Daddy. A first-class ticket and an all-expenses-paid trip to Barbados next week." Kimberly moaned louder. "How could I possibly say no to my two favorite guys." She dipped, gave Slugger a kiss, and then stood.

Darius frowned. *Fool, are you crazy? You can't afford that shit anymore.* Unbeknownst to Kimberly, both her trip to the Caribbean and her line of credit were being cancelled first thing tomorrow morning. But right now, Darius needed to cum inside Kimberly's hot juicy pussy that resembled a chocolate-dipped strawberry oozing with whipping cream.

Kimberly's feminine fingers caressed his chest, slid inside the grooves, then aggressively snatched open his shirt. Buttons bounced on the blacktop, then rolled downhill into the grass. "I'ma pussy-whup you today. And don't hold back," Kimberly dictated. The wetness of her tongue outlined the definition in Darius's chest, tracing the indentions underneath each mound. The cold air, saliva, and gnawing pressure of the metal ball made his nipples hard and his dick harder.

Unbuckling his belt, Darius pinched his zipper. Kimberly's hands grasped his wrists.

"Oh no, Daddy. Don't steal Mama's joy. I know how you like it." Bending over, Kimberly spread the lining of her coat over the lawn. "I'm gonna do you proper."

Darius's eyes zoomed in on what his dick couldn't resist, so he unfastened his pants and gripped Kimberly's ass, burying his face between her chocolate lips with their sweet strawberry fleshy center. Softly, Darius French-kissed her clit. In one fluid motion, his tongue swept her shaft, circled her vagina, and then teased her rectum. Saliva drizzled down to Kimberly's vagina, saturating her clitoris and dripping onto the coat. With his pants hugging his upper thighs right below his ass, Darius gripped his erection, spanked Kimberly's pussy with his dick, and gradually entered her, savoring the warmth of every fraction of an inch until his hips pressed flush against her ass.

Tilting his face toward the heavens above, Darius's body floated into Kimberly's. "Aw, yes. I miss my pussy gurl. I wish you could feel how good this shit is."

The cold breeze, Kimberly's hot pussy, and the openness of the outdoors heightened his sexual emotions. When a bluebird perched on his porch and whistled, Darius sang, "Yeah, dawg. You know how good this feels."

Slowly Darius repenetrated Kimberly as deep as he could. He paused inside her paradise. His eyes journeyed to the back of his head. Pussy was so good. Tight. Juicy. For a moment Darius was pussy-paralyzed.

Until Kimberly's hand reached between his thighs, grabbing his balls, and he humped again. This time with more depth. Squeezing gently then a little harder, Kimberly rotated his nuts in her hand then deeply massaged his extended dick, the rod between his dick and his nuts, almost making him explode inside her pulsating pussy. Easing his penis out, Darius removed his pants, admiring the cream coating his shaft. He circled his bulging head around Kimberly's opening then slipped back inside before their juices evaporated in the chilling wind.

"Yes, Daddy. Fuck me! Fuck your pussy, Daddy."

Yeah, Kimberly was appreciative to see him. Fancy had lost. Fancy could've been jockin' him. Kimberly's ass amazingly clapped, making a smacking sound each time she tightened her muscles around his dick.

"Not yet, Slugger. Hold on. Don't let her take you out like a punk man. Stay strong," Darius pleaded. "Hold out for a few more minutes, dawg." Quickly pulling out, Darius removed a condom from his back pocket. "Whew! Damn. That was close."

As Darius ripped the packet with his teeth, Kimberly faced him, holding his hands, then whispered, "Don't cover him up. I haven't tasted him yet."

Spitting the paper into his palm, Darius said, "Aw, shit." His heartbeat increased as Kimberly squatted in those sexy shoes then firmly massaged his pre-cum and her saliva into his dick.

"Incredible," was all Darius could say before Kimberly's slippery silver ball vibrated across his nuts. Her lips traveled up his shaft, over his head, gradually taking in as much as she could.

If Kimberly knew how good Darius's dick felt inside her mouth and pussy, she'd stand in line to trade her pussy for a dick. The real reason women were jealous of men wasn't because men cheated but because women didn't have dicks. Damn, Kimberly's mouth felt ridiculously unbelievable! "Oh my God!" Darius yelled into the wind.

Kimberly's hand was in motion with her head as Darius clamped his hands on the side of her temples, closed his eyes, and then forced Slugger deeper down Kimberly's throat, until his engorged head bypassed the hardness in the roof of her mouth and nestled into the soft tissue area that felt just like pussy. Kimberly gagged. Darius pushed deeper, saying, "This shit is so outrageously good." Any nigga that said he was faithful was lying or he was crazy.

Gripping his hips, Kimberly forced Darius back, patted his thighs, and mumbled, "Slow down. You're choking me."

"I'm, sorry, baby you know how I get when I'm in the zone," Darius said, unrolling the condom up his shaft. Turning Kimberly back around, Darius pushed her against one of the frosty white columns. Kimberly parted her cheeks, welcoming Darius's big, strong, and long dick. Pumping swiftly, Darius started fucking the shit out of her like a dog in heat. Trying to match his pace, Kimberly bounced on his dick as Darius thrust harder and faster until the explosion he'd wanted—"Here it comes!"—to give to Fancy—"It's yours!"—escaped his nuts.

"Ooohh, ddaaammmn! Shit! Goddamn! Woman, your pussy is unbelievable." Darius humped, pumping a few more times until the slackers—the last group of sperms—exited his penis. Slapping Kimberly's cheeks then picking up her coat and his pants, Darius said, "If your pussy could cook, I'd marry it. Believe dat. Let's go inside."

Kimberly laughed. "You are so stupid. You act like you haven't had sex for months," she said, trailing Darius.

Nodding, Darius replied, "Yup, you could say that. I need my shit tuned up every day."

Retreating to his bedroom, they showered, and then lay across Darius's circular bed. He clicked a few buttons on his remote and replayed the videotape from their recent outdoor session on the lawn so Kimberly could see herself in action.

Pointing, Kimberly said, "Hey, that's pretty neat. How did you videotape us? Can I have the tape?"

Darius recalled the day he'd met Kimberly sitting courtside at a Lakers game with some guy. Kimberly's date left during halftime, and by the time dude returned, Kimberly had given Darius her cell number. Initially he started not to call but one night he was bored lounging at his home in L.A. with no place to go, so he called Kimberly—like he'd done with Fancy—and invited her over. Kimberly was direct. Said she didn't fuck for free but was worth everything she got in exchange, and she was right.

"Of course not, you know better than to ask me a crazy question like that. My entire house has cameras so don't try anything stupid when I leave you here while I'm at my brother's funeral tomorrow."

Rolling onto her stomach, eyeing the plasma screen on the wall, Kimberly said, "Well, you taped us without my consent. *All* I want is a copy of that tape."

Mounting Kimberly, Darius pressed his head at the opening of her rectum. "I'll dub you a copy of this tape. If you let me—"

Kimberly kept watching television. "You don't seem sad about your brother being killed. Don't you care?"

Rising up on his knees, unstraddling Kimberly, Darius asked, "Where'd that come from? Of course I care. I'm just relieved that it wasn't my dad. And I'm sorry that it wasn't my other brother, Kevin. I still have to catch up to his stealing ass and when I do, it's gon' be curtains for that jokester because—"

The phone rang, interrupting his thoughts. Darius leaned over, peeped at the caller ID. It was Ciara. Jokester. Trickster. One and the same. Darius answered, "What the hell you want?!"

Calmly Ciara asked, "Let me speak to Kimberly."

Frowning, squinting, Darius stared at Kimberly. "What the fuck you doing telling Ciara to call my damn house for you?!"

Briefly rolling over, looking at Darius, Kimberly turned onto her side, continuously admiring herself kissing Darius's nipples on the big screen and said, "Darius, you play too much. I didn't tell Ciara to call me here."

Slamming his hand against the speaker button, Darius said, "Ciara, whatever you have to say to Kimberly you can say to me."

"Thanks, Darius. Kimberly, at Wellington Jones's request, I'm casting you for the lead actress in my new film *He's Just a Friend*. We both agree that you're perfect for the role. Young, talented, and scintillating."

Kimberly leaped to her feet. "Oh my God! Oh my God! Ciara, are you serious?!" Kimberly shouted the words again, doing a full split in midair. Jumping up and down on Darius's ten-thousand-dollar spread like she was on a trampoline, Kimberly sang, "I'm gonna be a star," repeatedly.

"Sit your ass down!" Darius yelled, jerking the black oriental spread from underneath Kimberly's feet, watching her collapse onto his bed. "Ciara, you can't do that! Wellington can't do that! *He's Just a Friend* is being produced by my company and you know it!"

Ciara interjected, "Correction, your parents' company. You're broke, remember? I've negotiated to do the casting for all films for

Somebody's Gotta Be on Top Enterprises. Wellington felt that was the least he could do since you screwed up my companies with your lying ways. But if you need help finding a job, I could use a gardener to clean up the manure you've left in my backyard. Darius, you've convinced me that having a dog is a better companion than having your trifling ass for a husband."

For the first time in years, a woman had made Darius speechless and he hated Ciara for that shit. Now Kimberly knew more than he'd intended to tell her. Was he that bad? That doggish? "You're a whore. Remember that. Solomon. Donavon. Allen. And God knows who else you've slept with. Fuck you, Ciara!" Darius yelled into the speaker.

"You already have, remember? I'm pregnant. With your son. So don't try that 'I'm not the baby's daddy' nonsense with me. 'Bye, Darius. Kimberly, congratulations. I'll see you in my office first thing Monday morning."

After disappearing for months, when had Ciara's ass gotten back from her sabbatical? Forget his mother and Wellington, Ciara was the first person Darius was visiting when he got to L.A. "So you're back working in your of—"

"I didn't call to speak with you, Darius. And don't show up at my office."

Click.

"Kimberly, don't bother unpacking your shit. You're in cahoots with Ciara so you've gotta get up outta my crib. Right now. Put your clothes on." Darius dialed the driver who'd left two hours ago. "Man, I need you to come by immediately."

Kimberly protested, "Darius, you can't be serious. I thought you'd be happy for me."

"I'm very serious. Get your shit and get out."

Kimberly had served her purpose.

CHAPTER 4

If Fancy could've separated the orgasms from the individuals, truth from illusion, or pain from pleasure, she wouldn't have sexed so many men nor would she have slept alone in her bed most of the time. Instead, she'd be lying next to her fine-ass husband every night, whoever he was. And Fancy damn sure 'nuff wouldn't have been lonely sitting in the midst of thousands of people at the Oakland Paramount Theatre listening to but not hearing the funniest man in America, Chris Rock, tell jokes that had Desmond and seemingly everyone else except her roaring with laughter.

Unbuttoning the waist of her pimento suede low-rise pants, Fancy slid her hand underneath her orange lace thong, inhaled, pressed her middle finger against her engorged clitoris, closed her eyes, and quietly exhaled. After leaving Mandy's office, and before Desmond picked her up for the comedy show, Fancy had taken a vow of celibacy, and after only a few hours her vagina adamantly protested, but Fancy wanted a break from men. Well, not completely. What Mandy made Fancy realize was that Fancy required time out from d-jaying different men. D-jaying, disc-jocking, riding, fucking, having sex with, whateva. All Fancy knew was Miss Kitty was officially on sabbatical and the next brotha was going to have to work overtime just to get a whiff.

Thinking back on her past affairs, maybe love, in many ways, was like having an orgasm. She had to experience her first life-altering high and heartbreak in order to appreciate the next. Understand the ex. Then learn how to become the best mate she could without hording or dumping her emotional baggage on everyone else.

If anyone in heaven was listening, Fancy asked for forgiveness if she didn't find the humor in not knowing her father, not loving her mother, and having to learn through trial and tribulation how a man should treat a woman. A role model would've been nice. A few times Fancy secretly observed her girlfriend, SaVoy. Since SaVoy was a Christian and all and was raised by her father and she was still a virgin, Fancy figured SaVoy had to know how a good man treated his woman.

But when SaVoy accepted Tyronne's proposal, a man who was more of a thug than the derelicts Fancy's mother dated and was nowhere close to the refined millionaires Fancy had dated, Fancy figured SaVoy's prayers either weren't specific enough or SaVoy, like Fancy, had no definition of a real man.

The crowd became consumed with laughter again, interrupting her internal monologue as Chris cursed some woman out. Not literally. Chris joked about her being in the mistress protection program. Fancy rolled her eyes at Chris then contrived a chuckle trying to join in the laughter with Desmond, but Fancy didn't have a clue what Chris's point was. Her self-imposed frustrations had nothing to do with anyone in the theater. Mistress—the word echoed in her mind. Yeah, Fancy, too, had believed she was in that program last year dating a married man. Turned out Byron wasn't married at all.

Softly sighing, Fancy eased her hand from under her thong then interlocked her warm, moist fingers with Desmond's, thinking the only New Year's resolution she needed this year was a revolution. A revelation. Someone to confirm that one day she, too, would be happily married to a financially secure man, preferably a man wealthier than Chris Rock. Scanning Chris's impeccable chocolate complexion, his large, bright white teeth, and his Delco Cabana leather jacket, money had definitely improved his appearance.

Starting with her honeymoon, Fancy would settle down, fuck

her rich husband beyond satisfaction, and then stay in bed, elevating her legs over the headboard, welcoming each of his sperm racing to fertilize her eggs. But did Fancy really want a husband or simply to have a baby for a wealthy man to secure her financial position?

Fancy had witnessed that married couples begrudgingly living in matrimony for years were happier after their divorce, and single people once married seemed the happiest of their existence—that was, until the honeymoon ended. Having worked diligently to conquer the man of her dreams—wealthy, attractive, successful, young— somehow Fancy's fantasy had unfolded into an endless saga, spiraling into a sweat-drenched nightmare Fancy had last night about giving birth to a stillborn child. Or in her case, having had that abortion. Painful. Terrifying. Yet in many ways satisfying. Fancy would rather exercise choice than rear a dysfunctional child by herself like her selfish mother had raised her. What if Desmond was the father? He couldn't afford to take care of them.

Fancy had learned that maturity came with time. Wisdom came in time. And happiness, well, that was something she'd searched for as long as she remembered through the eyes of men. Why couldn't her men make her life joyful and drama-free? Why did she expect them to?

In retrospect, things between Byron and Fancy could've worked if Fancy had trusted him from the beginning. Perhaps if Fancy hadn't memorized that number on his cell phone, then dialed the number as soon as she'd gotten home. Fancy vividly recalled being taken aback by the sound of a sleepy but sultry voice that had answered, "Hello." Instantly Fancy had assumed that the bitch on the other end of the line had to be Byron's wife.

"Huh." Fancy exhaled, squeezed Desmond's hand, and then continued her thoughts. Fancy felt pretty damn foolish to have independently drawn such a conclusion before affording Byron the opportunity to explain that Mrs. Van Lee, who had Byron's last name, honestly was his sister.

Unless a woman was Oprah Winfrey, Venus or Serena Williams, or some other household name, married women ought to give up the self-identity crisis bullshit and use their husbands' last names.

That way Fancy would've at least had a clue of who she was stalking. The old Fancy would've still fucked a woman's husband then eagerly sent him home right after he sponsored her rent. Fair exchange was no robbery. After sucking his dick real good, he'd be happy, Fancy would be sheltered and satisfied, and his wife could sleep peacefully at night knowing her husband loved her enough never to leave her over a piece of ass.

Unfortunately Fancy didn't discover the truth about Byron's sister until after Fancy showed up at the woman's front door, pretending to be an appraiser working in the area doing comparables, sat in her dining room socializing, and then ran away when Byron's sister's water unexpectedly broke, forcing her into labor.

Maybe if that—*Pow!*—sound of a gun signaling the start of a race blaring in her mind hadn't triggered Fancy to sprint so fast that she saw herself crossing the threshold of the woman's front door before Byron could question how she'd gotten his sister's address, Fancy would be Mrs. Fancy Van Lee not Miss Fancy Taylor. Now Fancy realized that that unnecessary confrontation was all her fault. How could her man have explained an unasked question?

Except for that mishap and the fact that Byron had strangled her and left her for dead stranded on that mountain overlooking the Golden Gate Bridge, Byron was ideal marriage material. Or was Dez, the man who'd searched in pitch darkness until he rescued her off the mountain, ideal marriage material?

If only Fancy had trusted Byron and not called the police to report the Mercedes he'd bought her as a stolen car because he'd taken the car back. Naw, fuck that. Fancy was pissed. Fancy had earned that damn Benz! What man gave a woman a drop-top convertible or any gift then repossessed the item? Yeah, she'd accepted the car back but not until after she'd made Byron feel guilty about hurting and abandoning her.

If only Fancy hadn't carried her insecurities, baggage, broken heart, sleepless nights, disappointments, resentment, and fucked-up past relationship issues into Byron's life, they'd be married or at least still engaged. Now that Byron wanted to forgive her, it was too late for them to develop a healthy relationship—she thought.

The mental scars of Byron's fingers choking the life from her precious temple were indelibly etched in a place Fancy called her "sabotaging subconscious." Fancy had somehow managed to fuck up every single relationship she'd had. Even if Fancy took Byron back, she'd never trust him again. Fancy knew because she'd played that lead role before. Lying to herself about how the relationship could've worked.

Fancy, if only you hadn't, or, Fancy, if you had been just a little bit more patient, or less demanding, or more sensitive to his needs . . . Fancy quietly blamed herself because most of her relationships ended in disaster. Truth was, her insecurities and inability to trust men ended her relationship with Byron years before they'd ever met, including the night they'd met at the New Year's Eve gala Desmond had proudly taken Fancy to.

Squeezing Desmond's hand again, Fancy continued her thoughts. Fancy loved Desmond, she thought. Yeah, in her own special way, she did. But New Year's Eve a little over a year ago, Desmond had spent two whole paychecks to take Fancy to a gala where she'd already plotted to meet a rich man well before Desmond had picked her up from her condo. Time revealed Byron was that man. Now Fancy realized there was nothing Byron could've done to make her trust him and there was nothing Desmond could've done to gain her love. Intentionally Fancy had used a good man, her best friend, Desmond, to find a better man. Or she believed Byron was better simply because he was richer.

SaVoy was right when she'd warned Fancy, "Stop using Desmond before you ruin him." Too late. Fancy was responsible for changing Desmond's loving, considerate, selfless attitude toward women. The next woman, probably Trina, would be handed Fancy's Olympian-burning torch with which she'd emotionally scared Desmond, but Fancy would try to heal his broken heart as best as she could before Desmond left her house tonight.

The same emotional trauma held true for another one of her sponsors, Adam. Except Fancy never wanted to marry Adam but somehow ended up feeling betrayed when Adam married someone else and stopped sponsoring her rent, manicures, and hair weaves. Actually, Fancy had stopped fucking Adam when she met Byron because she believed Byron was all the man she needed. Byron. Now the thought of his name made Fancy laugh aloud. What a joke.

What the hell had Chris said that had Desmond holding his stomach instead of her hand? Whatever. Fancy continued mentally entertaining herself with thoughts from her past because Fancy was getting too old to depend on a man. Funny how the men Fancy had, she didn't want, and the man she'd always dreamt of having, she never had.

Like Desmond. Desmond was too accessible, too poor, and too immature. But Desmond was the only man who truly loved Fancy just the way she was. Regardless, that didn't change the fact that Desmond wasn't established like the rich men Fancy was accustomed to dating, and Fancy refused to settle.

Sadly, Desmond was leaving her tomorrow. Trina was single, never married, and from how Desmond bragged, anxiously awaiting his arrival. Damn, Fancy couldn't believe she was jealous of another woman she'd never met. But Fancy had met Desmond's current woman, Carlita. Carlita was admittedly more woman than Fancy but Carlita was too old for Desmond. She'd offered to relocate with Desmond but he refused her while urging Fancy to go with him. How would Fancy and Desmond look together? What would people think? Fancy dressed in her designer wardrobe fit for a runway in Milan, and Desmond a college student kickin' around campus in denims.

Fancy had seen Desmond out of his blue jeans and felt his naked flesh making love to every part of her body and soul but that wasn't enough to convince Fancy to be his woman, let alone his wife. Fancy couldn't continue hurting Desmond. But she had convinced Desmond to return the engagement ring he'd bought for Carlita and buy a friendship ring for her. Fancy loved Desmond. She thought.

Fancy was certain there was a reason why she didn't have a man.

Didn't trust men. She wished she could say it was because she wanted every man to be just like her father. And although Fancy wasn't a Christian like her best friend SaVoy, Fancy thanked God that her exes were nothing like the blue-collar, alcoholic bar patrons Fancy remembered as a little girl, who'd fucked her mother Caroline at hours when decent, respectable men were asleep. They never stayed. In the middle of the night, they'd just cum and go, and the more they'd cum the more Fancy hated her mother for loving them. Why couldn't Fancy have said all of this to Mandy earlier?

The suitor Fancy hated most, Franze, was thankfully killed by his jealous wife. Caroline worshiped Franze. If Franze said jump, Caroline didn't ask how high, she'd simply jump as high as she could. But no matter how much Caroline did to please Franze, he was never satisfied. Was any man ever truly satisfied?

Caroline wanted Franze so badly that when he started slapping her face, she felt the pain as a sign of caring, claiming she shouldn't have made him upset. Fancy was glad Franze was dead because if his wife hadn't killed his black ass, Fancy would've eventually beaten his brains out of his head.

Guess his wife grew tired of the beatings, too. The palms of Franze's heavy hands landing against Caroline's cheeks gradually turned into fists pounding her eyes. Sometimes old bruises, before healing, became new bruises. When one eye opened, he'd close the other one. Fancy hated Franze. Still did. Because Franze was the reason Fancy lied on Caroline's ex, Thaddeus.

The first time Fancy witnessed Thaddeus hitting Caroline, she dialed 9-1-1 then sat on the steps of their blue porch and waited for the blue police car with the blue flashing lights to arrive. Since childhood Fancy had hated everything associated with blue, and Desmond being a blue-collar worker and all didn't help her to like him, but she loved him. She thought. Fancy thought this because she didn't know what love was. But after her last session with Mandy, Fancy discovered that she wanted to be loved.

"Are you o—" the policeman had began to ask.

Before that officer, dressed in a dark blue uniform, completed his sentence, Fancy had hysterically cried. Flashbacks of black eyes turned blue covering her mother's face sent her into a frenzy.

"He raped me!" Fancy yelled, reaching to wrap her arms around the cop's waist. Thaddeus had never touched her, but before Fancy experienced her first menstrual cycle, Franze had stolen her virginity, causing her to bleed vaginally, and then threatened to beat and kill her if she told anyone. Rape was another reason Fancy wanted to kill Franze. But since Franze was dead, Thaddeus would pay for all the men who abused her and her mother. The police officer's fingers swiftly clasped around Fancy's then twelve-year-old wrists before Fancy could grab his gun.

Struggling to break his grip, Fancy's voice escalated. "My mother's boyfriend raped me! And he's inside beating my mother. I want you to take him away from here! *Now!*" Fancy screamed until the word trailed down her throat and fake tears rolled down her then chubby cheeks. Suddenly lights throughout the neighborhood had popped on one at a time, just like her gross fat cells had melted away one pound at a time as Fancy had starved herself down to a size seven.

Without questioning her, Fancy watched the cops enter their house and later exit, handcuffing Thaddeus while escorting him out in his blue boxers. One of the officers placed his hand on top of Thaddeus's bald head like a fitted cap, forcing Thaddeus into the back of the police car behind the caged divider where he belonged. Racing barefoot onto the porch, Caroline scrambled to tie her robe around her naked protruding waistline just as the patrol car drove off.

Placing both hands on her lumpy hips, Caroline had stared at Fancy and demanded, "Fancy, what in the world did you tell them?"

Looking up at her mother's bleeding blue face, Fancy told the truth and a lie at the same time. "To protect you, I told them he raped me."

Caroline's hands shot toward heaven as she yelled, "What! Fancy, no! Why?"

Since Caroline couldn't protect herself, somebody had to protect Fancy's mother. Good or bad, Caroline was the only mother Fancy had and Fancy was her only child.

"Maybe the cops will beat Thaddeus until he turns black and blue like he beats you so he can see how it feels. I hate men! I hate you! I hate myself! I wish I were never born! I hope they keep him and never let him out of jail!"

Rolling her eyes, Caroline had replied, "Fancy, it's not that simple. Thaddeus is going to jail but when he gets out he's going to be angry with you and angrier at me."

Heartlessly Fancy stared Caroline in the eyes while the blood in her veins sizzled, then whispered, "Then I'll just have to make sure he never gets out."

Gripping her hand now, Desmond softly asked, "Are you okay? You're trembling and your palm is sweating." Tracing her hairline, his fingertips affectionately lifted her damp hair, laying the wet darker strands atop the dry ones.

The heated air inside Fancy's lungs quietly bypassed her deflating chest and exited her nostrils as Fancy lied to Desmond once more, pretending she was fine. Truth was, Mandy was right. Fancy could've been one of America's top supermodels, perfect figure, flawless hairweave, name-brand designer clothes, including her underwear, but mentally Fancy struggled to stop suppressing the real woman inside. Whoever she was. Selfishly, Fancy wanted Desmond to stay in Oakland to console her. What would happen if Fancy told Desmond the truth? For once, Fancy could just tell Desmond that she loved him.

She thought.

Back at her condominium, Fancy decided to forego celibacy for the night. Removing Desmond's shirt, she licked his nipple, lightly grazing his other nipple with her nails. Fancy desperately needed Desmond. Her hands floated lightly over Desmond's body, remembering each hairless curve, each firm muscle, his birth mark and flesh moles.

Laughing, Desmond said, "Chris Rock is a stone fool. He still got me laughin' and I can't even remember the jokes."

Fancy wasn't joking when she said, "Dez, I want to make love to you tonight," laying him backward on her bed then caressing the nape of his neck. Her lips gently pressed against his tasty chocolate lips, journeyed to his smooth cheek, along his protruding collarbone, and then down to Desmond's sexy chest.

Desmond stopped laughing and uttered, "Fancy, what are you saying? What does this mean?"

Straddling Desmond, Fancy told him the truth. "I love you, Dez. And tonight I need for you to love me. Inside and out."

Rolling Fancy onto her back, Desmond quietly undressed Fancy, dropping her pants to the floor on top of his. Easing below her navel, Desmond buried his face in Fancy's bush. Inhaling the inviting fragrance of a good piece of sushi, Desmond sniffed and sniffed and sniffed then held his breath. "I want to remember your scent. Every time I want you in my mouth"—Desmond's fingers parted Fancy's vagina—"I'll eat a California roll or a fresh piece of coconut to remind me of your taste." He licked and sucked then licked his lips. Without looking up at Fancy, Desmond said, "I love you," as though she was the only woman he'd ever loved.

Fancy's clit shaft became more engorged when Desmond's lips wrapped around her mound and delicately sucked her juices. Fancy trembled.

Playfully forcing Desmond onto her king-sized pillow-top mattress, Fancy pulled the chord, parting her ceiling-to-floor patio curtains. Full moon. Lots of stars. The bright string of lights circling Lake Merritt was all the illumination they had, but that was enough brightness for Fancy to see how lovingly Desmond's eyes sparkled. Fancy pressed the power button on her universal remote and romantic melodies resounded—"If this world were mine, I'd give you . . ."—throughout her condo.

Waltzing to her dance pole, Fancy untied the red velvet ribbon. At a snail's pace her fingers tightened around the cool steel. Keeping her eyes fixed on Desmond, Fancy's body freely swung to the side. Slinging her hair and swaying her hips, Fancy teased her breasts. Spreading her vaginal lips for Desmond to see Miss Kitty, Fancy made love to the pole as if she were sliding up and down on Desmond's dick. Gripping the pole with both hands, Fancy flipped upside down, split her legs to form a T, and then gradually brought her thighs together.

"Damn, baby. You look so good. I didn't know you could dance like that. I want you, Fancy," Desmond said, propping his naked body against her pillows. His throbbing erection slid between his fingers as he massaged his dick up and down while keeping his eyes on Fancy.

The coolness of the pole excited Miss Kitty so Fancy gyrated, releasing a mild orgasm, reserving the urge for a massive climatic release. Letting her arms hang freely, Fancy cat-walked along the carpet until her knees and then her feet safely touched the floor. Like a cat, Fancy crawled toward the bed.

On hands and knees, Desmond eased behind Fancy, parted her legs, and flicked the tip of his tongue on the bulb of Fancy's clit.

"I don't want you like this. I want your big hard dick inside me," Fancy gracefully protested as her elbows buckled and the rest of her body collapsed onto the floor. Lying on her back, Fancy looked up at the starlight reflecting off of Desmond's face and moaned, "Make love to me, Desmond. Right here." Fancy patted the carpet. "Right now." She parted her legs wide.

Desmond's head slid down her shaft, releasing a trail of pre-cum as he penetrated Fancy. Hugging Desmond, Fancy closed her eyes. Her hands cupped his ass, pulling him into her hips grinding toward his. Her pussy got wetter and hotter, so Fancy arched her back, thrusting her ass toward the floor, forcing Desmond to hit her spot. "Hold him right there. Don't move."

In tiny circles, Fancy slowly drained her fluids. Damn, that never-ending orgasm felt so stimulating she didn't want the moment to end. Suddenly her legs started trembling uncontrollably so Fancy paused, surrendering control to Desmond's rhythm.

Penetrating her, Desmond groaned, "It's right there at the head, baby. Fancy, I want to cum inside you." Desmond's head moved deeper.

Fancy squeezed her muscles, releasing her sensational orgasm. "Cum with me, Dez. Cum with me now," Fancy whispered.

"I'm cumming, Fancy. I'm cumming, damn, you feel so good." Desmond's entire body quivered as Fancy met his intensity, releasing her fluids. They squished in their sweat, meshing together their cum.

Desmond fell asleep on top of Fancy with his dick lingering inside her. Normally, Fancy would've taken a shower and gotten in bed but she wanted to have Desmond inside of her forever, or at least until sunrise.

CHAPTER 5

Day by day. Hour by hour. Minute by minute. Every single second. Life was a series of experiences strung on a timeline. None relivable. Some unforgettable. Each forgivable. Paths crossed, space to space, yet people seldom met, even when face-to-face. Like a puzzle missing a piece, a heart skipping a beat, no one's life was complete.

The winter morning was bittersweet. Heavy rain poured in the Bay Area, pushing a cold front—near forty degrees—and unusual high winds that whistled unfamiliar tunes over Darius's skylight, waking him throughout the night. Dark clouds shielded the sunrise, disguising the morning as night. Why did showers pour on funeral days, adding despair to an already depressing gathering? A unity of family and strangers, who ordinarily wouldn't mingle in the same setting or see one another outside of holidays, reunited to console the grieving.

Darius lay in his colossal donut-shaped bed with his hands clasped behind his head. "I hate going to funerals. This is a waste of my time. Why am I even going?" Darius said, then answered himself. "If it weren't for my dad, on the real I wouldn't go."

Brighter thoughts of meeting his dad's family encouraged Darius to sit on the side of his bed. "I'm about as close to Darryl, Jr., as a stranger lying dead in the cemetery," or his next-door

neighbor, whom he rarely saw. Michael Baines, a real estate tycoon, had owned the home next to Darius's Los Angeles house for
years, and they'd met twice in passing. Darius wasn't in L.A. today,
he was in Oakland out of obligation, not respect, for his half
brother's burial but mainly to avoid dealing with his mother and
Wellington.

How was Darius supposed to exhibit sadness for his brother
when frankly he disliked Darryl, Jr.? They'd met for the first time
when Darius was twenty. In that same setting, Darius's mom had
arranged for Darius to meet face-to-face his real dad, his other half
brother Kevin, and his half sister Diamond, whom he'd hadn't
seen since. Unfamiliar family. If the truth be told, Darius really
didn't know any of them, including his father.

Shortly after meeting Darryl, Jr., Darius hired him, trying to
help his brother—more like brotha—out with a steady, decent paying job, and just like Kevin, Darryl was a loser, a liar, and a thief.
Maybe if Darius's mother hadn't lied for so many years, Darius
could've helped the brother more and Darryl, Jr., would still be
alive. Who knows, Darius's positive influence throughout their
childhood may have kept Darryl, Jr., from hanging on corners with
narcotics dealers. Supposedly Darryl, Jr., wasn't selling drugs, but
being around that many runners so frequently made everyone sus-
picious, including their father.

Darius lumbered to his spacious bathroom, admired the gold
fixtures, Jacuzzi tub, and stand-alone shower. Everything Darius
owned was compliments of his mother's generosity. She'd put his
name on one of her bank accounts when he was born, and she'd
given him his own platinum credit card when he turned thirteen.
Moms. What would he do without her? What if his mother were
the one lying in that coffin today? Or his dad? His real dad. Or
Wellington? Darius blinked repeatedly, rinsing his tears down the
black marbled drain. Wellington didn't have to raise him.

"Lord, I've got to be more appreciative of my mother. I don't
know what I'd do without her. Please don't ever take her from
me," Darius said, splashing warm then cold water on his face. His
prayer wasn't realistic but what was the point of asking God, the

man who walked on water, a miracle maker, for ordinary treatment. Oh, damn. What if he'd indirectly just asked God to take him first? For clarification, Darius added, "Lord, please don't take me first. I know how You are so I thought I'd better make myself clear." Darius brushed his teeth then stepped into the shower. Hot steamy water swarmed the enclosure like a sauna.

Fancy. "Hmm, what's Ladycat doing?" Was she thinking about him? Waking up to some other man? Byron? Opening the door, a trail of water dripped from his body as Darius picked up the cordless phone lying on his nightstand. When Fancy answered, he said, "Ladycat, what's up? I sensed I was on your mind so I decided to call."

"Hey, Darius," Fancy replied. "I was just on my way out."

"On your way to work, huh," Darius commented. "That's good."

"I wish. I don't have a job yet. Anyway, I gotta go. You wanna get together later?"

The smile in Fancy's voice resonated through the receiver. Darius smiled, too. "Yeah, that's cool. Actually I could use some cheering up. I'm on my way to my brother's funeral."

"Aw, Darius. I'm so sorry. I didn't know."

"I'll be all right. I'll call you later. 'Bye, Ladycat." Maybe he could get some sympathy pussy from Fancy later.

Darius hung up then tossed the phone on his bed. The sultry sound of Fancy's voice made him feel better. Even though Fancy didn't know him or his brother, she seemed to care. Since his mother had turned on him, and Ashlee wasn't communicating with him, Darius could use Ladycat as a lover and a friend. He'd given Fancy that nickname the moment he saw her gracefully prowling the room collecting sponsorship checks at Byron's fundraiser.

Life was great when things went well. Like his high school graduation when his mom bought his first Rolex or the days when Ma Dear cheered for him at his basketball games. Basketball. "Some day soon, boy-ie." Darius daydreamed about playing in the league but his only wish today was that his half brother Kevin didn't show up at the funeral. "If he shows his face, I'ma have the cops arrest his ass for laundering my money," Darius said, talking to himself. Kevin had created more drama in Darius's life than all the women gelled together.

Posing in his three-way mirror, Darius admired his black single-button suit. He gathered his locks into a ponytail and eased on his sunglasses to hide his contrived expressions of remorse. "Good." When Darius stepped outside, the limousine was parked in his circular driveway.

Scanning the lawn and easing into the car, Darius smirked, recalling his unforgettable adventure with Kimberly. "Bitch! Ciara. Giving Kimberly a lead role without my permission." Knowing the amount lead actresses were paid, Kimberly would have more money than him. Would Kimberly continue fucking him at every request?

"Forget about Kimberly and focus on Fancy," Darius said, staring out the window.

"Excuse me, sir, but I didn't hear you," the driver said.

"Females, man. I'm just talking out loud."

This was possibly Darius's last chauffeured ride for a while so he'd use the driver all day and throughout the night and worry about paying the bill later. At least he'd have the car long enough to impress Fancy and hit it. To make certain Fancy gave up the pussy tonight, Darius decided to splurge beyond measure. After the funeral, he'd need to have more than his dick sucked. Massaging his erection, Darius imagined fucking Fancy in every hole possible, including her ears.

The driver doubled-parked in front of Whitted-Williams Funeral Home. "Hey, man, I'm gon' need you for the rest of the day and night. I'll call you on my cell when I'm ready. And when I say I'm ready, I'm ready, so wait right here."

Entering the empty parlor, Darius stopped in the doorway. "I must be in the wrong place." There were six people including himself. Squinting through his dark shades, Darius recognized Darryl Senior, and his wife, Diamond, and Kevin seated in the front row of aligned folding chairs. Darius should've known Kevin would be sitting next to their father, sucking up. And there was a homeless lady sitting in the back, brushing a matted wig.

Stretching his arm, Darius bent his elbow then glanced at his watch. "Maybe I have the wrong time. Surely this can't be everybody." Since the service hadn't started and Darius expected more people to arrive, he sat in the last row behind the strange woman. Less time to pretend he was distraught over someone shooting his half brother in the head.

Turning to him, the homeless woman stared at Darius, then whispered in an eerie tone, "There is death all around you."

Had Darius stepped into a live horror scene? If he ran outside, would the limo driver be dead or gone? Removing his glasses, belligerently Darius eyed the queer woman. A dripping-wet sweater draped her shoulders. A shopping bag stuffed with newspapers and a soggy loaf of French bread rested on the folding chair beside her. What the heck was she going to do after grooming that wig?

Cynically she stared back so Darius said, "Of course, lady, in case you haven't noticed, this is a funeral parlor."

Leaning her flabby arm over the back of her chair, she moved closer to him then whispered, "I know that. But everything around you is dying slowly, even your spirit."

Darius slid his plaid cushioned chair back two feet and said, "You don't know me," then stood.

"Your mother can't always fight your battles like you expect her to. It's time you accept responsibility for your actions and become the man your grandmother envisioned you'd become."

Whoa. The strength in Darius's legs escaped slowly, collapsing him back into the green chair. If he suddenly had to run away to save his life, he couldn't. This homeless woman had captured his attention. Darius mumbled, "How do you know Ma Dear?"

"She's sitting beside you. She's always beside you."

Gazing toward the cushion, the indention was wide. Blinking, Darius looked at the homeless woman. She closed her eyes then quietly said, "Only one of those babies is yours. But the son that is yours, soon after he is born, he will die. So will one of your parents. Next year. Death follows you." She opened her eyes.

"Gee, thanks lady." Darius stood again.

"Right now you are sad but, like when you were a child, you will find happiness again. And you will remarry but not the woman you think you want. For the first time in your life you will genuinely fall in love and you will marry the woman you fall in love with. But before that happens you will suffer. Tremendously."

Waving his hand at the floor, Darius said, "I'm here for my brother's funeral. Let me get away from you. I've heard enough of your foolishness, old woman."

The homeless woman replied, "I may be foolish."

Darius continued walking toward the front, near his family. Midway down the aisle he heard her say, "But I'm not broke. Goodbye, Darius." When Darius turned to see her face once more, she was gone.

"Hey, son," Darryl Senior said. "Darius, come sit next to me. Kevin, move over one seat," their dad said, ushering Kevin to the middle of the row.

Darryl Senior leaned his head on Darius's shoulder and started crying. What was Darius supposed to do? Hug his dad? Pat his back? Nothing? The only grown man Darius had seen shed tears was Wellington. Had Wellington pretended? Was Darryl Senior faking? Darius handed his dad a monogrammed handkerchief with the initials *DL* inscribed for Darius's Law. Darius made the rules, he didn't follow them.

"You have no idea what it's like to lose your firstborn. Darryl Junior may have not been perfect but he was mine. Just like you and Diamond and Kevin. Why would anyone kill my son?" Darryl Senior sobbed heavily.

Forcing tears, Darius wrapped his arm around his father's shoulder. Tears streamed down his face onto his black suit. Leaning over his father, Kevin rubbed Darius's back. Swiftly Darius shifted his eyes, squinted at Kevin, and mouthed, "Don't you ever touch me again, you thief."

Hunching his shoulders, Kevin lip-synced, "Aw, come on, brother. Forgive me. Please."

Darius's body tensed as he silently replied, "Forgive you? Like, hell. I'ma whup your ass if you don't give me back my money."

"But—" Kevin stopped talking when their father stared at him.

Some guy dressed in a cream-colored robe entered the room and stood behind a podium. Darius and seemingly no one else knew this person. Darryl Junior had a complete stranger conducting his ceremony? The funeral was nothing like when Ma Dear died. There was standing room only then. Pastor Tellings, who'd known Ma Dear for years, had preached a brief but powerful sermon. Darius never sang "I Won't Complain" at Ma Dear's funeral because before he opened his mouth, he passed out. Maybe he could sing the song for his half brother. Who was that strange woman? Darius wondered. Then her voice echoed in his mind, "There is death all around you. Death follows you."

Darius's legs lifted him to his feet. His mouth opened as he faced his family and began singing.

His dad cried, nodding with approval. Kevin's eyes turned red and watery. Maybe Darius should forgive Kevin because when Darius's day came to lie in a coffin nothing would matter more than how people remembered him. His women. His money. His career.

Immediately after Darius stopped singing, the pastor—if he was a pastor—asked, "Would anyone like to say a few words?"

Clearing his throat, Darryl Senior stood and said, "Um," I would." He paused.

Kevin bellowed from his gut, "Take your time, Dad."

Ass kisser, Darius thought.

"As my son's spirit has ascended into heaven, I would like for everyone to remember Darryl Junior as a man with a childlike nature, who died trying. Trying to fit in. Trying to love others. Trying to find himself. His purpose in life. Trying to be accepted even in situations where he knew people didn't like him. Laughing when there was nothing to laugh about, all along crying out for help on the inside. Darryl Junior gave his all. His last. And a little too late, tried to follow in Darius's footsteps. Darius, you have no idea how much Darryl Junior admired you. Darryl praised your success all the time in our presence. I admire and love you, too, son." Darryl Senior's tears forcefully choked the remaining words out of his throat. "Those drug dealers on the corner didn't kill my son. Darryl Junior's desperate desire to belong to a group that loved him, killed him. We should've been that group. I failed my son because I could've been that group. Let Darryl J be an example and let us"—he spread his arms wide—"starting right here, right now, not allow the lack of love in this family to kill another member."

Hurrying to uphold his father's weakening body, Darius placed his dad's arm over his shoulder and helped him to the nearest seat, which required Kevin to move over again.

"I love you, Dad," Darius whispered drying his father's tears then his own.

The guy in the robe read the eulogy that Darryl Junior's mother handed him. Strange, but she was expressionless during the entire service. Darius wondered how his mother would react if he were the one dead. Hopefully, not like Darryl Junior's mom. Why wasn't she crying? Something was definitely wrong between his father and her but now wasn't the time to probe.

The pastor said, "You may now view the body before the casket is closed."

In a semicircle, everyone viewed at the same time.

"Son," Darryl Senior said, "come over to our house."

"When, Dad?" Darius asked, amazed at how Darryl Junior's face was reconstructed while thinking about his date with Fancy.

"Now. For a family dinner. I want my family together today."

Damn. His dad's timing was off. Darius didn't have time to socialize with them. Reluctantly Darius answered, "Okay. What's the address?" Darius had never been to their home.

"Ride with me," his dad insisted.

Now that was not happening. Darius couldn't be at the mercy of a depressed, grieving individual even if it was his dad. "I'll have my limo driver follow you."

Thankfully, Darryl Senior didn't live far. Sunshine had replaced the rain brightening the day. His dad lived in Fremont off of the Stevenson exit of Interstate 880. Driving toward the hillside, the limo parked in front of a home that resembled M.C. Hammer's mansion, encompassing almost one square city block. Darryl Senior privately showed Darius his enormous trophy room while Kevin and the other family members scattered to separate parts of the house.

"Wow! Dad, this is incredible! So you played baseball, football, soccer, and ran track, too. Damn. This is tight." Looking up at the walls, Darius froze. Scanning the huge frames, Darius closed then opened his teary eyes. "You have pictures from all my championship games." Pointing, Darius continued, "That's the game when you put me on your shoulders after we won." Pointing again, "And that's the game when you autographed my jersey. And all those pictures when you coached me at Georgetown. Dad!"

Darryl Senior tossed one of his championship rings to Darius. "You'll be earning your own pretty soon."

Snagging the ring above his head, Darius briefly thought about the day Maxine threw his engagement ring at him and how he'd caught her ring the same way, then Darius bounced on his tiptoes and said, "This is sweet. Yeah. Hell, yeah." Thumping twice on his chest, Darius said, "I can do this." Darius placed the ring on his finger then gave it to his dad.

"I can tell you've got plans. I just wanted to show you what you can accomplish if you stay focused. Just always remember to treat people right, because you can't accomplish anything by yourself and you never know who you're going to need. You can come by anytime you want. Anytime, son. My house is your home." Darryl Senior accompanied Darius back to the limousine.

Darius was so excited he phoned Fancy from the car.

"Hel—"

Darius interrupted Fancy. "Ladycat, I'm on my way to pick you up! I have so much to tell you."

"Well, I'm glad you're in a better mood. Let me get ready. I'll see you in—"

"A half hour!" Darius said, ending the call.

The driver cruised and Darius floated on air. Having his dad in his life was the best high he'd ever had. More exciting than any of the material things his mother had given him. Darius called Fancy again.

"We're here. You want me to come up?"

"No, I'm on my way down."

Fancy strutted up to the limo drenched in amethysts and diamonds, wearing a long-sleeved, red leather dress with a sheer waist, and off-white thigh-high boots with red metallic heels. Her nails, hair, and makeup were immaculate. Darius knew Fancy was the woman for him. Ladycat was a woman of his caliber that would definitely complement his image.

"So where're we going?" Fancy asked, sitting next to him.

"Wherever you'd like. This is your night." Darius was so hyped Fancy could take complete control if she wanted.

"Okay, let's take a stroll down the pier next to Skates Restaurant and watch the sunset. Then we can go shopping at Tiffany's in San Francisco and have dinner at Silks restaurant."

Yeah. Right. Hopefully Fancy wasn't serious. But just in case she was, Darius added, "Then after dinner we can spend the night at my place."

Fancy smiled. Darius wanted to hold her but opted not to so he could keep Slugger from getting massively swollen on their first date. When the driver parked in front of the pier, Darius cradled Fancy into his arms, lifted her out of the limo, and quickly placed her on her feet.

"Here we are," Fancy said lowering her dress. "Let's walk to the end." As they strolled, Fancy grasped his hand and said, "I'm glad we have this time. I really want to get to know you."

Darius concealed his frown. Fancy was getting too serious too soon. All he wanted to do was have a good time. "Yeah, we have plenty of time for that when I return. I have to go to L.A. in a few days. But I'll be back."

Grazing the planks of the pier, careful not to sink her heels between the boards, Fancy asked, "So what had you all excited earlier?"

"Aw, man!" Darius cheesed. "My Dad, former NBA All-Star Darryl Williams, Sr., he's wonderful. I saw all of his trophies and championship rings for the first time today, and he said I'ma be just like him! I love my dad!"

Fancy's eyes drooped, jaw dropped, and cheeks descended toward her chin. "That's nice. I wish I knew my dad or felt that way about my mom."

"Ladycat, what's wrong?"

"Nothing. Can you take me home?"

"Home? No way. We came out to have a good time and I'm not going to let you go home and mope. Trust me. I have family prob-

lems, too, so I do understand. You'll be okay. I'll take care of you."
Who'd spoken those words? Darius bit his bottom lip. Dude, stop
trippin' over this female.

There they stood. Hand in hand at the end of the pier. Two of
the most attractive people in the universe, and they both had issues. Darius sensed whatever troubled Fancy was equally depressing as his problems. Darius and Fancy silently stood on the pier
until the sun burst into a huge ball of rays expanding from the
ocean into the heavens then faded into the water. Then Darius took
Fancy to San Francisco as she'd desired, to the private members-
only club they'd both frequented. When Byron showed up acting a
fool, claiming Fancy was his woman, Darius took Fancy home.

"So you want me to come up?" Darius asked then said, "I don't
want to be alone."

"Not tonight. Maybe next time. I'm tired." Fancy kissed Darius's
jaw. "Thanks. I had a great time and you were a perfect gentleman.
Call me tomorrow."

Oh, hell no. Fuck that gentleman bullshit. If Fancy thought she
was pimpin' Darius Jones, she was wrong. The limousine driver ex-
ceeded the speed limits to get Darius home. Darius had no intention of dialing Fancy's number ever again. His dick was hard and
his bed was lonely. Pumping his erection up and down, Darius
stared at his ceiling. After all the money he'd spent, another night
of masturbation.

Females! Fuck!

CHAPTER 6

Darius must've been crazy if he thought Fancy would fall for the "wine, dine, and then bang the hell out of Miss Kitty until his dick was satisfied" routine simply because he was rich, handsome, and spent lots of money on their first date. Fancy had enjoyed dining with him but she was serious. Miss Kitty was on hiatus. She was protesting again, clenching her muscles and stimulating her own G-spot, but Miss Kitty might as well stop acting a fool and get used to being solo because it would be a while, a long while, before she felt the stiffness of a man's erection penetrating her walls. Typically Fancy would've given a man as wealthy as Darius all the pussy he wanted but Byron, Adam, and Harry proved that that approach backfired every time. It was time to implement patience.

Lacing up her cross-country track shoes, Fancy stepped onto the treadmill, warmed up for ten minutes with a brisk walk at level three, and then increased the speed to six. While jogging, Fancy watched CNN on the flat screen television in front of her.

"Drop down and get your eagle on, girl," blared through Fancy's cellular phone. Quickly she answered, ignoring the NO CELL PHONE sign posted on the wall, as the guys running on treadmills along side her at Club One Fitness smiled.

"Hey, Byron. What's up?" Byron was the first person Fancy expected to hear from after seeing him at the members only club.

"Missing you. I apologize for the way I acted last night. I had no right confronting you in front of Darius."

Hell, he had no right confronting her at all. Byron's voice dragged like he had a bad hangover. "And I'm sorry for the way I mistreated you over the phone the last time we spoke. Are you enjoying the Benz?"

Byron could never give an apology without countering with something that was supposed to make Fancy feel guilty. "You can have the car back any time you want." Fancy refused to become attached to Byron through his car again.

"No, baby. I've decided it's yours. That's why I'm calling. I want to take you to DMV. Today. To transfer the title into your name."

Reducing the treadmill's speed from six to four, Fancy continued running and sweating. "Oh, really?" Fancy inhaled through her nostrils and out her mouth. "You do know you don't have to go with me to DMV. If you're sincere, just sign the title over to me and I'll register the car myself."

"I just want to talk to you Fancy, that's all."

Whenever a man said, "That's all," he was lying. The same as when anyone had told Fancy, "It's okay if you don't," or "I really don't mean to hurt you but . . ." All lies.

"What's the real reason you wanna see me?" Fancy asked.

The men beside Fancy frowned. Fancy nodded, then winked at the good-looking, muscular brotha to her left. The guy to her right would definitely prefer having a cheeseburger over eating a woman.

"Look, forget it. If you hadn't played all those childish games searching through my pants, checking my cell phone, and showing up at my sister's house, you'd be Mrs. Van Lee. Darius doesn't deserve you, baby. Darius is out for one thing and one thing only. Sex. Just like that night he convinced me to take you home from the club and swing back to hang with him and his boys and Desire and her friends. You can't trust him. When you get ready for a real man, call me."

Silence lingered on both ends. Had Byron realized what he'd said? Normally Fancy would've gotten upset. Byron wasn't worth her time. But Byron did have a big dick and lethal oral skills. Miss Kitty knocked twice. Three times. Fancy pressed the end button on her phone and increased the speed up to seven and sprinted. He'd call back.

To avoid lusting over Byron, Fancy's mind drifted, thinking about moving her bedroom set into the bedroom where it belonged because now that she was unemployed, the morning sunrise in her living room was awakening her before she was ready to get up. But how would Fancy move her dance pole? She couldn't. Never mind, the bedroom stayed in the living room.

Maybe Fancy should give Byron back his Benz so he wouldn't have a reason to call and she wouldn't be tempted to suck his sweet dick like a lollipop. Byron obviously ate all the right foods because his cum was so tasty Fancy could dip strawberries in it for dessert. If she kept the car, Byron would continue feeling like he had control over her. No more. This time Fancy was for real. Fancy Taylor was taking complete control over every aspect of her life. Why was it so difficult to do the right things?

Doing a quick twenty laps around the indoor track, Fancy completed fifty push-up, sixty arm curls, showered, and spent her usual thirty minutes in the steam sauna—in ten, out five, in ten, then out five again to avoid passing out like this one woman who stayed in for almost sixty minutes straight. Someone should've told her moving into the sauna was not the solution to losing all that fat overnight, but at least she was at the gym. Maybe Fancy could convince her overweight mother to join. At almost a hundred dollars a month, Fancy doubted Caroline would make the sacrifice physically or financially.

Completing her morning workout, Fancy exited the club, waving good-bye to her future real estate clients; most of them were on the basketball court getting their run in. Joining Club One Fitness was a major investment. The fee was astronomical but worth every penny because the Warrior basketball players, the Raiders, doctors, lawyers, dentists, the Oakland A's, Brian Shaw's fine ass—since he'd retired from the Lakers—Previn, Frederick Morris, and several other millionaires frequented the gym throughout the week.

Fancy stood outside the glass double doors in front of Wells Fargo, debating whether to get a shake or go home and study for her real estate quiz. The growl in her stomach answered for her. Walking pass Waldenbooks and GNC, Fancy noticed a familiar face.

Not her again. *No, she did not take off her matted wig, shake it in midair, and put that rug back on her head and pick up another wig. City Center really needs to keep the derelicts off the premises*, Fancy thought watching the same homeless woman she'd seen by Mandy's office sitting on the bench outside Jamba Juice with a grocery bag stuffed with newspaper and a loaf of bread. Fancy stood near the door fumbling in her backpack for money to buy an original Razzmatazz smoothie.

"Give it away," the homeless woman said, applying short uneven strokes to that matted hairpiece. Unlike on the day Fancy first noticed the homeless woman sitting on a bench across the street from Mandy's office draped in dingy clothing, her gray sweater was now freshly white.

Was she following Fancy? She'd better not beg for money. Eyeing the women, Fancy continued digging feeling for dollar bills.

"Give it away," she said again.

Skeptically walking over to the bench, Fancy said, "Excuse me," rolling her eyes, "but who are you talking to?"

She pointed directly at Fancy's forehead, reminding Fancy of how she'd done Mandy, so Fancy glanced over her shoulder then back at the woman. "What the hell?" Fancy dug deeper in her bag and handed the woman a dollar.

Shoving Fancy's hand away, she said, "I don't need your money, honey. Starting today. Give it away."

"Don't touch me." Wiping her hand on her backpack, Fancy exhaled heavily then grunted, "Give what away?"

"Your love. Who are you saving it for? No matter how much you love someone today you still have enough love in your heart to love them tomorrow. But start with loving yourself."

Fancy's head moved side to side. "You're crazy. Leave me alone. And stop following me!"

Rocking back and forth, the woman closed her eyes. Without opening them she said, "You want to be a millionaire, don't you?"

"Who doesn't?" That was a stupid question.

"But *you,* my dear, *desperately* want to become a millionaire. That's why you went back to school. And I do see financial blessings all around you."

Now she had Fancy's attention. Someone was giving Fancy positive news about her future. Fancy smoothed her hands over her waist-length blazer and listened.

Rocking, the woman gazed intently at Fancy and said, "Don't worry. Your millions of dollars will come later this year. In fact, within the next four to six weeks, you'll earn a lump sum of money. Excuse me, your light is unusually bright so I must close my eyes again. The man in your life is your future husband."

Yeah, right. "If you're so psychic, help me out. What's his name?"

"I can't see his full name. But his name starts with a D. I will say this: choose carefully because I see interference from several men. Don't cling to the familiar and don't fall in love with the wrong guy."

"But how will I know when I'm in love?" Fancy asked, moving one step closer.

The homeless woman leaned backward, shaking her wig, "Oh, I don't know if you want to hear the truth."

"Just tell me."

"The man you will fall in love with, you will love him so deeply you will take a bullet for him."

Fancy's chin pressed against her throat. Her eyes lifted toward her eyebrows that were stretching into her forehead. "Take a bullet? As in voluntarily get shot? You really need professional help."

Ignoring Fancy, the homeless woman replied, "Pray. Get closer to God. You once believed in God when you were a child. He's waiting for your return. And don't take the easy road. You are going to suffer and be hurt. Like never before. But don't let that stop you from giving away your love every single day."

Why had Fancy solicited this psycho's opinion? "Look, I've got to go, you don't know me."

Rocking back and forth the woman continued, "Forgive your mother and beware of your father, for he has a vendetta against you. If you don't do anything else I ask you to do, take a self-defense class next week. Your life is dependent upon it."

"First off, I don't know who my father is." Tears swelled in Fancy's eyes. "Besides, I thought you just said I was going to be a millionaire. Now you're telling me someone is going to try to kill me if I don't kill myself first. You're crazy, lady."

"Perhaps you're right. I've prayed that God take this gift of sight from me. But I've never been wrong. Good-bye, Fancy."

Racing inside Jamba Juice, Fancy realized she was listening to a lunatic homeless woman. A homeless woman prophesizing her life? Could she be right? What did she know anyway? Fancy changed her mind and decided to order a Peach Pleasure with a protein boost and one ounce of wheatgrass.

"What's your name?" the cashier asked.

"Fancy." Fancy paused then screamed, "Fancy! How did she know my name?!" Fancy left the cashier holding her ten-dollar bill then ran back outside. A couple was sitting on the bench hugging and kissing. Fancy ran down the escalator toward the BART transit station. The homeless woman, seated by the window, waved good-bye.

Fancy stood frozen watching the woman brush her wig as the train pulled off, whistling through the tunnel. The mysterious woman was gone. *If you don't do anything else I ask you to do, take a self-defense class next week. Your life is dependent upon it.*

What did that crazy woman know?

CHAPTER 7

A mother's work was never done. Didn't matter if her child was ten, twenty, thirty, forty, or older, a mother always cared. Regardless of whether her child was single, married, divorced, a clergyman, a convict, or a loner. A mother's undying love for her child was unconditional.

Jada sat at the breakfast table sipping hot coffee with hazelnut and cream. The *Los Angeles Times* was spread flat and wide across the onyx tabletop. Scanning the unemployment section for Darius, Jada said, "There is no way my baby is going to find a suitable job through these advertisements. I'm going to have to call in a few favors from some of my top clients."

Retrieving her cell phone, Jada dialed the cellular number for the manager of her Bank of America branch. Waiting for him to answer, Jada refreshed her coffee.

"Good morning, Mr. Riley. This is Jada Diamond Tanner." Jada always emphasized her middle name because it was a direct link to her business.

"Yes, of course. Good, morning. My accountant did send the check for our last contact, didn't he?"

"Yes, but that's not why I'm calling. I need your assistance. My son Darius needs a job for a few months until he starts college."

"It's good to let these youngsters work for someone else. I made all four of my children get intern positions while they were in college."

"Oh, but Darius needs a paid position. Darius's father wants him to earn and live off of his own money."

Laughing, Mr. Riley said, "That Wellington Jones certainly understands investments. That's why I keep my investments through him. Jada, consider it done. I can use Darius in my office immediately. Have him call me early tomorrow morning."

Feeling relieved, Jada turned to the world news section. What a tragedy. The death toll had climbed unbelievably. Over two hundred thousand people killed in a tsunami. Jada scribbled a reminder to send money to the forgotten people suffering in Rwanda.

Reversing her thoughts to her son, why had Darius grown up without any true friends? And the friendships Darius had acquired, they hadn't lasted. Was it because he was an only child? Jada had ensured Darius always had the best tutors and played basketball since second grade, but she hadn't encouraged him to develop friendships. Was she so busy juggling her life, her marriage to Lawrence, her business, and her affair with Wellington that she'd neglected to spend quality time with her son, making sure all of his needs were met? Educationally. Physically. Socially. Emotionally. When Darius didn't have Ma Dear, he had baby-sitters. But Darius never had friends.

Jada flipped to the sports section. As a teenager in high school, Darius was closest to K'Nine. Even when Darius went to Georgetown and K'Nine went to the University of Maryland at College Park, they partied together whenever possible. After K'Nine's sophomore year, when he was drafted into the NBA, Darius distanced himself when K'Nine became friends with his Atlanta teammates. Jada sensed Darius was jealous of K'Nine so she offered him the executive vice president position at her company in L.A. Offering Darius that job proved to be a mistake, but it allowed Jada to separate Darius from his father and head coach, Darryl Williams, Sr.

Eventually Darius had to know his real father but Jada didn't want him to find out accidentally. What if K'Nine and Darius had both gone to the pros at the same time? What if Darryl Senior really delivered on his promise and got Darius into the NBA?

Switching to the local section, Jada thought about the day she gave birth to Darius. Wellington was at the hospital with her, not Darryl. Wellington cut Darius's umbilical cord. Slept at the hospital every night with them. Even when Wellington's son's mother Simone questioned Wellington, saying, "Are you sure Darius is your son? He looks nothing like you," Wellington never asked Jada. Later Wellington confessed his suspicions about being Darius's father, but said, "I was so happy being a part of your life again, I guess I didn't want to know the truth."

Darius was five years old when Wellington doubted the paternity. Over the years, Jada and Wellington had raised Darius together. And Jada would be lying if she said she cared about Wellington the second as much as she did her own son. She'd seen the same change in Wellington when his look-alike, Wellington the II was born. For twenty years Wellington was Darius's father. Lawrence, for ten of those twenty, was more of a surrogate dad. And Darryl Senior. for the last two plus years was finally raising Darius.

Wellington was always there for them. Through Jada's ten years of marriage, Wellington was the disciplinarian for Darius. Wellington flew back and forth on short notice whenever Darius was sick, and to attend his games, and to see Darius off to college.

Perusing the entertainment section, Jada imagined what her life would be like if she'd married Darryl Senior instead of Wellington. Instead of Lawrence. Life was full of what ifs. But the one thing Jada was certain of was that she wasn't going to be forced to choose between her child and her husband. Because that conclusion was drawn the day she became pregnant. No man would ever come before her child. Her son was her responsibility and no man could force her to abandon her son, not even her husband. But had she in some way abandoned Darius?

Glancing over the obituaries to see if any of her clients or anyone else she knew had died recently, Jada pushed her Georgetown coffee mug aside. Darius wasn't perfect. Neither was she. Jada had her share of skeletons, disappointments, and deception. Lying to Lawrence when they were married about not having sex with

Wellington. Well, maybe she hadn't lied, because during the intimate moments she'd shared with Wellington they were making love, not having sex. She could use countless explanations to justify her past but that wouldn't change all the lies she'd told.

One consistent truth was, from the night they'd met at Will Downing's concert, Jada's heart was always with Wellington. Even when he called off their engagement and married Melanie Marie Thompson, Jada was still in love with Wellington. Wellington married Melanie because Melanie had gotten pregnant by him and Wellington, being a man of great character, wanted to make an honest woman out of Melanie, as if that were possible. Melanie's expected triplets and Wellington's evil mother, Cynthia, who never liked Jada, sabotaged their engagement.

What if Cynthia had never interfered in their relationship? What if Cynthia hadn't lied to Wellington over thirty-five years about his biological father? What if Jada's baby would've been for Wellington? What if?

Jada tossed the newspaper into its recycle rack. Her personal life was in shambles. When was Darius going to stop avoiding giving Wellington that check? More than anything, Jada simply missed and wanted to see her child.

Having to choose between being loyal to her husband or supportive of her only child was ridiculous. Jada went upstairs to their bedroom. How could she please both? Darius was spoiled and it was her fault, giving her child more than even he imagined. But why not? She was wealthy and, well, he was her only liability. Jada sat on the edge of the bed and stared at Wellington.

Selecting a tie from his rack, Wellington asked, "What's wrong, baby?"

"Wellington, we can't just cut Darius's finances off leaving him destitute. He's grieving over his brother's death, for goodness sake, and he is trying to get his life together." Jada watched her husband loop his necktie several times. She could've done it for him but she was too emotional not to intentionally choke Wellington.

"Jada, when are you going to let Darius grow up? He needs to learn responsibility. I'm tired of his carelessness and inconsidera-

tion for others. Three babies, Jada. Darius has three women pregnant. It's best that he doesn't have our money. And he'd better get
a job by the end of this week or he'll be homeless."

"Not my son, Wellington Jones. As long as there's breath in my
body and a roof over my head, Darius will never live on the
streets."

"I'm done with this conversation. You act like you're the only
one who raised Darius."

"I never said that."

"I didn't say you did. You don't have to. After all I've done for
you. For Darius—" The doorbell rang, interrupting Wellington's
response. Wellington and Jada looked at one another.

"Are you—"

Interrupting Jada, Wellington asked, "No, you?"

"No," Jada said, slipping her partially naked body into a black
silk robe. She followed Wellington downstairs.

When Wellington opened the door, there stood Jada's baby.
Darius's face was long like a child who'd just discovered there was
no Santa, with his mouth closed, his chin hung low. His eyes were
red and watery.

Welcoming Darius into her arms, Jada said, "Honey, come in.
Are you okay?"

Darius leaned into his mother's bosom. "Naw, Ma. I was disappointed you didn't attend the funeral yesterday."

Pushing Darius back, Jada said, "Baby, I didn't know Darryl
Junior that well."

"But you do know me, Ma. I expected you to be there for me."

Wellington interjected, "There you go again, thinking your mother
owes you something. Sit down in the living room." Wellington left
then returned with the insurance check. Wellington handed the
check to Darius and said, "Sign this so we can get the business back
up and running before the release of *Soul Mates Dissipate*."

Joining Darius in the living room, Jada said, "It's okay, honey.
It's not that serious. Just sign the check and we can deal with the
rest later."

"That's my business and those are my films. I ain't signing shit!"

"Wellington, he does have a valid point. We gave Darius his own company. Why don't we discuss this business arrangement now and you can explain to Darius the details?"

Wellington countered, "There's nothing to discuss."

Darius remained silent, staring at Wellington.

"I disagree. Wellington, I think we as a family should discuss why you felt the need to take over Darius's company."

"Because Darius screws everything he gets his hands on, that's why. When he gets his life in order, if he ever gets his life in order, he can have his company back. End of conversation." Wellington stared back at Darius and said, "I'm glad my son is nothing like you."

Jada shouted, "What the hell is that supposed to mean?!"

Darius leapt from the sofa and two inches from Wellington's face. "Fuck you! And your son!"

Wellington's fist landed in Darius's chest. "Who the hell you think you're disrespecting? Yeah, that's right. Stand up again so I can knock your sorry ass back down."

"Wellington, if you hit my son again I swear I'll hurt you!"

"Your son?! Your fuckin' son! That's right!"

Drawing back a fist, Darius yelled, "That's right!"

Wellington cocked his fist in midair.

Standing between Darius and Wellington, Jada screamed, "You two cut it out!" Breathing heavy, she placed her palms on their chests, then pleaded, "Darius honey, just sign the check."

Darius snatched the check from Wellington's grip, scribbled across the back, then threw it on the table.

"There, you satisfied? Everybody's happy now."

"Honey, everything will be all right." Jada wrapped her arms tight around Darius's shoulders. "You did the right thing."

Wellington picked up the endorsed check.

Darius protested, "I need some of that money, Ma. My bank account is low."

"Then you'd better get off your ass and get a job," Wellington said, leaving the room. He yelled from the foyer, "I'm going to the bank, then to meet with my client. I have a late appointment," then closed the door.

Massaging his chest, Darius said, "Ha, client, yeah, right. I bet that appointment will run after midnight, too."

Frowning, Jada sat next to Darius on the sofa and quizzically asked, "Honey, what's that supposed to mean?"

"Nothing, Mama. I need a half mil until school starts."

Shaking her head, Jada said, "I can't right now, honey, your father will get upset. But I'll see what I can do next month after Wellington calms down. Okay? But I do have some good news. I got you a job at a bank. You can start tomorrow." Jada reached for Darius's hands.

Avoiding her touch, silently Darius stood, exited the room, and then slammed the front door.

Jada desperately wanted to give Darius the money but maybe Wellington was right. Maybe it was time for her to let Darius grow up.

CHAPTER 8

Real Estate Finance was more challenging than Fancy had anticipated, particularly remembering all the intricate details between a fixed rate and an adjustable rate mortgage (ARM). Fixed interest rates remained the same for fifteen, twenty, or thirty years with no prepayment penalty. Adjustable rates fluctuated for the first one to seven years based on prime rates, but the initial rate for an ARM was below market as opposed to fixed rates, giving the homeowner initially lower payments. Then there were the conversions and assumptions only applicable to ARMs. The no-money-down programs, balloon payments, silent second mortgages, owner financed mortgages, the mortgage money market, sources for supply and demand for financing, loan processing, the primary lenders' right to sale of the mortgage in a pool of loans to another lender in the secondary market immediately after closing, because most primary lenders didn't service mortgages, and so much more. And all that information was disseminated in one class, leaving her to take four more required courses and three electives.

Pressing her middle finger against her temple, Fancy arrived a few minutes early to class and drove into the asphalt parking lot that was perpendicular to the street. "I have a newfound respect for brokers." The only remaining spaces were in the rear, behind the building. Sitting in her car, Fancy speed dialed Darius's number.

Darius delightfully answered, "Hey, Ladycat. What's up?"

"On my way to class. I just called to hear your voice and let you know I was thinking about you." A half smile brightened Fancy's spirit.

"Now that's what I'm talkin' 'bout. You want to hang . . . I mean get together after your class?" Darius asked.

"You're in Oakland? I thought you were in L.A."

"Yeah, I had to get away from my parents. They were truly stressing me the hell out."

"Well, class ends around eight. Meet me at my house at nine-thirty. 'Bye, Darius."

Fancy hung up the phone and dialed Caroline's number hoping her mother's voice mail would respond on the fourth ring so Fancy could leave a brief message.

"Hi, Fancy," her mother cheerfully answered on the first ring.

Fancy shouldn't have called. Why did she torture herself by trying to foster a relationship with her mother? Hesitantly Fancy replied, "Hi, Mom." Calling Caroline "Mom" felt awkward and Fancy wasn't sure how long she'd wait before reverting back to using her mother's name, because Caroline hadn't changed. With nothing better to say, Fancy asked, "How was your day?"

"Wonderful!" Caroline shouted. "Marvin is taking me to Rubicon's in San Francisco for dinner tonight. You've been so many places, Fancy. Have you been there?"

A man didn't have to do much to impress Caroline. A movie, a meal, or a drink at a bar, were more than sufficient to convince Caroline to open her legs. But Marvin was better than the blue-collar workers Caroline customarily dated. Fancy had courted enough rich men to know that Marvin was too wealthy, too attractive, and too sophisticated to be genuinely interested in her overweight out-of-shape mother, who would rather spend over four dollars a day on a Venti Caramel Frappuccino at Starbucks than pay three dollars a day or less for a membership at a decent gym.

Caroline shouldn't get her expectations up too high with this Marvin guy because he couldn't possibly love Caroline. But from what Fancy had heard, Marvin, like all the rest of Caroline's men, was certainly enjoying how good Caroline sucked his gigantic dick.

Casually, Fancy replied, "No, I haven't been to Rubicon's."

"Really? You mean I'm going to a place you haven't been? I promise to tell you all about my date with Marvin tomorrow.

Rolling her eyes, Fancy exhaled.

Caroline continued, "I really snagged a winner with Marvin. I love him so much. I think he's going to ask me to marry him."

Hardly, Fancy thought, replying, "I've heard good things about Rubicon's but Roxanne's in Larkspur is better and more expensive. Ma, be careful. Have you asked Marvin what he sees in you?"

"What's that supposed to mean? Are you jealous of me, Fancy? You think I can't date a man with money like you. You're the only one good enough to date a Byron or a Harry or an Adam or this new rich guy you've met, Darius."

Gee, thanks for bringing up old memories, Fancy thought as she said, "Don't be ridiculous." If Caroline knew how Byron and Harry had abused her, Caroline would rejoice believing Fancy's men were just like hers, and that was a lie. Fancy's standards were definitely above her mother's.

"I don't have any reason to be jealous of you. I've dated lots of wealthy men and I just know how they are, that's all. They spend very little on women who readily sleep with them and lots of money on good-looking women who demand quality goods and services."

"Well, you don't know anything about my Marvin."

Not true but not worth disclosing. "Ma, you met Marvin at a bar. And you haven't known him that long."

"So, he stopped in to have a drink. I served him well. Later that night he served me very well."

"That's what I mean. He's using you."

"Fancy, sometimes I want to be used. I'm not getting any younger and I'm not trying to save myself. Every woman is either using or being used, including you. The difference is I don't care. Marvin makes me happy. I love him. I. Love. Me. Some. Marvin. And I'm going to have a good time tonight. Oh, yeah. What fork should I use first?"

What fork? Caroline should learn to love herself. She probably didn't know Marvin's middle name, his parents, or where he lived. "I'm sure you'll figure it out. Just do whatever Marvin does. That'll make him happy. Well, have a good time. I've gotta get to class."

"Okay, Fancy. 'Bye."

Caroline was so selfish she seldom inquired about Fancy's day or how Fancy was feeling. "I love you" rolled off of Caroline's tongue when she raved about her men. Whateva, Fancy thought, shaking her hair behind her shoulders while retrieving her backpack from the trunk.

Walking in fifteen minutes early, Fancy could've talked to her mother a little longer but she had already listened ten minutes more than she wanted. The front seat on the end was Fancy's self-proclaimed reserved desk and after their first class, everyone understood not to sit in her space.

Opening her Finance book to Chapter Eleven, there were numerous terms to learn and problems to solve. While the mortgage calculator helped, it still took Fancy longer to get the right answer—when her results were correct—than most other students. Fancy attentively watched the instructor go over returns on investments, returns of investments, passive income, and what items qualified and which ones didn't. The amount one could carry over to the next tax year and the various income tax brackets and the corresponding percentages allocated for each bracket. A single person earning $7,150 only had to pay ten percent of his income while a single person earning over $319,000 a year had to pay thirty-five percent of his income. In federal taxes? That didn't include state? Or city? Oh, hell no. Since Fancy had never filed a single tax report, she was shocked.

Raising her hand, Fancy asked, "Why do I need to learn about taxes to sell real estate?" Quietly all heads turned in her direction. Convinced her good looks weren't holding their attention, Fancy defensively commented, "The only dumb questions are the ones that aren't asked. Don't act like some of y'all weren't thinking the same—"

Mr. Riddle, the instructor, a white man with white fuzzy hair and a big red bumpy nose, interrupted, "Fancy, the best agents think

ahead of their clients. Investors need to know the pros and cons of
new acquisitions. And first-time home buyers need to know how
much they can write off when buying a home."

"But that's their accountant's job. Not mine."

"Then you'll never become a top agent. Maybe you should get a
day job and forget about selling real estate."

Cupping their hands over their mouths, Fancy's classmates
chuckled, mumbling to one another.

Arching her back and sitting tall in her chair, Fancy firmly
replied, "Well then, I guess I'll just have to master passive income
and every tax-related impact on acquisitions."

Mr. Riddle smiled and began scribbling a math problem on the
white board with a black erasable marker. His khaki pants buckled
into a wedge inside his butt and thighs.

Now Fancy understood why rich—make that wealthy—people
donated millions of dollars to non-profit organizations. That was
how Fancy was able to solicit so much money from philanthropists
while helping Byron fund-raise for his company. And Fancy would
never forget the seventy-five-thousand-dollar donation Darius gave
Byron without reservation. Whatever happened to that woman
who was with Darius that night? Ashlee Anderson.

Mr. Riddle's eyes lingered a little too long on Fancy's breasts as
he moved on to mortgage amortization. He jotted principal and
interest payments, then added taxes and insurance to the final payments. Mr. Riddle amortized fifteen, twenty, and thirty-year mortgages. If a buyer made a twenty percent down payment, he didn't
have to pay for private mortgage insurance (PMI). PMI, which
guaranteed lenders' repayment of the loan if buyers were to default, had no direct benefit to the homeowner that paid the
monthly bill. Maybe Fancy could get some one-on-one tutoring
from Mr. Riddle to help her learn the course material versus mem-
orizing formulas and data for the exam. Fancy felt empowered
knowing one day soon she'd help lots of families purchase homes.

"Fancy, what answer did you get for number four?" Mr. Riddle
asked.

Why did he have to choose her? Fancy hesitated then answered,
"Six point one seven five percent."

"Did you amortize the loan over a thirty-year period with a monthly principal payment of $3,768 with or without the balloon payment payable in twenty-five years?"

Mr. Riddle was intentionally trying to confuse Fancy. She wasn't sure. Massaging her temple, Fancy boldly replied, "With."

Everyone in the class snickered.

Changing her answer, Fancy quickly said, "Without."

Mr. Riddle shook his head, making Fancy realize that Harry's property management company functioned very differently from real estate sales and acquisitions. If she had made a mistake on calculating a tenant's rent, it went unnoticed. But Fancy was committed to completing Real Estate Finance, Appraisal, Economics, Practice, and Legal Aspects consecutively. She'd show them. She didn't know the answer today but eventually she would.

"Fancy, you cannot guess when dealing with people's money. Just like numbers are absolute. You must be confident and correct. Every time. Or you'll be labeled as incompetent. You can stay after class if you'd like and I'll break down the figures for you."

"Thanks." Those students were laughing at her now but when Fancy took her exam with them, she was passing the first time. That was her goal. To pass everything the first time. Fancy refused to be like those students who had to repeat the exam and sometimes the course because they didn't understand the subjects.

After everyone had left, Mr. Riddle sat next to Fancy and said, "Fancy, I see something special in you that I seldom see in most of my students."

Fancy smiled then asked, "What's that?"

"Determination not to fail. You see many students come in here with the hopes of passing the course. You are determined to pass this class and I want to help you. I'll share a few secrets that, if used properly, can make you lots of money."

The corners of Fancy's mouth spread wider. "Really?"

Mr. Riddle took a piece of paper and began scribbling. "Like your times tables, memorize these basic equations so that when you are speaking to your clients, you not only sound intelligent but you are. For every transaction, act like it's your money you're calculating and investing. Know the pros and cons of each deal. Most importantly, learn your market and always maintain the utmost integrity when dealing with clients. That way you get lots of referrals. That's how I make my money. I don't solicit clients anymore. Now people come to me. For advice. For investment tips. And to sell their property. But I'm getting old, and it's time for me to take a few students under my wing and teach them what I know. I'll teach you but you must promise me you'll never sell your soul to make a deal."

Nodding, Fancy said, "I promise."

"Don't spend your commission before or after you earn it. Reinvest your commissions into real estate acquisitions. Rich people don't stay rich by giving away their money. From this day forward, consciously think about every single thing you spend your money on. Don't sell a family a house they can't afford, and negotiate the highest commission split you can with your broker going in. Since you haven't placed your salesperson's license with a broker, I'm going to do two things for you. One, personally refer you to Kees Realty and Mortgage in San Leandro. Howard will teach you more than sales. Howard will teach you how to make money. And two, I'll give you a lucrative referral. The more business deals you close, the more money you ask for from your broker until you, my dear, own and operate Fancy Realty and Mortgage. You can do it."

Fancy gasped as tears swelled in her fluttering eyes, and softly said, "Wow, no one has ever had this much faith in me. Thanks, Mr. Riddle."

"It's not the faith I have in you that makes you special, Fancy, it's the faith you have in yourself. I didn't choose you. Your confidence chose me. You already look like a millionaire. Now it's time to become one. I'll be here early tomorrow evening. Five o'clock. You are welcome to come anytime before the seven o'clock class," Mr. Riddle said, standing and straightening his inexpensive pants that gathered in his crotch beneath his small pot belly.

Standing, Fancy shook his hand. "I'll see you at five sharp."

Skipping to her Benz, Fancy remotely unlocked her door. "This is the beginning of a new life. A new me. For the first time in years, I'm genuinely happy." Tossing her purse and backpack over the driver's side seat onto the passenger's side, Fancy started to turn around and sit in her car, but before she backed up a black leather glove covered her eyes, nose, and mouth.

"I could kill you right here," a manly voice said, whispering, "right now. But I'm going to make you suffer, you little bitch." Quickly he slid his muscular arm underneath her elbow, across her back, and under her other elbow, forcing her arms close together, then hoisted her arms toward her neck. "You think you can just misuse me and get on with your life. Wrong, bitch!" he grunted. "You're coming with me."

Fancy's and Mr. Riddle's were the only cars in the back lot. Fancy couldn't see around the building to the street and no one walked along the back sidewalk. Each time Fancy inhaled, the glove blocked her nostrils. Panicking because she couldn't breathe, Fancy frantically kicked her boots, desperately attempting to puncture his shin but continuously she hit nothing but air.

"Hey, you! Get away from her or I'll shoot! Let her go, pal! I'm not asking you again!" Fancy heard Mr. Riddle yelling in the distance, but couldn't determine how close he was to her because she couldn't turn around. Gun shots fired in the air. The police station was three blocks away but where in the hell where the cops when she needed them?

"This isn't our last encounter, princess," the mugger said, slamming Fancy's body face-first against her car then running across the street. Mr. Riddle fired one more shot, wounding Fancy's assailant in the left leg. Holding his thigh, her attacker limped then fell into the passenger side of a sports utility vehicle that suddenly appeared. Snatching him inside the vehicle, tires screeched and smoke trailed as the driver sped off toward Hegenberger Road. The force of the mugger's arms had pushed Fancy into the roof of her Benz. Blood gushed from her nose. Fortunately she had a soft convertible top or her face would've been seriously damaged. Briefly Fancy reflected on Mandy's comment, "Heaven forbid if you were to become disfigured." Mr. Riddle raced over, lightly touching her shoulder.

"Are you okay? Who was that guy?"

Turning to face Mr. Riddle, Fancy pressed her fingers inside her nostrils then sarcastically answered, "Oh, that was So-and-so. We do this all the time." Fancy raised her hands toward the midnight sky then said, "Like I'm supposed to know!"

If you don't do anything else I tell you, take a self-defense class this week. Your life is dependent upon it, echoed in her mind.

Massaging her arms, Fancy said, "But I won't be here early to-morrow. I need to take a self-defense class. Depending upon what I learn, maybe we can stay late. But just to be safe, I'm parking on the street."

"You can't. That's a no-parking zone. The police will tow your car. I'll reserve you the space directly in front of the school. And I can teach you self-defense."

The police? Tow her car? Right. "Well, I'll park as close as I can to the street. But I'm never parking all the way back here again. And no thanks. I need a professional." Fancy started her engine.

"I am a professional. Marksman and black belt. I could've killed that guy but he wasn't worth it. He'll think twice before attacking someone else. But it's up to you. If you don't find a class, let me know."

"Thanks."

"Are you sure you're okay? Maybe I should call an ambulance or follow you home."

"Thanks, Mr. Riddle. I'll be fine." Suspiciously Fancy closed her door, wondering if Mr. Riddle's offers were legitimate or pretentious. Was Mr. Riddle legally carrying his gun? Fancy honestly cared only about her safety and was relieved Mr. Riddle had saved her life.

On her way home Fancy constantly searched all her mirrors, rearview and sides, and looked over her shoulder to make certain no one followed her, including Mr. Riddle. Who would want to harm her? Why? Driving into her garage, the ring tone of her cell phone distracted Fancy. Grabbing her purse, Fancy left her backpack on the passenger seat.

"Dammit," Fancy said, then answered, "Hey, Darius. I apologize. I forgot we had a date tonight. I was in class."

"Don't give me that bullshit! You said you got out of class at eight. It's almost one o'clock in the fuckin' morning. You didn't even have the decency to call me! I could've made other plans!"

Exhaling heavily, Fancy meticulously said, "Trust me, I know what time it is. I know you're upset. I already apologized once." Fancy unlocked her front door, removed her shoes, and then stepped onto the snow-white carpet in her sunken bedroom area. "Look, I can't talk right now. I have a lot on my mind. Can I call you in a few days or next week maybe?" Tossing her purse on the loveseat, Fancy removed all her clothes then lay across her bed.

Darius yelled, "I wasted a grip! A thousand dollars to take you out tonight! And you all casual and shit about this! Hell no, you can't call me."

"Okay, 'bye." Not needing another headache, Fancy hung up the phone. Fancy would call Darius next week anyway but right now she had to boot up her laptop, go online, and find a self-defense class.

Surfing websites Fancy thought, "Damn, Fancy you work out all the time. How could you panic like that? If he does come back, he'd better be ready for a royal ass-whipping."

CHAPTER 9

Who in their right mind would apply for a job that didn't list a base salary? Employers needed to stop wasting Darius's time trying to save their company a dollar. Relaxing on the plush leather sofa in his recreation room, Darius powered on his plasma television, retrieved his crystal snifter of Rémy Martin Louis XIII from the end table, kicked his feet up on the ottoman, and shook his head.

Sipping scotch for brunch, scanning the employment section of the *San Francisco Chronicle*, Darius thought, What a joke. "No experience necessary. Make up to ten thousand dollars in less than one month." For whom? The owner? The company? Doing what? If the job paid that kind of money, they wouldn't advertise the position in the paper, withhold their physical address, phone number, and omit the company's name. "Fax resumé to (415) 555-...," an unnamed person. That "up to" income crap implied that after spending his money and exhausting his time, Darius could work his ass off and not earn shit.

Darius used to post his job openings for Somebody's Gotta Be on Top at craigslist.org, quoting the starting hourly income, his mailing address, and phone and fax numbers. During his initial phone interview, if a person wasn't articulate Darius didn't invest time in a face-to-face interview. Leaning his head back, Darius's locks rolled behind his shoulders as he gulped the last shot of scotch. Setting the snifter aside, folding what should've been labeled the *un*employment section, Darius dialed the eight hundred number exclusively reserved for privileged wealthy clients and waited to check the balances in his accounts. Hopefully he could forego working for someone else for a few more months.

An automated voice announced, "You have been selected to participate in a survey. Please ask the representative to transfer you after the call. The representative will not know you've been selected until you ask to be transferred."

Immediately the next voice Darius heard was a live, overly friendly representative. "Thank you for calling. How may I provide you with excellent customer service?"

"I'd like to get the balance on my account." Darius couldn't recall budgeting. Before Wellington's irrational behavioral change, Darius had spent money without caring about a balance or doubting if he had enough cash or credit to cover his expenses.

"What's your account number, mother maiden's name, and place of birth?"

Answering the questions, Darius wished his mom's last name was legally Tanner instead of Jones and his was Williams versus Jones. His mother never used Wellington's surname anyway. The last name Jones had absolutely no connection to his legacy and in the moment while waiting for the representative to respond, Darius decided that he'd legally change his last name before going pro.

Happily she replied, "Mr. Jones, as of today you have five thousand dollars in your checking account, all of which is available to you immediately."

Lowering the volume on his television, Darius shouted, "Five what? You must mean five hundred thousand."

The representative slowly articulated, "Five thousand, Mr. Jones. Four figures."

The only other time Darius's heart raced faster was during sex. "What about my money market?"

"Zero balance, Mr. Jones."

"C.D.?"

"That account is closed, Mr. Jones."

Sitting on the edge of his sofa, Darius yelled, "Are you serious?! I can't live off the interest of five thousand dollars."

"I apologize, Mr. Jones. We actually show a pending transaction from Luxury Limousines for fifteen hundred, so you actually have thirty-five hundred dollars. All of which is available to you today. And I'm also showing there were several lump-sum withdrawals from your accounts."

"When? By whom? For what?" Darius's eyes narrowed as his toes curled gripping his socks. That conniving, thieving brother of his. Darius wished Kevin were the one dead. Next time Darius saw Kevin, Darius was kickin' his ass on the real.

The representative casually answered, "Today. A cashier's check in the amount of four hundred ninety-five thousand dollars was issued payable to a Jada Diamond Tanner."

Jumping up and down on his sofa, Darius screamed, "My mother! These are my accounts!"

"But her name is still on the accounts, Mr. Jones. Is there anything else I can do to provide you with excellent customer service?"

"Yes! Stop calling me Mr. Jones!" Darius slammed the cordless on the base. "Fuck a survey!" Snatching the phone into his hand— nose flaring, lips tightly pressed together, eyes squinting, heart racing, and breathing heavily—Darius paced the floor adjacent to his pool table, furiously dialing his mother's cellular.

"Hi, honey." Cautiously his mother asked, "How are you?"

Picking up the eight ball, Darius yelled, "Broke! What have you done?! Why did you withdraw four hundred ninety-five Gs from my accounts? Zeroed out my money market? And closed my C.D.?" Darius squeezed the solid glass black ball so hard his hand ached.

"Wellington says you can have back all the money after you get a job."

"He's not my daddy! Why do you keep listening to him? I bet he wouldn't treat his little precious Wellington the Second that way. Fuck him!" Trading the eight ball for number one, the place Darius used to hold in his mother's heart, Darius hurled the ball— *Smash!*—shattering the plasma television.

"Darius, you can have any attitude you damn well please! Like it or not, Wellington is my husband and he's been a real good step-father to you! For twenty years he was the only father you knew—"

"And whose fault is that!" Picking up another purple ball, Darius slammed it into the liquor cabinet. "My real daddy ain't no scrub. He starred in the NBA! Remember? He's celebrity."

Carelessly his mother agreed, "You're right. Then ask Darryl for some money, honey."

"Forget you!" The remaining balls, all except the eight ball, flew one at a time, breaking stereo speakers, the glass coffee table, and expensive statues. "Be happy with your lying ways and your cheating husband who flies back to Oakland to service his clients. And unless Melanie Thompson is his client, he's serving her his dick real good. Wellington always wanted my business. Melanie probably convinced him to take it over. He can have my business. He can have Melanie. He can have you. And you can fuck both of them again at the same time if you want!"

Moms was stuck. For a moment she didn't say anything. When she spoke, Darius heard the disappointment in her voice. Eventually she'd find out somehow.

"Stop your lying! Darius, honey, look. You can have the money back as soon as you get a job. Any job. Stop making me miserable with your lies."

Darius slammed the cordless on the base and the last ball, the eight ball, into a framed photo of him with his grandmother.

"Fuck!" He'd missed. He meant to destroy the picture of him with his mother, not his grandmother. Forget his mom. Darius didn't need them. Walking around his house, Darius thought somebody's daughter was going to have to pay for his devastation and frustrations.

Darius picked up the phone and dialed Fancy.

"Hey, Darius. What's up?"

She seemed chipper, Darius thought, responding, "On my way to pick you up. You ready?"

"Sure, where to?"

"I can call my limo driver. I'm sure he can be at my place in a few then we can go wherever you want."

"Sweet. I'll be waiting."

Closing his recreation room door, Darius phoned the limousine company and was pleased that his driver would arrive in a half hour. After waiting thirty minutes, Darius grabbed his suede jacket and headed outside. "Whew! Good." The driver had arrived. Dressed in a black patent leather and suede-like cap, the driver was leaning against the passenger door. Hopefully his fifteen-hundred-dollar charge would clear Darius's account, but if not, by the time Luxury Limousines discovered he was broke, Darius's dick would be satisfied and his date would be over.

"Hello, Mr. Jones," the driver greeted him, gripping the door handle.

Darius didn't respond. When the door opened, Darius settled into the backseat and poured a glass of Louis XIII. He downed it then refilled his glass, downing shots until he arrived at Fancy's condo building. Darius retrieved the outgoing numbers from his cellular database and dialed Fancy.

"Hey, we're downstairs. Don't keep a brotha waiting." By the time he arrived at Fancy's, Darius was so horny he could fuck anything with a pussy, including a cow. Darius wasn't toasted but he felt good. Aroused. Upbeat. When the driver opened the door, Darius's bottom jaw hung.

Shaking his head, Darius thought this sistah was incredible. But damn, look at her now. "You look exquisite."

Darius was feelin' that short silver satin dress that clung to Fancy's protruding nipples and flared around her hips, outlining her curvaceous ass. Darius reached for the brown mink coat draping Fancy's arm then held her hand until she was inside.

"Thanks. I'm so excited tonight. I passed all of my Real Estate Finance quizzes and I take the brokers' exam in eight months."

"That's cool. Maybe I'll buy a home from you."

"No doubt," Fancy said seductively, smiling.

Darius's hand eased up Fancy's bare thigh. Fancy grabbed his wrist, applying excruciating pressure to his inside vein with the ball of her thumb, and said, "Please don't do that."

Snatching his arm away, concealing his pain, Darius half smiled then replied, "Damn! What's wrong with you? Your legs are so sexy and soft I had to feel them this time." Darius massaged his wrist.

"Not without my permission. Please."

Shaking his arm, Darius asked, "Then may I?"

"Maybe some other time. Tonight I want to enjoy my success and get to know Darius Jones a little more. Like, what's life like for you? This intuitive woman advised me that I'm going to become a millionaire this year, so I'd like to know from a millionaire does having all that money make you happy? I want to know how you feel about women. About me. About relationships. What's your middle name?"

Darius reflected upon the homeless woman's words to him then said, "Damn, can't we just enjoy the moment?"

Fancy frowned, saying, "Pardon me. I thought we were."

Darius exhaled. Fancy was fucking up his high and adding to his stress but Darius was with her now. Regardless, he still had to pay the driver so he deserved to feel more than legs.

"Okay, being a millionaire is the only life I've lived so I don't have a comparative basis. I don't have a middle name. I'm not in a relationship. I think relationships are a waste of time. I—"

"Slow down," Fancy said, stroking his hand.

Darius rubbed his hand from her fingers past her elbow up to her bicep then touched the side of her breast. Fancy pulled away.

"Oh, so you can touch me but I can't touch you. What's up with this sudden attitude? You weren't acting like this the last time we went out."

Letting go of Darius's other hand, Fancy nodded. "You're right. I respect that. I won't touch you again without asking. I've been through a lot since our last date, and, well, I don't want to talk about it. But why do you think relationships are a waste of time?"

This trickster was trippin'. Darius would have to bang Fancy's skull hard against the headboard just for the hell of it, to knock some sense into her. "Because women these days are fake, they're phony." Darius scanned Fancy's makeup, eyebrows, and lips. Damn, her lips sparkled like candy. He continued, "You don't know if it's their real hair, lips, ass, eyelashes, alias, or what."

Checking out Fancy's body, Darius said, "I don't have time to fan through all the smoke screens of Barbie-doll leeches who feel just because they have big titties, a small waist, nice ass, and track-star legs that if they fuck you you're obligated to take care of them."

Smoke made Darius think about saving Ashlee from the fire. How was Ashlee? Had her face healed from the burns? At first Darius had wanted Ashlee pregnant with his child but now, after what that homeless woman said, he didn't. Darius prayed none of those kids were his. What was he thinking about? That self-proclaimed telepathic psycho didn't know him. What intuitive woman had Fancy met?

"You're right, Darius."

"Huh." Fancy's breasts solicited his attention so he responded to them.

"I'm up here. Look at me, Darius. I'll be honest with you. I'm not ashamed to say that I've only dated millionaires or guys who've sponsored all of my expenses. Fair exchange is no robbery and if a woman doesn't know her worth a man sure as hell won't. But I'm tired. Tired of pretending to be interested when I'm not. Tired of faking orgasms in bed. Tired of accommodating horny-ass men with phone sex. Whatever, you name it, I'm tired. Right now I'm in a different space."

Oh, great. Darius had caught a born-again virgin in the midst of her holy transformation. What a joke. Once a trickster, always a trickster.

"I'd like to have another friend to replace my only male friend who recently moved to Georgia. And I'm hoping that person is you. I want to get to know the real Darius. The one that bleeds when he's cut, cries when he's sad, and struts when he knows his shit is on point. I love your arrogance, but like me I know you have a vulnerable side. That's the side I want to know. The child inside of you and the powerful intelligent man that owns and operates Somebody's Gotta Be On Top Enterprises. I'm not interested in having sex with you. If we grow closer and decide that's what we want, fine. If not, that's okay. At least I'll have you as my friend."

Fine was right. Fancy smelled edible. What had she said? Her erect nipples distracted Slugger. Darius would convince her to take off those panties later—Fancy was probably wearing a thong or nothing at all—when they got to his place.

"Let's go to Scott's in Oakland. Jack London Square," Darius instructed the driver although they were already in San Francisco. Darius refused to pay top price for filet mignon and caviar if Fancy was serious about not giving up the pussy.

CHAPTER 10

Darius had proven himself Fancy's greatest challenge. His sexual interest and advances were flattering but Fancy was determined to reveal the best intangible assets Darius had to offer. Dining at Scott's was nice but clearly, once again, Darius had expectations of fucking and that wasn't happening. Why couldn't he appreciate her desire to get to know him better? And if Darius thought rides in plush limousines to a few three and four-star restaurants would convince Fancy to give up the pussy, he was wrong.

Hell, Fancy didn't eat much food and although she didn't have a lot of money, she could afford to feed herself. Thirty dollars at Berkeley Bowl bought more than enough fresh fruits and vegetables for three meals a day for an entire week. Berkeley Bowl's liquid echinacea, One-A-Day Vitamins for Women, eight ounces of aloe vera juice mixed with equal parts of cranberry juice, and CKLS from the Black Muslim Bakery on San Pablo Avenue kept Fancy so healthy she couldn't remember the last time she was sick.

Strutting into Nellie's Soul Food for breakfast, Fancy was pleasantly surprised to see her best friend SaVoy Edmonds sitting alone at a table for four near the register. Breakfast was Fancy's biggest meal of the day. Fancy didn't understand people who ate a light breakfast, a moderate lunch, and their heaviest meal of the day at dinner, shortly before going to bed knowing all those metabolizing calories were sure to convert into fat cells primarily around their waists.

The restaurant was filled with blue-collar truckers in blue jeans, businessmen, and what seemed to be neighborhood patrons talking loud. As she passed their tables, Fancy smiled, quickly diverting her attention to SaVoy before any of the men garnished the courage to approach her. Nellie's, located on the corner of Third and Adeline—a few blocks away from Caroline's house on Seventh Street near Market—was the only place Fancy ate at once a week. The white lace curtains were the fanciest of the restaurant's bland décor, but the food Fancy selected from the menu was healthy. Especially the collard greens seasoned with smoked turkey. Nellie never used pork and Fancy liked that because she didn't have to worry about any part of the pig, accidentally or intentionally, ending up on her plate.

SaVoy's smile radiated across the room brighter than her canary turtleneck sweater. The banana-colored corduroys were nice but, glancing at SaVoy's feet, those chocolate-colored Timberland boots were seriously clashing and too masculine for her outfit.

"Hey girl, how are you?!" Extending her arms, Fancy embraced SaVoy then continued, "Where've you been hiding? You're looking good." SaVoy would look better if she'd worn a pair of jazzy calf-high three-inch-heel boots. Men enjoyed admiring a woman who dressed like a lady. With so many females in the East Bay dressing like guys these days, Fancy easily turned heads everywhere she went.

SaVoy's pale, almost white complexion, firm cheekbones, and long straight hair were attributes from her Caucasian mother, whom SaVoy had only met once about a year ago. Fancy was glad she wasn't the only one who'd never heard her mother say "I love you." Although SaVoy never spoke about her mother, SaVoy and Fancy shared the same pain. At least SaVoy had a father who adored her more than any man ever could, including Tyronne.

"You look good yourself. I was going to ask you the same thing. Although you stopped returning my calls, you know I pray for you all the time, Fancy. Girl, you must've gotten a job at a clothing store dressed up so early in that micro-mini business suit and thigh-high boots."

Pinching the edge of her aqua-colored skirt, Fancy smiled. Bright colors any time of the year were magnetic. The vibrancy cheered Fancy, and Fancy's constant smiles made people around her happy, too.

Pulling out a wooden chair, Fancy replied, "Thanks. You know me. Actually I just stopped in to get a bite to eat before heading to the gym. Never know who I might meet in transit. But I should have a real job by the end of the day." Grabbing a napkin, Fancy brushed a crumb from the seat then sat facing SaVoy. "I'm claiming a much better life this year. And for starters I'm placing my salesperson's license with a real estate company today and I'm taking classes for my broker's license. So when you and Tyronne get ready to purchase your home"—Fancy slid her business card across the table—"buy it from me."

Holding a small tablet in her hand, the waitress interrupted, "Excuse me but can I get you ladies something to drink?"

Was she preparing to write down a drink order?

Fancy answered, "Yes, and you can take our food orders, too. I'll have an orange juice and vegetarian omelet, no toast."

SaVoy said, "And I'll have an orange juice, French toast, two eggs scrambled, and Canadian bacon, with toast."

"I'll get your drinks right away," the waitress said, walking to the next table still holding the pad in front of her.

Declining to comment on SaVoy's selection of double toast, Fancy noticed SaVoy had gained a few pounds.

SaVoy looked at the card. Smiled. Then said, "Congratulations. I bet I can have Pastor Tellings let you do a seminar at our church."

"You are so determined to get me to church, and having my own seminar will work. Let me know when. Unfortunately I have to work for someone else until I learn the business first but I'm definitely opening my own office by the end of the year." The intuitive woman's voice echoed in her mind: *You need to get closer to God.* Fancy wasn't forcing a spiritual relationship with God or anyone else. "How's Tyronne?" Fancy asked, not honestly caring.

The sparkles twinkling in SaVoy's eyes must've blinded her common sense because like Fancy once was, Tyronne still was a user.

"Tyronne is truly wonderful. I love him so much. Every day I'm with him is heaven on earth."

Fancy's eyebrows reached for her hairline. "Really? Would you die for him?"

Frowning, SaVoy asked, "What kind of question is that?"

"Yes or no?"

Responding defensively, SaVoy said, "I don't know."

"Never mind. You don't have to tell me because I'm taking a break from men. But I had a great date with Darius Jones the other night," Fancy lied, name-dropping. Now SaVoy's eyebrows reached for her hairline.

"Fancy, please don't get involved with Darius. He ruins everyone he comes in contact with. Darius is Satan's offspring. You'll end up hurt like his ex-fiancée who, thanks to Darius, has—"

Fancy interjected, "And Tyronne isn't the devil himself? You don't know Darius. How dare you tell me how to live my life when you're engaged to a thug?" Darius had been engaged? Fancy would question him later.

SaVoy protested, "You don't know my fiancé. Tyronne is not a thug. He never was. Just because he's streetwise and up on your game, you don't like him. And he doesn't like you either."

"And why might that be? Because I'm up on his game? Whateva, but you need to give me the same respect I give you. I'm not asking your sanctified opinion about Darius. He's hot, sexy, and arrogant. I like him. A lot."

The waitress quietly placed the food in front of them then softly said, "If I can get you ladies anything else, let me know."

SaVoy squinted at Fancy for a moment. "You're right. God forgive me. I apologize. But I doubt that it's Darius you like. It's his money, and at this point, from what I've heard from *reliable* church members who were close friends with Darius's grandmother and still friends with his mother, you probably have more money than Darius. I was just trying to be your friend and warn you. You talk to Desmond lately?"

Picking the mushrooms out of her omelet, Fancy decided not to respond to any more of SaVoy's comments about Darius. "Desmond called yesterday. He's settled in his dorm. Getting acclimated to law school. But I can tell he misses me. Maybe after he gets his degree, I'll give him a chance."

"You are still a trip. Desmond doesn't want you. Desmond called me yesterday and told me he decided to move in with Trina to save money."

SaVoy hadn't changed. She still wanted to be the one who knew every damn thing first. Or at least before Fancy. Maybe SaVoy was right about Desmond living with Trina, but Fancy didn't care because if she wanted Desmond, she could have him at any time regardless of what woman was in Desmond's life.

"As long as Desmond is happy I'm happy for him." Now Fancy was just picking at her food, not eating at all. "The person I need to ask you about is Tanya. How is she?" Fancy questioned if Tanya was ever really her true friend. Tanya was more of a friend by default because she'd met Tanya and SaVoy at the same time while in high school.

"Has it been that long since we've spoken? Wow, Tanya had a baby for William, a beautiful little girl, so she moved back in with him."

Fancy's head moved from side to side. "I guess she wasn't strong enough to make it on her own. Having his child isn't going to change his controlling, abusive ways."

"I disagree. Being a father is changing the way William treats Tanya. They do come to church together. Regularly."

Church didn't change anybody, Fancy thought. Unless William wanted to change, Tanya would still be subjected to his nonsense.

"How's your mom, Fancy?" SaVoy asked, chewing her last piece of French toast.

"Caroline is Caroline. She's still too big but she has lost weight. Down from a size twenty-eight to an eighteen. Supposedly engaged to some rich guy she met one night while she was working the bar who's never going to marry her. I don't talk to Caroline much because, as usual, her man is her life."

"But you've got to be happy for her. Don't be jealous. She's your mom. I'ma call and congratulate her later."

"Whatever." Fancy tossed her napkin over her plate, laid twelve dollars on the table, and then stood. "I've gotta go catch my spin class with CoCo. I'll call you about the seminar. Oh, yeah. SaVoy, tell your mother I said hello whenever you speak with her again. You should call her. She is your mom."

The sparkle in SaVoy's eyes had vanished earlier after SaVoy had begun defending Tyronne. Fancy's heart was satisfied watching the tears swell in her best friend's eyes as Fancy turned and walked away. SaVoy was no better than Mandy and neither of them was better than Fancy Taylor. Maybe SaVoy would think first before using her subtle Christian conniving ways to condemn and judge Fancy or anyone else. If it weren't for the real estate seminar and being the maid of honor in SaVoy's wedding, Fancy wouldn't call SaVoy again.

Strutting out the same way she'd came in, Fancy hopped in her car, bypassed Caroline's house, drove several blocks to Fourteenth Street, and parked in City Center's garage. Spin class was full as usual. Fancy pedaled extra fast to work off her frustrations. She wanted so badly to see what Darius had to offer but he'd become standoffish. She needed some dick in her life.

Fancy pumped faster than the other cyclers. Now that she had her salesperson's license, she had to meet this broker who'd quickly teach her the business. Since Mr. Riddle recommended Howard Kees, Fancy would stop by Howard's office after her workout. She started to skip CoCo's floor exercise and killer abdominal workout but Fancy hadn't earned her six-pack by taking shortcuts so she stayed.

After class Fancy announced, "I'm a licensed realtor so anyone who needs to refinance or purchase a home, you can see me anytime." Fancy flashed a millionaire's smile then headed toward the locker room. The eucalyptus steam relaxed her body. Fancy showered then eased on her wrinkle-free miniskirt, single-button blazer, and matching thigh-high boots. On her way out of Club One, Fancy glanced to the left, considered going to Jamba Juice, and then thought about the homeless woman. If she was there, maybe the homeless woman could answer a few more questions for Fancy.

While she was contemplating this, a tall thin woman tapped Fancy on the shoulder.

"May I have one of your cards? I'm going through a divorce. My husband wants to buy me out. I was avoiding looking for my own home, I guess because I didn't want him to leave us, but when you announced you're a realtor that was my sign to move on."

Did Fancy ask for the woman's life history? Was Fancy going to become a therapist like Mandy? Holding her business card, Fancy followed Mr. Riddle's advice, pulled out her Palm Pilot, and said, "Give me a number where I can contact you." After Kelly gave Fancy her information, Fancy gave Kelly a card. "I'll call you later to set up a time to meet tomorrow." Mr. Riddle had advised Fancy not to allow more than twenty-four hours to elapse with an interested buyer, saying, "If they go with someone else so does your commission." Opting to avoid any possible contact with the wig woman today, Fancy turned right and headed to the City Center garage to get her Benz and drive to Howard's office.

When Fancy walked into Kees Realty on MacArthur Boulevard, a voluptuous, dark-complected woman said, "Hi, I'm Denise. May I help you?"

Smiling, Fancy said, "Yes, I'm here to see Howard Kees."

"Do you have an appointment?" Denise asked, peering at Fancy.

"Uh-huh. Mr. Riddle sent me."

"You must be new," Denise said, scanning Fancy's clothes. "Nice outfit. But it's going to take more than a pretty face and a great body to work here. Have a seat."

Fancy gave Denise a "Whatever, you're only a receptionist, honey" look.

Denise picked up the phone, and a moment later a handsome, dark-complected, fiftyish gentleman with salt and pepper hair, wearing eyeglasses, a casual no-name brand button-up shirt, and loose-fitting khaki pants like Mr. Riddle's, entered from a back office.

"So, Riddle sent you, huh?"

"Yes," Fancy said, standing and shaking his hand firm like Mr.

Riddle had instructed her in his self-defense class. That way Howard would sense her self-confidence and strength, like Darius had when Fancy gripped his wrist. Mr. Riddle had said if a man contested her strong grip to beware, because he may be interested in more than business.

Howard said, "Come into my office."

Mischievously, Fancy turned toward the receptionist then politely answered Howard. "Thanks."

Denise said, "Oh, by the way, Fancy, I'm Denise *Kees.*" Then she smiled at Howard and said, "Daddy, I'm going out for lunch. I'll deposit the escrow funds while I'm out and I'll be back in thirty minutes." Sliding on her designer sunglasses, Denise picked up her Prada purse and softly tucked her shoulder-length hair behind her ear.

Fancy rolled her eyes at Denise then noticed the bachelor's degree awarded to Denise Kees hanging on the wall above her desk. Cornell University. Whatever. Maybe Mr. Riddle was wrong about this arrangement. Fancy wasn't working for some spoiled daddy's girl. Denise had better be thankful that the old Fancy hadn't entered Howard's office, because by the time Denise returned from lunch, her daddy would've been lunch and Fancy would've been his top agent and business partner.

CHAPTER 11

Jada gave Wellington a traditional good morning closed-mouth kiss before he eased out of bed at five-thirty. She admired the way her husband's bald head matched his hairless face, all except his thick eyebrows, which Jada was certain he'd shave, too, if he wouldn't look like a freak, to rid himself of gray hairs. The pubic hairs surrounding Wellington's big dick were clipper-shaved every week, so close he barely maintained a shadow. Her husband's body was tighter on the inside. His skin, with time, had lost some of its elasticity but Wellington was still fine as ever. He was her Samuel L. Jackson in action. Confident. Handsome. Charming. The best lover. And a damn good dresser. Aging had actually complemented Wellington in many ways. Good looks coupled with almost being a billionaire fed his ego and drove him to acquire wealthier clients at every opportunity. Like, as he'd professed, the client he was scheduled to meet in Oakland today.

Normally Jada would lay out her husband's clothes while he showered, then she'd go downstairs to the kitchen and prepare a light breakfast. They would read the business sections of the *New York Times, Los Angeles Times,* and *USA Today* then discuss their plans for the day. How many times had Wellington lied to her? When Jada heard the water running in the bathroom, she raced downstairs to Wellington's office, and did something she hadn't done before with any man, searched his private property, his Palm Pilot.

Powering up today's calendar, Jada read: *Dept Flt #333 @ 8:00am from LAX. Arr SFO 9:10am. Meet Carey Car @ baggage claim. PU 3 dozen roses. Go2 Victoria's Secret. Lunch in SF @ noon The Cheese Factory. No other appointments. Return Flt #334 @ 6:00pm next day. Arr LAX @ 7:10pm. PU 1 dozen roses 4 Ba.*

Jada tried to remember when Wellington had stopped sending her roses. After they'd met, Wellington sent the same arrangement of one red and eleven yellow roses every week; even after she'd married Lawrence, Wellington sent the flowers to her office. After Jada married Wellington, he'd stopped sending anything. But why? Did he still love her like she loved him?

Powering off Wellington's Palm, Jada wondered what to do. She could cancel his travel arrangements. Confront him. Or do nothing at all. She hurried upstairs to the bedroom. Wellington's smooth body glistened with beads of water.

He asked in an expecting tone, "Breakfast ready?"

"Yes," Jada lustfully answered, her hazel eyes lingering on his dick. "You are breakfast." Her tongue captured the liquid drops covering his neck from his shoulder to his ear.

Gently pushing her away, Wellington said, "You keep that up and I'm going to have to reschedule my client's appointment. Where are my clothes?"

Ignoring his plea, Jada kissed Wellington's erect nipple then whispered, "You'll be on time. But first you need to take care of mama. She's sizzling." Jada placed Wellington's hand between her thighs. Her pussy pulsated in his palm. When he opened his mouth to speak, Jada eased her tongue inside, then, pressing her firm breasts against his chest, she massaged his dick to a firmer erection.

Saturating her wet body with chocolate cocoa butter lite oil twice a day after taking a cool shower kept her skin firm. Wellington enjoyed hot steamy showers which were more relaxing than hers, but Jada knew cold water and a good moisturizer would preserve her skin's tightness.

Stooping to his waist, Jada sucked Wellington's bulging head and massaged his balls while gliding her taste buds in the crevice underneath his head. She licked. With grave passion, Jada sucked her husband's dick like a caramel pop.

"What's gotten into you? Damn, that feels good, ba. Can I get this every morning?"

"Morning," Jada said, stroking his pre-cum into her mouth. "Noon." Jada licked each of his nuts. "And night."

Wellington's body quivered. A palatable tartness oozed through the skin of his shaft. Jada was pleasantly familiar with that taste that came right before Wellington was about to explode in her mouth. She stopped, shoved him backward onto the bed, and straddled him.

Rotating her hips front and up, then down and back, then front again, repeating her rhythm, Jada's vaginal walls caved in around her husband's elongated shaft. Nice and slow Jada continued her groove. Wellington reached between her legs and began teasing her clit with his middle finger. Small circular motions, lubricated by the external flow of vaginal fluids secreted from Jada's clitoris, heightened her sexual energy, causing her hips to move faster.

Squeezing her nipples, Jada moaned, "Oh, baby, my juices are flowing all around the big juicy dick. You make me feel so good, I love you. Fuck me a little deeper, daddy."

Each time Jada lowered herself onto his dick, she forced her hips lower, taking more and more of her husband inside her until it felt like Wellington's dick pressed against her navel.

The white of Wellington's eyes was all Jada saw when he grunted, "Ba, your pussy drives me insane. After all these years, how do you keep her so ti—"

Exhaling, Jada moaned, "Aw, yes. This is my dick. Whose dick is it?"

Wellington's eyes opened wide.

Questioning him again, Jada stared into her husband's eyes and asked, "Whose dick is this?"

His eyes shifted to the left before answering, "Yours, ba. Only yours. Always yours. I love you so much."

Jada whispered, "Then give me this cum. All of it," hoping he'd have none left to give to any other woman.

Jada knew Wellington well enough to tell he was lying when he'd said, "Only yours. Always yours," because underneath his almost convincing tone, his voice trembled nervously.

"*Yeeesss,*" her husband hissed, cumming so hard his dick continued throbbing long after his orgasm was over.

Jada continued sitting on top of Wellington and in that moment she admired the man she'd fallen in love with twenty-three years ago and married three years ago. Maybe she should trust him because whether or not Wellington was having an affair, Jada was not divorcing her husband.

Glancing at the digital clock on their nightstand, Wellington's eyes widened. "Damn! I'm late. Ba, I gotta go." Hurriedly her husband re-showered, dressed, and dashed out the door in less than ten minutes. Since Wellington still owned his home in Half Moon Bay, carry-on luggage wasn't necessary.

Sitting naked on Wellington's side of the bed, Jada sadly picked up the cordless phone, staring at the numbers so long that her vision merged them into one black spot. A teardrop fell between openings of the number zero. Drying it off the receiver, Jada dialed her secretary and said, "Cancel my appointments for today. I'll be in tomorrow."

Jada's heart ached like never before. With the exception that she hadn't convinced Wellington to give Darius back the money or his business, everything in her marriage seemed so right. In the short time Wellington had taken over Somebody's Gotta Be On Top, Darius's business had become a cash cow, bringing in new film productions, the most recent in the higher eight figures.

"But Mrs. Tanner, you have a client who took the red-eye in from New York to meet with *you* today."

"Dang-gon-it. That's right. Tell Zen to meet with him. Tell her to negotiate contingent upon my approval. I'll be back by six. Schedule a seven o'clock dinner with my client at a five-star restaurant near LAX and we'll finalize everything before his return trip to New York tonight. 'Bye." Terminating the call, Jada speed-dialed her travel agent. "Have my driver pick me up in an hour. Book me a flight to SFO for ten o'clock this morning returning at four o'clock this evening."

Jada showered, inhaling the scent of Wellington's masculine shower gel which lingered inside the enclosed doors. Trying to convince herself everything was all right, Jada questioned if she should stay in Los Angeles and negotiate the fifteen-million-dollar contract herself or risk losing the deal if her client refused to meet with Zen. Brushing her long hair, which Wellington begged her not to cut for years, into a ponytail, Jada eased into a black pantsuit. She concluded her marriage was worth more than any contract amount. But would following Wellington save her marriage if she'd already lost him to another woman?

All the way to San Francisco, Jada contemplated taking the next flight back to Los Angeles but something inside guided her toward the Carey Car driver holding up a sign that read, "Jada Diamond Tanner." Merging onto Highway 101, the driver exited the last San Francisco exit before crossing the bridge into Oakland. Twenty-five minutes later, at eleven forty-five, Jada was passing time at Macy's shop-looking in the women's lingerie department when she heard a familiar voice.

"Could you have this gift-wrapped for me, please? I'll be back around two to pick it up."

Melanie Marie Thompson. There she stood, the same perfect size ten. Melanie's plastic face filled with botox made her eyes bulge at the cashier. Melanie must have lived many miserable years single with no husband of her own, but obviously she was trying to hold on to her youthfulness. Jada shivered. Melanie's face looked frozen. Dead.

Quickly Jada turned and went upstairs to the furniture department one floor below The Cheesecake Factory. She sat in a reclining chair that was comfortable but not comforting to her, but at least her suspicions were over. Waiting until twelve-thirty, Jada rode the escalator from the furniture department that led directly into the restaurant, sat in a corner of the bar area facing the hostess counter, and watched her husband, seated on the outdoor patio, feed calamari, avocado egg rolls, salad, and strawberry cheesecake to a woman who'd wrecked their engagement twenty-plus years ago.

Unbeknownst to Jada back then, Wellington had fucked

Melanie several times before he'd suggested the ménage à trois that Jada had eagerly agreed to. But how did Darius know about that? And how much did her son know? Did Darius know that Melanie had eaten her pussy and sucked Wellington's dick during their ménage à trois? Did Darius know that Melanie claimed a pregnancy that convinced Wellington to marry her instead of his mother? Once Melanie miscarried the triplets and confessed the children weren't Wellington's, Jada thought that was enough to keep Wellington away from Melanie's conniving ass forever.

Tired of watching her husband cater to Melanie, Jada paid her bill, walked outside to the patio, and stood in front of her husband. "You care to explain this?"

Quizzically, Wellington looked up at her and asked, "Ba, what are you doing here?"

"Me?" Two fifty-plus-year-old women and an older man fighting on the rooftop would've been ridiculous but Jada swore if Melanie opened her mouth, Jada would put her fist in it.

Wellington stood. "Melanie, excuse us. Ba, let's go downstairs to the furniture section and discuss this."

"Wellington Jones, don't you touch me!" Jada jerked her arm away then stared up at her husband. Thrusting words between clenched teeth, Jada said, "All I want from you is an explanation. Why would you throw away our marriage on this . . . ?" Jada wanted to call Melanie a tramp but knew the person she had to address was the man looking down on her.

Melanie remained silent, staring up at the cloudless sky while squeezing her tongue into the fork's grooves, savoring the cheesecake.

Wellington angrily articulated, "Twenty fucking years I have lived with your lies, but I suppose that's different. It's always different for you, Jada. As long as you're the one lying and cheating it's okay. You don't think I know about your so-called business dinners with Darryl."

"Wellington, we were only talking about getting Darius into college and the NBA. That's all. I wasn't feeding him strawberries and whipped cream and whatever else you sat here feeding her."

"You may as well have, you never told me about your dinners."

"Oh, I see. You're trying to justify this bitch!"

Melanie whispered, "You a trip. Don't forget about her over-night trip with Darryl."

Wham! Instinctively Jada backhand-slapped Melanie in the mouth. Blood seeped into the crevices of Melanie's white teeth as her chair fell backward onto the cement. When Wellington raced to help Melanie up, Jada pointed her finger in his face. He flinched, knowing Jada would strike him, too. "I'll see your ass at home, not tomorrow, tonight."

Jada stormed out of the restaurant. Damn, she hated that Darius was right. But even though she knew the truth, there was no way she'd give her husband to that whore because that was exactly what Melanie wanted.

CHAPTER 12

Waking up in his home away from home, in Los Angeles, in his bed, today was the single most important day of Darius's life. Darius hadn't been in L.A. since signing over his insurance check to Wellington. Darius missed Oakland a little but he missed talking with Fancy a lot. Fancy was the one woman who didn't care about Darius Jones the millionaire. Once his life was in order, maybe he could be faithful to Fancy.

The last few weeks, Darius had stopped communicating with everyone except his father. Darryl taught Darius how to invest time in himself. To seriously organize his future. Hassle free. Drama free. And while the last couple of weeks Darius had been pussyless, it wasn't by his choice but Darius had accepted his father's advice and practiced dick control.

Darius had discovered a new inner strength. The headaches that accompanied the orgasms were no longer worth his time. Spending time with his dad was priceless. Darius had taken Darryl Senior up on his offer of visiting anytime. Every day for fourteen consecutive days, at eleven o'clock in the morning, Darius had visited his father's home in Fremont.

Running five miles a day gave Darius time to talk with his father. Lifting weights, Darryl spotted him first, and then it was his turn to stand over his dad, helping to hoist the three hundred pounds, balancing the bar back onto to the rack above his dad's head.

Some things Darius was glad to learn, some not. Like it was cool understanding his love of women was no different from his father's. The only difference was that Darryl Senior respected the women in his life, including Darius's mother. Except for the time he refused to accept responsibility for Darius's mom's pregnancy. His dad admitted how stupid he was because the one child he could've helped the most, he'd helped the least. Until now. Darryl had said, "Son, from now on you can depend on me. Forever. For anything." Darryl's lifelong commitment empowered Darius. His dad had confessed that the way to keep a woman in his good graces was to treat every woman like she was important, but treat his woman like a queen.

L.A. was where every illusion could become reality and every sexual fantasy was two degrees of separation. Darryl reclined in the passenger seat of Darius's Bentley.

"Well, son. How do you feel?"

Grinning, Darius glanced at his dad, then at the road ahead, and said, "Man, I'm so excited I might jump out of the gym when I see my teammates and coaches again."

"Be cool. Never let any of them know how excited you are. Let your talent and the skills I've taught you do the talking."

With his seat fully reclined, Darryl's long legs almost touched the glove compartment. Darius wished he'd grown another two inches to six-nine like his dad but he'd stopped growing in high school. His dad's coal black hair was sprinkled with strands of gray. Darryl looked distinguished. Intelligent. His thin mustache was well-trimmed, hovering above his square chin. Quickly, Darius looked at his dad, then in the rearview mirror at himself, and then focused on the road ahead wondering if he'd ever cut his locks.

"All the working out we've done in the last few weeks," Darius commented, thumping on his chest. "I've gained five solid pounds of muscles. I'm stronger. Faster. More athletic. Why can't I flex?"

Pointing toward the Sunset Boulevard exit, Darryl exhaled and signaled for Darius to turn right onto Westwood, then said, "Every player on UCLA's team wants to go pro. You are going pro. That's why you have to stay cool."

"I don't get it." Shrinking in order to make someone else appear better wasn't Darius's style.

"You get out of life what you negotiate, not what you earn. Remember that. When your teammates stop passing you the ball, you will get it. You have got to touch the ball at least once every single possession. You can't act as if you're the shit because if you do, that's how they'll treat you on the court. Like shit. Be cool."

"Aw'ight. I suppose." More than anything else, Darius wanted to play professional ball, so he'd listen to his father's advice.

"And another thing," Darryl said, motioning toward the campus. "You have to make amends with those women who might be carrying your babies. Any negative press and you'll be cut from UCLA and you'll never go pro. You don't want a bad rep and the media following you twenty-four-seven."

Darius knew every road leading to UCLA but he was letting his dad direct him today in every way. "Honestly, Dad, the only one I care about is Ashlee. Desire and Ciara can kiss my ass."

"Boy, didn't anything I said sink in? You've got a lot to learn about women. Don't you know women can destroy you? Be careful where you stick that dick of yours. And take it from me, never tell a woman to kiss your ass."

Nodding, Darius said, "I've learned my lesson. Now I make sure I use a condom all the time."

"Good."

Darius parked near Pauley Pavilion. "They need a new facility. Maybe I'll buy them one when I go pro."

Darryl shook his head as they walked inside and greeted the coaches. Darius beamed as the coaches commented on Darryl's championship rings. One on each hand. His dad could've worn all four.

"Thanks for awarding my son a scholarship."

"Based on the tapes you've sent, Darius didn't need your endorsement to earn a Bruins scholarship. He's the real deal. And based upon how he practices with the team, we expect he may just start."

Darius nodded, then stopped when his dad looked at him.

The coaches introduced Darius and Darryl Senior to the dean of business, the players, then gave them a tour of the campus and the dorms. No way was Darius living on campus in those small rooms. Darius would commute or buy a place closer to the university, which reminded him that he had to visit his mother today for money since he was broke and starting school soon.

After the interviews Darius signed the National Letter of Intent and Scholarship contract. The drive to his mom's was painstaking. Silently, Darius drowned in thoughts of facing his mother and Wellington again without a job.

Parking in his parents' circular driveway, Darius asked his dad, "What do you think about me changing my last name to Williams?"

"Really? Son, that would be great but you've already established a reputation with the last name Jones."

"But it's not my father's name. It's somebody else's father's name. And I don't want my children, your grandchildren, confused about their family history."

"That's solid thinking. You'll be successful regardless, so if you want to change your name, I'd be honored to go to the courthouse with you."

Darius hugged his dad and said, "Thanks." But he wasn't looking forward to seeing his mother. Slowly he approached the huge double doors and rang the bell. Darryl stood beside him.

His mom was cheerful, dressed in a lavender dress and matching open-toed shoes. "Hi, Darius. Hey, Darryl. Come in."

Following his mother to the family room, Darius briefly reflected on their last encounter when Wellington hit him. Punk. Standing in front of the sofa with Darryl beside him, Darius said, "Hi, Mom. I just dropped by to show you I signed my scholarship and NLI for UCLA. I start taking classes this summer and my dad has been working me out every day, so technically I have a job."

Stretching across the chaise, his mother said, "That's good, honey."

Darius spoke barely above a whisper, "You can give me back my money and my business now because going to school and playing ball are two full-time jobs."

"That's nice," Wellington said, walking into the room. "We'll see about the money. You can forget about the business. I've taken that over."

"Man, ain't nobody talking to you. You probably spending my money on Melanie."

"Darius!" his mom yelled. "Stop it!"

"It's true." His mom had proof and she was still defending her cheating husband.

Wellington yelled, "I don't have to explain anything to you, kid."

Darryl interjected, "Oh, but you do." Looking at Jada, he continued, "Is that true?"

Wellington protested, "Man, don't go there. You're in *my* house."

Jada shouted, "Our house!"

"Fine, then I'll leave until they're gone," Wellington said, turning toward the door.

Darius remarked, "Tell Melanie I said hello."

"Darius Jones!" his mom yelled.

"Sorry, Mom. I just don't understand why you're letting him control everything. I'm your son. I need your help. I don't have any money."

"When you start school full-time, I'll give you back all of your money and a little extra."

Wellington reentered the room and shouted, "He doesn't deserve it! No! You! Will! Not!"

Darryl yelled at Wellington, "Man, I'm not going to allow you to disrespect the mother of my child or my son. Jada has spoken."

"Your son!" Jabbing his pointing finger into his own chest, Wellington said, "This is one man who raised your damn son when you were busy chasing women." Wellington pointed at Darryl. "And the two you did raise, they both turned out to be crap."

Darius watched his dad walk over to Wellington, stopping just inches away. Darryl's chest blocked Wellington's face. "You say one more word about my boys, any of them, and I'll make certain you won't again."

Shaking his head, Wellington backed out of the door. "Jada, if they're not gone when I return, I'm calling the police. I will not be threatened in my home."

"Our home!"

"Whatever." Wellington exited though the kitchen into the garage, then slammed the door.

Squeezing on the chaise next to his mother, Darius said, "Mom, I'm sorry about Melanie."

"Honey, don't be."

"So you're going to divorce him, right?"

"I married Wellington for better or for worse. Our marriage will be fine."

Darius stood, looked down at his mother, and then said, "Dad, you ready?"

"Yeah, son. Let's go."

His mother was fooling herself. Darius was shocked because his mother was a powerful woman who was totally submitting to her husband and he hated her for that. Maybe she felt guilty about lying to Wellington all those years. Darius was just glad, come next month, as his mother had promised, he'd be living in style again.

CHAPTER 13

Every closing brought some sort of closure and, with the home-owners' desire, welcomed a new beginning for life. For Kelly Martin, the closing on her single-family home brought closure to her separation and soon-to-be divorce from a husband who'd emotionally abandoned her years ago. The excitement of a fresh start with her kids and her personal trainer—although, thanks to Fancy, Kelly had vowed not to let him move into her new place—was liberating.

Waiting for Howard to arrive at the closing, Fancy sat in the lobby and dialed Darius's number.

"Hey, Ladycat. What's—"

"Wish me well! I'm at my closing."

Darius replied, "I can do better than that. Let me take you out for a celebration tonight."

"You are so wonderful! Here comes Howard. I'll call you back later," Fancy said powering off her cell phone.

Joining Howard, Fancy entered the meeting area.

The six-hundred-square-foot conference room at the title company was filled with a long cherry wood table, twelve swivel cushioned chairs, a family of four, Howard Kees, the escrow agent, the seller and her agent, and Fancy. Fancy's body tingled all over as she realized that making money had become equally as enjoyable as having sex, although she did miss talking with Darius. He'd stopped calling and since he hadn't returned her last phone call, she refused to call him again. That was a smart idea because Darius would eventually phone her. Sex. When was the last time Fancy had had sex? Miss Kitty danced like it was her closing and she was getting some new or used accommodations to satisfy her needs.

This was not the time to think about getting fucked. From what Fancy had heard from Byron and others, her ex-boss, Harry Washington, was spreading rumors about her being a whore and a thief. Typical of a scorned man but when Fancy finished taking all of Harry's clients, Harry would have a genuine reason to call her a crook. A bitch. Whateva. But Fancy promised herself, in time, she'd get even with Harry.

Fancy couldn't believe she was about to close on her second FHA-insured loan. Skeptical about classroom teachings versus reality, shockingly what she'd learned in class from Mr. Riddle was actually true. Government-backed financing helped lots of families and singles who otherwise couldn't afford to purchase a home become homeowners. With that type of promise from Uncle Sam, Fancy could sell every renting American a home! Especially since more than fifty percent of renters were paying more money to their landlords than it would cost them to pay their own mortgages. Fancy was dedicated to educating renters, starting with her first-time homebuyers' prequalification seminar at SaVoy's church following this Sunday's eleven o'clock service. Fancy had even decided to attend church before the seminar, give thanks for her many blessings, and pray that Darius returned to her. Making money was cool but having no one to share in her success was saddening.

Kelly was serious and diligent about finding a property and Fancy was glad she was Kelly's agent. Fancy had driven Kelly to fifteen open houses before Kelly fell in love with a three-story, four-bedroom villa in Kensington. With FHA's maximum home limit of $601,692 for the Bay Area, Kelly made the minimum three percent down payment of $18,051, qualified for a $100,000 grant from the city, and took a silent second in the amount of $380,257, backed by the seller, payable in fifteen years. After Kelly and her husband sold their home, by court order Kelly would receive seventy-five percent of the proceeds because she had sole custody of their children. With the sale of their home, Kelly would have more than enough money to pay off her second mortgage. Otherwise, Fancy would've recommended Kelly purchase a less expensive home for her family.

Kelly's three kids, ranging in age from four to twelve, were equally excited. Before the closing, Fancy had advised Kelly that if for any reason she ever defaulted on her mortgage, she should do two things.

"First, I want you to immediately request a forbearance agreement from your lender. Then I want you to call me. If you wait until your mortgage is in foreclosure, I can't help you obtain a payment plan but I can help you sell your home."

Mr. Riddle had taught Fancy that if the home was worth more than the loan a lot of lenders foreclosed on homeowners instead of offering a repayment plan for their delinquency. Then the lender sold the property for a profit with no obligation to compensate the homeowner.

Mr. Riddle had said, "Always encourage a homeowner to sell if he can't afford to maintain the mortgage. One, he won't have a foreclosure on his credit report. Two, in California, property in even the most distressed neighborhoods appreciates, so he should at least get enough money to relocate. And stay abreast of the FHA maximum loan limits and homebuyers information posted at HUD.gov and FHA.com."

With a new career on the horizon, Fancy felt confident and empowered handling Kelly's escrow. In order to expedite the signing of numerous papers, last week Fancy had met with Kelly and they reviewed every word—especially the ands, ors, shalls, and ifs—of every document on the table today. Fancy had also explained to Kelly the closing fees, interest rates, seller's three-percent credit, and loan points. The escrow agent handed the package to Fancy. Fancy passed it along to Howard, who gave it back to Fancy.

"Review it," Howard insisted.

Fancy reviewed each page, ensuring the proper documents were enclosed. "Let's get started," Fancy said, handing the package back to the escrow agent.

"Since you've purchased a home before, Ms. Martin, you should be familiar with the documents but I'll explain each one," the agent said, eager to earn his fee.

"Fancy gave me a copy of the package along with the loan papers a week ago and I've read every word. So unless you have additional or revised forms, all I need to do is carefully review the inserted language, rates, fees, and sign my name about fifty times."

Howard proudly winked at Fancy. Fancy nodded, and two hours later Ms. Martin and family were handed the keys to their new home. Fancy handed Kelly a small crystal cat that dangled on a gold link keychain.

"What's this for?" Kelly asked, smiling.

"To celebrate your new beginning. And to remind you that, like a cat, a woman has always got more than one life. You're the mother, the head of household, the financial supporter, cheerleading coach, escort driver, and you're dating the finest personal trainer in the Bay Area. I'll call you in a week to see how things are going."

Fancy walked outside with Howard. "Okay, Miss Taylor, you're clearly on your way to the top. Lunch is on me."

Oh, hell no! And have Denise call questioning about what was taking her daddy so long to get back to the office? "Thanks, but I'll have to take a rain check. I'm showing three homes in Montclair to a prospective buyer"—Fancy glanced at her diamond watch—"in about an hour."

"Well, excuse me. Go make that money. Don't forget to stop by my office later. It's time to start teaching you about acquiring investment property. Starting in Las Vegas, not California."

Smiling, Fancy said, "I'll see you at the office around six," then skipped to her Benz. Her commission check wasn't enough to invest in a home after she deducted her income taxes and paid her rent. But if the homeless lady was correct, Fancy would soon be rich beyond her own imagination.

Fancy hurried to Montclair to meet her prospective buyer, Mr.

Drexel, as he called himself, insisting on being addressed by his last name. When Fancy parked in front of the three-story, five-bedroom home, a tall, handsome, muscular black man dressed in a business suit and sunshades, with a neat low-cut mustache and short-cropped afro, stepped out of a white BMW and smiled.

Extending his hand, his deep greeting was charming. "You must be Miss Taylor. I didn't expect such a beautiful woman when I scheduled the appointment over the phone."

Cha-ching. Mo' money. Fancy shook his hand firmly, saying, "And you must be Mr. Drexel."

She punched in the code on the lockbox, and the box sprang open. Fancy retrieved the keys and unlocked the front door. Silently, Mr. Drexel immediately toured the entry-level floor. He nodded, then said, "I'll tour upstairs on my own for a moment if you don't mind."

Casually Fancy replied, "Not at all, go right ahead." It was common for buyers to view homes without agents following them around. In fact, unless Mr. Drexel had a lot of questions, Fancy preferred waiting.

Fancy walked into the kitchen, placed the keys on the counter, and dialed Caroline's number from her cellular.

"Hey, Fancy. I was just leaving with Marvin. We're going to Clear Lake. Can you believe that? Marvin is going golfing. He loves to golf. I've never been to Clear Lake so I'll have to call you when we get back tomorrow. 'Bye."

Obviously, Caroline hadn't been there because otherwise she would've known that most of the rich guys took their convenient women to northern California, away from San Francisco, and then left them alone in the lakefront homes or resorts until they were tired of hanging out with their buddies, only returning whenever they were ready to have sex.

Searching her purse, Fancy placed her business card on the counter to let the homeowners' know she'd shown their house. Several other cards from various realtors were now stacked underneath Fancy's.

Fancy went into the living room. Taking in the panoramic view, she whispered, "One day I'm going to own a home like this." But she wanted to make money investing in real estate so Mr. Riddle had advised her to follow the advice in the book *Rich Dad Poor Dad* and buy income property first, and purchase her dream home later.

Twenty minutes had passed so Fancy tiptoed upstairs. "Yoo-hoo. Mr. Drexel, where are you?" There was no answer so Fancy proceeded to the basement. "Mr. Drexel? Are you down here?"

Still there was no answer, so Fancy raced back upstairs to the top level and opened a bedroom door. Closed it. Opened another bedroom door, walked around, closed that door. Fancy peeped out the window. Mr. Drexel's car was still parked on the street so Fancy opened the third and fourth bedroom doors. Closed them. Then Fancy approached the master bedroom. Slowly Fancy opened the door. Her heart pounded against her breast. "God, please don't let me find this man dead. I promise to go to church Sunday." Relieved she'd heard a voice downstairs, Fancy rushed to the entry level.

"Yeah, honey. The house is perfect. I want to make an offer on this one but you should see it first. How soon can you get here?" Mr. Drexel paused, then said, "Tomorrow is fine. Take an early flight so I can take you to brunch at the Carnelian Room."

Fancy's heels clicked along the hardwood foyer to the front door. Mr. Drexel was standing outside on the porch talking on his cell phone.

Stepping outside, Fancy asked, "Where'd you go? I was looking all over for you."

Ending his call, Mr. Drexel grabbed the knob and closed the door.

Right before the click, Fancy yelled, too late, "Don't!" Then she whispered, "My keys and purse are inside."

"Oh, my goodness. I'm so sorry. I was so excited I had to call my wife."

Damn, think, Fancy, think. "If you can take me home, I have an extra set of keys. I can get them and come back."

"That's the least I can do. I'm so sorry." Mr. Drexel dialed his phone and said, "Honey, you won't believe what just happened. I locked the realtor out of the house she was showing me. Now we *have to* buy the house. Don't bother flying in tomorrow, I'll make an offer in the morning. Okay, darling. I love you. Good-bye."

Fancy felt stupid for leaving her purse and keys on the counter. But Mr. Drexel was friendly and Fancy wanted to make sure she had his purchase agreement ready for signature early tomorrow morning. A few more deals and she could request a ten-percent increase in her commission.

Adjusting the seat in Mr. Drexel's car, Fancy asked, "So, where are you relocating from? And what is your first name? And are you sure your wife doesn't need to see the home first?"

"Oh, I've been here for a while. My wife, she lives in Kentucky, and maybe you're right. Maybe she should see the house first."

"Is that your wedding band on your pinky finger?"

"Yes and no."

The baguette band set in white gold sparkled but Fancy knew better than to keep asking marital questions. "Do you have kids?"

"Two."

"Are they in school?"

"One of them is in the second grade."

"And the other?"

"She graduated from high school years ago."

"Montclair is an excellent choice. They have one of the best school districts in the entire Bay Area." As Mr. Drexel parked in the circular driveway at her place, Fancy politely said, "Thanks. I'll be right back."

The doorman, Mr. Cabie, smiled and said, "Hello, Miss Taylor. Another client?"

"Yeah. I need to borrow the keys to my condo."

Taking the keys from the doorman, she pressed the elevator button for her floor. Fancy raced to her unit, retrieved the extra set of keys for her car and condo from the nightstand, and hurried back downstairs. Mr. Drexel's BMW was gone.

Fancy questioned Mr. Cabie. "Where'd my ride go?"

"I don't know, Miss Taylor. He left as soon as the elevator door closed. Maybe he'll be right back."

"Yeah, maybe you're right," Fancy mumbled, getting back on the elevator. "If he doesn't—oh, shit!"

Rushing inside her unit, Fancy dialed 9-1-1. The operator forwarded her to the police, claiming locking her keys inside a home wasn't an emergency. Fancy hung up and dialed Howard on his cell phone to bypass his probing daughter, Denise. "You have reached the voicemail of Howard Kees." Fancy hung up and dialed the office.

"Kees Realty," Denise answered.

"Denise, this is an emergency. I need to speak with Howard."

"He's in a meeting with a client. Can I help you?"

"Interrupt him! This is important!"

"First off, you need to stop yelling at me. My daddy is in a meeting, so either you talk to me or call him back in an hour."

"Fine." Fancy exhaled heavily. "I locked my purse and keys in the house I was showing in Montclair. I need a ride to the house right away."

"Hold on. Let me call the owners and see if they're there."

Why hadn't Fancy thought of that? Maybe because her multiple listing service data sheets with the phone numbers were inside her car.

Moments later Denise returned. "They're not answering. How'd you lock your keys in the house?"

"Actually, I didn't. My client closed the door while we were outside talking."

"What?! Where are you?"

"At home."

"I'm on my way." Denise hung up the phone.

Waiting in her condo for Denise, Fancy's home phone rang. Oh, shit! Darius. "Hey, Darius."

"Hey, Ladycat. You ready for our hot date tonight? My driver is picking you up in an hour."

"Damn, I forgot again. I can't go out tonight."

"You're kidding, right? Not this bullshit again. You know how long I had to beg my moth—"

"Darius, I'm so sorry. Calm down. An emergency came up. If

you'd like, you can come by after I get back." Fancy stepped onto her balcony, watching for Denise's car on the street below.

"Come by and what?" Darius questioned.

"Just chill at my place. We don't have to go anywhere."

"Oh, that's cool."

"I don't cook so bring something healthy, to eat."

"I'll bring something healthy, all right."

"No meat. Food, Darius. Food. Denise is downstairs. I gotta go. See you at eight."

Fancy raced to the elevator, through the lobby, bypassed Mr. Cabie, and hopped in Denise's car. Denise drove fast, taking Highway 13 into Montclair. When they arrived at the house, Fancy's car was gone.

Ringing the doorbell, the homeowner answered. "My house isn't available for showing after hours. You ladies need to contact your realtor."

"We are realtors," Fancy answered. "I left my purse in your kitchen. May I come in?"

"No, you may not. Wait here while I check."

When the lady closed the door, Fancy commented, "She's a trip."

"No, actually she's smart," Denise said. "She shouldn't trust us any more than you should trust your prospective clients."

"Sorry, there's no purse in my kitchen," the woman said when she came back, then closed the door again.

Denise looked at Fancy and said, "He has your purse, too. You have to change the locks on your condo. I can call the locksmith."

"She's lying. He can't have my purse because the house keys were in the kitchen." Fancy raised her hand to ring the doorbell again.

Grabbing her hand, Denise said, "Are you crazy? We could lose our licenses or have them suspended. You can't harass a home-owner. Just let me call a locksmith to re-key your locks."

"I'll change them tomorrow. Darius is coming by tonight."

"Fancy, I thought you knew the rules. Never put down your purse, keys, or the keys to the house while showing a home to any-one."

"I've had enough for one day. I'll deal with this tomorrow. Take me home."

Questioning whether she'd continue showing homes to strangers, Fancy had never imagined that anyone would rip her off. What if Mr. Drexel had attacked her like that stranger? Damn, well, at least she had Darius to comfort her. Then again, why did horrible things happen to her whenever she planned a date with Darius?

CHAPTER 14

A woman knew instantly whether or not she'd fuck a man. He didn't have to encourage, persuade, or entice her because once she determined she was sucking his dick, all he had to do was show up. Anywhere. Her house. A restaurant with a private restroom. His friend's house. Her friend's house. A dressing room in a department store. Or the backseat of his car.

Fancy decided tonight was the night she'd let Darius taste her pussy. Preparing a tub filled with lukewarm water, one gallon of homogenized milk, and sixteen ounces of natural honey to sweeten Miss Kitty, Fancy pampered her body like she was prepping dessert, softly kneading the mixture into her pubic hairs for five minutes. An extra squirt of honey, instead of her usual chocolate, onto her fingertips and Fancy rubbed the syrupy texture into her vaginal lips and shaft. Miss Kitty became engorged with every stroke so Fancy cupped herself and said, "Damn, I can't wait to fuck Darius." She moaned, sprinkling milk on her kitty, then sat in the white porcelain oversized tub. Warm vanilla sugar candles lined the perimeter of her tub, her vanity, and burned throughout her bedroom.

Not knowing where her house keys, her purse, or her car were, and not having much confidence that the police would locate any of them, Fancy felt relieved that when she'd ask Darius to stay with her, he promptly said, "Yes." Now all she had to do was convince Darius, without asking him, to kiss both sets of her lips, caress her breasts, and stroke Miss Kitty until she purred.

Hopefully Darius wasn't a disappointing lover. He didn't brag about what he could do so that was a good sign. Men who did all that damn talking about how good their dicks were, Fancy learned while she was in high school, were all lies. Her best lovers never boasted about their skills or the size of their dicks. But when they had a chance to prove themselves worthy of a second session, like Byron, they fucked like they were auditioning for a lead role and she was the producer.

Byron. What was he doing? Fancy wanted to call him. If Darius faked on her tonight, Fancy was not reneging on her promise to Miss Kitty. She'd call Byron. Leaning her head back on the inflated white satin pillow, Fancy thought it had been too long since she passionately held a man in her arms and had a man cuddle next to her in bed. She wasn't trying to win an award for preserving Miss Kitty or break any woman's record for retaining her virginity. Fancy's goal tonight was to release her pent-up frustrations with a man she loved—Darius. She thought.

No matter how much you love someone today, you still have enough love to love them tomorrow, echoed in Fancy's mind. So it was okay for Fancy to love Darius. Emotionally and sexually.

Stepping out of the tub, Fancy dried the bottom of her feet, then walked around her house until the milk and honey drops absorbed into her skin. Touching her forearm, the light stickiness lingered on her fingertips. The double ring tone on her phone meant that Darius was downstairs.

Fancy answered, "Yes."

Opening her door three inches, Fancy raced to her bed and layered a red satin sheet atop her down feather comforter. Since Fancy's building was secured with a twenty-four-hour doorman, and only the office manager and selected board members had keys to the lobby entrance, Fancy ignored Denise's advice to immediately change the locks. If anyone made it to her front door or inside her unit, Fancy would fault and sue the homeowners' association for so much money, they'd gladly give her her own unit.

Mr. Cabie said, "Miss Taylor, a Mr. Jones is here to see you."

Seductively, Fancy said, "Send him up."

Fancy slipped into a green thong and matching robe then sat on the loveseat in her bedroom and waited for Darius.

Peeping in, Darius's locks swung through the crack before his face.

"Stop peeping. Come on in."

"Oh my goodness" was all Darius said when he saw Fancy dressed in a robe and high heels. Her hair and makeup were flawless as if she was on her way out, not in. Gently Darius embraced Fancy, inhaling her hair, her neck. "Damn, you smell edible. What is this?"

Noticing Darius's erection through his sweats, Miss Kitty knocked twice. Fancy motioned for Darius to sit on the loveseat beside her and gave him an abbreviated version of what happened while showing the house to Mr. Drexel.

As she spoke, Fancy noticed a few of the bulbs on the necklace of lights around the lake were out. Fancy tried counting them so she wouldn't appear anxious as Darius secured his strong arm around her shoulder.

"So you said the dude looked professional and he had on a business suit?"

"Yeah, but I don't want to talk about him anymore. I'm just glad you're here." Laying her head in Darius's lap, she let Darius stroke her hair. When Fancy felt his erection, she wanted to nibble on his dick through his sweatpants but instead, pretending she was startled, Fancy lifted her head. Gently Darius's hand pressed her head back in his lap.

"Relax. He's under control. I know not to try anything with you, trust me. But you're sending a brotha mixed signals looking and smelling good. But you do know we both like you."

"I like you, too," Fancy said, struggling to maintain her nonchalant composure when she really wanted to rip off Darius's clothes, straddle him, and ride his dick until they were both exhausted and satisfied. Patience.

"I've never met a woman in the midst of becoming successful. I always meet women who are already millionaires. I guess that's why they don't trip on having sex. Either they want you or they don't but they don't play games. I've heard about your reputation. Don't play games with me, Fancy. You won't win."

Where in the hell did that comment come from? And what had Darius meant? Sitting up to face Darius, Fancy said, "If you're comparing me to your other women, don't. And I don't give a damn what you've heard or who told you." Fancy tightened the belt on her robe. Darius had fucked up her good mood but not Miss Kitty's. She was tumbling. "What I need to figure out is how am I supposed to get around until the police find my car?"

Darius chuckled. "You can forget about getting that car back. Mr. Drexel, or whatever his real name is, has sold that Benz. Don't worry, Ladycat, you can use my spare car. It's kinda big. It's an Escalade but I know you can handle the size." Darius smiled, thrusting his pelvis upward. "I'll bring it by for you tomorrow."

Insulted by Darius's conflicting comments, Fancy thought one moment Darius was complimenting her, the next insulting her, now offering his car. Fancy did need transportation but was Darius for real or lying just to have sex? Before Darius changed his mind, Fancy suggested, "I can come and get it at seven in the morning," then lied, "I have several homes to show," to make her request seem urgent.

"Naw, I said I'll bring the car over. And the first place you need to go to is the Department of Motor Vehicles and get another license before you start driving around in my car."

"Fine. By nine?"

"Okay. Damn, can I get a kiss?"

Darius didn't have to offer his car to have sex with Fancy but he'd better not be lying about his offer. Tilting her head, Fancy puckered her lips then teased, "But all you can have is a kiss."

Darius's incredibly soft, melt-in-your-mouth lips meshed into hers. The way he navigated his tongue throughout her mouth, Miss Kitty knew Darius had great oral sex skills. The moment he touched her breasts, the sweet sensation rushed Miss Kitty, arching Fancy's back.

"Not yet," Fancy said, sandwiching her sticky thighs together to absorb the juices soaking her thong.

Parting her thighs, Darius said, "Let me see her. I know she's wet."

Slowly, Fancy lay across the sheet, halfway slid off the thong that was restricting her flow, then waited as Darius pulled her thong over her knees, down her legs, and then over her feet. Darius held the emerald lace, sniffed, then seductively commanded, "Spread your legs. Let me see her. Um, damn, what is that smell? You smell sexy. You got me so hard I just wanna give this." He slid his huge dick from underneath his blue UCLA sweatpants.

Like a ballerina, Fancy's legs parted parallel into a full split, seemingly without her assistance. She paused.

"Damn, you're limber. That's sweet." Gently parting her vagina into three sections, Darius said, "She's almost as cute as you. Let me see you work her out on your pole."

"Sure, but not—"

"Tonight. I know."

"Then let me taste you. And next time maybe you'll do a dance for me."

Darius's tongue softly parted her lips. "Oh, she's sweet and sticky." His slippery tongue slowly journeyed up one side of her shaft. Pausing at the top he gave Miss Kitty a kiss, and then his tongue continued down the other side. Miss Kitty pulsated with joy as Darius explored her inner lips. His lips rested at the top of her shaft again, softly pressing. Then he kissed down her shaft. Fancy wanted to scream. All the frustrations from the day's activities floated from her body.

"Damn, you taste like cotton candy. I could eat you forever." Continuing his lip-tation, Darius's kisses turned into sucks starting at the top of her shaft all the way down to the very tip of her clit. Juices eased from it. Miss Kitty was wet on the inside, too. Darius sucked a little harder, then his tongue traveled inside her walls again. Fancy wanted to cum so badly her thighs clamped over Darius's ears.

"Not yet," Darius whispered, placing his palms inside her thighs, moving them outward. "I'm enjoying your taste too much. I want to take my time."

Damn, but could Fancy take her time? Inhaling deeply through her nose and slowly out her mouth several times, Fancy was able to lessen her orgasmic flow.

"That's good," Darius whispered, sliding off his sweatpants and his sweatshirt.

Aw, damn. Darius's cobra-shaped body was beautiful. If only with his body, Fancy was definitely in love. Caramel. Smooth. Muscular biceps, chest, shoulders, and his waistline was incredible. Fancy was pleased that Darius wasn't bulging like those weight-lifters on steroids. Simply pure athletic. Graceful. The body Fancy had envisioned on Kobe was nothing compared to Darius's. Easily Darius looked ten times better than any basketball player she'd seen or met but Fancy had never dated a potential professional athlete.

Darius repeatedly teased her breasts, her butt, the crevices in her fingers and toes for well over an hour, then redirected his attention to Miss Kitty. "You want me to put him in after you cum?"

Fuck it. The biggest dick she'd seen was staring in her face. Fancy was burning up inside. "You have a condom that fits?"

Darius whispered, "Of course."

"Then, yes. I do."

Rolling on his condom, Darius's lips captured her entire shaft and sucked gently. This time when Fancy came to the edge, she came hard and long. Darius positioned his head outside her pussy then slowly penetrated Fancy. Fancy continued cumming. Miss Kitty suctioned hard.

"Damn, you feel so good. Can I put him in the back door next?"

"No, I don't do that," Fancy lied.

"Then turn over."

Ignoring Darius's request, Fancy said, "You are a much better lover than I anticipated," then ran her fingers through his locks. Fancy looked into his eyes to see if she could vibe with the real Darius. Exchanging breaths, when Darius exhaled, Fancy inhaled. Fancy waited until he inhaled then she exhaled. "You are so beautiful." Fancy's fingers caressed his chest as she leaned forward, kissing Darius's lips.

Each time the thickness of his penis climbed her walls, Fancy clamped onto his head and squatted lower. Attentively, she responded to Darius's body motions with her emotions, hoping to connect on a level she'd never experienced before. She waited until Darius was ready to release himself and came with him, holding him closer. Tighter. Lovingly. Afterward, Darius scooted down, lay his head between her breasts next to her heart, and neither of them moved. Darius's lean caramel flesh peacefully rested on top of Fancy until the morning sun's rays kissed their bodies.

Awaking in the same position, Fancy whispered, "I don't want just another relationship, Darius. I want you. All of you."

"Don't say that," Darius mumbled. His lips grazed her nipple. "You don't know what you're asking for."

"Yes, I do. For the first time, I think I'm falling in love. With you. But I'm not sure. But what I do know is, I need somebody who loves me for me." Pausing, Fancy wondered how Desmond was doing in Atlanta, then continued, "And I was kinda hoping that person would be you." How could she be sure when she'd only had sex with Darius one time? But that first time felt like they'd been together before. Did great sex define love? Or did love define great sex?

"Well, don't," Darius protested. "This may sound crazy but a homeless woman told me that death follows me. She said I was going to marry but not the woman I want. So I can't want you. Besides, I have to go back to L.A. tomorrow to get ready for college and I'm not sure when I'll be back here in Oakland."

Fancy focused on the part of Darius's statement that was most important to her future. She wanted to tell Darius about her encounter with the homeless woman but Fancy needed more information on his relationship. "Are you engaged to someone?"

Quickly Darius replied, "No."

"Are you planning on proposing to someone?" Fancy asked, teasing one of his locks.

"Not anymore. I told you I don't believe in relationships."

Exhaling, Fancy said, "You know what?"

"Tell me."

"I don't know if you recall me mentioning it, but I met a homeless woman, too. She said someone was going to try to kill me and I needed to take a self-defense class. I took that class months ago and nothing has happened."

"Yeah, I hear you. We must be two strange individuals. How many individuals meet crazy homeless people?" Darius held Fancy tighter. "I'm sure it's not the same woman. You wanna make love to me again? I need that."

Make love. That sounded so delectable but not nearly as sweet as the man who'd asked. Fancy whispered, "Yes, I do."

CHAPTER 15

The quality of life for Darius rapidly declined. Being back in L.A. with no money was almost as depressing as not seeing Fancy for eleven days. Fancy called every morning to say good morning and each night to tell him good night. If Darius was busy in his dorm room talking to his roommate, Lance, or allowing females that showed up nightly at his dorm door to entertain him, he didn't answer Fancy's calls but was happy the next day listening to her sexy messages.

Fancy was special. So special that Darius spent a few more of his last dollars to visit Fancy for the weekend. When Fancy confessed she needed someone to love her, Darius wasn't man enough to admit that he, too, needed someone to love him. Darius wanted and needed to hold Fancy in his arms again. This time, when he saw Fancy, Darius would share his deepest feelings.

"We'll begin our preboarding of first-class members only. If you're seated in first class, you're welcome to board at this time," the chipper flight attendant announced.

Darius sat at Gate 72 holding a boarding pass for group five and a novel he'd recently purchased at an airport bookstore, *The Preacher's Son* by Carl Weber, hoping some guy had more issues than he.

Observing the nearby passengers, Darius realized that flying coach was reserved for medium- to low-income to the unemployed penny-pinching travelers with bad credit or too many goddamn unruly kids. Anything less than prime, including interest rates, was definitely not created for Darius, but thanks to his hypercritical, scheming stepfather, Darius could no longer afford to spend the additional hundreds of dollars on a first-class ticket.

Now that Darius's mom knew that Wellington wasn't the ideal husband, she still wouldn't divorce him. His mother adored Wellington. Darius had no proof, but his instincts told him that somehow Melanie was involved in running Somebody's Gotta Be On Top. Otherwise, why did Wellington protect Melanie instead of his mother? A piece of ass was never more important than the wife. Even Darius knew that. His mom didn't know that he was aware of everything that happened at The Cheesecake Factory that day, but a man as powerful as Darius had many eyes in many places watching many people, including Fancy, all the time.

Wannabe employees, actors, or sponsors would call or leave messages on his voice mail pretending they knew him well by saying, "Hey, Darius. Just called to say I saw your girl in the city today shopping Neiman Marcus. Give me call so we talk about my upcoming project. I want you in on this man. My number is . . ." Most of the callers, Darius barely remembered, but the information was always welcomed.

Reflecting on how his mother had gotten furious at him, screaming, "Darius, you will do anything to hurt me!" Darius had only tried telling her what she should've already known. Wellington was no good.

Smack!

Darius's face burned with bad memories of almost striking his mother back. "Are you crazy? That's my face! What'd you hit me for? Wellington's the one you should be going off on." That was the first time his mother or any woman had slapped him. What gave her the right? Tired of defending himself against Wellington, Darius gradually peeled away his mother's fingers then angrily articulated, "Don't you ever hit me again."

Reliving the moment, Darius's throat tightened. Clenching his back teeth, his jaws twitched recalling how his mother ignored his demand and continued, "Just because you hate Wellington, don't try to make me hate him, too!"

Men knew one another's vices but Darius would've never told his mother about Wellington's two-year affair with Melanie Thompson if Wellington hadn't stolen his money and his company.

Damn, Darius couldn't continue letting Fancy drive his uninsured Escalade but perpetrating his lifelong style of spending lots of money on the finest women, Darius didn't know how to ask for his car back without pissing Fancy off. Women. Wasn't that some shit? Darius Jones, trippin' over what started out as a quickie. A "wham, bam, thank you for your time" dime piece. A "let him bust a nut and then he was done" chick. Months later, Darius was struck and stuck.

The friendly flight attendant smiled at Darius then announced, "This is the last boarding call for flight two, two, seven to Oakland."

When had he missed his seating number? Longing to hold Fancy in his arms once more, Darius fingered his locks, zipped his black leather jacket, brushed his black slacks, and then boarded the ten-thirty Friday morning flight at Los Angeles International Airport.

Fancy was the only person who understood his plethora of problems or cared enough to listen. Eventually Darius would have to find a reason—legit or not—to dismiss Fancy. Her clever technique of persuading him to express his feelings and disclose personal information was extremely upsetting. Sure, some people had acquired knowledge of some segments of his life but no one had uncovered Darius's vulnerabilities. Until now. Until Fancy.

There was a part of Darius encased within his ribs, on the left side of his body, pounding against his chest that genuinely loved that sultry woman. Being with Fancy was different from sexing his ex-fiancée Maxine, his step-sister Ashlee, all his faceless one-nighters, the chicks that boldly came to his dorm, and his soon-to-be ex-wife Ciara.

Maybe Darius desired Fancy because she was more physically fit than all of his women combined. Or because Fancy had sucked his dick better than Kimberly. Or perhaps because Fancy wasn't with him for his money. Or at least he hoped not. Or simply because Fancy had confessed, "Darius, I've never been in love. I want to learn how to love you unconditionally so that if my life depends upon your survival, I wouldn't have to think twice." What bothered Darius the most was, when he wasn't with Fancy he wanted to be with her. And that was the difference.

Who was he fooling? He was falling in love. Rummaging through his past affairs, a short time ago Darius believed he loved Ashlee, and two years ago he was sure he was in love with Maxine. He'd never loved and barely liked his wife. But Fancy . . . Darius exhaled, thinking aloud, "Nothing has ever felt like this."

For the first time true love was riding more than his jock. And Darius hated it. In the midst of blinking, when his eyelids touched, Darius yelled inside his mind, *Fuck this dumb shit! Love is for suckers. Punks! Wimps! Willing to relinquish control of their emotions. Darius Jones! Get your shit together, man!*

Opening his eyes, Darius stored his bag, claimed the aisle seat in row twelve next to his assigned middle seat, daring anyone to ask him to move, fastened the seat belt tight across his lap, punched ten on his cellular, and then hit the talk button.

"Hey, Darius," Fancy eagerly answered. "I'll pick you up in front of baggage claim at noon. I can't wait to see you. I miss you, baby. And I have a surprise for you."

The last surprise Darius had received was a twentieth birthday party from his mother. Then he'd stood in a room filled with his fiancée Maxine, his mom's four executives, all of whom he'd fucked, and his early birthday date, Kimberly Stokes, who'd worn only a pair of stilettos and a short red coat, rotating his present between her chocolate thighs in front of a mound of mousse on the dessert table. Darius's mom vowed never to surprise him again. Women. If Fancy would listen for two seconds or inhale, Darius could answer.

"Hey, Ladycat. I—"

"Oh, Darius. Oh, sweetheart, you won't believe what happened to me yesterday. Two things. One, the police found my Benz so I can give you back your Caddy, Daddy. And two, Mr. Riddle, my real estate instructor, introduced me to this tycoon who's giving me an exclusive listing on his ninety-four-unit waterfront complex in San Francisco! Not forty-nine like the football team. Ninety-four units!"

Darius knew Fancy had zoned out when she started calculating aloud her seven-figure real estate commission as if he weren't on the phone. "Let's see, if the property sells for the asking price, two hundred million dollars, times six percent commission, divided by two, times her sixty percent is . . . damn! Howard is going trip out! Can you believe that? Darius? Did you hear me?"

Yeah. He'd heard everything except the dollar amount. Hanging up, then powering off his phone, Darius unbuckled the seat belt, retrieved his carry-on from the overhead compartment, and dashed down the aisle through coach into first class, and out the door.

The flight attendant yelled, "Sir, wait! This plane is departing immediately."

Without looking back, Darius replied, "I know!" then hurried to the parking shuttle.

Pursuing Fancy was a huge mistake. He couldn't date a woman who had more money than he. It took four months for Fancy to give up the pussy. She asked too many damn questions. And bragging about her newfound success was unattractive for any woman. So what if she'd closed on four houses last month, had three new deals on the table, and was closing on two investment properties in Las Vegas. And she'd better not give his pussy to that real estate tycoon Riddle introduced her to, some old dude who was supposed to give her an exclusive.

Rich men promised females anything to get laid. Why didn't Riddle list his friend's property for sale? If Fancy was going to be Darius's future wife, she had to quit dealing with so many rich men, especially Darius's competition, Byron Van Lee, who seriously wanted to marry Fancy. Darius wished he could get back the seventy-five grand that he'd generously donated at Byron's charity event last year where he'd first met Fancy.

Cruising out of short-term parking onto Century Boulevard in his burgundy Bentley, Darius laughed at himself. "You're the only arrogant youngster imitating a millionaire who has rich parents that literally won't give you a dime. What the hell are you doing driving around with your entire savings in your pocket?" Darius glanced at his image in the rearview mirror. His three hundred and sixty locks had grown halfway down his back. Two had detached from the roots due to stress but Darius reminded himself that he was still an irresistible brotha. Thick cocoa lips. Chiseled chin. A solid six-pack complemented his snake-long dick.

Months ago Darius could've cashed Fancy's four-, five-, and six-figure checks repeatedly. Darius parked in the garage space marked CMCA for Ciara Monroe Casting Agency, next to Ciara's S600 Mercedes, rode the elevator with a bunch of wanna-be millionaires, and then entered his wife's office.

Ciara's new receptionist was consuming versus earning her salary, frivolously chattering on the phone.

"Hum-um. Excuse me, but is Mrs. Jones in?"

Pivoting in her chair, she whispered into the receiver, "Yeah, uh-huh. Girl, hold on," then replied to Darius, "I'm sorry, I didn't hear you come in. We don't have a Mrs. Jones here. What company are you looking for?"

"One more uninformed comment like that and you're fired. Get off the phone and learn your job. Yes, you do have a Mrs. Jones. Ciara."

The secretary's glittered, glossy lips suctioned against her teeth. "Oh, you mean Ms. Monroe. I didn't know she was married." The thirty-something-year-old provocatively dressed woman's eyes roamed Darius's six-foot-seven stature, lingering between his pockets. "Oh my." She looked up then said, "Ciara is in with a client. Do you have an appointment?" Twirling her hair, her tongue rotated in the corner of her mouth. She smiled.

"That's your damn job, too! Get off the phone and check your calendar." Darius could've slapped the phone she held in midair from her hand as she waited to resume her conversation. He could've fired the airhead but she wasn't worth his energy. Instead, Darius strolled down the hall, punched in the digital code to unlock Ciara's door, and entered her office without knocking. "Ciara, we need to talk—"

Darius's body stiffened as his feet suddenly stopped. Ciara gyrated with the vibration of an electrical dick long enough to accommodate two pussies at the same time.

Reaching for her purple panties sprawled on the floor, Ciara yelled, "How did you get in here? Get out!"

Darius laughed, then said, "You'd better get used to that phony plastic black bologna 'cause you'll never feel Slugger again." Clenching his crotch, Darius hoisted his hard-on up and down several times.

"Fuck you, Darius! You arrogant bastard."

The word bastard lingered momentarily. Darius thought, "Maybe once upon a time when I didn't know my biological father. Bump that. I'm not letting some female degrade me. Not at all."

Ciara pointed toward the door. "Get out! Now! If I didn't have a business to operate I swear I would've stayed out of the country, as far away from your inconsiderate ass as possible. I hate you!"

"You know you want this stiff dick inside you. Let me help relieve some of your frustrations. Let me counter some of that hate with some good lovin'." Darius locked the door and then suggested, "You're already pregnant so if you want the real thing, why don't you give your husband some of that"—Darius whispered—"sweet creamy pussy? She's already moist."

The beige personal-sized blanket lying on Ciara's maroon leather loveseat was stained. Darius knew Ciara well enough to recognize she was on the verge of cumming. "You know you want to feel this Mandingo rod of flesh sliding in your hot pussy." Darius maneuvered his dick up his thigh and removed Slugger from his pants. Slowly he pumped from the head to the base deep into his nuts while gazing into Ciara's eyes. "Mmm, he wants her."

Ciara's breathing became rapid. Her nostrils flared so wide Darius saw the hairs inside her nose. "Aw, yeah. That's my spot," Darius said, squeezing pre-cum from his head. "Look at that. I know you're hot. I am, too. Breast milk is oozing from your plump nipples. Let me lick." Darius's tongue traced his lips, leaving a thin coat of saliva.

Ciara's double-Ds had increased to double-Es during her pregnancy. Crumpling the blanket then stuffing it into a black leather handbag, Ciara said, "Darius, you know what your problem is?

You're lovable. But you don't how to love. You're right. I am horny but I'm not desperate."

Oh, snap. The fake dick retracted several times with one press of a button. Ciara tossed what was now a compact umbrella case into the same bag. Damn, what a hellava transformation.

"C'mon, let me taste you," Darius pleaded, kissing Ciara's gigantic, dark cherry-painted lips while rubbing his engorged head against her clit. Darius unfastened her soiled blouse, unsnapped her soaked bra, dabbed her wet nipples with his fingertips, and then gently sampled her milk. "Mmm, sweet." That would be a lucky kid sucking on those tits every day. His index finger probed between Ciara's bushy luscious lips, spreading them apart. Warm, thick cum juices saturated his fingertips. Unbuckling his pants with one hand, Darius massaged Ciara's cum into her clitoris, causing her to jerk several times. She didn't stop him so he whispered, "Turn around."

Ciara was hot and tight and already pregnant so Darius didn't bother putting on one of the condoms in his back pocket. Easing the head in, Darius fantasized maybe he should fuck Ashlee and Desire, too, since they hadn't delivered the babies they'd claimed he fathered. Pregnant pussy was sin city. Made Darius wanna holla. He'd never felt anything so stimulating and climactic since he'd broken Maxine's virginity. Darius withdrew to avoid prematurely ejaculating. Slowly he reentered Ciara. Stroking back and forth, savoring the sensation, Darius penetrated Ciara a little more with each thrust. She trembled with convulsions as her muscles throbbed along his shaft.

"Yes, daddy sho' nuff knows you wanted this big dick, gurl."

This probably wasn't a good time to ask for the money Darius needed but what choice did he have? He was practically broke. But first he had to let the cum in his balls explode. Ciara's hips popped and rotated Slugger into her pussy pocket tucked away in the deepest socket of her vagina.

"Whew," Ciara said, spitting Slugger out like a wad of bubble gum, laughing. "Thanks for the stress release. I knew I married you for a reason."

Darius blurted, "Ciara, I need a million dollars," holding his limp dick.

Ciara's smile converted into a frown. "What you need is a conscience, muthafucka," she replied, cleaning herself with baby wipes then putting on fresh underwear and a different outfit. "Get out of my office."

Neatly, Ciara folded the clothes she'd taken off and placed them in her leather bag along with her other accessories, and then stored the bag in the empty bottom drawer of her lock-type file cabinet.

Wondering what else was in that bag, Darius asked, "Can I have one of those?" pointing to the white cloths.

Ciara's secretary buzzed on the intercom. "Ms. Monroe, your one o'clock is here."

Tossing the blue box, Ciara said, "Just in time. Good, send her in in five minutes," then spayed cinnamon air freshener toward the floor.

Meticulously Darius cleaned Slugger and folded him away. Unlocking the door, he said, "I'll wait in your conference room until you're through but I'm not leaving without a check. Don't forget I'm still legally your husband and I'm entitled to half of everything you own."

"Then sue me, Darius. That's how you kill every spirit around you. You'll fuck over someone every chance you get. Even your mother. But right now what you need to do is get the hell out of my office before I call my media contacts and let everyone know how screwed up your life really is."

The homeless woman's voice echoed between Darius's ears. *Death follows you.*

Kimberly Stokes, Darius's number one piece, walked into Ciara's office wearing one of the mink coats Darius had bought her over the years. Kimberly was still his number one sex buddy. He hoped.

Kimberly smiled. "Oh, Darius. Hi. It's a pleasant surprise seeing you here. I thought you were supposed to be in Oakland."

"Yeah, I was." Darius nodded upward at Kimberly then said, "Call me later. Better yet, stop by my place when you leave here."

Shaking her head, Ciara's eyes shifted to the corners and narrowed. Before Ciara embarrassed him further, Darius closed her door, this time from the outside of her office.

Where in the hell was everybody driving at noon? Interstate 5 was a parking lot. Inching along the freeway to his exit Darius thought, "Kimberly's not going to stop by after talking to Ciara."

Darius entered his home and lay across the sofa, letting the television watch him. How much was his plasma screen worth? Looking around his home, Darius realized he could get a lot of money if he sold some of his stuff. Or he could write a check from one of his accounts to the other, then withdraw the funds the next day before the check bounced.

Awakening to the ding-dong tone of his doorbell, Darius switched channels to his outdoor monitor. Kimberly. She'd showed up at three o'clock. Darius acted as if he was happy to see her. Slugger was overjoyed. Maybe he could get a financial return on the investments of all the shit he'd bought Kimberly.

"Hey, baby. How've you been?" Darius greeted Kimberly, knowing he didn't give a damn about her anymore.

"Great. I'm so excited about my starring role. Can you believe it? I'm going to be an icon. A household name!" Kimberly tossed her jacket onto the chaise.

Not another female flaming about the success she hadn't earned. Darius had to deflate Kimberly's ego. "Not. Only actors with substance and history are icons. Not actresses. But I do wish you well. Let me get that credit card back I gave you. You won't be needing my resources anymore."

Unzipping her Coach purse, Kimberly handed Darius the platinum Visa and said, "Here, take it. That's why I stopped by. This account is closed. You don't know how embarrassed I was standing at the jewelry counter in Tiffany's when they told me the card was declined. I made him run my diamond earrings twice."

"You're joking. Right?" Twice? She'd tried to run his shit twice? Darius's dick went limp.

Kimberly's head swung side to side. "But you're right. I don't need your money."

"What the hell! This is bullshit!" Darius paced his living room floor watching some beer commercial. When the sexy woman in a bikini lounging on the beach licked her lips, Slugger got hard again. Darius's hands rested on Kimberly's waist. "Give daddy some brain, my head hurts."

Darius kissed Kimberly. The room darkened. Kimberly's forehead wrinkled. Her eyebrows drew close together, almost touching. The picture on the big screen disappeared. The date and numbers on the digital clock erased. The lights vanished. Darius flipped the light switch. Pressed the TV remote. Nothing.

"Wait here."

As Darius journeyed through his place—bedrooms, family room, garage—flipping switches and pressing buttons, every electrical unit was off. Darius peeped through his vertical blinds. It was still daylight outside so he couldn't tell if his neighborhood had a power outage. He raced out to the white utility truck blocking his driveway.

"Hey, man. What's going on?" Darius asked, zipping his pants.

The utility man dressed in orange overalls asked, "You didn't get the disconnection notice?"

"This is bullshit, man. You've definitely made a mistake. Not my house. Turn her electric back on, brotha. I'll straighten this out tomorrow."

Of all times to see his next door neighbor, Michael Baines. Darius turned his back to Michael, facing the electrician.

Loudly, the electrician said, "Sorry, man. Can't do," and put the key in the ignition.

"I've got a fine-ass honey inside, percolating anxious for me to do her. Just this one time."

The electrician slammed his door as if he was the one annoyed, rolled down his window, and replied, "I need my job so I can go home and get laid. No sense in both of us missing out."

Walking back inside, Darius lied, "The electrician made a mistake. Everything should be taken care of shortly. We don't need lights," he said, rubbing Kimberly's nipples through her thin blue sweater.

Kimberly held Darius's hands. "No, but we do need hot water."

"It'll be back on shortly, I told you. By the time we're done, you can shower."

Kimberly's lips tightened. She glanced up at Darius and said, "Then why did the electrician leave?"

"Don't question me. After all I've done for you! The only lip service I want from you is below the waistline!"

Kimberly's arm stretched back. Darius's fingers wrapped around her wrist, inches from his face. Pushing Kimberly away, Darius angrily said, "Get your trifling gold-digging ass out of my house before you make me—"

"Do what, Darius? Get a job. Stop trippin'." Kimberly picked up her jacket. "Ciara told me you asked her for money. And that your parents are still cutting you off financially until you officially start school because summer school doesn't count. Baby, I've earned everything you've given me and more."

"I'll make sure someone else gets your part."

Kimberly smiled, then started strutting toward the front door. "Too late. I signed the contract today." Tossing her fake horse hair over her shoulder, Kimberly snapped her fingers twice. "Can you say millionaire?"

Darius opened the door wide and yelled, "Get out! Looking at you is making me sick."

Still grinning, Kimberly said, "In a few hours it won't matter, now will it?" She paused, then continued, "Oh yeah, I almost forgot. You'll be fine. Dogs can see in the dark. Good-bye, Darius." Kimberly left abruptly.

As he slammed the door, Darius's cell phone rang. The last person he wanted to talk to was Fancy, but she was the closest person he had to a friend.

"Hey, Fancy. What's up? I missed my flight. You still want me to come and keep you company?"

"Sure, come on." Fancy was still enthusiastic.

Darius's boarding pass was in his pocket so he could exchange it for another pass and stay at Fancy's place in Oakland for the weekend until he figured out how to come up with some money. Darius couldn't wait until the semester started. Going to UCLA and playing basketball were his future jobs. Until then, he'd have to come up with something, but working for someone else wasn't in his plans. Think, Darius. Think.

Kevin Williams. Why hadn't Darius thought of his thieving half brother before? Last time they'd spoken at the funeral, Kevin claimed Wellington had frozen all of his accounts and assets. How foolish of Darius to have believed two liars. Kevin's ass owed him over a million dollars. It was time for Kevin and Wellington to pay. One way or another, Darius would recoup what was rightly his.

CHAPTER 16

Fancy enjoyed another fabulous night until the dawn with Darius in her arms. She hadn't imagined Darius as a homebody, but he didn't want to go out to dinner, he wasn't hungry, and at her request, he denied allowing her to spend the night at his house. They ordered a vegetarian pizza, and when the pizza arrived, Darius disappeared into the bathroom for fifteen minutes. Consuming two-thirds of the pizza, they watched all three *Scary Movie* flicks, laughing until their stomachs hurt from those hilarious Wayans brothers. The following morning when Fancy suggested going to breakfast, Darius declined.

Fancy asked, "Well, how about dinner tonight?"

Removing the plastic from his freshly dry-cleaned slacks, Darius said, "Naw, I'd better not make plans. I might have to fly back to L.A. tonight. If I don't, I'll come back by."

"Darius, I'm not the type of woman who wants to stay at home having sex every night without going someplace. So if you want to take me out tonight, call me by noon. If not, I might make other plans."

Darius slipped his crewneck short-sleeved navy shirt over his head and said, "That's cool." Darius kissed Fancy's lips. "Don't make any plans, I'll call you later."

Escorting Darius to the door, Fancy thought, "He must be crazy if he thinks I'm going to sit around wasting my time waiting for him to decide if he wants to take me out." Fancy closed the door and then changed the linen on her bed. Glancing at the corner of her living room, Darius's shoes, jeans, and button-up shirt were still there. Quickly Fancy packed his belongings in a black trash bag and placed the bag inside the closet in the back room where she kept her clothes. Racks of clothes on wheels were situated throughout the room like a miniature department store. No man, including Darius, was making his mark on her without making a commitment.

Tossing her throw pillows onto her loveseat, Fancy paused when her phone rang. "Good, he called soon," Fancy said before looking at the caller ID. Byron's name was displayed where Darius's name should've been.

"Good morning, Byron."

"Good morning to you. What are you doing tonight?"

Fancy hesitated and then said, "Nothing. Why?"

"I have a referral for you. Can I take you out?"

A date would be nice, Fancy thought, asking, "Where?"

"You know me. Don't ask. You wanna make some money or not? Maybe we can become partners and you can donate a portion of your commission proceeds to my nonprofit for every referral. Besides, I miss you, Fancy."

Byron was hallucinating if he thought Fancy would agree to give his organization money on his terms. "I need to see you, too," Fancy said, realizing she'd have to tell Byron about Darius eventually.

"Cool. I'll pick you up at six. 'Bye."

Fancy didn't know why she had agreed to go on a date with Byron minutes after Darius had left her place. Was it necessary for her to go out with Byron? Fancy could've told Byron about Darius before she hung up the phone. Darius was obviously upset about something but refused to discuss his problems. His deep laughs during the movies were mostly genuine, but there were times when Darius should've been laughing with her and either didn't respond or his burst of laughter was poignantly delayed. The same distant responses Fancy gave Desmond at the comedy show, Darius had given Fancy last night.

Byron's devious ways annoyed Fancy but his promise to send her a client justified one last face-o-face date. Plus, Fancy wanted to give closure to her estranged relationship with Byron and let him know she was dating his friend.

Slipping into a sweatsuit, Fancy rode the elevator to the lobby, greeted Mr. Cabie, then crossed the street. Jogging along the trail, Fancy wondered if she could have a meaningful relationship with Darius.

If only Mandy would forgive her. Why did she have to call Mandy a bitch? Fancy convinced herself that her outburst was the real reason Mandy refused to see her. Fancy could talk with SaVoy, but SaVoy was too judgmental. Caroline was too busy. And Desmond was . . . Glancing at her wristwatch, it was before five in Atlanta, maybe she could call Dez. "Never mind," Fancy said to herself. "If Desmond wanted to talk to me, he would've called by now." Trina must have persuaded Desmond to marry or agree to marry her by now. Especially since they were living together.

Fancy's legs sprinted the three and a half miles around Lake Merritt in less than forty-five minutes. Returning home, sweaty and confused, Fancy soaked in a tub of herbal essence homemade tea mixtures wrapped in packets of cheese cloth and fresh red and white rose petals from the bouquet Darius had given her last night. No milk and honey bath for Byron, but her pampering baths weren't about Byron or Darius. Regardless of the stress in her life, Fancy was going to age gracefully and no man would have her looking ten years older than her actual age, like Caroline. Fancy wondered how Marvin was treating her mother and if Caroline was still acting like a little kid.

Stepping out of the tub, Fancy dried her feet, then went to her closet bedroom, selected the crimson baby doll dress and matching open-toed sling-backs trimmed in coral blue, then hot-curled the ends of her hair. Swooping her weaved strands into a circle atop her head and off of her face, Fancy bent the ends then applied her makeup. Men had no idea what women went through to prepare for a date. Selecting the ruby earrings Byron had bought, and the diamond necklace Harry gave her, Fancy was almost ready for her last date with Byron.

The double ring tone of her phone indicated Byron was in the lobby. Instead of answering the phone, Fancy slipped her dress over her body, stepped into her shoes, grabbed her purse, dabbed perfume behind each ear and between her breasts, and hurried downstairs. When the elevator door opened, Darius stood in the lobby holding another bouquet of roses.

Frowning, he asked, "Where are you going?"

Dammit. She should've answered the phone. "Out. You said you were going to call back by noon."

"No, you told me to call before noon. I told you not to make plans."

"Darius, it's too late. I have plans already," Fancy said, staring at Darius's Escalade in the circular driveway.

"What nigga you goin' out with?"

Mr. Cabie busied himself, pretending not to overhear their conversation.

"It doesn't matter. I'm not going back upstairs. I'll call you when I get back." Fancy prayed Byron didn't arrive before Darius left.

"Well, let me in before you leave and I'll wait for you."

Darius was insane if he thought she'd let him roam her condo alone. Men were actually nosier than women. Sneaky. Distrustful. Shaking her head, Fancy said, "I'll call you when I get back, Darius."

Squaring his shoulders, Darius yelled, "This is bullshit! Don't call me ever again!" He walked away.

Fancy yelled back, "When are you going to grow the fuck up and stop acting like a spoiled-ass kid! You don't want a commitment but you want to control where I go! I told you I wasn't staying home tonight. I'm glad you're leaving! And don't come back!"

Darius opened then slammed the lobby door. As Fancy waited for the elevator, Byron drove into the driveway.

Damn! Hoping Darius had left and wasn't parked on the street, Fancy strutted through the lobby and eased into Byron's car. Fancy hadn't been on a date with Byron in months.

"You look nice. I like that dress," Byron said, opening the car door to his BMW.

"Thanks. So where're we going?"

"To a concert, dinner, then to my place."

"Concert and dinner is cool but not your place. Mine."

"Lighten up. I heard you're seeing Darius and I just saw him leave. He's probably upset because he can't afford to treat you the way I do."

Fancy was in for a long night. Ignoring Byron, she admired the new condo development off of Harrison Street and Jack London Square and asked, "How much do you think that building is worth?"

"About a hundred million."

"Are you serious?"

"You have a license, look it up on the MLS and see what the asking price is."

"Yeah, I will. So how many clients do you have for me?"

"One right now."

"Cool, but just so you know, I'm not dating Darius," Fancy said, staring ahead at the building in Jack London Square that once housed TGI Friday's. Seemingly overnight the restaurant had closed and no one knew the real reason. Fancy had researched it, discovering Oakland's waterfront was being rehabilitated, including the Old Spaghetti Factory and every business in that building. All Fancy cared about was the real estate value. One day she'd sell commercial properties.

"I don't care about Darius. In fact, don't mention his name when you're with me. You're with a real man now. One who should be your husband."

Byron's name didn't start with a D so according to the homeless woman's prediction, he couldn't be her future husband. Besides, Fancy was through with Byron and his big dick. Miss Kitty knocked twice. Darius's dick was bigger and better. Miss Kitty knocked twice more. *Cut that out.* Fancy pressed her thighs together. "How much do you think that building is worth?" Fancy asked, pointing at the Park Hotel.

"Look, if you don't want to go to the concert and dinner at Yoshi's, we don't have to."

"No, it's fine." Why was it that Byron could talk about his business for hours but now that she was interested in making money, he didn't want to discuss the properties?

Dinner at Yoshi's was nice. Fancy ordered sushi. Byron ordered steak. Byron didn't want to discuss real estate and Fancy wasn't interested in having a relationship. Quietly they ate. When they entered the intimate concert area at Yoshi's, they sat up front. Byron pulled his chair close to Fancy and placed his arm around her shoulder. Instantly Fancy moved his hand.

"Please, we're not in a relationship so let's not pretend."

"Fancy, you know I love you. I didn't invite you out as a friend. I invited you out as a lover. And my love."

"You never said anything all through dinner. Not one word." Byron had stared at Fancy the whole time. Eerie. Irritating. She couldn't tell what he was thinking. One minute he seemed calm, the next he acted as though he was jealous of her. Now that Fancy had her own money, she noticed the men in her life were treating her differently. She didn't need them anymore. But they needed her to need them. "You never once mentioned your friend who's supposed to be my client. There probably is no client, Byron. My time is valuable. If you're going to play games, and all you want to talk about is getting back together, let's go."

Byron asked, "What about the show?"

What about the show? Was that all he had to say? Fancy stood and started walking toward the door. "I don't care about the show. Take me home." Fancy was compromising herself for a ghost client.

Exiting the concert room and entering the lounge area, Fancy wished she'd stayed inside because Darius was seated in an oversized chair facing them. Like he was intentionally waiting for her to come out. Had Darius followed them to Yoshi's? Fancy tried to slow her pace but Darius immediately headed in their direction.

Patting Byron on the back, Darius sarcastically said, "I see she's yours tonight. Enjoy yourself, man."

"Oh no, you don't," Fancy said, following Darius outside. "You are not going to treat me like a piece of meat."

Standing outside, Darius yelled in Fancy's face, "What the fuck you doin' with that nigga? I thought you were my girl. I should've known better than to trust your ass."

"Darius, it's not what you think! And I'm not your girl. And I'm not his girl! You can't just decide arbitrarily that I'm yours! Byron and I were giving closure to our relationship. That's all." Damn, why had Fancy said, "That's all"?

Byron walked by Fancy and Darius and said, "Closure. Yeah, right. I'll see you tomorrow night," and kept on walking. Darius turned and walked in the opposite direction. Men were scandalous just like women. Fancy had no plans of ever seeing Byron again after he fronted her in Darius's face.

Hailing a taxi, Fancy's heart ached because she didn't want to lose Darius. She loved Darius. She thought.

CHAPTER 17

Since Darius had enough credits from his prior years at Georgetown, he entered UCLA as a junior and was exempt from the mandatory "live on campus" policy for freshman basketball players. At Darryl's request, Jada paid for a dorm room anyway. Darryl had said, "Son, you'll have fewer distractions if you live on campus. Your room is too small to host parties and when the females crash your dorm room offering sexual pleasantries, at least you'll have your roommate to witness that you didn't rape them." Dad always tried to predict the outcome of every situation before anything occurred.

Darius had asked his dad, "So you think I'm going to spend every night in this shoebox?"

"Son, you have to make sacrifices in life to become successful." Darryl's eyes shifted toward Darius's roommate then back to Darius. "You know what we discussed earlier."

"Yeah, I know." One was not to name-drop his inside connections to the NBA draft to his teammates. Darryl had informed Darius that his coaches and teammates would make assumptions, but Darius was not to confirm nor deny their statements.

After breaking up with Fancy, Darius returned to Los Angeles. Chilled for a week. Attended his psychology classes. Basketball workouts because, according to NCAA rules, the team couldn't officially practice for almost another three months. Darryl's advice to Darius regarding Fancy was, "Don't trip. There'll be another Fancy knocking on your door every night. Focus on school and basketball." Darryl was wrong. There'd never be another Fancy. Fancy was the reason Darius had to respond to Ashlee's demand to see him.

Starring out the window into the clouds, Darius thought about how his life, overnight, took a different direction. The woman he hadn't seen in eight months, Ashlee, had called him. And within a few hours, Darius was on his way to Dallas. The coach plane ride seemed the longest mental and physical trip Darius had taken, including the descent into Dallas, Texas.

While in flight, Darius could not believe that a terrible kid with a cast on his leg continuously kicked the back of his seat, the person who sat next to Darius snored, and Darius's seat wouldn't recline. During the flight Darius ignored the kid he could've strangled by reading the second half of *The Preacher's Son,* figuring some brotha had to have more problems than he, and Darius was right. Dude was a straight trip.

"Aw, shit." Darius closed the book, unbuckled his seat belt, then stood. The plane, only a few feet from landing, suddenly was on an incline back into the sky. Rattling and shaking, the 757 shook so hard Darius fell into his seat, not sure they'd make it up or down safely. Darius silently prayed, "God, please don't take me out like this. Don't let my mother have to identify me by my teeth. Please, Lord, please."

"Everyone, please remain calm and seated with your seat belts fastened," the not-so-chipper flight attendant announced. "There were crosswinds on the ground and for your safety we were instructed to circle around until given clearance to land."

Dallas-Fort Worth always had ground crosswinds. That shit wasn't new. "Who in the hell gave clearance for landing? Whateva sleepy overworked muthfuckin' air traffic controller is in that tower, fire his ass!" Darius shouted.

A few "Yeahs!" and "That's rights!" roared throughout the plane.

When the flight attendant held her head in her lap, Darius

closed his eyes. If she was scared, he had cause to be terrified. After circling around three times, Darius almost regurgitated as the plane landed safely on the runway. Everyone except Darius clapped as he retrieved his carry-on and headed to the exit door before they arrived at the gate.

"Sir, for you own safety, please re—"

"This is for my own safety. I ain't movin'," Darius said, standing in front of the attendant.

The door opened and Darius dashed to the taxi stand because his mother refused to pay for a driver. The anxiety stirring in Darius's abdomen made the taxi ride from DFW airport to Presbyterian Hospital an eternity.

Ashlee had called at two in the morning and told Darius she went into labor prematurely so Darius convinced his mother to buy him a ticket he couldn't have purchased with his last few dollars. Moms was undeniably in denial; trying to keep from losing Wellington to the same woman twice, she'd become obsessed with chasing her husband. Darius was too emotionally tied to Fancy, so he was glad his full-time class schedule would start soon.

The hospital lobby was cold like a morgue. Quiet. The smell of sick people reeked throughout the corridors as Darius exited the elevator onto the maternity floor. What if Ashlee's baby wasn't his? Oh, shit! What if he was dead? Or going to die? "Stop buggin' out, man. That old homeless lady who claimed she was predicting your future didn't know you. Her ass was crazy."

Darius stood outside Ashlee's door. What the hell, he was here now. And whether or not the baby was for Darius, Darius wanted to see him. Her. Since Ciara had given him back her engagement and wedding rings, and since Darius originally had bought the engagement ring for Ashlee, he would propose to Ashlee if the child was his. But he was in love with Fancy and he needed money, so on his way to the airport, Darius had pawned a twenty-thousand-dollar engagement ring for five grand. He had the wedding band in his pocket along with the money, ready to hand everything to Ashlee for the baby. Darius prayed Ashlee had a boy.

"Hey," Darius whispered, quietly entering Ashlee's room. "You doing okay?"

Ashlee didn't look okay. She was paler. Eyes puffy. Hair scattered all over her head. Her stomach protruded as though she hadn't delivered the baby. Lawrence sat in the corner in a huge chair. He stared at Darius and didn't speak.

Darius wanted to curse Lawrence out for interfering with his relationship with Ashlee. "Hello, Mr. Anderson," Darius said, remembering how his real dad told him to keep his enemies close, and if Darius was lucky, out of the media when Darius turn pro.

Lawrence stood and said, "Ashlee, darling, I'll be back in an hour. Hopefully he'll be gone by the time I return." Lawrence kissed his daughter's forehead.

"Thanks, Daddy, for understanding," Ashlee said, hugging her father.

When Lawrence exited the room, Darius kissed Ashlee's lips. "Is it a boy? I miss you. How are you?"

Ashlee's smiling eyes resembled the look Darius used to see on his mother's face whenever he walked into a room. "We're fine. And yes, it's a boy."

"Can I see him? Where is he?" Darius asked, wondering if the baby resembled him.

"He's in the nursery." Ashlee pressed a button on the side of her bed and said, "Nurse, can you bring Junior in, please?"

Darius smiled, hoping Ashlee could see the excitement in his eyes.

The nurse replied, "Certainly, Mrs. Williams."

The sparkle in his eyes glazed over. No, Darius did not hear the nurse say "Williams." He wasn't prepared for that shit. "Williams? What the hell?" Standing over Ashlee, Darius questioned, "Ashlee, you have something you need to say to me?"

The nurse entered and handed the baby to Ashlee. "No, please," Ashlee said to the nurse. "Let Darius hold him."

The nurse dumped the kid in Darius's arms like he was the father. Darius wanted to move his arms but then the kid would fall on the floor. Instead, Darius scratched his locks, wondering what to do next. Darius couldn't yell with the baby in his arms.

"Darius, I apologize. I wanted you to be here with me and I

couldn't tell you over the phone. But I wanted you to see him. He's so beautiful. I want you to be his godfather."

"This is a joke, right? I took the first fuckin' flight, a red-eye flight that almost crashed, to be here for this. You apologize for being late or stepping on someone's foot, Ashlee. Not for making a man fly over a thousand miles to tell him it's not his baby." Darius shouted, "Why is everybody fucking with me? You of all people kickin' my ass when I'm already down. Please tell me you're not playing me for a fool, too."

Propping the pillow behind her back, Ashlee cried, "Darius, we're family. I love you. Can you think of someone other than yourself for just a moment?"

The kid was kinda cool and hella tiny, barely heavier than a bag of sugar. He weighed five and half pounds. Except for the wrinkles, Darius thought the baby favored him. A little. "So you married Kevin because he's the father? You married him after he stole all of my money?"

"Darius, can't you see? Kevin was trying to be like you. He's really a nice man."

"Nice man, my ass. He's a thief! All he wants is your money. Ashlee, is this my son? Because if not, I'm out. I have to get back to school and back to my woman."

Ashlee closed her eyes momentarily then said, "My dad was smart enough to draw up a prenuptial."

"Your dad let you marry this clown and he won't let you speak to me on the phone!" The baby started crying. "Oh, damn. I'm sorry. All I want to hear you say is whether or not he's mine. I need to hear it from your mouth, Ashlee."

"He's hungry." Ashlee extended her arms and uncovered her breasts. Holding his head with one hand and her breast in the other, she directed the baby's head toward her nipple. Darius's dick got hard so he sat in the only chair across the room, the one Lawrence occupied earlier. Did she mean to uncover both of her titties? Watching the little fella breastfeed made Darius reminisce about doing Ciara in her office. Ashlee patted the baby on the back, then asked the nurse to come and get him.

Darius stood, stretched, then walked over to Ashlee and said, "I demand a paternity test."

"I agree. That's fine."

Darius was tired of Ashlee's charade. "I really don't have anything else to say to you. I will be a father to my son but I can't be Kevin's son's godfather."

"That's fine, Darius. I don't know why I expected you to be a man about this."

"This is bullshit! Be a man about what? I'll arrange for the test before I leave." That meant another phone call to his mother for more money because there was no way Darius was spending his money to find out the truth. "I love you too much, Ashlee, to play games."

"No, you love yourself too much," Kevin said, entering the room.

Darius turned to witness a shorter image of himself. Kevin had grown locks, was sporting a Rolex, and his clothes were top-of-the-line designer down to his shoes. Without speaking a word, Darius's hands clamped around Kevin's neck and tightened.

"Darius! Don't!" Ashlee yelled. "Let him go!"

Darius slammed the imposter into the wall, sending a framed photo of daisies crashing to the floor. "Nigga, if you don't pay me back my money . . ." Darius choked his half brother until Kevin couldn't suction an ounce of oxygen. Huge veins popped out of Kevin's neck. Tears swelled in both men's eyes. Darius was hurt that Ashlee had betrayed him. Darius could beat Kevin's ass and feel better. But there was nothing Darius could do about the pain Ashlee had caused him. The entire situation was Ashlee's fault. If only she'd been faithful.

Ashlee yelled, "Nurse! Nurse!"

Darius had zoned out and forgot Kevin couldn't breathe. Kevin's face was red, his body limp. The veins in his neck spoke the words he couldn't. Peeling his fingers away, Darius's imprint remained. Ashlee was in the background, still screaming. As the nurse entered, Darius punched Kevin in the face, knocking him to the floor.

"You lucky I don't have my gun with me or I'd blow your fucking brains out. You have two days to get me money or else the next time I see you you'll be saying hello to your other brother. My brotha."

Walking out, Darius mumbled, "Why is everybody fuckin' with me?"

CHAPTER 18

Did it matter who was right or wrong? Fancy was willing to forgive Darius; for what, she didn't know, but whatever was keeping the two of them apart was driving her insane. Fancy keyed in sixty-nine on her cellular phone to call Darius.

Darius answered, "Hey, Lady—"

Fancy pressed the END button. Maybe later. Fancy had to keep the promise she'd made to herself and not call Darius. Nothing good had ever materialized from relationships in which Fancy cared more about the man than he cared for her. And perhaps it was too late to adjust her feelings, and she was truly in love, but her actions didn't have to dictate her love for Darius. It was okay to wait for Darius to call, and through her reactions reassure him that he was loved. If Darius wanted Fancy, he'd have to pursue her.

Darius had ended their relationship, shutting her out. He refused to communicate his feelings about their issues but he'd talk nonstop about basketball. Fancy had grown irritable, listening to Darius brag about himself simply to hear his voice while holding on to threads of hope of repairing their relationship. What could she do to stop obsessing over Darius? Fancy didn't want to visit her mother but she had to do something to avoid thinking about Darius so much.

Visiting her mother was difficult but Fancy's lime green strap-up four-inch heels, which crisscrossed up her legs to her knees, crept up Caroline's blue stairway. Fancy cringed as she knocked on the door. She wasn't in the mood to spend time with Caroline but she couldn't spend another day in her condo keeping herself from everyone except her clients.

Opening the door, Caroline said, "Hey, Fancy. Come on in. What brings you by?" Caroline's hair was a mess. Uncombed. Rough around the edges. She could use a touch-up. The thin, floral print cotton robe loosely covered Caroline.

Following Caroline into her bedroom, Fancy said, "Just wanted to say hello to my mother. Since you've got a new man you don't return my calls anymore."

Caroline had the same full-sized bed, scratched wooden headboard, nightstands, and dresser with a wood-trimmed mirror she'd had for God knew how many years. One day Fancy would buy her mother a new bedroom set. Fancy sat on the same side of the bed as Caroline, a few feet away from her mother.

"Now, I know you, Fancy, and you never just want to say hello. I hear the real estate business is going well for you."

"Yes, it is. I have a nine-figure deal in the pipeline, and when it closes I'll be a millionaire."

Caroline's eyes widened. "Really?"

The conversation wasn't intended to center on Fancy or her money, so Fancy answered, "Yes, really. How's the man in your life? Mr. Marvin."

Fancy's mother had a man and Fancy didn't. Where was Darius? What was he doing? Who was he doing? Was he thinking of Fancy? Missing her? Or laughing with some other woman? Holding her in his arms the way he once held Fancy?

"He's wonderful. We're engaged. And I'm pregnant." Caroline smiled wide.

Fancy's jaw dropped at the same time. "Pregnant? Mother, at your age? You're too old to have a baby."

"If that fifty-seven-year-old woman can have twins, I can have a baby, too. I'm not even forty."

"I don't believe you. You're a lousy mom. You have to have an abortion."

"Fancy, this is not your life. It's mine. I know I wasn't the best mother to you. I wasn't ready for a child when I had you. And if I could've understood then what I know now, that being a woman doesn't guarantee you'll be a good mother, I would've listened to your father and aborted you with the money he'd given me."

Standing over Caroline, Fancy refused to cry. Not yet, she told herself. Not yet. "Well, at least this baby will know its father and hopefully have a mother that can tell him or her that she loves them."

"So that's why you came. You finally worked up the courage to ask me who your father is. Sit down."

Not really. Fancy wasn't sure if she sat because her legs were weak or because she finally had a chance to know who her father was. Fancy sat next to Caroline on the bed, holding her own hands. "Wait. You haven't told me all this time. Maybe I don't want to know."

"No, you have a right to know. But promise me you'll make an appointment with Mandy to discuss this."

Fancy sprang to her feet and said, "Naw, that's okay." Maybe Fancy should apologize for having called Mandy a bitch but if knowing her father was going to be all bad, Caroline should keep her secret. "Maybe I'm better off not knowing him. I gotta go."

"Sit, Fancy," Caroline said, patting the empty space next to her. "You remember the day you called the police and had Thaddeus arrested?"

"And?"

"I'm so sorry, baby. But Thaddeus is your father."

The weight of Fancy's body slumped to the floor. Kneeling, she yelled, "Mama, no! How could you? So you let me lock up my father without telling me? What in the world were you thinking? He'd forgive me? Or he'd never be released from prison? He's out, Mama!" Fancy cried, "What am I supposed to say to him?"

"I'm so sorry, Fancy. But I know you'll think of something." Caroline began crying as she continued sitting on her bed.

"Don't you cry. I hate you! Now I see why you can't tell me you love me. You don't love yourself. How could you!" Fancy stared at the blue closet, remembering the day Franze had raped her then locked her in the closet until she promised not to tell. Looking at her mother, Fancy said, "I wasn't trying to hurt him. I just wanted my mother. To myself. But you were too busy getting laid to notice. Just like with this Marvin guy. Every man in your life comes before—" Fancy stood, forcing back her tears. "All I ever wanted was you and for you to tell me that you love me. And you still can't give me that. That's okay. One day I'll find somebody to love." Fancy loved Darius and hoped he loved her, because right now Fancy needed to be held.

Caroline sat there crying hard, as if she was the one wounded. Now Fancy hated her mother and felt bad for incarcerating her father. She left Caroline's house without saying good-bye. From now on Fancy would just call her mother Caroline like she had done most of her life because she had never felt like Caroline was her mother.

Picking up her cellular while driving, Fancy dialed SaVoy's number. She really wanted to talk to Desmond, but he didn't answer her calls after five o'clock. The time in California was two-thirty but five-thirty in Atlanta. Mandy really was the only one Fancy should talk to but she wasn't taking or returning her calls. Realizing SaVoy was at church, Fancy terminated the call.

Fancy drove to Mandy's office, parked across the street on University, and turned off her car. Fancy was so hopeless that if the homeless woman she had seen before was sitting on that bench, Fancy would talk to her. What was Fancy thinking? It was Sunday and Mandy's office was closed. Fancy cruised down University and sat in her Benz outside Skates restaurant, again contemplating if life was worth living.

Now that Fancy had money, she still wasn't happy. If she left town, she would still be alone. If she stayed in Oakland, she'd still be lonely. If she killed herself, she'd be free of all the madness. All of her sadness. Reluctantly Fancy sat in her car outside Skates restaurant looking over the waves splashing against the boulders.

"Damn!" Fancy said when she saw Michael Baines drive into the parking lot. "Fancy, you've got to stop forgetting things." Instantly Fancy regretted that she'd agreed to meet Michael Baines. She wanted to change the location because the only reason she'd come to Skates was to reminisce about her first date with Darius. Skates was their special place. Maybe it didn't matter anymore. Why did she continue thinking about Darius when he probably had a woman or several women in Los Angeles?

The phone rang, interrupting her thoughts. It was Darius. Every time Fancy thought of checking out, someone Fancy cared for checked in. She cleared her throat and answered, "This is Fancy Taylor, your realtor of choice," wanting Darius to hear her professional voice. Darius had replaced Desmond. Fancy didn't want to rush him but she had to get inside soon for her dinner date. She didn't want to risk losing her lucrative deal.

"Hey, Laydcat. You busy?"

Ladycat. Fancy missed and loved the way Darius seductively pronounced the syllable "cat." Except this time he didn't sound sexy at all. Fancy lied, claiming, "I have a client on the other line," to give herself time to regroup. Her chest was aching. Fancy could hardly breathe. Closing her eyes, Fancy forced back tears. It felt so good hearing Darius's caring voice.

"That's okay. I shouldn't have called."

Fancy was angry at Darius for distancing himself from her but couldn't display that energy lest she pushed him farther away.

"Darius, wait. Please, don't hang up." Fancy kept her eyes closed, fearing if she opened them Niagara Falls would emerge. "I miss talking to you. I'll only be a second."

Fancy clicked over to her dial tone, inhaled deeply three times while counting to ten, and then switched back to Darius. "Hey, you okay? You sound down." Fancy cheered herself up to listen when she was the one who needed to talk.

"I wish I could say I'm okay but I'm not. Remember when you asked me about my last girlfriend?"

"Yes." Now that Fancy loved Darius the person, she wasn't sure she wanted to hear what he had to say. Fancy wanted him back in her life. And she didn't want to become Darius's friend, listening to him talk about other women.

"Well, it's complicated. I thought this woman from my past was pregnant for me. Turns out the baby is my half brother's kid."

"Oh, no. Your brother slept with your woman? When did you

find that out?" Fancy was relieved that whoever this woman was, she wasn't a threat to their relationship.

"Yesterday. I wanted to thank you for letting me crash at your place back when. I didn't want to be alone but didn't know how to tell you that I needed you."

"That's great to hear because I didn't want to be alone either. You can come back anytime you'd like, but what about your brother?" Fancy had to know what was on Darius's mind without getting caught up in her emotions. What if he loved someone else?

"I don't want to talk about Kevin. He made me so mad I almost killed him. Fucking my sister."

Frowning, Fancy asked, "Fucking your sister? I thought you said this woman was your ex-girlfriend."

"Damn. Like I said, it's complicated. One day I'll tell you the whole story."

"If you want to see my therapist, I can give you her number." Maybe if Fancy gave Mandy a referral, Mandy would give Fancy an appointment. Glancing at the clock in her car, twenty minutes had passed and Fancy was twenty-five minutes late.

"A therapist. I'm not crazy."

"Neither am I. I'm only suggesting. What I'll do is when we hang up, I'll call and leave the number on your home voice mail."

"Whatever, I gotta go. 'Bye."

Fancy wasn't suggesting Darius hang up. He made her nervous. Fancy knew he was hurting but he cut her off before she finished talking. Before she could tell Darius her problems, he was gone. She should be glad because, knowing Mr. Baines, he wasn't going to wait much longer.

Praying Darius was in Oakland, Fancy dialed his home number instead of calling back on his cell. "The number you have reached is not in service. There is no additional information for . . ." Fancy redialed the number and got the same message so she hung up and called Darius's cell phone, hoping he'd answer. He didn't, so she left Mandy's number on his voice mail then said, "I love you, Darius. I want us to work things out. You have no idea how much I truly miss you." Quietly crying, Fancy held the phone for moment and then hung up.

Michael walked out of Skates, bypassed Fancy's car, got into his Range Rover, and drove away. Had he seen her? Glancing at the time on her cellular phone, Fancy dialed his number.

"Baines," was how he answered.

"Hello, Mr. Baines, this is Fancy. I was in the parking lot when I saw you leaving. I can wait if you'd like."

"You were in the parking lot when you saw me arrive. If you're not serious about making money, don't waste my time. I'll find someone else to do this deal." He hung up.

Was talking to Darius worth losing over a million dollars? Definitely not. Fancy would have to find another way to deal with balancing her career while trying to love Darius.

CHAPTER 19

Ladycat had undeniably become precious. Darius found himself daydreaming about Fancy. Wanting to be with her more and more, talk to her. But his male ego had decided that Fancy, like all the rest of the women in his life, couldn't be trusted, so he stayed at his home in L.A. to avoid visiting her. Reluctantly, Darius stopped returning and answering her calls, knowing that soon Fancy wouldn't call him anymore.

There were only a few more weeks before their exhibition game against a foreign team. Darius was going insane. The few hours spent for his declared major in Business Econ combined with workouts weren't enough to occupy his time. Like now. Darius had almost four hours to do nothing but wait for practice to start. His one class for the day was over and his homework was done by noon. What the fuck did full-time students with no jobs or extra-curricular activities do all day? Hang out on Venice Beach?

Lounging on his sofa, watching the news, Darius prayed that neither Ciara nor Desire was pregnant with his child. Initially, he had been pissed because Ashlee had married Kevin without his permission, but not anymore. In retrospect, God had answered one of his prayers. But if one of the other kids was his, either way Darius would come out a loser. "Lord, thanks for letting Ashlee's baby be for Kevin. That's one down, and please let the other two not be mine, too." The thought of being dedicated to either one of those tricksters for the rest of his child's life was depressing. Damn, why did Darius have to think about life or death, reminding him his child was supposed to die?

"Fuck!" Darius yelled, hurling the remote across the room.

Pissed with the conniving women who'd complicated his life, Darius was pleased that his mom had reconnected his electricity and his home phone, and against Wellington's wishes, written Darius a small check for ten grand after he'd told her how he'd pawned the diamond ring for cash. Surely his mother didn't want that to end up in the newspaper, or the fact that he was determined to forge her signature on a check to pay his bills.

Darius dialed Ciara's office. After the fourth ring the recorded voice mail message stated, "You have reached CMCA . . ."

Exactly four hours remained before practice so Darius hung up, got in his car, and drove to Ciara's office. His basketball gear was in his dorm room, a place where Darius spent as little time as possible to avoid the groupies who were becoming increasingly bold about knocking on his door. At least on Fridays, Saturdays, and Sundays Darius kept his personal adventures private. Monday through Thursday the coach demanded he live on campus and, regardless if his roommate, Lance, was in the room, Darius handled his sexual business.

Ciara's secretary no longer forwarded Darius's calls, and Ciara had stopped answering when Darius dialed her cellular and refused to respond to his messages, so Darius decided to show up unannounced, again hoping to walk away a free man.

Darius entered Ciara's lobby and scanned behind the counter. Not a soul in sight. "Good, hopefully Ciara had enough sense to fire that lazy nosy chick," Darius said, bypassing the secretary's empty desk.

Darius stood outside Ciara's door, pressed his ear to the glossy wood, and listened.

"Mmm, yeah. That feels so good. Suck a little harder."

"Mmm, hmm."

The moaning and groaning turned him on, causing Slugger to swell and his breathing to increase. "Impeccable timing, she's at it again," Darius thought. Licking his lips, Darius punched in the code, held the knob, and then quietly cracked the door open. His eyes bucked in disbelief.

Kimberly Stokes's head was buried between Ciara's pregnant thighs.

Darius entered, saying, "Hollywood! Hollywood! Now I bet this scene would gross millions opening night at the box office. Let's tell your media contacts about this." He took several snapshots with his camera phone while Kimberly was still on her knees.

"Darius! What the hell?" Ciara's stomach rolled up as she propped herself up on the loveseat.

Smiling as he took another photo, Darius suggested, "I can wait outside 'til you're done cumming." Closing Ciara's door behind him, Darius waited in the lobby, looking at the pictures he'd taken with his phone. No way would Darius fuck Ciara and Kimberly at the same time but they needed some dick in that equation. So that was the missing component. Ciara and Kimberly were bisexual lovers. Was Kimberly doing Ciara by choice? Or was that how she'd gotten her role? "Don't know how I missed that one," Darius mumbled, surfing through the stack of *Variety* magazines on the rectangular glass-top coffee table.

Soul Mates Dissipate was on the cover of the most recent issue. That was his damn project. Darius's mother had invited him to the premiere but Darius declined, telling his mom, "That's like being a guest in my own home." Darius had produced that film. When the credits rolled hopefully they'd show Darius Jones, not Wellington Jones. "Go. Steal my credits and have fun with your lying husband." Maybe Darius should storm the red carpet and take Fancy with him so she could see he really was a successful businessman. At one time anyway.

"Darius, Jones!" Ciara's arms swung spastically above her stomach. "How do you keep getting into my office without my permission?"

Biting his bottom lip with a half smile, Darius replied, "Now, if I told you that, I couldn't get in anymore." Darius grinned at Ciara. "Look, I came by to congratulate you on the premiere tonight but I see Kimberly beat me to it. Just in case the baby is mine, I think we need to have a decent relationship. And to simplify things, you need to sign these divorce papers." Darius handed Ciara a yellow envelope.

Tossing the package on the coffee table, Ciara firmly said, "Leave them with me. I'll give them to my attorney. After the baby is born, I'll make that decision."

"Ciara, I've met someone else." Darius picked up the package and handed it to Ciara again. "I love her and I don't want to make a full commitment to her until I bring closure to our relationship."

"I know. Fancy Taylor. Realtor. She lives in Oakland on Lake Merritt. She's cute. Young. More your speed. I couldn't care less what the hell you do with your little playmate but I say when we get divorced. Right now you're worthless," Ciara said, slapping the package from Darius's hand. "You're a liability not an asset. I'm waiting to see if my stock will increase if you go pro. If you stay broke, trust me, you won't have to ask me to sign those papers again. Now get out of my office."

Ripping the magazine into four uneven sections, Darius tossed the loose pages toward Ciara. "When are you going to stop, Ciara? Huh? When? You dyke!" Darius's fingers locked around Ciara's arms. Thrusting her back and forth Darius continued, yelling, "You dyke. Sign those goddamn papers! I don't want to be married to you another minute!"

"Darius, are you crazy? Let me go! You're pissed because you can't finish what the fuck you've started! Who's the dyke now, Darius?" Ciara yelled louder, toward her office.

When Darius turned to see if Kimberly heard them, Ciara whirled her arm into a circle, broke loose, slapped Darius hard across his face, and then yelled, "Kimberly, call the police!"

Kimberly raced out of Ciara's office, wiping the moisture from her mouth. "Let her go!" Kimberly yelled, racing back into Ciara's office.

"You will sign these papers," Darius grunted, releasing one of Ciara's arms then reaching for the fake jewel pen on the secretary's counter. The same damn pen Ciara had used to get his attention the first time they'd met at a meeting, claiming it was a family jewel worth ten thousand dollars. Darius should've left that imitation pen on the conference table. But no, Ciara had gotten the contract Darius should've been awarded for *Soul Mates Dissipate* so the only way for him to steal the contract from Ciara was to marry her. Big mistake. Darius could've stolen the contract without committing to Ciara. Narrowing his eyes, Darius said, "Don't you ever hit me again." Then, in disgust, he shoved Ciara toward the sofa.

Darius's eyes widened as Ciara's feet slid from under her watermelon-sized belly. He tried to catch Ciara before the back of her head hit the sharp edge of the coffee table but their hands missed the connection. He'd meant for Ciara to land on the sofa. As she lay unconscious in an expanding puddle of blood, Darius froze. His body trembled with fear. He whispered, "Get up, Ciara. I'm so sorry."

Barging out of Ciara's office, Kimberly said, "I— what have you done to her?" Then kneeling over Ciara, she screamed. "*Nooooooo!*"

"I didn't do anything to her. And what were you doing in her office that you didn't come out here until she called your name?"

"You wanted me to come out and get caught up in some more of your wrongdoings? Please, I've already witnessed too much. You'd better pray she's not dead," Kimberly said, holding Ciara's bloody head in her lap.

Ciara's body was lifeless.

"You didn't see shit! She slipped. It wasn't my fault! I swear it wasn't my fault. I didn't touch her." When Darius heard the long, piercing, familiar sound of sirens, he raced out of Ciara's office, down the stairway to avoid the possibility of running into the police, got in his car, and drove away.

Six hours later Darius was sitting in his Bentley in front of Fancy's place in Oakland. Darius needed to talk to Fancy but hadn't called so he'd tried bribing Mr. Cabie with a hundred-dollar bill to let him go up to Fancy's condo without calling.

Mr. Cabie refused, simultaneously dialing Fancy's number. "Miss Taylor, Mr. Darius Jones is here to see you. Uh-huh. Okay. Sure thing, Miss Taylor," Mr. Cabie said, hanging up. "Miss Taylor said to park across the street and wait fifteen minutes in your car."

"This is bullshit! What man is up there that she has to ask me to wait fifteen minutes so she can get rid of him before I go up?"

"I can't answer that question, sir."

When Mr. Cabie didn't say, "Sorry, sir," Darius figured some other man was seeing his woman. Darius glanced down the street for one of Byron's cars. Quite a few Jaguars and Mercedes were parked along Lakeside. The lights were on and a function was in progress at the Scottish Rite Temple so Darius couldn't identify any of the vehicles. Darius got in his car, started the engine, and then looked upstairs at Fancy's balcony.

Ladycat was on the balcony dressed in stilettos, a thong, and a red sheer negligee. Slowly she danced, teasing her body. Squeezing her breasts. Cupping her clit. Rubbing her thighs. Fancy turned around and slid the negligee over her cheeks. Taking a dildo, Ladycat eased the head of it into her mouth, licked the black dick like a lollipop, then slid it down the front of the thong. Hanging one leg over the rail, Ladycat humped that hard stick of rubber like it was the real thing. Darius wasn't sure how much more he could watch without assisting. His heart pounded against his chest when Fancy moved her thong aside and penetrated her asshole.

"Aw, fuck." Slugger definitely wanted to participate. Darius unzipped his pants and popped out his ridiculously swollen dick. He started stroking himself. Ladycat shook her head then curled her pointing finger. Crossing the street, zipping his pants, Darius was damn near run over twice but didn't care.

Mr. Cabie signaled Darius to keep going. When the elevator door opened, Ladycat was waiting in the hallway with one heel on the carpeted floor and the other braced upon the decorative table. Her legs gaped wide. Darius could smell the memorable honey sweetness of her pussy.

"Let's go inside," Darius whispered.

"No, I want you right here."

"What about your neighbors?"

"Who cares. Fuck me, Darius. Right here," Fancy urged, unbuckling his pants. She sucked his dick so good Darius came twice in the hallway. Once they were inside her apartment, Darius buried his face in Fancy's pussy and inhaled deeply. Slow, long, sticky licks pleased his palate. He smothered Miss Kitty with kisses until Fancy's body stopped quivering.

Rolling onto her stomach, Ladycat spread her cheeks and said, "You can put him here," pressing her finger against her asshole.

Darius wanted to ask if she was sure, but he didn't want her to change her mind so he quickly put on a condom and penetrated her from behind. Gently he entered her rectum; reaching his hand around her hip, he massaged her clitoris. His eyes rolled to the back of his head as he came again.

Darius was drained. Exhausted. He stumbled to the bathroom, flushed the condom, showered, and returned to bed. Holding Fancy in his arms, he said, "I want you to move to Los Angeles."

Softly Fancy replied, "I can't. My client base is here in Oakland. But I will visit often."

"Yeah, like you visit Byron."

Sighing, Fancy looked at him and said, "Darius, don't do this to us again. Can't you just be happy and appreciate the beautiful time we just shared together?"

Darius wanted to tell Fancy about Ciara but couldn't. Now Darius feared the police were after him. He needed an alibi and safe haven to hide in, otherwise he wouldn't have left L.A. But Fancy was right. Darius didn't want to spoil their incredible moment. Without saying another word, Darius turned his back to Fancy, pulled the covers up to his neck, curled into a fetal position, and went to sleep hoping he wouldn't hear any sirens in the night.

CHAPTER 20

Lying in bed next to Darius, Fancy suffered from insomnia. Fancy tossed so much she couldn't sleep. The digital clock projecting on her ceiling read two-thirty. Fancy closed her eyes, trying to force herself to fall asleep. Opening her eyes to look at the ceiling, the time was now two thirty-five. Seemed liked a half hour had passed. Who was dumping trash down the garbage chute this time of the morning? Fancy thought listening to the familiar sound coming from her back room.

Darius slept. Turning and ruffling the covers, he mumbled, "It wasn't my fault." First his legs stretched from the head to the foot of her bed. Then he curled into a ball. Then he mumbled some more. What was wrong with him?

What was his problem? Darius had acted strange the entire night, abruptly asking her to relocate. Darius was too arrogant to be insecure but his actions dictated otherwise. He kept curling into a fetal position and apologizing to someone in his sleep. Dreams were never what they appeared so someone could've been apologizing to Darius. Maybe his mother.

Fancy's imagination worked overtime, trying to decode what was going through Darius's mind as he restlessly slept with his back to her. Finally easing her naked body from under the covers, Fancy crept to the bathroom, trying not to awaken Darius so she could hear if there was something more important Darius would say in his sleep after she returned.

Vigorously brushing her teeth, Fancy rinsed her mouth, leaned over her vanity, closed her eyes, and splashed cool water on her face. Opening her eyes, Fancy's lips spread wide, exposing her tongue to scream when a masked man appeared in the mirror behind her. Was she dreaming?

Swiftly, his long thick fingers covered her mouth and nose. "Scream and I'll shoot you."

Fancy mumbled, flapping her tongue against his palm, "Take whatever you want. Please don't hurt me."

"Shut up, bitch," he grumbled, pressing his hand tighter to her face.

The excruciating pain silenced Fancy, numbing her face. All the techniques Mr. Riddle taught her in self-defense escaped her. What did he want? Why hadn't Fancy listened to Denise? Was it Mr. Drexel?

Think, Fancy. Think. On the verge of crying, Fancy couldn't focus with the cold steel pressing hard against her spine. This was a time when having body fat would've helped. Tears traveled down her face. One behind the other. What if he pulled the trigger? Intentionally or accidentally?

"Shut up." He shoved the cold gun deeper into Fancy's side, then placed the barrel against her temple as he removed his mask, dropping it to the floor.

With her mouth uncovered, that was Fancy's chance to yell for Darius. Her mouth opened wide, but the screaming inside her head never escaped her lips.

Quickly he covered her mouth again and said, "Do you remember me?"

"Mr. Drexel. Why?" Tears poured again. Then Fancy remembered Mr. Riddle had instructed her to stay calm and remember as many details as possible. Gradually Fancy stopped crying, noticing the diamond wedding band was not on his pinky finger.

"Look closer, bitch. Picture me without hair. Without a mustache. Picture me fat and out of shape."

Fancy photo-snapped his face in her mind, constantly shaking her head. Who was he?

Then Mr. Drexel said, "Why didn't you visit me in prison?"

Watching her eyes enlarge in the mirror, Fancy shut them tight. It was her father. But why? Through closed eyelids, Fancy began crying again, wishing she was dead. Caroline had no idea how she'd ruined Fancy's life. Why hadn't Fancy asked her father's last name or told her mother by name who'd stolen her car and purse? Or was Drexel his real last name? Fancy didn't know.

"Oh, don't cry now, princess. Save those tears because you are about to know exactly what it feels like to get fucked in your ass. You know what they do to men who go to prison for rape? I'ma show you. Let's go."

"Daddy, I'm so sorry. I didn't know. Honestly, I made a mistake." The words were only in her head because her mouth was still covered. Maybe Fancy shouldn't fight him. She didn't deserve to live after taking away his freedom.

Where was Thaddeus taking her? He couldn't get out of her building without being seen by someone. Fancy swiped all the unlit glass candles from her vanity, sending them crashing to the floor hoping to awaken Darius. The crackling noise was barely loud enough for Fancy to have heard. How stupid to have carpet in the bathroom.

Fancy's father led her into her extra bedroom, which she'd converted into a closet, and then quietly closed the door. *Strip!* The duct tape ripped from the roll. Thaddeus gnawed the edge with his teeth while holding the gun. He covered her mouth, bound her wrists together behind her back, and then partnered her ankles so tight the bones crunched together. Fancy panicked. The words "You're hurting me" lingered in her mind. In that moment, Fancy heard, "Most people hope to pass. You are determined not to fail." But how was Fancy going to escape alive?

"You sure are pretty," Thaddeus said, shoving his tongue inside her ear. "You've always been pretty. Fancy, I told your mother to abort you, but no. Her dumb ass took my money, went to the abortion clinic while I sat outside in my car waiting for her, then six months later when it was too late to kill you, she tells me she didn't do it. She couldn't do it. Well, consider yourself lucky because you should've been dead a long time ago. But be sure that tonight I am going to kill you. Oh yeah, you never told me how your mother was doing. Don't worry. I'll kill her lying ass tomorrow. You're all her fault. But you sure are pretty. It's been ten years since I've had a real woman." His clammy hands fondled Fancy's breasts as she lay helpless like a mummy. Thaddeus sucked on her nipples while removing his dick from his slacks.

My God, he's really going to rape me, Fancy thought, closing her eyes.

"Don't close your eyes," he whispered, "I want you to remember me from your grave." Then Thaddeus rolled Fancy over, facedown, and straddled her. Fancy felt his cold stiff erection penetrating her cheeks. Ramming his dick into her butt, Thaddeus grunted, "Uuuhhhhhh."

A silent scream was trapped behind Fancy's sealed lips when Thaddeus's dick hit her pelvis bone and slid up the crack of her ass onto her back. He'd missed. *God, please help me. I promise to go back to church.* Then Fancy heard, *If you don't do anything else I ask you, take a self-defense class. Your life is dependent upon it.* The homeless woman's voice echoed in her mind. Fight, Fancy! Fight!

Thaddeus lifted his pelvis. When Fancy felt the head of his penis circling her asshole, swiftly she sprang to her feet, blocking his thrust. She locked his nuts between her feet and dug her toenails deep into his flesh, trying to disconnect his balls.

"Bitch!" Thaddeus yelled, grabbing himself.

Fancy kicked backward like a donkey, knocking Thaddeus to the floor. Maximizing the strength in her legs, Fancy stood. Whirling about the room using her shoulders, Fancy forced every designer rack in the room on top of Thaddeus then rammed her shoulder into the door repeatedly. Turning backward in attempt to unlock the door, Fancy heard Darius yell from outside the door, "Fancy! What's going on?!"

Fancy rammed her shoulder into the door harder and harder, mumbling, *"Help!"*

Darius turned the knob. "Move out of the way!" he yelled.

Thaddeus stood. Some of Fancy's best clothes hung from his body. "I'ma kill you, you little bitch! Where's my gun?" He scrambled underneath the clothes and scattered racks on the floor. "This time I'm going to have a real reason to go to prison."

The door flung open. Darius froze standing naked in the doorway with his arm extended and his gun pointed at Thaddeus's chest. Thaddeus pointed his gun at Fancy then at Darius. Darius froze as Thaddeus pointed the gun.

Who or what are you willing to die for? echoed in Fancy's mind. Closing her eyes, Fancy stepped in front of Darius.

"I love you, Daddy. I love you, Darius."

Pow! Pow! Two shots in the dark. Both to the heart.

CHAPTER 21

Somebody's Gotta Be On Top's gross potential had earned an unprecedented $1.1 billion in less than three years according to the movie magazine. Jada, amazed and uninformed by her husband, speed-dialed Wellington's private number. So that's why Wellington wanted Darius's business. That sneak. Jada could've walked down the hall to Wellington's office, but she was upset with Wellington's behavior and being within striking distance of him at any time was not good.

Wellington answered, "I suspect you've seen the article by now. I don't have time for this. What do you want to know this time?"

"Nothing. It's simple. Wellington, you will give Darius back his company. End of discussion," Jada insisted.

"Or what? I'm part owner, too, remember? And don't act like you haven't benefited. I'm the one who gave your public relations firm an exclusive on all publicity for every film produced by or in conjunction with Somebody's Gotta Be On Top."

"And you're also the one paying Melanie to option new films. But I'm squeezing her ass o-u-t. Just so you know, my attorney recommended a legal separation but I'm filing for divorce." Jada emphasized, "And I've decided to sell my ownership interest to Darius and help him force you out of his business."

"That's the stupidest thing I've heard you say since I've known you. Darius doesn't have time to run this hectic business."

Jada thought Wellington would comment on the divorce, but he didn't. She affirmed, "Then I'll help him."

"You don't have time either. And I'm wasting my time having this conversation." Wellington hung up the phone.

No, he did not hang up on her. Wellington had become bolder since their encounter at The Cheesecake Factory, inviting Melanie to his office against Jada's demands. Melanie worked in Oakland but Wellington claimed since she was practically her own boss she accepted every detailed assignment she could in Hollywood, and as long as she was in Hollywood, he'd gladly accept her assistance and use her contacts. Jada doubted Melanie had a job at all.

Prepared for battle, Jada had worn her flat heels, black pantsuit, stud black diamond earrings, and secured her hair into a neat bun before she'd left home.

Darius was right again when he said Wellington would never deprive his biological son. Little Wellington, although he'd soon graduate from kindergarten, never went without. Wellington spoiled his child and Simone, Wellington II's mom. Once Simone had gotten over Wellington, she took advantage of every opportunity to send little Wellington to their house while she and her husband traveled at Jada and Wellington's expense. Jada tried telling Wellington that Simone was padding her budget but all he'd say was, "Let me handle my son and Simone."

How could Jada have been so trusting, believing that her husband would never cheat on her? Maybe because Jada had never been unfaithful to Wellington. At least not since their marriage. Or perhaps since Jada made it her full-time job—with the exception of joining a swingers club—to satisfy Wellington sexually. Or so she'd thought. Jada had too many clients and potential clients to risk being labeled a swinger.

Leaning over her huge cherry wood desk at Black Diamonds, Jada stared into its customized glass top. Between the desk and the glass, Jada had inserted an array of color photos of the most important people of her life: her mother, Ruby, and her dad, Henry; Darius; Wellington; and herself. Unexpectedly, Jada's head fell closer to the desk. Stretching her neck upward, Jada smoothed her bun behind her head.

Why couldn't she instill in her child the same morals her parents fostered in her? Love. Respect. Honesty. Well, maybe like most people, Jada selectively chose when to utilize her values and with whom. Self-esteem was something Jada developed with time and no matter how much her parents believed in her, Jada's life didn't change until she started believing in herself. Jada's dark complexion gave her a complex for many years. But after her father sent her to a dermatologist, had their dentist correct her crooked teeth, and sent her to the M.A.C. cosmetic store for a complimentary makeover, Jada realized the color of her skin was never the problem. Collectively, the small inadequacies adversely impacted the way she felt about herself. Years later, low self-esteem was the least of Jada's concerns.

Every picture of Lawrence, including the pose of Lawrence proudly hugging Ashlee on her first day of kindergarten, had been removed from the collage after Jada divorced him. Jada tapped on the quarter-inch-thick transparent glass. Lovingly, Jada smiled at her favorite photo. A once wrinkled and torn image of Jada with Darius and Wellington had been restored and centered amongst the group. That was one of many photos that Darius had spitefully damaged then mailed back to her when she didn't attend any of his basketball games at Georgetown. Values? Did Darius have any? Did Wellington? How could Jada repair her marriage? Or would she simply replace her snapshots of Wellington with someone else? Swiftly, her eyes looked toward the glass-top. Jada shook her head again.

Gazing into Wellington's photogenic alluring brown eyes, Jada wearily hummed as the puffy bags underneath her hazel eyes became alarmingly visible. Tugging at her cheekbones, Jada said, "My goodness. When did all this happen? I've got to get some rest."

Glaring at herself, Jada nodded, contemplating divorce. Acting civilized toward Wellington throughout the day, any day, at home or at work, was suddenly agitating. To minimize their arguments— make that her arguing, his ignoring—Wellington had retreated nightly to one of the guest bedrooms while Jada slept—three hours at best per night, twenty minutes on, forty minutes off, and so forth—alone in their bedroom.

Most days Jada gladly left earlier than Wellington in the morning, worked later well into the night, and although she considered living at the Ritz Carlton for a few weeks to emotionally regroup, she'd have too many personal items to pack and take along. Irrespective of the quality of any hotel, sleeping in a bed God only knew how many others had slept in, had sex in, had died in, wasn't something Jada would volunteer to do for an extended period of time without insisting on using her own linens. Propping her elbow on the desk, Jada braced her forehead in the palm of her hand and closed her eyes.

Years ago, Jada and Wellington had agreed it was a fantastic idea for them to lease additional office space in San Francisco's financial district. Wellington Jones and Associates, Somebody's Gotta Be on Top, and Black Diamonds still occupied the same understaffed office area downtown on Montgomery Street near Market Street. But fortunately and unfortunately, Jada's Los Angeles office was down the hall from Wellington's newly combined headquarters of Somebody's Gotta Be on Top.

Jada's face slipped off of her hand, stopping inches from the glass top as her horrid dream of Wellington and Melanie blissfully dating crashed. "And we were happy, or so I foolishly thought. Okay, Jada. Get up and get out of the office." Ten A.M. Four hours of sleep over the last forty-eight and ten more to go before quitting time. Slowly entering her private rest room, Jada splashed cold water on her face, removed then reapplied her moisturizer and makeup.

Feeling refreshed, Jada bypassed her receptionist and said, "Forward my calls to Zen. I'll be back at noon."

Turning right toward the elevators, Jada stopped, made a one-hundred-eighty-degree turn, bypassed her office, and entered Wellington's. "Is Mr. Jones in?"

Wellington's receptionist answered, "He's in with a client but if you want to come back, he should be available shortly, Mrs. Tanner," as if Jada were also a client.

"No, thanks. I'll wait," Jada said, proceeding to the visitor's area located opposite Wellington's office. Settling into the black leather vibrating chair, Jada's head rested snug into the neck massager. She turned off the television.

Tick. Tick. Tick. The pendulum inside the grandfather clock swayed, hypnotizing Jada as her eyelids eventually submitted to her restless body and closed.

Reminiscing about her first date with Wellington in Carmel, Jada tried to recall the last time she'd turned Wellington into a human sundae, dousing him with whipped cream, strawberries, chocolate, and cherries. Or the last time she'd given him a shower massage. Or the last time he'd taken her on an excursion. Or rubbed her feet. Or brushed her hair. Or simply held her hand in public.

Tick. Tick. Tick. Jada's eyeballs rolled upward under her lids. They'd become so consumed with work and so familiar with one another that Jada thought she was investing quality time with her husband when, now that she thought about it, all she was really doing was squeezing him into her free time. But everything between them seemed so perfect. Was Melanie doing the things Jada used to do? Was Wellington sharing his time, money, heart, or all three with Melanie?

Tick. Tick. Tick.

Blinking slowly several times, Jada opened her eyes and glanced around the dark room. The vibrating chair was still. The office was quiet. Looking at the lighted clock, Jada whispered, "Six-thirty? Can't be." Jada checked her wristwatch. Sure enough, she'd been in the same position for eight and half hours. Jada patrolled Wellington's office. Everyone was gone.

"So did he just leave me here sleeping or did his secretary forget to mention I was waiting?" Wellington easily could've missed her slumped in that huge chair. Well, as long as she was here, Jada's nails clicked on Wellington's door. Jada held the doorknob, turning it slowly. The last time she'd searched Wellington's belongings, she wasn't pleased. What difference did it make? If she found nothing, she'd love him more. Maybe invite him into the bedroom with her tonight.

Quietly entering Wellington's office, Jada closed the door the same way. "Let's see. Where do I begin?" Jada imagined fucking Wellington in his office. That would be a first if only the session wasn't in her mind.

Jada sat behind Wellington's desk and opened every drawer. The last drawer on the bottom right-hand side was filled with condoms and lubricants. Jada removed everything from the drawer, placed the contents on Wellington's desk, and then put everything back. What was her point? The next drawer up was empty. The top drawer was filled with airline itineraries. Shuffling through the stack, each trip had two reservations. One for Wellington. The other for Melanie. Jamaica. Canada. France.

"My God. How could he?" Jada mumbled, closing all the drawers. She'd seen enough. The dancing box on Wellington's monitor lured Jada's hand to the mouse.

Searching for more divorce ammunition, Jada's wrist wiggled along the Lakers mouse pad. Wellington's computer was on-line twenty-four-seven. Clicking on the drop box, her husband's cookie history had numerous triple-X Web sites: girls on girls; guys on girls; guys on guys? When Jada clicked on Wellington's mailbox icon, an endless list of daily messages from DeliciousMelanie were displayed. Should've been MaliciousMelanie. Jada couldn't convince herself to double-click on any of Melanie's messages. Scanning the topics, one subject read, "Contract for Somebody's Gotta Be on Top."

Jada instantly double-clicked on the e-mail from Melanie to Wellington.

"Thanks for making me a partner in every way. I'll continue managing the San Francisco office until you've convinced Jada to convince Darius to sign his thirty-three-and-a-third interest over to you. I mean us. Then we can combine our percentages, force Jada out, and start selling stock shares to our partners. BTW, our daughter needs a new nanny. You want us to stay in San Francisco or move to L.A.? Since I'm spending three days a week in L.A., if we relocate we can save money by closing the San Francisco office and you could see Morgan more often. Think about it. We love you."

Jada printed the message then forwarded it to her inbox. Closing the e-mail, Jada had no idea what to do next so she sat motionless, wondering how much Darius knew about Wellington's wrongdoings.

"Ha, ha, ha. You are so silly." A female voice resonated in the air right outside Wellington's door. Quickly Jada scurried to Wellington's adjoining conference room, leaving a hairline crack in the door.

"You won't be laughing when I put this big dick inside you."

What? Was that her husband? Talking nasty?

"Well, we'll have to see," Melanie said, entering Wellington's office while unbuttoning her blouse.

Slam!

Wellington forced Melanie's back against the wall, lifted her skirt, and inserted his finger into her vagina. "You're already ready. Damn," Wellington said, licking his finger.

"Don't think finger fucking is going to get you off the hook again," Melanie moaned. "You promised me a big dick and that's what I want, goddammit."

Jada waited. For what? She wasn't sure but she couldn't move. Jada expected Wellington to open one of his condoms after unzipping his pants, but he didn't. Wellington massaged his dick over and over to no erection. "Suck him for me," Wellington said, sitting on the edge of his desk, double-clicking on the girls on girls Web site.

"And? What's in it for me this time? Huh?" Melanie asked, bobbing her lips toward Wellington's crotch. "I want half of the company. Mmm, if you didn't taste so good, I would've left you alone a long time ago. And there's no way in hell I'd be your mistress." Melanie slurped and sucked hard, letting saliva escape her mouth as she massaged Wellington's erection.

Jada watched her husband lean his head back in ecstasy. "You always did suck my dick the best, you know that. Damn, I'm ready to blast off in your mouth, baby."

Wellington's dick was more soft than hard. He couldn't fuck with that erection, Jada thought, flushing one eye closer to the crack in the door.

Melanie sucked harder. Her hand stroked faster until Wellington yelled, "Aawww! Yes! Yes! Back your pussy up on this dick, bitch, and let me fuck you. And make your pussy suck the Ruler."

Strangling Wellington's semi-hard foot-long erection in her hand, Melanie guided Wellington inside and began to ride him like a pony on a carousel. "Rub my pussy, you sexy caramel bald-headed muthafucka."

Pushing Melanie forward, Wellington stood, squatted, and then stroked his hand between Melanie's legs while humping her from behind like a damn dog.

"That's it. Now tell mama. What's your fantasy, daddy? Mama will do whatever you like."

"Um-hum," Wellington moaned.

"You want me to wrap my juicy lips around your head and suck your dick some more," Melanie moaned.

Wellington nodded, then said, "Oh yeah," thrusting his dick deeper like he was trying to keep from slipping out.

"Well, I'm sucking your dick right now while Jada is licking dem big-ass nuts, daddy. That's right. She's doing you, too. Remember how I licked Jada's pussy? That's the same way your secretary is licking your nipples. Put your tongue in her mouth. That's right. You have all of us at the same time."

"Aw, shit," Wellington groaned, closing his eyes.

"I'm sucking this chocolate dick real good, daddy. But I'ma let Jada have a lick. You want her to taste your dick, daddy?"

"Oh, hell yes," Wellington groaned humping inside Melanie slower and deeper.

"Hold this pussy in your hand. Don't let go. If you let go, I'ma spank you. Stroke this tiger before she bites you. Keep stroking her. I'ma lick your asshole while Jada deep-throats your dick, daddy. Um-hum. Fuck me harder. Because I'm getting ready to fuck you. You want me to put my finger in your ass?"

"Aww, yeah. Kiss between my asshole and nuts first, baby."

"I got you, daddy. I know your spot. I got you. My finger is slowly slipping inside you. Squeeze my finger while I press against dem colossal nuts from the inside. Jada, suck my man's dick. Suck it, bitch. Suck—"

"Who you calling a bitch?!" Jada yelled, slamming the door against the stopper.

"Aaahhhhhhh!" Melanie screamed.

Wellington yelled at the same time, drizzling cum down the side of his dick. "What the fuck?"

Wellington scrambled, pulling up his pants. Melanie pulled down her skirt.

"Oh, no. Don't stop. You two lovebirds carry on. I'm too pissed to even go off," Jada said, sternly eyeing Wellington. "Don't come home tonight. Or tomorrow. Or the next. And you," Jada said, looking at Melanie, "he's all yours. But my son's business is not for sale. In fact, effectively immediately, I'm taking over Darius's company until he decides what he wants do with his business." Jada turned to leave Wellington's office, stopped, faced Wellington, and said, "Oh, yeah. I almost forgot. Give Morgan a kiss and a hug for me." Wellington had gone too far. This time there was reconciling to do.

CHAPTER 22

"What's up, Big D? You ready for the exhibition game tonight?" Lance asked, lying on his back, palming the basketball with one hand above his head.

Lance was six-foot-five, two inches shorter than Darius, weighing two hundred twenty pounds. Starting at the point for three consecutive years, Lance desperately wanted to play professionally. NBA. Overseas. He didn't care where as long as he continued playing basketball. With the new NCAA rule, Lance and every other player including Darius could play on scholarship for five years instead of four. So if Lance didn't go pro after his senior year, he'd decided to stay the additional year to play ball and work on his Master's. Thanks to Darryl Senior, Darius wouldn't need more than one year before making his move into the pros.

Lying in his bed across the room from Lance, Darius said, "Man, I'm about to give them the business. I need to touch the ball every play. Don't forget. Don't let me starve on the court, man. You feed me and I'll make sure my dad takes care of you, too."

"You know I'm a team player and I'm quick with my passes, so if you want me to give it up, you gotta work to keep your ass open, man."

Somehow the last part of Lance's statement didn't sound quite right. "When you alley-oop, I'ma already be in the air. When you bounce, I'm there, baby. And when you fast break, I'm faster. I'll be waiting for you to get to the other end."

Tossing the ball in the air, Lance said, "You got a lotta shit on your mind, D. I can tell. Whatever it is, whoever she is, leave that bitch on the bench. I want to win a championship this year. And for the first time since I've been here, we have a damn good chance to go all the way."

Darius kept staring at the ceiling. "I'm cool, L. My dad is on his way over to help me straighten out this shit. Besides, this is just an exhibition."

Hurling the ball at the ceiling, Lance yelled, "Don't say that shit, man! All you fuckin' rich kids are just alike. Don't have to work for shit! Think everything comes easy!" Haphazardly, the ball ricocheted around the room, slowing to a low bounce next to Lance's bed.

"Chill out, man. I don't apologize for having money." Actually, Darius had spent eight of the ten grand his mother had given him and was hoping she'd be at his game today to see how hard he was working.

"That's your fuckin' problem, D. You don't apologize for shit. Not for the way you misuse these women. You don't have to fuck them just because they show up at your door, our door. And the way you brag to me about your dad getting you into the pros. And you never say you're sorry for the times you show up late at practice and everybody has to run suicides for your selfish ass. You think you're better than us but you're not!"

Darius stood, walked toward the door, and said, "The honeys are perks. Like fringe benefits. Don't hate on me because you don't use yours. And it's not that I think I'm better than you. You know I'm better than you and that bothers you. Stop shrinking, man. Show up for your shit and claim it! 'Cause if you think I'ma give anybody slack on or off that court, you trippin'." Darius opened the door. "Oh, hi, Dad. Come in." Turning to Lance, Darius said, "By the way, for a white boy you got some mean ball handling skills. You must've grown up playing with the brothas."

Lance stood, shook Darryl's hand. "Hi, Mr. Williams." Responding to Darius's comment, Lance threw Darius a fast ball then said,

"How many times I'ma have to tell you, I'm not white. I'm Canadian. When you travel to Canada, we call you American. Not black."

"That's cool." Darius flipped the ball back to Lance. "But you still white to me. I'll see you at the team dinner before the game. Later, man."

Tapping Darryl on the shoulder, Lance asked, "Excuse me, Mr. Williams? You mind if I ask you a few questions about the NBA next time you come by?"

Darryl patted Lance's shoulder, smiled, and then said, "Not at all, Lance."

Walking outside the dorm building, Darryl said, "Darius, you have to learn how to respect your teammates."

"What did I do wrong this time?"

"Once he told you he was Canadian, you should've acknowledged that and not followed up with what you said. Politics, son. I keep telling you this entire game is full of politics. The sooner you learn how to become an ambassador, the more support you'll get and the less problems you'll have. What if Lance refuses to pass you the ball? Changing the subject, your mom called me. Said she wants to have breakfast with us."

Damn, Darius thought, but wouldn't say aloud. Probably a setup to take something else away from him. Riding along Interstate 5, Darius said, "Lance is good people and I will apologize to him before the game tonight." Darius quietly drove to his mother's house while his dad preached more life lessons. Cruising into his mother's circular driveway, Darius said, "Thanks for being my dad, man. I love you."

"I love you, too, son. Let's go in before your mom comes out here."

Frowning, Darius said, "Hey, mom. How are you? You don't look well." What was wrong with his mother? Darius knew Wellington was cheating on his mom, but if his mother's baggy sad eyes and depressed spirit were the results of infidelity, Darius would never cheat on Fancy. His mother was once so beautiful; now she'd aged five years in less than one.

"Hi, baby. Hi, Darryl. Come on in. Have a seat at the breakfast table."

Moms had biscuits, turkey bacon, grits, eggs, and fresh fruit in serving dishes on the table.

Darius's spirit was dwindling with his mother's. Darius sat next to his mom, across the table from Darryl. "Where's Wellington?"

"Gone. He left. We're getting a divorce. Don't ask any more questions about him. We're not here to discuss Wellington."

Darryl commented, "So maybe after breakfast we can discuss us being a family."

"There is no us, Darryl. All we have in common is Darius."

Darius reached for the bowl of grits. Darryl grabbed his hand. "You can't eat that on game day. You'll lose your stamina before halftime. You can eat plenty of eggs, all the turkey bacon you want, and a bowl of fresh fruit. That's it."

Reaching for the eggs, Darius asked his mother "You coming to my game tonight?"

"Yes, of course."

"Is you-know-who-coming?" Darius asked staring at the grits.

"I doubt it but I don't know."

"Ma, I love you. I'll take care of you. I can move in with you tomorrow and take care of you. I don't know what I'd do if anything were to happen to you."

Jada slid Darius a deposit slip across the table.

Leaping from his seat, Darius yelled, "Yes! Thanks, Mom! I love you! I love you! I love you!"

Darryl looked back and forth from Jada to Darius, then said, "He's acting like you just gave him ten million dollars."

"I did," Jada whispered.

Darryl stared at Jada then at Darius, and shook his head. "Give it back, son."

Sitting next to his mother, hugging her tight, Darius frowned at Darryl and said, "What? You're kidding, right?"

"Darryl, I didn't give the money to Darius. He earned it from the movie *Soul Mates Dissipate*. It's rightfully his. It's his first payout. There's more coming. And soon, Darius, you'll have your company back. I'm buying Wellington out of your business in exchange for not asking for interest in his company."

Darryl asked, "What about your business? I remember the day we sat at your mother's table and you said you were starting your own business. I knew you didn't need me to become successful. I'm proud of you. And I believe I know you well enough to say, within two days you'll be back to taking care of yourself. But will Wellington have interest in Black Diamonds?"

Jada tried to smile but couldn't. Her eyes stretched more than her lips. "You don't stop loving someone overnight or within two days. I still love Wellington very much. I just can't accept the things he's done." Jada squeezed Darius's hand. "Honey, did you know Wellington has a daughter?"

Darius and Darryl responded in unison, "What! You're kidding, right?"

"Morgan."

"I—" Darius's cell phone rang, interrupting his comment. "Hello?"

"Darius, Ciara insisted I call you and tell you she's in labor. She wants you to meet her at the hospital in fifteen minutes. In case you don't recognize my voice, this is Ciara's sister—"

"I know, Monica." Exhaling heavily, Darius became overwhelmed with relief. He knew Ciara wasn't dead because no one, including his parents, had questioned him about the accident. Fluttering his eyelids, Darius withheld his remorseful tears.

Monica hung up.

"What's wrong, son?"

"Ciara is in labor. She wants me to meet her at the hospital."

"Let's go," Darryl said, standing.

"I can't go. I have a big game today." The real reason Darius didn't want to go was because he was scared. He hadn't called Ciara since she had slipped, fell, and hit her head in her office, fearing something bad might have happened to the baby.

Jada said, "You have to go, sweetheart. She's your wife. I'll meet you there in a half hour."

Darius protested, "She's my wife only on paper. I don't love her." Darryl stared at Darius. "I know. Politics."

While Darryl drove to the hospital, Darius constantly looked at his watch. Two hours before he had to be back on campus with his teammates or he wouldn't play.

"How long will it take her to have this baby?" Darius asked, stopping at the information booth.

"Son, she might not deliver until tomorrow but if you visit her now, you can come back later after your game is over."

Darius asked the information clerk, "What room is Ciara Monroe in?"

The information clerked scanned her computer and said, "We don't have a Ciara Monroe."

"You have to. Maybe she's not in the system yet because she's still in labor."

Darryl asked, "Do you have a Ciara Jones?"

"Yes, we do. She's in the delivery room. Here are your visitor passes. Take the second bank of elevators to the fifth floor."

Outside Ciara's birthing room, Darius prayed again that he wasn't the father of Ciara's child. When Darius and Darryl entered Ciara's room, two Los Angeles police officers stood blocking the door.

"Are you Darius Jones?" the short and stocky cop asked.

"This is bullshit, Ciara!"

Darryl interrupted the police officer. "What do you want with my son?"

The officer handed Darryl a piece of paper. "I see," Darryl said, handing back the paper. "Clearly you've got the wrong Darius Jones. My son isn't a murderer or a thief." Instantly Darius's eyes connected with his dad's. Neither of them said anything. "I'm his father, Darryl Williams."

The police said, "We know who you are. Darius Jones, you're under arrest."

"What for? My dad just vouched for me. Let me go!" Darius said, stepping backward.

"Son, I'll be at the precinct when you get there." Darryl shook his head at Ciara and said, "When we take over Somebody's Gotta Be On Top, your contract will be terminated immediately."

Ciara sat in that fuckin' birthing chair breathing heavy and rubbing her stomach. "I don't think so, Mr. Williams."

"Pick one," the officer said answering Darius. "The murder of Thaddeus Drexel. Check fraud in Dallas, Texas. Credit card fraud around the country," he said, gathering Darius's hands behind his back. "Thanks, Ms. Monroe, for being cooperative."

Darius didn't know how to tell the officer that it was self-defense without making him tighten the handcuffs more. Darius hadn't allowed himself to really think about Fancy until now. Fancy was either crazy or she honestly loved him. What woman would almost take a bullet for any man?

Scared that Ciara had reported him to the police for assault, Darius had left Fancy's condo before the cops had arrived and after he'd shot Thaddeus. Ceasing all communications with Fancy, Darius hadn't seen nor spoken with her since he'd shot Thaddeus, but until now Darius hadn't known Thaddeus was dead because Fancy hadn't called him either. Darius's heart ached not knowing Fancy's whereabouts. Now Darius was on his way to jail, and if they didn't know about Ciara's incident, which was honestly an accident, Darius was certain they'd find out before releasing him.

"Man, I don't know what the hell you're talking about. I'm innocent, man. I've got bail money in my pocket. Let me call my mother."

Tightening the handcuffs, the officer said, "You can call her from the precinct."

"I'll call her, son. Don't worry. Just be cool," Darryl said, then hurried out of the room.

"That's too tight, man. I got a game tonight. Don't hurt my wrists."

"The only place you're going to play ball is in prison. Let's go," the cop said, escorting Darius to the patrol car.

Women. If Darius hadn't fallen in love with Ladycat, her past wouldn't have endangered his future. By and by, Darius was beginning to think the homeless woman was right when she'd said, "Death follows you," but wrong when she'd claimed, "You'll be happy again."

CHAPTER 23

Two weeks had passed since the incident. Accident. The shooting. Since that day, the only two places Fancy frequented were her broker's classes and Howard's office, consuming herself with studying and working. Denise tried consoling Fancy by saying, "It's not your fault. If anyone breaks into your home and tries to rape you, they deserve whatever they get. Including death."

Fancy hadn't returned to her condo since Darius had killed Thaddeus. *Pow! Pow!* constantly rang in her ears as though she'd pulled the trigger. Now, whenever a car backfired, she jumped. The thought of going to gatherings where the audiences cheered, collectively clapping or stomping, made Fancy visibly uncomfortable. Wringing her hands, shifting in her seat, trembling, in addition to constantly looking over her shoulder, had become habits she hoped to break someday.

Shortly after Darius fired his gun, five cars with flashing blue lights lined the crowded street and circular driveway beneath Fancy's balcony. Oakland policemen came quickly, undoubtedly because of her address, but by the time they'd arrived, Darius, against Fancy's plea—after untaping her mouth, hands, and feet—had left instantly. Abandoning Fancy in her greatest time of need. He'd left her alone at home with a dead body bleeding all over her designer wardrobe.

Pow! Pow! Two shots to the heart and Thaddeus's flesh and blood splattered all over Fancy's naked body. With all the cops in her condo, a bath would have to wait so Fancy sheltered her body with a long, brown, thick robe. Later that night the paramedics arrived but left shortly after Thaddeus was pronounced dead.

One police car and two officers remained until the coroner removed Thaddeus's body from her condo. After hours of intimidating questioning by multiple officers, Fancy showered, washing away memories of a neglected childhood, a horrible father, a spineless mother, and an absent lover. What else could go wrong?

Fancy packed a small suitcase, and when the officers left at daybreak, Fancy left, too. She'd respond to the nosy board members that were in and out of her apartment when she returned. If she returned.

Fancy wanted to go to church and beg for forgiveness, but she wasn't sure if it was too late to call upon the Lord in her time of need, since she hadn't praised him in her moments of glorious success. Being spared her life, twice. Having more money in the bank than she'd ever earned before. Finally knowing what it felt like to love someone, that true love brought pain and pleasure. Both feelings were extreme beyond measure. Beyond comprehension. Dictating irrational behavior. And although in her heart Fancy didn't want to, she'd stopped calling Caroline. Maybe if Thaddeus was serious about killing Caroline, Fancy had saved Caroline's life. Make that Darius had saved Caroline's life.

Lodging at the downtown Marriott on Tenth and Broadway, Fancy opened her suite door and picked up the newspaper then tossed it into the unread pile on the sofa. Pouring herself a cup of orange juice—Fancy didn't drink coffee let alone from a guest-room pot—randomly Fancy selected a newspaper and removed the dirty rubber band to review the real estate section.

When Fancy unfolded the paper, her heart almost stopped beating. Fancy gasped. "My God. Darius? On the front page? Arrested?" Glancing at the date, two weeks old, Fancy read the headlines aloud: "Poor Little Rich Man Arrested for Fraud and Murder."

The story read, "Darius Williams, formerly known as Darius Jones, purportedly the number one draft pick for the NBA, son of former NBA star Darryl Williams and mega-publicist Jada Diamond Tanner, owner of Black Diamonds, was arrested for credit card fraud for purchases totaling over a million dollars. Darius Williams was also booked on check fraud for depositing a fifty-thousand-dollar check payable to Somebody's Gotta Be on Top enterprises into his personal checking account after he no longer owned the company. As if that wasn't enough to get Darius kicked off his college basketball team, this next charge might just slam dunk his basketball career. Darius Williams has been charged with the alleged murder of Thaddeus Drexel, an ex-convict . . ."

Frantically, Fancy dialed Darius's cell and home phones, hoping someone would answer. *Think, Fancy. Think.* Suddenly Fancy realized, after having asked Darius a gazillion questions about his past relationships, his childhood, and his goals, she'd failed to request contact information for Darius's parents. What if Darius had been shot in her condo? Who would Fancy have called? No one. Not Darius's mother or father, or even the brother he hated. She would've had to call information then wait until Monday morning to call his mother's company. Now Darius wasn't answering his phone and Fancy didn't know how to contact him.

Booting up her computer, Fancy logged onto the college Web site and then dialed the coach's business office number. No answer. "Damn, it's Saturday." Nervously Fancy dressed in the one outfit—peach low-rise pants, a burnt orange shirt that buttoned across her breasts exposing her navel, and pair of high-heeled shoes—she'd hung in the hotel closet for two weeks and had worn once while in transit to check into the hotel. Nervously Fancy packed her travel bag then headed to the airport and took the next flight, first-class, to Los Angeles.

An hour and a half later, sitting in the back of a luxury Town Car at LAX surrounded by dark tinted windows, Fancy asked, "Where do they normally take law offenders?"

Turning, looking over his right shoulder, the driver replied, "Depends on what crime they've committed. Blue or white collar? Male or female?"

"Male. Murder. Allegedly. Credit card fraud. Allegedly," Fancy said, dialing Darius's number again.

"Probably IRC over on Bauchet."

"What's IRC?" Fancy asked.

"The inmate reception center."

"Take me there."

Lifting his eyebrows, the driver stared at Fancy.

"Don't sit there staring. Let's go."

Driving along Interstate 5 to Highway 101, glancing in his rearview mirror at Fancy, the driver commented, "You do know that they're not all innocent, right? How do you beautiful women get caught up with these deadbeat guys?"

Pressing the END button on her cell phone, Fancy stared at the driver in his mirror. "You don't know me. Here's my business card."

Accepting her card, the driver replied, "I'm not questioning your status. Obviously you can afford to pay me two hundred dollars an hour. All I know is these dudes get caught up committing crimes and then they convince their women to bail them out. I hope you're not expecting him to repay you."

Silently, Fancy questioned herself. Why was she voluntarily doing so much for Darius? Would Darius have done the same for her? Tipping the driver, Fancy eased on her sunglasses and hurried inside like she was hiding. After waiting for hours, and discovering fortunately Darius hadn't been transferred, Fancy posted his astronomical bail then waited several more hours until he walked out. He was unshaved and unkempt. Fancy only cared about the man on the inside. Darius's eyes were red and puffy like he hadn't slept for days.

Wrapping her arms tight around Darius's waist, Fancy said, "I'm going to stand by you throughout your trials."

Darius removed her arms and stepped back. "Thanks, but you've done enough for me."

"Oh, you don't have to thank me for getting you out. But I was surprised you were still here. Why didn't your parents get you out?"

Shrugging his shoulders, Darius shook his head. "My dad was going to get me out then he suggested I chill. I don't know why. Knowing him, he had a reason. But after I found out I'd killed a man, I needed time to myself. Taking your dad's life killed a part of me. I can't quite explain it. But I'll never be the same. I had time to reflect and think about my life. All the wrong things I've done. But you have no idea what it's like in here. It's hell. I don't know how people survive years behind bars caged like animals. Being treated as less than human. All I know is I'm innocent and I won't be back. But you've done enough for me. It's all your fault I was in here in the first place. If you had changed your locks like Denise told you, I wouldn't be here."

Tucking her hair behind her ear, Fancy objected, "What about the checks and credit cards? Are those my fault, too, Darius?"

Darius shook his head, but Fancy couldn't determine if he was agreeing it wasn't her fault or disagreeing like he didn't understand. "No. But seriously, I am innocent of all those charges. I don't know what the hell they're talking about or trying to prove, but not me. Propaganda is a muthafucka and the information in the paper was all wrong. I ain't gon' be just another brotha to put in the system. I didn't do shit."

When Fancy opened her arms to console Darius, he pushed her biceps down and away from him. Tears welled in Fancy's eyes so she fluttered her eyelids. "I haven't been back at my house since the shooting. But I did get a copy of Thaddeus's autopsy and death certificate. Thaddeus was terminally ill. You shot him but you didn't kill him. His real cause of death was cancer. The doctors said Thaddeus knew he only had a month to live. I guess that's why he didn't care about killing me. But if my mother would've loved me, I would've never lied on Thaddeus when I was a little girl. Darius, I told the police Thaddeus raped me. I didn't know he was going to have to serve ten years in prison. But once I'd lied I didn't know how to tell the truth without the police locking me up for perjury. I just wanted them to take Thaddeus away from our house and never let him come back."

Darius's arms shot toward heaven the same way Caroline's had when Fancy had told her the truth. Didn't anyone understand Fancy's position?

"You did what? Get out of my face! I don't ever want to see you again. If you had your own father arrested, there's no telling what you'll do to me. You probably had something to do with this fraud bullshit, too!"

"I promise you, Darius, I don't know anything about the fraud situation. I was a little girl," Fancy cried, reaching out to Darius. "I didn't know what to do. I was scared. Haven't you ever been afraid?"

Pushing her away again, Darius said, "But you were old enough to know right from wrong. You sent an innocent man to jail! For ten years! Now he's dead! And I'm the one who—"

"Killed him," Fancy said, completing Darius's sentence.

Darius turned his back to Fancy then walked away.

"Wait, Darius. Where are you going?" Fancy pleaded.

"Home."

"Can I go with you? So we can talk."

"No. There's nothing for us to discuss. I don't ever want to see you again. And I'll make sure I pay you back your bail money."

Fancy followed Darius outside.

"Get out of my face, Fancy! You're a liar!" Darius cried. "You're just like all the rest!"

CHAPTER 24

Darius had lied to himself again. Fancy wasn't like all the rest. Not even close. Never had he secretly shed so many tears for a woman, any woman, not even his mother. When Darius returned home from jail, he wanted Fancy to stay with him. But if she lied on Thaddeus, she'd really fucked up an innocent man's life. How could Darius forgive Fancy? Was it his place to grant Fancy forgiveness? All Darius knew was that his heart ached, and his life wasn't the same without Ladycat.

Fortunately, luck had a way of saving his ass, and his nine lives must've been renewed. The day Darius was arrested and while Darius was in jail, three new credit cards were established in his name. The checking account in question was closed. And his half brother Kevin was arrested at a bank in Dallas and charged with numerous counts of fraud.

Ashlee's baby's father was a proven thief. Darius wondered how Ashlee was feeling now that she'd become a single parent married to a convict. Better yet, how was Lawrence? That wasn't his problem, but the fact that Darius still loved Ashlee created a dilemma. Should he pursue Fancy or make amends with Ashlee? Forget Ashlee. Darius wasn't raising Kevin's baby. Hell, he didn't want to raise his own, and continued to pray that neither Ciara nor Desire were the mothers of his child. Children. Hopefully the results of his paternity test with Ciara and her son would be in the mail when he returned home for his basketball road trip to Oakland.

Darryl Senior had used his connections to ensure Darius wasn't transferred from IRC to another location before his hearing, and simultaneously Darryl had traced Kevin's fictitious business, NyVek. As much as Darryl hated turning Kevin in, he'd said, "Son, I know God has good things in store for you. In your heart you want to do what's right. Now's your chance. You can never disappoint me. Just make sure you don't disappoint Him."

Darius was happy and angry at the same time. Happy because all of the charges against him were dropped, including charges for the murder of Thaddeus, and because his scholarship was still intact. Darius apologized to his roommate Lance, his teammates, and coaches. Everyone except Fancy.

Fancy gave an incredible creditable statement with documentation at his hearing about what actually happened. Darius was glad he had his gun on him that night or his basketball career would've ended, because there was no way he would have let Fancy take a bullet for him. But Darius was still amazed that Fancy had risked her life to save his. And she'd taken the first flight out of Oakland to bail him out of jail. Why couldn't Darius return her love unconditionally? Darius had decided that if he found his lady, if it wasn't too late, this time he'd legitimately try.

The security cameras at Fancy's condo had captured Thaddeus sneaking through the garage and up the back stairway with a black mask on, the same mask that was recovered as evidence from Fancy's condo.

The condo Fancy no longer lived in. That pissed Darius off. The fact that Fancy had moved without telling him. No new address. She'd changed all of her numbers. Darius didn't know how to contact Fancy's mother, Caroline. Last Darius had heard was from Mr. Cabie who'd said, "You didn't hear this from me Mr. Williams, but Miss Taylor is living at in Oakland Hills. I'm only telling you because I know she misses you."

Fancy had bought a penthouse in Oakland Hills. Ironically the same penthouse unit Darius's mother once owned. But when

Darius questioned his mother, his mother wouldn't discuss the details or give him Fancy's new numbers. Darius couldn't show up unannounced, and doubted the new doorman would let him go up to Fancy's unit anyway.

"This is bullshit," Darius mumbled.

Darius had to find out from Mr. Cabie when he'd stopped by to say hello, hoping to get a private dance from Fancy on her balcony, that Fancy was gone. Darius had guessed that throughout his legal ordeal, his mother and Fancy had become somewhat close. He had to warn Fancy not to trust his mother before something bad happened. Darius was certain that his mother had an ulterior motive for selling Fancy her condo. But what?

"Hey, man. You all right?" Lance asked, nudging Darius.

"Yeah, man. Just got a lot on my mind," Darius answered, leaning his head against the emergency door window of the 757.

"Hey, man. You makin' me nervous. Let's switch seats. You gon' make this plane crash if you keep leaning on the exit like that."

Although they were close to landing at Oakland International Airport for UCLA's game at Cal Berkeley, Darius didn't argue. Darius wanted the aisle seat anyway. Propping the pillow behind his head, Darius stretched his legs. Damn, Darius missed Fancy. All they'd been through. Darius knew she wasn't perfect, but neither was he. Who was Darius to judge her? That was the man upstair's job. But as much as he loved Fancy, every time Darius saw her, he flashed, dwelling on the negativity. What was up with that?

Lance interrupted his thoughts and asked, "Hey, man. Your girl coming to see you play tonight?"

Slouching in his seat, Darius said, "Don't know. Maybe."

Secretly Darius had hoped to see Fancy sitting courtside at his game, wearing the sexiest outfit in the gym, with no panties on, just for him.

When the plane landed, Darius gathered his bags, rode quietly on the team's chartered bus, and when they checked into the Claremont, Darius settled into his shared room with Lance. Darius remembered how he'd treated Ciara to a complete spa package—massage, facial, pedicure, and manicure—at the Claremont spa, prepping her for their first lovemaking session. That's how Darius had won Ciara over. Pampering her in every way. Lying across his bed, Darius wondered if he could ever win Fancy back.

Darius picked up his cell phone and dialed zero-one hoping Fancy would answer.

"Hi, Darius. You calling about Kevin?"

"Kevin? Hell no, I'm not calling about no Kevin," Darius said. Looking at his caller ID, Darius had dialed Ashlee's number by mistake. He'd meant to dial one-zero.

"Well, looks like he's going to have to do some serious time. How did I ever get caught up in such mess with you and your brother?"

"Just lucky, I guess. Or naïve. Look, I gotta make another call. I'll call you back tomorrow." Hearing Ashlee's voice convinced him he was finally over Ashlee Anderson. Williams. Whatever her last name was now.

"Wait. Darius, don't you have someone to ask me about?"

"No. I don't."

"I was expecting a call from you sooner. I filed an annulment divorcing Kevin when I read the results of our paternity test."

"Ashlee, I have a big game and I don't have time for your childish adventure. First you want me. Then you want Kevin. Now that you know what I tried to tell you all along, that Kevin was a thief, now you want me back. I'm over you, Ashlee. I'm in love with a beautiful woman."

Ashlee barely spoke above a whisper. "You don't have to take my word. Read your test results. I was wrong about Kevin being the father. And just so you know, I changed our son's name to Darius Jones, Junior, right before he passed away. He lived three weeks and two days. And your name is on his death certificate as our son's father. 'Bye, Darius." Ashlee hung up the phone.

"Fuck!"

The homeless woman's words haunted Darius again: *The son that is yours, soon after he's born, he will die. So will your father. Next year. Death follows you.*

How could Ashlee drop some shit like that on him before a big game? And now that Darius had changed his name, his son—his dead son—had the wrong last name.

"This is bullshit!" Darius threw his Rolex against the wall.

"Hey, man. Save that aggravation for the Bears. Let's go."

Lance was right. Darius's son was dead and Darius had to hear that bullshit over the phone as though Ashlee was a damn journalist delivering some insignificant fucking news report, like the weather forecast or traffic conditions. His son was dead.

"This is bullshit, Lance, man. Why do females do shit like this? They don't think men have feelings, too? She just called and said my son died, man," Darius cried.

Lance's eyes swelled with tears. "Big D, I'm so sorry man. I didn't know you had a kid. Let's take that shit out on Cal for real, man, 'cause you can't bring back your son. But you can win this game for Lil' D. I'ma feed your ass all night long, D, to keep this off your mind, man."

Darius's inner tears were tears of anger. Hatred. Darius was ready to decapitate somebody. When the hosts announced his name and jersey number, twenty-three, Darius ran toward Cal's coach, shook his hand, then dashed back toward his teammates. Darius stood there bouncing up and down on his toes, stretching his biceps. Halfway through warm-up Darius saw her—Fancy. He couldn't believe she was seated courtside next to SaVoy. Regulations prohibited him from leaving the floor during warm-up and game time to socialize, so Darius nodded and grinned at Fancy. She smiled a ray of sunshine into his heart.

Darius's team was ahead by twelve points at the end of the first half; Darius scored twenty-three points. Seven free throws. Four dunks. Two fifteen-footers and two layups. Fancy cheered each time Darius scored. The second half, with Lance's continuous help, Darius eerily scored the same twenty-three points the same way. The final score: UCLA, 82; Cal, 79.

Before Darius could talk with Fancy, the reporters were in his face shoving microphones and asking questions.

"Darius Williams, are you going pro after the season? How does it feel being back on the basketball court with a new name and an outstanding game? You've overcome some tremendous obstacles. Do you think you can take your team to the NCAA Championship?"

Darius politically answered like Darryl had taught him. "Right now I'm just giving my all to the game and to my team. I live, eat, and breathe basketball. I feel back at home on the court. Yes, I have overcome some tremendous obstacles. If God is for me, then who can be against me? I'm going to do my part to get my team to the championship. But I couldn't have played this well without my teammates. Especially Lance. Especially Lance. We're winners. And winners never quit."

Looking in Fancy's direction, Darius noticed his next-door neighbor Michael Baines in her face, grinning. Michael hugged Fancy as they walked away together with SaVoy trailing.

"Excuse me," Darius said to the reporter then ran across the court.

"Fancy. You wanna get together and talk later on? I'll be here until tomorrow morning."

"Sorry, Darius. I can't. Michael and I have dinner plans with Mr. Riddle and a new client who's interested in purchasing *several* apartment complexes. We can do breakfast, if you'd like."

"I thought Howard Kees was your broker."

"He is," Fancy replied, partially turning away.

With extra bass in his voice, Darius said, "I'll call you later tonight."

"Okay," Fancy said, pausing and kissing Darius's cheek as though he was her brother and no longer her lover.

Back in his hotel room, Darius lay in his bed and waited until midnight to call Fancy. She answered on the first ring.

"Hey, Darius."

"So what's up?" Darius asked, throwing the covers off his flaming hot sweaty body. Darius was angry with Fancy. But her voice was so sweet and innocent.

"Nothing much. Just missing you," Fancy said.

"That's not what I heard."

"Here we go. It didn't take long for your attitude to kick in. What did you hear?"

"You tell me."

"Darius, stop trying to find a reason to be upset with me. What are you talking about? I don't have time for this, baby. I have to meet a client in the morning for breakfast."

"Baby? Breakfast? A few hours ago we were going to breakfast."

"You didn't confirm. And we need to finalize the client's purchase offers. He's buying four multifamily properties."

"So now I need to confirm. And don't call me 'baby.' Do you call all those guys you've fucked baby, too? Maybe that's why you won't sleep with me anymore because you're too damn busy opening your legs and selling your pussy to the highest bidder? You probably don't even have any got damn real estate clients. I heard that's just a front for your hookin'."

Sniff. Sniff. Darius heard Fancy's sobs through the phone, confirming his beliefs.

"Hookin'? Are you crazy? I don't know what the hell you're talking about!"

"Does the name Harry Washington sound familiar? My boy Byron told me that Harry is putting out the word on the executive circuit that you're a prostitute and a thief. Harry says he's going to have you arrested for credit card theft."

Fancy became silent, then quietly said, "Darius, I never told you this, but Harry raped me."

"Oh, like Thaddeus raped you?"

"I've got to go."

"Go! Go get your money on trick! I wouldn't pay a dime to fuck your trifling ass!"

"I hate you! I hate you, Darius Jones! Williams! I thought you were my friend. I thought you were different! But considering you're a good-for-nothing bas—" Fancy paused. "No, I'm not going to stoop to your level," Fancy said. "Congratulations, Darius. Good game."

What the fuck had gotten into Darius? That was the future Mrs. Williams and Darius was acting a damn fool because she'd played him in front of his teammates, and he had to hear that shit on the team bus all the way back to the Claremont. Lance was the only one who was cool. When they'd gotten back to their rooms, Lance called his mom and dad, showered, then went to bed before midnight.

Darius picked up the phone and redialed Fancy's number.

"What, Darius? Haven't you insulted me enough?"

"Ladycat, I apologize. I love you."

"I love you, too, Darius. But the conversation we just had has nothing to do with love. I have an important day tomorrow. Good night." Ladycat hung up the phone.

Well, at least she was still speaking to him. Certain Lance was pretending to be asleep, Darius's roommate had already heard too much of his personal business. Darius realized being part of a team meant he'd have no personal business. Darius would give Fancy a call after he got back to his house in Los Angeles. And he'd better not run into Baines.

CHAPTER 25

Lying in her bed, watching the early sunset through the patio window, orange, yellow, and red hues layered the mountaintops beneath a cloudless sky. Tall evergreen trees swayed gently in the breeze. Fancy knew she'd forgive Darius for his harsh words. He didn't mean what he'd said. Over the past years, Fancy had learned a lot from her sessions with Mandy. How to depersonalize situations, accept responsibility for her actions, and then stand in her own truth. Most men possessed an inept ability to communicate effectively with women, so instead of saying what they honestly felt, they'd psychologically devalue themselves, then mentally or physically abuse their woman or women. Once again, something weighed heavy on Darius's mind but instead of telling Fancy, Darius held in his anger and misdirected his aggression toward her.

Harry and Byron were partially to blame for Darius's insecurities, not Fancy. Shallow men hid behind egos, money, expensive cars, nice homes, designer clothes, good looks, or whatever other attributes they believed magnetically attracted women to them. And when all those qualities failed, well, men disrespected and degraded other men and ultimately hashed out their frustrations on women. Innocent women.

Women, like sports, were gaming competitions for men. Harry

was upset with Fancy because, with Mr. Riddle's help, Fancy had become Harry's number one contender and Fancy wasn't stopping until she took Harry's place in the real estate industry. One day Fancy would meet Harry face-to-face again, and when she did, Fancy would blow Harry the biggest kiss, thanking him for making her better than him.

Fancy refused to shrink ever again to boost any man's self-esteem, including Darius and Byron. Fancy wasn't sure if Byron wanted her as much as he wanted to win her from Darius as if she was some prize trophy to sit on his shelf of countless accomplishments.

Perhaps Mandy would accept Fancy's call today. Mandy's words were constantly in her mind. "Love is defined for self, Fancy. I cannot give you a description or write you a script or prescription for love. Listen, if you don't know where to begin your definition of love, think about this. Who or what are you willing to die for?" Finally, Fancy had an answer.

Cuddling under the down comforter, Fancy had already proven to Darius that she would die for him. Why had Fancy really jumped in front of Darius? Maybe it was because Fancy didn't believe she deserved to live. Thaddeus was sent to rot in a jail cell with men who'd brutally raped him because he was charged with raping her. Indirectly, Fancy had killed an innocent man. And she'd aborted her baby. That was another life or death choice she'd made. How could Fancy forgive herself? Fancy would gladly trade places with Thaddeus if she could. Fancy's cell phone rang, interrupting her thoughts. She was relieved for the break in her mental sabotage and happier that Darius's name appeared on her caller ID.

"Hey, Darius."

Darius blurted, "Ladycat, I want you to move to L.A."

Darius's statement took Fancy aback. Way back. "Whoa. Where'd that come from?"

"I've decided that I want you here with me."

So typical. Once a man decided what he wanted, the woman was supposed to be equally or exceedingly excited. Not Fancy. Where was Darius's consideration for what she wanted? "Darius, I can't.

I've established a notable reputation and the business clients I service are in the Bay Area. Besides, I'm not moving in with any man as his live-in girlfriend that he can kick out whenever he wants."

"You don't have to work, Ladycat. My mom gave me ten million dollars. I'll take care of you. And if you want, I'll marry you. We were meant for one another."

Calmly Fancy questioned, "If I want? Darius, that's not the way to make a commitment or a proposal." Mandy would've been proud of Fancy. Fancy knew Mandy would when Fancy told Darius, "I'm open to discussing our possibilities of having a future together. I love you. Very much. Enough to be your wife. But the way you degraded me over the phone the other night, we're not going to pretend that that didn't happen. And if it happens again, I'm terminating our friendship. I'm not going to create, perpetuate, nor allow your unacceptable behavior. I don't put myself down. After all you've done I've never put you down. And I'm not going to allow you to bring me down by lowering my self-esteem or making me completely dependent upon you. Darius, we have to support one another. In so many ways, we already have. And just like you, I have goals, too. One is to own and operate my own real estate firm by the end of next year. My success is not about you. It's just that now that I know how to take care of myself, never again will I allow a man to *solely* take care of me. Not even you." Silence lingered. Did Fancy hear Darius sniffling?

"My heart is aching. I've never felt for any woman the way I feel for you. I've tried to forget about you, but I can't. I've already lost my brother, my son, and I'm scared of losing you. I'm not sure how much more rejection and death I can handle. I need you, Fancy. And I'm not accepting no from you. Fancy, I do want to marry you. Don't wait until I go pro to make up your mind. Just think about relocating."

"If you think I want you for your money, there's nothing to think about. Good-bye, Darius." Fancy hung up the phone and hugged her pillow tight.

Unlike when Mandy spoke those words to her, Fancy's good-bye to Darius wasn't final. Desperately, Fancy wanted to be with Darius but she wasn't going to let him mistreat her. If Darius genuinely wanted Fancy today, he'd want her tomorrow. And no matter how difficult it was for Darius, he would respect Fancy.

Picking up the phone, Fancy dialed Mandy's number.

"Hello, this is Dr. Sinclair's office," the receptionist answered.

"Hey girl, this is Fancy. I'd like to schedule a *much* needed appointment with Mandy."

"Sorry, Fancy." The disappointment in the receptionist's voice stunned Fancy's desires for the much needed therapy. "Mandy adamantly refuses to put you back on her schedule. I've already asked her ten times and she's warned me not to ask her again. I need my job. But I can give you the number for the referral from Mandy."

"No, thanks."

"Fancy, wait. Don't hang up. Most people don't realize it but Mandy's home phone number is listed on-line in the white pages. Not her address, just her phone number, but you didn't hear that from me."

"Thanks." Fancy hung up the phone with no one to fault but herself for her rejections. Obviously Mandy wasn't going to permit Fancy to disrespect her again. Fancy sighed with frustration. "I guess that's what Mandy meant about standing in my own truth. Huh. She's going to show me by example. That's okay. I'll be fine."

Fancy thought about the people she'd isolated to protect her emotions and the ones she'd rejected based on her standards, like her so-called friend Tanya. Tanya wasn't smart enough to be her friend. Because Tanya allowed William to control her, Fancy had stopped associating with Tanya months ago. Tanya had feelings, too.

Now Fancy knew why rich people suffered from depression. Fancy had money but she didn't have happiness. Not a mother, a father, Desmond nor Darius. Marrying Desmond was out of the question. Marrying Darius would be the biggest commitment or worse mistake of her life, but a chance Fancy was willing to take.

Fancy's heart ached particularly painfully when things didn't go well between her and Darius. Like tonight. Fancy wanted to call Darius back but didn't. Instead, with no destination in mind, Fancy got in her car and drove along Harrison Street onto

Interstate 580 East. To 680 East. Took I-5 South toward Los Angeles. Six hours later Fancy was sitting in Darius's driveway contemplating whether to knock on his door or check into a hotel and phone Darius in the morning.

Ringing Darius's doorbell, Fancy waited several moments.

Darius stood in the doorway and said, "Hey, um, Ladycat. Do you know it's three in the morning? What are you doing here? Are you okay?"

Fancy brushed past Darius into the living room. "I miss you, Darius." Fancy continued walking toward Darius's bedroom.

Hurrying, standing in front of Fancy, then blocking her path, Darius stuttered, "Um, well, you can't go in the bedroom. It's a mess. The maids didn't come today."

"I don't care about the mess. I care about you, silly. And I'm tired from driving." Maneuvering around Darius, Fancy opened his door and froze when she saw two naked women in his bed. "And you had the audacity to call me a trick. Who in hell are they?" Fancy asked, pointing.

Hunching his shoulders, Darius said, "I don't know."

"Don't know! You can come up with something more honest than that. I knew I should've stayed in Oakland." Turning on the lights Fancy yelled, "Y'all got ten minutes to get your shit on and get up out of here!"

The two girls, one black and one white, French-kissed and smiled at Fancy, then said in unison, "Join us."

"Oh, hell no!"

Darius grabbed her arm, closed the door, and said, "Let's talk about this in the living room."

Jerking her arm, Fancy slipped, losing her balance. "Whoa!"

"Aw, shit!" Darius yelled, breaking her fall. "Whew! I almost had a flashback."

The heels of Fancy's boots scuffed along the carpet like she was running. "Get off of me!" Bracing herself on her hands and knees, Fancy grabbed her purse then stood. "That's okay. They don't have to leave." Fancy turned and slowly walked away. When Darius didn't stop her, Fancy knew there was no respect and their relationship was over.

CHAPTER 26

"This is bullshit!

"Fancy has got to stop sitting courtside at my games with her male friends, clients, or whoever in the fuck those guys were." There was no way in hell Darius would marry Fancy now. Did she enjoy torturing him? Disrespecting him? Did she like that nigga's touch who was feeling up her leg, caressing her thigh? Darius hadn't seen him before. Fancy had lost her damn mind. Did she love the dude? Was he a bigger and better lover than Slugger? What made him so damn special? Fancy seduced his ear, as though she was considering giving him some pussy after the game was over. Dude sat there smiling. Grinning. Darius wanted to pop him in the face with the basketball. Had Fancy sucked his dick?

"What the fuck?" While Darius was dribbling the ball and trippin' on Fancy, his opponent had stolen the ball and there was no way Darius could catch him without drawing a foul. His opponent slam-dunked and the crowd went ballistic, screaming and cheering.

"Fuck!" Darius yelled, slapping his hands together before taking the ball out. Glancing at Fancy, dude was laughing, holding his stomach.

The referee gave Darius a warning. "One more profanity outburst and I'm giving you a tech."

Throwing the ball to Lance, Darius's opponent didn't simply block his shot, he hit the basketball so hard it flew into the fans three rows back.

"Fuck!" Darius yelled.

The referee signaled and then pointed toward Darius. "Technical on," he said, holding up two fingers on his right hand with his palm facing inward, followed by three fingers palm facing outward. Darius's head coach leaped from the bench onto his feet and jumped up and down while yelling at Darius. "Williams! What the hell are you doing out there?"

Lance pulled Darius aside and sternly said, "Chill out, D. Get your head off the fuckin' feline on the sideline. There's nothing over there more important than winning this game. Not even pussy. You'll have your pick of pussy in an hour."

Looking at Darryl Senior sitting next to his mother in the first row behind UCLA's team, Darius pressed his lips together, exhaled, and said, "You right, L. You right." Then he relinquished and let someone else take the ball out.

Darius's mother didn't have to use his father to get back at Wellington. And Fancy didn't have to flash some other brotha in his face or sleep with somebody else simply because Darius had allowed those two females from the swim team to please him the other night.

In his reoccurring dream last night, Darius did the butterfly and backstroked, tossing all night long until Fancy showed up at his front door at three o'clock, drowning his ménage a trois with her irrational behavior. That dream reoccurred every night after Fancy had shown up without calling. Darius shouldn't have opened the door. He wanted to put those women out when Fancy arrived unannounced, really he did, but those seniors weren't through seducing one another or sexing him. But Darius was caught off guard when Fancy was bold enough to open his bedroom door without his permission. Fortunately Fancy hadn't attempted to join them because Darius definitely didn't want to marry that type of freak. Those seniors were cool and all, serving their purpose, but neither of them were marriage material like Fancy.

"Get Williams!" Darius heard the coach yell after he'd dribbled down court and missed an easy-ass layup. Dude sitting next to Fancy was holding his fuckin' stomach again, this time bent over his own lap. The coach benched Darius the remaining four minutes of the second half. Postgame interviews went to the other starters on his team, including Lance.

While the commentator questioned Lance about Darius's performance, Darius casually strolled up to Fancy and waited for the explanation that he deserved. Fancy had better have a damn good one for humiliating him in front of millions of fans. Of all his games, Fancy would've chosen to show up at an ESPN nationally televised game.

"Hi, Darius. This is Desmond. Desmond, this is Darius. You didn't play well. Are you okay?"

Knocking Desmond's hand back into his stomach, Darius said, "Laugh at that, muthafucka." Darius didn't want no goddamn introduction. Darius said, "I remember you now. You're the dude from the church New Year's Eve. Don't your broke ass fuck my woman, man. You can't afford Fancy."

Desmond looked at Fancy. When Desmond opened his mouth to respond, Fancy said, "Darius, stop. Desmond is just a—Desmond is my friend. You are, too."

"Fuck that friend shit. I'm your man. And you're my woman. I'll talk to you later. Make this your last time showing up at my game sitting courtside letting some so-called friend feel up your ass." Darius walked away, then back to Fancy. "You know what. Better yet. Don't trip. You can fuck whoever you want. I'm through with you."

"You ready, Dez?" Fancy asked, ignoring Darius's comment. "'Bye, Darius."

Darius had fucked up again. Losing his cool in front of another man. Fancy was driving him insane. Dressed in her tight, low-rise black suede pussy pants that divided her vaginal lips and her hips right down the middle like a half-court line. Darius saw the imprint of Fancy's pussy so he knew everyone else, especially Desmond, had, too. The lace-up drawstring crisscrossed where a zipper should've been. The silver shiny turtleneck shielded Fancy's braless protruding nipples but not the diamond in her navel.

Already late, Darius ran to the locker room for the team's post-game meeting before getting into deeper trouble.

Soon as Darius entered the room all heads focused on him as the coach yelled, "Williams! What the hell happened out there? When you're on my court, you forget about everything else or sit your ass on the bench! I don't care if your mama is sitting in the center of the court butt naked licking on a lollipop, you run over, around, or through her to protect the ball! Then you score! Score, Williams, score! That's your job! Not watching some two-bit half-naked broad on the sideline. You almost cost us the game."

Picturing his mother without clothes was not a visual Darius entertained and he hoped none of his teammates had either. Speechless, Darius stood staring at the coach until the team was dismissed. Fancy wasn't some two-bit broad. She was his woman. But the coach was right and Darius knew he'd have the same or similar speech from Darryl in about an hour.

Driving fifty on the freeway to prolong his trip home, Darius wondered what was his mother's scheme for spending more time with his dad. And although Darryl was unhappily married, Darius prayed his parents didn't marry after all these years. Ashlee, Ciara, Fancy—why in fuck did women have to be so scandalous and revengeful?

Darryl was waiting in his car in the driveway when Darius arrived home. Parking next to his dad, and before they entered the house, Darryl lamented, "Son, let that be a valuable lesson on how women will try to bring you down. I keep trying to warn you about these females but you won't listen. When you're on that court, beating your opponent is the only thing that matters. Not Fancy. Not the guy she walked in with. Not me. Not even your mother. If your head isn't in the game, you need to be on the bench. Remember all the times I benched you at Georgetown? That's why. Don't mess up again. You're lucky y'all won this one or you would've lost your starting spot."

"What difference does that make? I'm going pro after this season anyway."

"Don't get cocky. You're not there yet."

Sitting next to his dad on the sofa, Darius said, "Remember when you said, 'You have no idea what it's like to lose your first-born'? And that Darryl Junior may have not been perfect but he was yours? Well, I found out."

"Son, what are you talking about?" Darryl Senior asked, placing his arm around Darius's shoulder.

As Darius cried on his dad's shoulder, he said, "I didn't even have a chance to be a father to him. I held him in my arms for five minutes, Dad, then I rejected him."

Passively, Darius listened to Darryl's monologue about Darryl Junior until his dad left his house. Then Darius sat on his sofa with a bottle of Louis XIII, no glass. Drinking from the bottle, visions of his son appeared. Tiny. Long. Pale. Wrinkled. Innocent. Small hazel eyes resembling Darius's mom's. Shiny straight coal-black hair like Darryl Senior. Cute toothless smile. That was until Darius started yelling at Ashlee, making him cry. His son's fingers, short but strong, gripping his pointing finger. Darius gulped from the bottle again.

Darius's son, whom he'd only held in his arms once, was dead. How could Darius love that little boy so much? Someone he honestly didn't know, when he didn't love or show love to the people he did know? Darius had rejected the flesh of his flesh because he thought, like Ashlee, that Kevin was the father. What was his cause of death? Ashlee had never said.

Fancy was probably fucking Desmond right now. Darius wanted to call but he'd been trampled over enough.

"Fuck that," Darius said, dialing one-zero anyway. The phone rang five times then went to voice mail.

In his attempt not to trip on Fancy, Darius powered off his cellular then turned off his home ringer. He set the thermostat to eighty degrees to heat up the Jacuzzi then took a long hot shower, letting the jet streams pound his sore muscles.

Stepping out the shower, the doorbell rang frantically. Shaking his locks, Darius said, "Groupies."

They always came to his front door. Not tonight. That's how his woman had gotten mad at him before. Sometimes it was hard to resist the groupies. Win or lose, after a game getting laid was one thing Darius could consistently rely upon. The adrenaline of having as many freaks as he wanted running nude throughout his house pumped energy into every vein. Looking down, Darius's dick was standing straight out, welcoming a charge. His hand wrapped around his long shaft. Long strokes. Slow strokes. Strong strokes.

"Fuck this. Why am I trying to do the right thing?" Fancy was probably riding that dude right this minute so why should Darius stand here beating his meat while Desmond was doing Fancy? Grabbing a towel, Darius wrapped his waist then walked to front door. They could rape him tonight if they wanted, he didn't care.

Centering his eye over the peephole, Darius froze. Uncontrollably, tears flowed. Without saying a word, Darius opened the door, stretched out his arms, and welcomed Fancy into his heart. Into his home. And this time, without hesitation, into his bedroom.

Trailing him, Fancy offered, "Darius, I can explain about Dez."

"Ssshh. You don't have to explain anything, Ladycat. All I need to know is that you love me and you want to be with me and me only."

Ladycat's lips kissed his eyelids, his cheeks, his chin, and then his lips. Cupping his mouth, her tongue gently pried apart his lips. Switching places, Darius stretched his lips wide then covered Fancy's mouth. Fancy held his face in her palms. Eyes to eyes with her, tears streamed down his cheeks. "I do love you, baby."

Darius picked up Fancy, carrying her to the Jacuzzi.

"Darius, wait! I still have my clothes on!" Fancy said, kicking off her shoes. One stiletto plopped in the Jacuzzi.

"Not for long, Ladycat."

Sitting Fancy in the tub, Darius's hands gripped Fancy's silver turtleneck sweater at the top and ripped it down the middle. Eagerly he palmed then kissed her sudsy breasts while patiently untying her suede pants underwater. Darius slid Fancy's pants halfway down her thighs to her knees, then leaned Fancy over the side platform of the Jacuzzi. Holding his dick in his hand, Darius circled Fancy's pussy under the water then slid the head up and down over her vagina.

Thrusting his dick one-third of the way inside her hot pulsating walls, Darius stroked again and the third time he hit deep inside Fancy's pussy pocket. Darius felt the dimples on the side of his ass deepen with every stroke. Darius fucked Fancy so hard, water splashed on her back, in their hair, and on the floor.

"Don't you ever give my pussy away to nobody. You hear me? Nobody," Darius commanded. When Fancy didn't answer, Darius said, "Come over here," positioning Fancy's clit in front of the jet stream. He stroked faster and harder; while the water massaged Fancy's pussy on the outside, Darius rode the inside.

Ladycat screamed, *"Daaaaaaaammmmmnnnnnnn! Yeeeeesssssssss!"* repeatedly. "Baby, please, I can't take any more."

Partially blocking the force of the jet stream, Darius rotated his finger on her clit under the water in front of the jet but refused to pull his dick out. Darius fucked Fancy harder. Turning his face to the side, simultaneously guiding Fancy's face, he tongue-kissed Fancy passionately, searching her mouth with his tongue.

The cum in his balls gained force and shot in waves through his shaft, exploding from his head inside Fancy's pussy pocket. The purse that Darius knew would shelter and secure his sperm for at least three days. Darius didn't care if one penetrated one of Fancy's eggs. In fact, Darius wished that Fancy would develop his seed inside her womb. Maybe she'd stop working. And definitely she'd marry him.

Darius eased his woman out of the Jacuzzi, toweled her off, and then lay her across the bed and smothered her clit with kisses, generating small orgasms that tasted like vanilla. Darius sucked Fancy's shaft from clit to base until Fancy showered him with the sweetest cream he'd ever swallowed. Softer and softer, Darius suctioned until Fancy was drained.

Darius whispered, "Baby, I love you."

Ladycat mumbled, "Um-hum. Me, too." The heavy weight of her hands rested on his locks where only moments ago she was pushing his lips against hers.

Quietly Darius lay his head on Ladycat's pubic hairs and snuggled into her crotch, inhaling her intoxicating aroma. Fancy must've sprinkled her pussy with some magical potion that made Darius want to eat her every time they made love. Wrapping his arms underneath her buttocks, Ladycat's pussy became his pillow and her strength became his new foundation for life. With Fancy by his side, there was no obstacle Darius couldn't overcome.

CHAPTER 27

Being with Desmond one more time was necessary for Fancy to see if his name was the name, beginning with D, of the person she was supposed to marry. After asking Desmond to fly to Oakland, and spending several days, all day, twenty-four hours a day with him, Fancy was positive that Desmond was not the one. Now Fancy no longer had to say, "I love Desmond. I think." Was it true that women matured faster than men? Had she outgrown Desmond? Well, Fancy definitely learned that being with Desmond for an extended period of time revealed certain things she hadn't known.

The saying "You don't know a person until you live with them" was a reality for Fancy and Desmond. After the first night at her penthouse, Desmond stopped picking up behind himself. Wet bath towels remained on her marble bathroom floor, jeans and T-shirts draped her vanity stool, and the unfolded newspaper decorated her living room coffee table until she recycled it daily. Desmond expected Fancy to figure out what was on the menu for breakfast, lunch, and dinner when her biggest and sometimes only meal of the day was breakfast. And money had become another problem. The lifestyle Fancy was accustomed to, Desmond couldn't accommodate, saying, "I'm a full-time college student now. Until I start practicing law, I'ma be broke." The Desmond Fancy knew would spend his last dollar to make her happy. But thankfully Desmond was only with her for one more day, so as with all the other days, Fancy would pay their expenses.

The real Desmond Brown had finally surfaced and Fancy didn't like him very much. Now that Fancy thought about their past, Desmond was pretending all along, trying to impress her. Desmond could've saved his money, her time, his time, and her money if he had been himself. Maybe Trina had spoiled Desmond, but there was no way Fancy would handicap any man by catering to his every need. If Desmond wasn't sleeping he was shadowing her every move. Fancy tried getting Desmond to stay a day or two with his best friend Tyronne while she showed houses and closed escrows, but Desmond claimed seeing how successful she'd become, he was thinking about becoming a real estate attorney.

Yesterday, Desmond had driven her Benz from Oakland to Los Angeles. Today, Fancy regretted that she had to take a six-hour drive back to Oakland trapped in a car with a man she wasn't in love with, who clearly still loved her. Or was it her looks that Desmond loved? Suddenly Fancy realized that appreciation, respect, dependability, and friendship were the qualities she still admired in Desmond. And love. In a sisterly way. A motherly way. Not the way a wife should love her husband. Seriously, Desmond was too clingy. Fancy wanted an independent man, like Darius.

Fancy loved Darius so much that she couldn't take her clothes off in front of Desmond when they had checked into the Ritz last night after Darius's game. Following her around the suite half the night, Desmond wanted Fancy badly. Groping. Grabbing. Himself, not her. Desmond's dick stayed hard. Obviously Desmond had something to prove, but not to her. The more Desmond tried, the more annoyed Fancy had become, and the more she longed to be in Darius's arms. Fed up, and before she flashed on Desmond, cursing him out, Fancy had gathered her purse, slipped on her shoes, and said, "I'll be back."

"Where are you going this time of night?" Desmond had asked, lying naked in bed with his heads leaning forward.

Fancy could've told him the truth and prayed Desmond would've been gone by the time she returned. Instead, she rolled her eyes to the top of head and then quietly closed the hotel door. Was she required to be hospitable under miserable circumstances?

Although Darius had declined her explanation after his game, Fancy hadn't taken Desmond to Darius's game to make Darius upset. What she wanted was for Desmond to see how talented Darius was. But all Desmond had done was laugh at Darius all night long, well after the game was over, agitating her more. Darius always played the role of having everything together, under control. During the game and last night, Fancy saw the Darius she'd waited to see. The little boy inside the man that yearned to be loved. By her.

Not trying, Fancy had pissed both of them off so when Desmond refused to leave her alone, Fancy took a chance and drove to Darius's house unannounced. If Darius would've had more groupies, then Fancy would've ended their friendship. For real that time. Spending the night at Darius's was wonderful for Fancy and horrible for Desmond.

Earlier this morning when Fancy returned to the Ritz from Darius's house, she valet-parked, then energetically, full of life, happily skipped inside the door wearing one of Darius's dress shirts tied above her waist. Desmond was sitting in the lobby with his luggage.

Desmond raced toward Fancy and authoritatively questioned, "Where've you been all night? Whose clothes are you wearing? And your hair is all flat."

Smiling, Fancy replied, "Why? Does it matter?"

With his lips twisted sideways, Desmond said, "Yeah, as a matter of fact it does."

Fancy continued smiling. "I had some unfinished business to attend to." If she wouldn't have blatantly pissed Desmond off, Fancy would've skipped all the way to their suite.

Moving closer to her, Desmond's voice angrily escalated. "So you abandoned me again? I could've stayed in Atlanta with Trina."

True. Glancing to see who was within ear range of their senseless and embarrassing conversation, Fancy noticed a well-known celebrity talking to an undercover security agent. Probably his bodyguard.

"Excuse me, Dez. I have to say hello to a potential client." According to Mr. Riddle, everyone was a potential client.

Following Fancy's stare, Desmond said, "Damn, that's Jamie! I have to say hello too!"

Fancy placed her hand on Desmond's chest. "Stay here, Dez. I'll be right back."

"That's what you said last night and you showed up twelve hours later. I'm going everywhere you go," Desmond insisted, dragging his luggage.

Retrieving a business card from her purse, Fancy handed it to Jamie. "Excuse me, Mr. Foxx. I'm Fancy Taylor, your realtor of choice. You were fantastic in the movie *Ray*. I've watched the movie at least twelve times. My favorite line was, 'You don't know how it feels to be blind and still be afraid of the dark.' Oh, that and, 'I'ma make it do what it do, baby.'" Flirting, Fancy winked at Jamie then smiled.

"Thanks," Jamie said, smoothly easing her card into his jacket pocket.

Desmond chimed in, "I'm your biggest fan, Mr. Foxx," emphatically shaking Jamie's hand. "My mama told me she saw you at the Oakland Paramount Theatre when you won the Bay Area Black Comedy Competition imitating handicapped people. Oh, that and you played the piano and everything. She said at the after-party you were standing alone and people were barely talking to you." Desmond looked at Fancy, then concluded, "One of these days I'm going to know what it's like from the people who ignore me now, man, to be all over me once I'm rich like you."

There Desmond went again, fantasizing about his unearned income. First Johnnie Cochran, now Jamie. Fancy shook Jamie's hand and said, "Nice meeting you," then walked away.

"Man, I gotta go with my girl. Be blessed. And I'll tell my mama you said hello," Desmond said.

How could Fancy have liked Desmond who annoyed the hell out of her? "Wait here in the lobby, Dez, until I get my bag from the room." Fancy figured if she slept in the car, the time would pass faster.

While Fancy was packing her bag, her cell phone rang.

"Hi, Mr. Baines. How are you?" Michael Baines had become Fancy's number one client.

"Call me Michael, please. Where are you?"

"In Los Angeles. Getting ready to drive back to Oakland."

"No, stay in L.A. My plane just landed. Can you pick me up?"

How could Fancy say no to a man who single-handedly grossed her over a million dollars on one deal? "Sure. I'm on my way."

Leaving her bag in the room, Fancy went downstairs and stood next to Desmond.

Looking up from the newspaper, Desmond asked, "Where's your bag? I'm ready to go."

"I'm not leaving. I've bought you a one-way ticket to Oakland and I've arranged for a driver to pick you up at the Oakland airport. Your full name will be on a piece of paper he or she will be holding. And they'll take you to the downtown Marriott. I've made a reservation for you, and in the morning the same driver will take you back to the Oakland airport. All you have to do is—"

"You are not abandoning me again! I came with you. I'm leaving with you."

"Desmond, please. I don't have time to debate this. My top client—one who wants to buy property in Los Angeles—is at the airport, and since I'm here I can make this deal."

"Whatever. I should've never taken you to that real estate office."

"Let's go," Fancy said, feeling more in control like a man than woman. Fancy could easily get accustomed to being in charge.

Dropping Desmond off upstairs at departures, Fancy zipped downstairs to arrivals and picked up Michael.

Opening the passenger door for Fancy, Michael said, "I'll drive."

Settling into their seats, Michael leaned from the driver's seat. His arms wrapped tightly around Fancy's shoulders. "Good to see you." When Fancy turned her head, the wetness of his lips pressed against her cheek, fractions of an inch away from her mouth.

Whew. Quietly, Fancy exhaled, wondering but unwilling to question what Michael's intentions were.

"I have several properties to see today. One I'm going to buy for personal use. You can have this seven-figure deal, too," Michael said, looking at her, "if you'll be my lady."

Speechless. Fancy didn't know what to say without blowing the transaction. "Well, let's see the house."

When Michael drove to the house adjacent to Darius's, Fancy's heart tried to beat out of her chest. Darius's car was parked in the driveway next to his mother's.

"I have the keys," Michael said, parking Fancy's Benz on the street with her tags facing Darius's house. "You okay?"

"Yeah, I'm fine," Fancy lied, getting out the car.

"This is not the house I'm buying. This is another one of my houses."

"Then why'd you park my car on the street? Let's park in the garage."

"Oil stains decrease your property value. You know that. Besides, we're not going to be here long. I just needed to drop off my bag and take a shower. That's all."

Michael's living room was beautiful and the only room Fancy wanted to see. Spacious. Everything was white accented in gold. Carpet, walls, mantle, fireplace, statues, picture frames. "I'll wait here," Fancy said, sitting in a high-backed cushioned chair like Mandy's. Looking at Michael's furniture, Fancy recalled calling Glide Memorial Church in San Francisco, welcoming them to everything in her old condo except her files. If she didn't have to file taxes, they could've taken the cabinets, too.

"Make yourself comfortable. I'll be right back."

When Michael disappeared, Fancy raced over to the window and peeped outside. Jada was frowning, pointing at Fancy's license plates. Darius frowned, too, then mouthed, "This is bullshit!" When they looked at Michael's window, Fancy ducked, closing the curtains. Fancy's new objective was to get out of Michael's house immediately. Fancy went to the living room to retrieve her purse and car keys.

Almost stumbling over Michael's feet, Fancy said, "Oh my gosh. You scared me. I thought you were in the shower."

Michael was now seated on the sofa dressed in a silk robe. An ice bucket chilling a bottle of champagne was on a nearby stand. "We never celebrated the closing on the San Francisco waterfront property. Let's have a toast to continuous prosperity."

Unlike Harry Washington, Michael was a man who could destroy her reputation with one phone call. Plus, she didn't want to risk losing a lucrative deal. If Darius truly loved her today, he'd still love her tomorrow. Fancy sat on the sofa next to Michael, drank several glasses of champagne, and then fell asleep. When she awakened in the middle of the night, naked in Michael's bed, Fancy knew she'd fucked up. The question was, how much?

CHAPTER 28

Life. Subject to change without notice.

Different day, same husband. Jada opened her hazel eyes staring into a space filled with years of wonderful memories and recently lonely moments. The horizontal position, lying on her back, was the same when she'd retired to bed as when she'd awakened this morning. She'd become a corpse in a coffin. Darius had lain across the foot of her bed last night but he was gone when she woke up.

If anyone would've told her she would divorced Wellington, Jada would've smiled and said, "Until death do we part, Wellington will always be my husband. Wellington is my soul mate."

Someone should've told her that "until death do we part" was a parable referencing the heart, not life. If one person stopped caring for the other, both were decomposing. Jada's feelings for her husband hadn't changed. But could her spark ignite a burning flame to save her marriage?

Wellington's hearty laughter resonated in her mind with fond thoughts as she continued gazing into the emptiness of their bedroom. How could he pretend their relationship was good after he'd had an affair? For years. How could she have not noticed his change? Probably because to her, her husband was the same.

Handsome. Fun. Loving. Kind. Polite. Strong. Successful. And while Jada didn't like Wellington very much, she loved him.

Jada was a few hours away from sitting face-to-face with Wellington. Hopefully she'd be civil. Whenever their divorce was finalized, she'd buy a home from Fancy. Selling Fancy her Oakland penthouse below market price was not intended to irritate Darius, although it had. Jada wanted to do something nice for Fancy for many reasons. Mainly because there was no way Jada could repay Fancy for saving Darius's life on many levels. Fancy had stood by Darius in his darkest times.

Jada had never seen Darius so afraid as the day he was booked for murder and fraud. Praise God Ciara hadn't pressed charges against Darius for assault and battery, the one charge that would've locked Darius up for years. Darryl had said a 242 was a chargeable crime and if Ciara had even mentioned to the cops that Darius had shoved her while she was pregnant, accidental or not, the district attorney would've pressed charges even if Ciara refused.

Of all the times Jada had held her son in her arms, she wanted to bail him out again that time, but Darryl insisted Darius stay a few days—three, maybe four—saying, "It won't kill him but he needs to sit still and think. And the only way our son is going to sit still is if we leave him behind bars for a few days."

Tears rolled down Jada's cheeks into her hair and onto her pillow. When Darius had gotten of jail, he'd come directly to her house. Stayed the night, lying across the foot of her bed, telling her more than he'd ever confessed before. Darius's vision of playing in the NBA made him so happy that she was happy for him. His insecurities with women had made him frustrated. His distrust of all women had made him bitter. The sadness Darius said he felt when thinking about Ma Dear had made him, at times, extremely depressed. But when Darius had begun angrily degrading Fancy, Jada poked Darius in the side with her foot and emphatically told him he was wrong for not embracing Fancy.

Jada had said, "Not many women will love you enough, honey, to almost die for you and then turn around and bail you out of jail.

Fancy loves you, Darius. She loves you in a way that I never could. For once, take a chance on love and open up your heart."

"But I'm scared, Ma. I know you love me unconditionally but what if Fancy stops loving me, like Wellington stopped loving you?"

Looking into her son's eyes, Jada had explained, "Everything in life is a gamble. When you have kids, you don't how they're going to turn out. But you do love them unconditionally. Like I love you. When you start a business, you don't know if you'll be successful. But you always strive for success. And in life, you will learn more from your mistakes than from what you do right. But only if you take chances."

Darius's eyes had glazed the way they did when he didn't see whatever was in front of him because he was lost in thought. "You're right. You're good to me, Ma, and I'll be a better son. I'll show you. And I'll talk with Fancy."

Jada felt all of the goodness in Darius's heart's intentions. She just hoped that Darius could appreciate Fancy before it was too late. When Darius saw Fancy's car at his next-door neighbor's, Jada had to explain to him how a woman could get caught up in a situation that wasn't what it appeared to be on the surface. "If you love Fancy, honey, then you must confront her with respect, not anger."

Dragging her body from the bed, Jada retrieved the plush green, purple, and gold towel set Wellington had bought her on their first trip to New Orleans for Mardi Gras. Showering, Jada could still smell the scent of Wellington's cologne in her mind. She brushed her teeth, combed her hair, and dressed in one of her conservative two-piece pantsuits so her emotions would be in sync with her appearance.

Noticing the flashing red light on her cell phone, she'd missed a call from Darius. "Mom, I just called to say I love you, thanks for always supporting and believing in me, thanks for everything, and I apologize for all the pain I've caused you. Call me when you get back in from your appointment, I'm going to spend the night at your place tonight so you won't be lonely. I don't want you to be alone. Oh, yeah. My dad said he'd gladly keep you company anytime." Jada chuckled. "Hope I made you smile with that one. Hugs and kisses, Mom. I love you."

Since Wellington was gone, Darius wanted to be the man of her house. But it wasn't Darius's responsibility to take care of her. Not on that level. If she were sick, yes. Because she was getting a divorce, no.

Driving along Interstate 5, Jada called Darius.

"Hi, honey. I'm on my way to my meeting with Wellington."

"Ma, you sure you don't want me to meet you there? I could have Lance take notes in class for me."

"No, honey. I'll be fine. But thanks. How are things between you and Fancy?"

"Thanks to you, Mom, great. She explained what happened. She says she's coming to my last games, even out-of-state games. I love her. And I love you, Mom."

"Honey, if you're serious about marrying Fancy, just remember that the love of a woman or a wife doesn't surpass that of your mother. A wife's unconditional love will make you complete as long as you realize that your woman is not your mother. In time, your wife will become much closer to you. She should be your best friend, your confidante, your support person, and ultimately the woman who will breathe life into your life, into your children's lives. I don't want you to make the mistakes I did. I lied for so long I'm still struggling to overcome my guilt. I do feel partially responsible for Wellington's actions."

"Bump that! It's not your fault, Mom."

"Darius, don't pacify me. Clearly all of this isn't my fault, but I am partially to blame and I can accept that. That's why I'm not freaking out. When you've done right by someone who has wronged you, you feel betrayed. Angry. Revengeful even. But when you are the one who's wrong, like you were wrong for marrying Ciara, you have to accept the truth and not blame others. I'm here now. I'll call you on my way home. Thanks, honey."

"Love you, Mom. 'Bye."

Jada parked in the garage then entered the room five minutes late. Jada's lawyer and Wellington's attorney were seated across the conference table from Wellington, reviewing the financial statements for all three businesses, including Somebody's Gotta Be on Top Enterprises, which her lawyer had already advised had turned a remarkable profit after the release of *The Honey Well* by Gloria Mallette.

The meeting, the first of several, was agreed upon to prepare a draft dissolution of marriage along with the stipulations and division of assets. The knots in Jada's stomach united, doubling her abdominal pain. Jada paced, trying to alleviate the pain accompanied by a migraine.

"Are you all right?" Wellington asked, seemingly concerned.

"I will be after this is over. I cannot believe this is how you want to end our marriage. Starting with a division of assets as opposed to developing an understanding of our issues."

Wellington's face was expressionless. "I think it's best. Darius is grown. My son is more of a nuance to you than a joy. And—"

Standing next to Wellington, Jada yelled, "Wellington, that's not fair! Don't you dare sit there trying to justify your behavior! What about this Morgan child?"

Wellington pushed his chair backward and faced her. "I told you, Morgan is not my daughter. Melanie—"

Looking down upon her husband, Jada wanted Wellington to hold her. Tell her everything would be okay. But she replied, "I don't believe you."

Rising to his feet, Wellington lamented, "Listen, Melanie asked me to help raise Morgan. Morgan has a father much like Darius's father was. But admit it. It's true. You don't want to help raise my son. Whenever he's over for the weekend, you conveniently have something else to do that keeps you away all day."

Wellington was inside her three feet of space. Jada stepped back. "If you hadn't left him with me every single weekend without checking my schedule, maybe, just maybe, I wouldn't have minded being around."

Wellington sat in his chair. "Ba, I didn't say anything because of my love for you. And I still love you. Always will, ba. But—"

"But what?" Jada said, sitting next to Wellington. "You'd rather be with Melanie."

Holding her hands, Wellington said, "Naw, ba. This isn't about sex or another woman. That's not it at all. Melanie could never take your place. To be honest, I don't know what the hell I was thinking of or if I was thinking at all. You have no idea how hard it was for me to accept the fact that Darius wasn't my son. Melanie was convenient and I needed someone to turn to. Look, if you don't want to do this today, we can think about this another month or so."

"And do what in the interim?" Jada asked, hoping for a favorable response but added, "Keep living apart. Keep walking by one another in the hallway at work and not speaking. What?"

"Talk. We can talk. Believe it or not, I do miss waking up to you. Reading the newspapers in the morning with you."

When Wellington gave in, Jada became angry. "You should've thought about all that before you started fucking Melanie in your office and everywhere else."

Shaking his head, Wellington said, "You're never going to change. As long as things go your way, you're happy. You lied to me, to Darius, to Darryl, to yourself, and everyone has forgiven you, but you can't forgive me because of what? Your selfish pride."

Not wanting to admit Wellington was right, Jada asked, "Did you make a decision on signing over your interest in Darius's company and did you schedule your doctor's appointment?"

"Not yet. And thanks for reminding me about my appointment. I'll call today."

"Wellington, like it or not, Darryl is going to run Darius's company. We didn't establish this company for our benefit. We established this company so that Darius would have his own business. And business-wise, you must admit, Darius did well."

Wellington looked at his attorney and said, "Reschedule this meeting in two months."

Jada's lawyer asked, "What would you like to do?"

Jada had almost forgotten the lawyers were there. "That's fine, but proceed with finalizing the independent financial reports and paperwork so when we do meet we won't have another delay. There's no need to drag this out. You can call me later with the first available date to meet."

"Wait, ba. We do need to discuss this. Can you guys step outside and give us a moment?"

Wellington's lawyer responded, "Sure."

Jada looked at her lawyer and said, "It's okay. You can leave. Call me later."

"Ba," Wellington said, patting the seat next him. "Come sit down."

Jada sat beside a man she thought she'd spend the rest of her life with but didn't want to share another day with. "What?"

"I want us to be friends. I don't want this divorce to get uncivil. Giving Darius back his company in the middle of production for Gloria Mallette's *The Honey Well* could cost millions. Especially since Ciara refuses to cooperate with Darius unless he remains her husband."

"That crazy woman needs to go on and sign the divorce papers. Darius loves Fancy. And Wellington, I'm no longer asking you to give Darius back his company, I'm telling you."

"Darius is part of our problem, too. Anything Darius wants, Darius gets."

"And how is that any different from your son, Wellington the Second?"

Wellington became silent then said, "Isn't this funny? We were friends for over twenty years. Now after less than three years of marriage, we're getting divorced."

"So do you want the divorce?" Jada asked.

"Never said I didn't. I said we could wait two months and you said you didn't want to wait at all. Fine, we'll handle this your way," Wellington said, approaching the door. "Seems to me you wanted out long before now."

"Wait one goddamn minute, Wellington Jones! What's that supposed to mean?"

"Just what I said. The things you used to do, you stopped. So I stopped."

"Like what?" Jada asked. "I still lay out your clothes, fix your breakfast."

"You call that breakfast?"

"This isn't about breakfast. What's this really about?"

"I'm done with you." Wellington exited the room.

Jada sat trying to keep her composure, waiting for the attorneys to enter the room, but they didn't. She'd forgotten she told her lawyer to leave. When Jada opened the door, the hallway was clear so she left.

What was the real reason Wellington refused to give Darius his company? Did Wellington honestly want a divorce? Did she? All Jada knew was she wasn't going to stay married to a man who flaunted his woman, a woman she despised, in her presence and her workplace. Wellington Jones could kiss her ass.

Being single at her age was not going to be fun. Jada still looked good but dealing with the men who were chasing young women, stealing their youthfulness trying to stay young, was not her idea of fun.

Jada's best girlfriend Candice had recently purchased a mansion in Beverly Hills after separating from her husband Terrell. Maybe Jada would visit Candice at her home instead of going to her big empty house. Their house was lonely without Wellington.

CHAPTER 29

Finally! Yes! Ciara had agreed to sign the divorce papers. This time she'd requested the meeting. Not at her office but at a neutral location. Since Darius had grown emotionally closer to his mother—spending nights and weekends at her house—his opinion of and respect for women had improved. Darius had developed a newfound appreciation of his mother.

His mom was intelligent, beautiful, and when she wanted to be, comical. Witnessing how depressed his mother had become living without Wellington and learning so much about his mother's struggles being an only child to parents who were also only children, had convinced Darius to seek professional help. His mother made him realize that he couldn't continue going through life alone without having friends, both male and female. She'd said, "But first, honey, before establishing true friendships, you must know how to be a friend. Then you must surround yourself with good people who have your best interests at heart. Not the ones who want to be your friend because you're a millionaire. You must know when to listen. When to give advice. When to be there. And when not to be there."

Focusing added attention to his appearance before he left his Oakland house, Darius's freshly twisted locks were gathered into a ponytail, exposing his clean-shaven face and emerald-cut diamond earring. Darius splashed on cologne then fastened his new Rolex on his left wrist. He dressed in an expensive, casual, tan button-up shirt with his diamond cufflinks and a pair of brown slacks. Not for his luncheon with Ciara but for his evening date with Fancy.

Nervously, Darius arrived at the address on University Avenue that the receptionist had given him. "Damn, there's no garages around here?" Darius mumbled, driving several blocks past Mandy's office toward UC Berkeley. Making a U-turn, Darius bypassed Mandy's office again and parked his customized Escalade diagonally, consuming two spaces in Kragen's parking lot. Somebody was sure to see his car but hopefully not him. And definitely not Fancy because Darius made certain to invite her to his place in Los Angeles while he was in Oakland for his appointment.

Standing at the receptionist's counter, Darius read the framed eleven-by-fourteen print: "Every smiling face isn't smiling. Every laughing voice isn't laughing. Every shut eye isn't sleeping. Every listening ear isn't hearing. Every broken heart isn't broken."

"Good morning," the receptionist said. "You must be Mr. Williams."

"That's right. Good morning. I have a nine o'clock appointment. Do I need to complete any paperwork?"

"No, Mandy prefers to ask the questions herself."

Pointing at the print, Darius said, "You know that last saying doesn't make much sense."

"Oh, but it will, Mr. Williams. Before you leave, it will. Mandy will see you now."

Stepping into Mandy's office, Darius felt awkward. Maybe he should pay his bill and leave.

Mandy frowned, staring, "Aren't you Mr. Jones?"

"Naw, Williams is my last name."

"You were Darius Jones before, right?"

Darius started to tell Mandy the truth, but didn't know why he lied, "No. Not me."

"Have a seat, Mr. Williams," Mandy said as she sat in a high-backed swivel chair reaching for a legal-sized yellow pad. "So what brings you here?"

"Life."

Mandy sat staring then asked, "Yours? Or someone else's?"

"Both."

"Okay, Mr. Williams. When was the first time you experienced love?"

Darius sat on the blue leather sofa smiling, scanning Mandy's bookcases. His eyes settled on *A One-Woman Man* by Travis Hunter. Why did they have two different covers for the same book? "My first time was when I was in elementary school. There was this girl—"

Mandy interrupted. "Not sex, Mr. Williams. Love."

"Um, I apologize," Darius said, easing his hand over his ponytail.

"Don't. We'll cover sex in another session. Today we're talking about love."

Darius sat staring at an unaligned row of gardenias. Slowly he spoke in an uneasy tone like something fluttered in his throat. "I remember . . ." Darius hurtfully smiled, recalling the print behind Mandy's receptionist desk, then continued, "As a little boy loving my mother more than anyone in the whole wide world. Mom, she used to *always* take care of me. I was always first. She gave me lots of hugs and kisses. She took care of me when I was sick. Her eyes sparkled like diamonds whenever I entered a room." Darius was careful not to use his mother's name or anyone associated with him. Especially Fancy's name because Fancy wanted so badly to meet with Mandy again. Now he understood why.

"What happened?" Mandy asked, scribbling.

"One Christmas when I was three, I recall telling my dad, 'I think I made Mommy sad, because when I walk into the room, her eyes don't light up no more.' My dad said, 'Mommy just has a lot on her mind and it has nothing to do with you.' I believed him. But today, I'm not so sure. What I realized as I got older was my mother was sad because my dad had another woman. As long as we were a family, my mother's eyes sparkled. But when Dad left, he took a part of my mom that I never got back."

"Let's focus on you, Darius. How did that make you feel?"

Clenching his back teeth, Darius's jaws flinched. "Sad. But that's when Ma Dear started loving me."

"Who's that?"

"My deceased grandmother. My mom's mom."

"Oh, okay."

Darius expected Mandy to say she was sorry to hear Ma Dear was dead, but she didn't so he continued, "Ma Dear always protected me. She told me when I was wrong but she still loved me the same no matter what."

"Darius, love is not defined by what people do for you. It is what you do for them that counts. The sparkle in your mother's eyes for your dad disappeared when you were three years old because the love she wanted to give to your father, she could no longer give. He'd moved on to another woman. Your mother's sadness internalized into an unspoken rejection. No one wants to feel rejected. Your sparkle is still there. Always has been. But your light inside your mother was blocked by your dad's light. And you were too young to know how to rekindle that sparkle. It wasn't your fault. But it's not too late. You must show your mother that you truly love her. Stop measuring love by what others do for you. Either *you* love someone or *you* don't."

"I'm an only child. My mother is an only child. And both of her parents were only children. I have one person I'd like to be a friend to. I have a lot of issues. When I was twenty, I found out that the man I thought was my dad wasn't my dad, and my real dad was a professional basketball player. I hated my mom for lying. I've tried, and although I'm closer to my mom, I don't think I can forgive her for lying to me."

Mandy stood and said, "We'll continue this conversation in our next session." Shaking Darius's hand and looking up into his eyes, Mandy said, "People lie all the time, Mr. Jones. I'll see you next week."

Darius smiled, but he wasn't smiling on the inside. "What does that saying, 'Every broken heart isn't broken,' mean?"

"The mind can make the heart believe things that aren't true. Most people who say 'I love you' don't mean it. They don't show it. But they've said it so much that they believe they're telling the truth. Insecurities, inadequacies, and fears rip the heart apart, but it's all in the mind. Not the heart. Good day, Mr. Jones."

What was the point now in explaining the truth—that Mandy was right, his last name was Williams? Darius stopped at the receptionist desk and scheduled his appointment for next week with Mandy. Walking across the street in a daze, Darius saw a big orange laminated sheet tucked inside his driver's side window.

"Do NOT attempt to move this vehicle or you will damage your tire."

"What the fuck?" Looking around, Darius saw a small-framed Asian woman walking toward him.

"Sixty dollas. I remove," she said, pointing up at a sign that read, Parking For Customers Only.

If his flight to L.A. wasn't leaving in an hour he'd go inside and straighten this bullshit out. Darius handed the woman three twenty-dollar bills and said, "Hurry up."

"Next time I charge you double for taking two spaces," she said, holding up two fingers.

Her comment wasn't worthy of a response. Racing to the Oakland International Airport, Darius valet-parked his car, ran to the kiosk and retrieved his boarding pass, bypassed the long security line, and followed the flight attendants into their security entrance. During the flight, Darius had time to reflect on his session with Mandy.

Mandy had him thinking and that was good. Leaning against the emergency door, Darius thought about Lance and sat up straight. Darius felt remorse for abusing Ciara. Marrying Ciara only to have access to her business was immature and wrong. Fortunately both of their businesses survived and thrived but he was at fault for stealing Ciara's heart. Saying "I love you" when he never had.

Flipping through a *Sky* magazine, the seventy-minute flight breezed by. He'd baited Ciara in but he hadn't force her to succumb to his charming ways. But a man guilty of misleading or mistreating a woman had to apologize. But was an apology enough? Retrieving his Bentley from short-term parking, Darius thought, what if Ciara granted him the divorce but never forgave him? Hopefully Ciara wasn't playing any more games to complicate his life. Parking in the lot at the restaurant in Malibu, Darius constantly glanced over his shoulder for police cars, sheriff uniforms, anyone visibly associated with the law.

Ending his college year and basketball season with his team having made it to the Final Four was great, but Darius doubted the team would go beyond the Sweet Sixteen without Lance and him. With Darryl's help, Lance was going to play professionally in Switzerland earning almost a million dollars a year.

Smiling at the hostess, Darius said, "Reservation for Darius Williams."

"Are you sure your reservation is for today?" she asked, scanning the list.

"Check Ciara Monroe."

"Oh, here you are, right this way, sir."

En route to the table, Darius avoided staring at the sexy women in thong swimwear playing volleyball on the beach. To Darius's surprise, Ciara had reserved a window table for two. Briefly Darius closed his eyes. The warm afternoon sunshine toasted his freshly shaved face.

Opening his eyes, Ciara looked amazing, strolling toward Darius dressed in a tapered crisp white business suit resembling the outfit she'd worn the day they'd met. Except today she'd worn a skirt that stopped several inches above her knees.

"To say you recently had a baby, you look great," Darius complimented her, pulling out a chair for Ciara. "Must be some sort of afterglow."

Lifting a brow, Ciara said, "Thanks, so do you. I know you're glad the basketball season is over so you can find out which NBA team you'll be playing on."

"Yeah, I am excited. But honestly, I'm more excited that you agreed to sign the divorce papers."

Ciara's hair was amazingly straight and layered against her head. Her luscious lips were covered in brown with a shimmering glittery gloss. Her breasts, bigger than before. Man, that kid was lucky.

Breaking his concentration, Ciara said, "Darius, the reason I wanted to see you was to tell you that I still love you. I'm not sure I'm ready to be a single parent."

"I can respect that. But I don't think it's me you love," Darius said, not wanting to have a relationship conversation with Ciara. "Let's open the results to our paternity test and then continue this discussion."

Lord, please, please, please. If the homeless lady was correct, and so far she was, then Ciara's child was not his. Removing the envelope from his pocket, Darius picked up the knife and slid the tip into the small opening on the side. The ridges sawed along the top from side to side. Carefully he removed the enclosed letter. Staring at Ciara, Darius unfolded the bottom, then the top of the page. Glancing at the results, Darius smiled, shaking his head, knowing his Ma Dear was smiling, too. He was not the father of Ciara's child.

"Let me see that," Ciara insisted, reaching for the paper.

Gladly Darius's fingers released the page.

"This can't be true. The only other person I was with was Solomon," Ciara whispered. "And he's dead." Pleading, Ciara said, "Darius, you have to be the father. Even if he's not your son. My baby won't have a daddy."

What in the hell was wrong with women wanting him to raise their kids? First Ashlee when she thought Kevin was the father, now, of all people, Ciara, the woman who practically hated him. Then claimed she loved him. Which one was it?

"I'm not willing to do that. I care for you but it's time we part and move on with our lives. Ciara, I'm in love with Fancy. And I want to marry her."

Tossing the paper on the table, Ciara hung her purse on her shoulder and scooted to the edge of her seat. "I'll call you after the draft selection."

Darius yelled, "Ciara, you are not going to force me to be a father to someone else's child!"

Whispering, Ciara stood over Darius, stared down into his eyes, and said, "You can go to jail or raise this baby. The choice is yours." She walked away.

Gripping Ciara's arm, Darius said, "Wait. Sit down. Let's talk," then released his grip. Exhaling, Darius said, "I don't how to be a good father to your son and be a true friend to the woman I love. What if you want more than I have to give?"

"You can start by visiting the baby once a week." Ciara spoke like she was dictating to her secretary.

Frowning, Darius asked, "The baby. What's his name?"

Ciara smiled, then said, "Darius Jones-Monroe."

Darius stood, shaking his head, and said, "Give the child his real father's name," then left the restaurant. He might need to call Mandy before next week. Ciara's decision not to sign the papers had nothing to do with the baby or Darius. Any single woman raising a child alone wasn't completely happy. That's why his mother married Lawrence. Maybe she loved Lawrence enough to be his wife, but more importantly she wanted a steady companion. Darius couldn't remember his mother ever dating before Lawrence. Not that she didn't; Moms didn't want to introduce him to any man who wasn't going to be a part of their lives. With all the gossip in Hollywood about Ciara being a single parent and a lesbian, Ciara wanted a celebrity husband to complement her and hush the film industry media critics.

Darius drove along Santa Monica Boulevard and dialed Fancy.

"Hey, Darius! Where are you?"

Why did women always question a man's whereabouts immediately after saying hello? "Just chillin'. Missing you. You ready for our trip to London this weekend?"

"For sure, daddy. I can't wait to pounce on your big dick while we're in the sky. I'll give you a sample when you get home."

"So is that all you want your future husband for?"

"Not at all. But Slugger does add appeal to your proposal."

Darius had so much on his mind that Slugger was limp. He sighed, then said, "The ten-hour flight will give us time to talk."

"Talk? What's wrong?" Fancy asked.

"Nothing's wrong. We just need to discuss a few details. That's all." Fancy didn't know about Desire, or that that was why Darius was going to London—to find out if Desire's son was his. Although Darius doubted Desire had told the truth, he had to make certain he didn't have children out in the world unbeknownst to him. Nor

did Darius want any newsbreaks hitting the paper about him before he went pro.

"Oh, no. Whenever you say 'that's all,' that's not all."

"You found a wedding gown yet, woman?"

Fancy laughed. The sweet melody in her voice indicated her
smile behind the laughter was genuine. "Yes, I have. My mother
helped me pick it out. It's so exquisite and sexy."

"Don't have my twins on exhibit. Those are for my eyes only,"
Darius said, driving by his house. He wasn't in the mood to make
love.

"Nothing wrong with a little foreplay on your wedding day."

"I gotta go. I'll call you back later."

Darius couldn't tell Ladycat the truth so he drove to his
mother's house. Maybe Mom could help him come up with a solution to please everybody. One thing was certain, Ciara was going to
have to sign the papers whether she wanted to or not. And Desire's
baby, Darius prayed, wasn't his.

CHAPTER 30

After all the disappointments lingering in her past, today was a day filled with wonderful surprises for Darius and her mother, and Fancy couldn't resist doing something great for herself. She deserved it. The seventy-five-degree temperature resonating from the bright burst of sunshine made Fancy happier. Gathering her designer purse and keys, Fancy skipped to the elevator, into the garage, and cruised onto the hillside. Pausing momentarily, she shifted her gear into park. The sweeping view of Oakland and San Leandro was calming. Houses, bridges, and freeways were filled with people in transit. Fancy wondered how many little girls in those homes were being abused and how could she help them.

Shifting into drive, Fancy cruised into the driveway at her old condo building on Lake Merritt and waved at Mr. Cabie. "Have a great day!" Fancy yelled, then drove away. The beautiful day graced the outdoors with joggers of all ages, kids on bikes, skateboarders, and roller skaters. Memories of times spent with Darius at her condo warmed her insides. Briefly Fancy thought about Thaddeus. But this was a day to give thanks and be grateful so Fancy refused to allow any negativity into her space.

"Lord, please forgive me," Fancy whispered, then drove to Caroline's—oops, she'd meant to say her mom's—house in East Oakland. Punching in the telephone number for the movers,

Fancy inquired, "I'm calling for the estimated time of arrival for the move of Caroline Taylor. When will the driver arrive?"

"Hold, please," the male clerk said.

A minute later he said, "They'll be there in about twenty-five minutes."

"Oh, good. Thanks."

Fancy parked in front of her mom's house then knocked on the door. When Caroline opened the door, Fancy stepped backward instead of forward. "Hey, how are you feeling?"

"Fine, considering I don't have a man. Come in."

Here we go, Fancy thought, slowly entering the living room and following her mom to the bedroom. This visit wasn't about her past so Fancy focused on her mother's concerns, sympathetically asking, "No, what happened?"

Plopping on the bed, Caroline replied, "Marvin told me he loved me. And like a fool I believed him. Now he's telling me he has a younger woman. Can you believe that?"

Actually, yes. Holding Caroline's hand, Fancy asked, "What about his baby growing inside of you? He can't just leave you pregnant like this."

Caroline rubbed her protruding stomach. "He can. And he did. I don't know what went wrong. We were so happy together. Baby, I'm too old to raise another child by myself."

This wasn't the time to say I told you so, so Fancy hugged her mom tight. Her mother barely knew Marvin. A few drinks, dinners, and good times did not make a woman marriage material. "Everything will be all right, Mom. I have a surprise for you. Hopefully it'll cheer you up."

Lazily, Caroline looked up at Fancy, partially smiling, and said, "I hope so. What is it?"

Removing the keys from her purse, Fancy said, "Remember the three-bedroom house in the hills close to my condo that you said you liked?"

Fancy's mom's eyebrows lifted as she stretched her spine. "Yeah."

Handing Caroline the keys, Fancy said, "Well, it's yours. The movers will be here any minute to move you."

Caroline stared into her palm. Tears dropped into her bosom. "Today? I haven't packed a thing."

"Don't worry, Mom. You're expecting. You can't lift anything heavy. I paid them to pack and unpack everything for you. All you have to do is shower and get dressed. You're going to L.A. with me today. I have a surprise for Darius."

The smile on Caroline's face didn't erase the hurt sitting in the windows of her eyes. "You're just full of surprises. Fancy, come here." Fancy's mom opened her arms wide. "I love you, Fancy. I always have. You were always so strong and so beautiful. You've always taken care of me. Even when I was too drunk to care for myself. I never felt like your mom. It just seemed like when your father and I broke up after I decided to keep you, one day I was single and the next day I was a kid, single with a kid, but not a single parent. I very much wanted to live my life the way I'd always lived it. Partying. Dating. And working just enough to make ends meet and meet the next guy."

The lump in Fancy's throat choked her. Fancy wrapped her arms as tight as she could around her mom and cried. "You don't know how long I've waited to hear you tell me you love me. I love you, too, Mom. And I forgive you. Please forgive me, too."

"Forgive you for what?" Caroline asked, heaving over Fancy's shoulder.

Fancy softly said, "For being ashamed of your obesity. For hating you because you loved your men more. For not trying to understand your pain."

Caroline's arms fell into her lap so Fancy sat back and listened.

"Yeah, child. Life for me as a child was rough. You think you had it bad. Not to minimize what I did to you, but I had to clean up from sunrise to sunset. Cook dinner every day from the age of ten. I wasn't allowed to go to movies or dances, or just play outside with my neighbors. I can't call them friends because outside of school I never played with them. Fancy, I never told you, but I've never graduated from high school. When I turned sixteen, I left home and never went back. Shortly afterward I was pregnant with you. I'd already had one abortion and didn't want to have another. When my mother died, I didn't go to the funeral. When my father died, I didn't go to his funeral. And when I became pregnant with you, I was happy. Until Thaddeus left me. Then when I had you, you were more of a burden than a blessing. Now here I am pregnant again with a child God knows I don't want."

God. Getting closer to God didn't mean that Fancy had to go to church every Sunday. If somehow, some way, she could dedicate her life every day by helping someone else, God would continue blessing her. "If you honestly don't want your child, I'll raise my baby brother or sister."

Caroline hugged Fancy then said, "Fancy, I can't ask you to do that."

Hugging her mother again, Fancy said, "You didn't. I offered. I'd rather raise him or her than have him or her go through what I went through. And you are going to go back to school. I'll pay for your education."

Looking at Fancy, Caroline's eyes sparkled with love. "Was I that bad of a mother?"

"Honestly, yes. Now let's go see your surprise."

"I don't deserve the house. You keep it," Caroline proudly said, "to help pay for my GED."

Fancy stood and insisted, "I said, let's go."

Caroline showered while Fancy selected the best casual outfit from her mother's closet. Caroline replaced her slippers with the flat shoes Fancy selected. Greeting the movers on their way out, Fancy said, "Here's the keys to the new residence. Move everything in. Don't forget to lock up this house and leave those keys at the new house, too. By the time you finish in about eight hours, we'll be at the new residence." Handing the driver a hundred-dollar bill, Fancy said, "Here's your tip in advance. Earn it."

En route to the airport, Fancy drove by her mother's new home but they didn't have time to go inside, which was okay because Caroline had toured it during the open house. Using valet parking at Oakland International, they flew the early afternoon flight to L.A. Upon their arrival, the driver was waiting, holding a sign that read: Caroline Taylor. Fancy called Darius from the car. "Hey, baby. Where are you?"

"In L.A."

"In L.A. where? I'm here, too. I have a surprise for you."

"You'd better learn to call ahead, woman. I'm at home. Baines is at my home, too."

"You sure know how to ruin a surprise."

"I'm sorry, baby. Come on over."

Knowing how predatory men were, Fancy was glad she hadn't slept with Baines. He hadn't given her any more deals but she'd gotten what she needed from him and figured Baines would make some other attractive young realtor the next millionaire. Caroline sat daydreaming out the window so Fancy left her mother deep in thought.

The driver parked in Darius's driveway. "Wait right here," Fancy instructed. "Ma, you can wait in the car, we'll be right out."

Unlocking Darius's front door with the key he'd given her, Fancy went directly to the bedroom, removed her clothes, pushed Darius onto the bed, and began ripping off his clothes.

"Can I get a hello?" Darius asked.

"Hello, baby," Fancy said, mounting Darius.

Surrendering, Darius lay back with his hands clamped behind his head. "Hi, Ladycat. Do your thang, woman."

Squatting on Darius's dick, Fancy moaned, "Hi, Slugger," squeezing Darius's dick with her pussy. Miss Kitty immediately pulsated. "Don't hold back, baby. Cum with me, daddy. Rub my clit. She's on fire. Oh, yes." Fancy rotated her ass into Darius's pelvis, tightening all her muscles.

"*Aaawww,*" Darius hissed. "*Yeesss. Yeesss. Yeesss,*" thrusting his engorged head deep into Fancy's pussy pocket.

Fancy felt Darius's cum throbbing, soaking her inside. Leaning into his face, Fancy kissed Darius, and then said, "I love you, baby."

"I love you, too. But we have to start using condoms. Where's your mom?"

"Oh, shit! I forgot my mom is in the car outside."

Darius smiled. "You got a one-track mind, woman. Get up off the dick."

Hurrying to shower, Fancy dressed again. By the time she was ready, Darius was, too. Smiling as the driver opened the back door, Fancy's mother was curled on the back seat under a blanket asleep. "Let her sleep," Fancy suggested. "She's pregnant."

Frowning, Darius's eyes widened. "For real?" he mouthed.

Nodding, Fancy motioned for them to sit in the front with the driver. The driver parked in front of the office building where Jada, Wellington, and Darius's offices were located.

"You're taking me to see my mother or my father."

"Neither. So how's Darryl doing with handling your company?" Fancy asked Darius while waking her mother. "We're here."

Looking around, Caroline asked, "Where am I?"

"L.A., mom. Let's go."

Darius helped Caroline out of the car. "My dad loves the movie industry. Now, if we can only keep him from trying to cast himself in every major male role."

Arriving at the tenth floor, Fancy said, "Lean over so I can cover your eyes. Both of you."

The three of them took tiny steps along the hallway until Fancy reached her destination. Uncovering their eyes, she pointed toward the sign.

Darius and Caroline read the inscription on the gold business plate: Fancy Taylor Realty and Mortgage.

"Ladycat, that's great! This is you?" Darius asked, picking Fancy up and swinging her around.

"Oh, baby." Caroline smiled. "I'm so proud of you. You have your own business."

Fancy nodded. "Yes. And when you get your degree, you have an office job waiting for you."

"That's nice baby, but mama likes working at the bar."

"So where're you going to live?" Darius asked.

Fancy batted her eyelashes.

Darius eyes widened. "You're moving in?"

Nodding again, Fancy said, "Yes, I am."

Sternly, with his deepest voice, Darius said, "That's not how you move in. We have to talk about this first."

"Ma, have a seat in my lobby." Fancy curled her pointing finger at Darius and said, "Oh, we're gonna talk all right." Grabbing Darius's hand, Fancy led him into her office, closed the door, kissed and licked Slugger to an erection, then sucked him, making Darius cum twice. After all the times Fancy had listened to Caroline, it was her mother's turn to listen. But Fancy had hoped that her mother had fallen asleep again.

CHAPTER 31

Yeah! The day Darius impatiently awaited had finally arrived. Not his wedding day. No boy-ie. Marrying Fancy could wait. Not for long but not tonight. Tonight, New York City, Madison Square Garden, the first round draft selection was going down!

Having arrived in New York two days prior to the draft, Darius had roamed every borough exhausting his nervous energy. He couldn't eat. Didn't sleep. His dad had traveled and hung with him nightly at Manhattan's clubs. Randomly Darryl had instructed the driver to stop at the various clubs he had frequented while balling. Darius had the best times with his dad. Pops still had it. Darryl had danced all night with women Darius's age, leaving the club early this morning around six when the sun was rising, leaving them nine hours to get ready for the event. After partying into the morning and then dropping Darryl off at the hotel, before Darius retired to his room, Darius had one more stop, to pick up Fancy.

"Sir, your party has arrived," the driver said, opening the limousine door.

"Oh my goodness," Darius mouthed, watching Ladycat stand on the curb at John F. Kennedy airport. Every baller had a beauty, some celebrity wives, but Darius had a queen and he'd planned on treating Fancy like royalty.

Fancy didn't like wearing pants on special occasions but insisted when flying, saying, "There's nothing sanitary about an airplane, not even in first class. People sneeze, breathe their germs, and fuck on the blankets." So Fancy always traveled with her own blanket. Her own sanitizers. Even her own toilet tissue. "People don't wash their hands after using the rest room but they don't hesitate to pass your drink from the flight attendant to you while cupping their fingers around the rim. Never let anyone other than the flight attendant touch your drink, and even then you're taking a chance because if the attendant washed her hands in the airplane rest room, that water is contaminated."

Grabbing Fancy's hips, Darius pulled her pussy close to his face. Fancy fingered his locks, meshing her breasts into his forehead, sending waves of pleasure throughout his entire body. Darius buried his nose between Fancy's thighs, inhaled, and then said, "Damn, you smell good. I miss you, baby. Come here let me hold you." Darius stood and hugged Fancy. They kissed, not caring who was watching or waiting.

On the limo ride back to the Ritz, Darius lay his head in Fancy's lap. Ladycat was so incredibly good to him. Unbeknownst to her, she made this day and every day, special.

Darius's mom and Wellington had arrived in New York a week ago to partake in his moment of honor but Darius hadn't seen them, nor did he want to see them, since they'd arrived. Wellington was up to something. Instantaneously, Wellington had adamantly changed his mind about getting a divorce and was being extra nice to Darius's mom. Maybe because Wellington surprisingly saw Darius step in as the man caring for his mom on a daily basis and his mom had eventually started going out with other men, including his Darryl, suddenly Wellington wanted back in. Suspiciously, Melanie had vanished but for how long was Darius's concern. Wellington could've stayed in Los Angeles. Darius hadn't invited him. His mom had.

When the limo driver opened the door, Darius kissed Fancy. "I love you, Ladycat. Thanks for coming."

"Wouldn't have missed this big moment for anything. I love you, too."

Did Fancy mean she loved him or was she simply responding in kind? Settling in their room, Fancy showered then slipped into sexy lingerie, a fuchsia lace see-through teddy with clear-heeled stilettos. "Relax, I'm going to do a celebration dance for you now and a victory dance on your face later."

With a woman like Fancy, Darius had no reason to be unfaithful. Fancy eased a CD into the player. Her hips swayed and dipped. Fancy kicked off her heels, first the right then the left, and stood on the coffee table holding her clit and teasing her nipple at the same time. Slugger sprang forth with his head protruding in search of Miss Kitty.

Licking her fingers, Fancy slowly moved her teddy aside, rubbed her shaft, and then whispered, "She missed you and she wants you." Unsnapping the crotch, her pointing finger curled, beckoning him. Fancy's eyes fixated on Darius's dick. Inhaling and exhaling rapidly, Darius moved closer.

Fancy guided her pussy toward Darius's lips. Gently Darius kissed and kissed again and again, then held his lips against Fancy's clit and inhaled as deeply as he could, then held his breath to savor the scent. Exhaling, his moist tongue filled the groove underneath the hood of Fancy's shaft, dancing and wiggling from Fancy's vaginal opening to her clit then back again. Dancing together, Darius kept pace with Fancy's movements. He licked and licked until Fancy aggressively grabbed the back of his head then thrust him closer. Tenderly suctioning the tip of her clit, drinking her juices, Darius grunted, "Uh. Um. Um. Um," moving his head.

Ladycat purred, "Ow. Mm-hmm. Ow, yes. Yes, baby. Oh, you make me feel so good."

The sound of Fancy's voice made Darius feel good. Darius suctioned in her shaft which was slightly shorter than the size of her pinky finger. In and out, in and out, Darius sucked. But not too hard and not too long, because the first time he'd done that to a woman her pussy blew up like a balloon and took days to deflate.

Fancy became more engorged. Her shaft throbbed in his mouth so Darius inserted his middle finger into her wet pussy, stroking in the same come-to-me motion she'd used moments ago. Kindly Darius pressed against her G-spot, finger-fucking her while taking all of her vaginal shaft into her mouth.

Ladycat danced on his finger and moaned until she finished fucking his hand. Easing off his finger, Fancy lowered her teddy straps, stepped off the table, and said, "I want you to fuck me, daddy. My pussy is so wet, hot, and ready for you. Damn, I'm still cumming."

Crawling onto the bed, Fancy kneeled on the edge, leaned forward, and spread her cheeks. Looking over her shoulder, she moaned, "Come and get her."

She didn't have to ask twice. Circling his plump head around her drooling pussy, Darius slid his dick halfway in. Fancy backed up on the other half and yelled, "Fuck me, Darius! You've got your pussy all hot and shit, don't tease me, baby. Fuck me good."

From zero to sixty Darius gave his woman what she'd requested, stroking deep, fast, and hard. Miss Kitty grabbed his shaft and held on for a ride that would last well over an hour.

Showering together, they laughed like children while dressing in their finest clothes. Darius stepped into his designer suit pants and eased into his tailored shirt. Placing his tie around his neck, Fancy said, "Let me tie that for you."

"You don't know how to do a tie, woman."

Meticulously, Fancy eye-measured the distance for both layers, smoothed her hand over the tie, then wrapped, looped, and tucked the knot better than he could. "There." Then she fastened his cuff links, held his jacket until he slid both arms inside, and buttoned his top button.

"You sure know how to spoil a guy," Darius said, thinking about Mandy's comments. Darius retrieved Fancy's spaghetti-strapped white pearl dress, slipped it over her head, zipped up the side, then eased on her shoes, buckling the straps. Choosing a perfume of his choice, Darius dabbed it behind Fancy's ears, then glided the tip between her breasts.

Darius proudly escorted Fancy to the limousine and said, "Thanks, baby. I feel so good."

Sitting inside, she said, "Me, too."

Darius held her in his arms all the way to Madison Square Garden. The last time Darius was at the Garden was years ago, when he was executive vice president of Black Diamonds. Now

Darius had his very own gem lying in his arms. Polished. Flawless. Perfect for him.

As they entered the Square, turning heads, Darius walked straight to the table, not wanting any other man to feast off of Fancy's glowing energy and bubbling personality. Mom, Wellington, and Darryl were already seated with his mother in the middle, preventing Darius from sitting next to her.

"Hi, Mom, Dad, Wellington," Darius said, sitting next to Darryl.

"You just made it on time, son. I thought they were going to start without you. Hello, princess," Darryl said.

"Hello, Mrs. Tanner, Mr. Williams, and Mr. Jones," Fancy said, following Darius's lead.

The commentator announced, "With the first pick in the NBA Draft, the Los Angeles Lakers pick . . ."

Fuck! Darius thought, immediately disappointed that he hadn't been selected by L.A. Having been labeled and treated like a celebrity in his hometown, Darius wanted to stay local. Especially since Fancy had opened her office in Los Angeles.

Ladycat held his hand. Darius wanted her to let go because his stomach was knotting up, forcing his bowels into his rectal canal. Darius needed to relieve himself but couldn't move, scared he'd miss his name being called, but also afraid that if he didn't go to the rest room, he'd have a childlike accident.

"With the sixteenth pick in the NBA Draft, New Orleans pick . . ."

"This is bullshit. I'll be back," Darius whispered, rising from his seat.

Darryl placed his hand on Darius's shoulder. "Patience, son. Your turn will come."

"When? They've called everyone except me. I've gotta go to the rest room, Dad. My stomach is killing me."

Removing his hand from Darius's shoulder, Darryl said, "Hurry back."

Walking swiftly toward the exit, Darius heard, "With the seventeenth pick in the NBA Draft, Atlanta picks Darius Williams from the University of California at Los Angeles."

Curling his fingers into a fist, Darius swung his elbow along his side until his fist aligned with his ribs and said, "Yes."

Tightening his butt cheeks, Darius strolled up to the podium, smiling as he was handed a cap with an "Atlanta" patch across the top. "The first person I want to praise is God. Then I give thanks for my deceased grandmother, Ma Dear. My mom, Jada Diamond Tanner. I want to thank my dad, Darryl Williams, my coaches at UCLA and the coaches at Atlanta, and last but not least my stepfather, Wellington Jones, and my fiancée, Fancy Taylor."

After relieving himself, Darius enjoyed hearing the remaining Draft selections. After his offstage interviews, Darius returned to their table. Everyone was smiling except Ladycat.

Whispering in her ear, Darius asked, "What's wrong?"

Fancy shook her head. Tears streamed down her cheeks so Darius dabbed her face with his handkerchief, tucking the initials DL under her fingers. With a half smile, she whispered, "Atlanta?"

Before Darius responded, his cell phone rang. Glancing at Ashlee's name on the ID, Darius excused himself from the table, walked into the lobby, and then answered, "Hey, Ashlee. Everything okay?"

"Yeah, I just called to congratulate you on your selection and your engagement."

"Thanks. I really mean that. How are you?"

"Just missing you. Darius, we had so much together." Ashlee starting crying. "Darius, I love you."

"Ashlee, please don't do this to me. Not now. I have enough on my mind right now."

"Promise me that before you get married, you'll come and visit me. I want you to visit our son's grave with me."

Why in the fuck did Ashlee have to bring up such sad shit during one of the happiest moments of his life? Darius pressed his thumb and middle finger into his eyes, forcing back tears. Nothing was more painful than losing his son. He'd only held the lil' man once. He was so tiny and so precious. And Darius thought he'd gotten over Ashlee, but damn, since they were kids, they'd been through everything together.

"Huuhhh." Opening his eyes, Fancy stood in front of him. Darius sniffled into the phone, saying, "I promise. I gotta go," then hung up.

"What did she want?" Fancy questioned, drying her tears.

"Why are you crying, Ladycat?" Darius asked.

Hugging Darius, Fancy said, "Because when you hurt, I hurt. What did she want?"

Since Darius and Fancy had agreed to be honest with one another, quietly gasping for air, Darius said, "Me. She wants me."

CHAPTER 32

All any mother wanted was the best for her child and since Darius was drafted into the NBA in the first round, Jada was elated. Despite all her problems and each of her concerns, Jada had so much to be grateful for. Her loyal employees like Zen, who could've quit or gotten fired after fucking Darius. Zen had become the person who ran her office daily, making sound decisions. Jada's phone rang nonstop from clients and friends with congratulatory comments and requests for NBA game tickets. Jada's best friend Candice wanted courtside seats. Jada wasn't even guaranteed seats that close. The day after Darius was drafted, stock in Black Diamonds increased thirty percent.

Hopefully, with his new career and with his fiancée Fancy, Darius would truly find happiness. Jada forgave herself for lying to Darius, Darryl, Wellington, and herself. And gave herself credit for the things she'd done well. Exceptionally well.

If only Jada had told Darius that Darryl was his father and Wellington wasn't, everyone's lives would've been better. Who knew? Perhaps if Jada had told the truth, Darius would've never gone pro. But then again Wellington probably wouldn't have married her, or perhaps he wouldn't have had an affair with someone she despised. What if Jada hadn't had the ménage a trois with Wellington and Melanie? Then Melanie would be just another woman. But she wasn't. Although Melanie was no longer Wellington's woman, during their affair Wellington hadn't been discreet about his feelings for Melanie or their relationship. Life was filled with what-ifs.

The great accomplishments Jada had made weren't predicated upon what-ifs. Jada had been a damn good mother to Darius, a wonderful wife to Wellington, and treated Darryl with respect when he didn't deserve it. Darryl walked into Darius's life after being absent for over twenty years and all of a sudden he was a hero. A saint who could do no wrong. Where was Darryl when Darius was sick? When Darius almost committed suicide when he thought he'd contracted HIV? Or when Darius almost had an emotional breakdown when Ma Dear died? Not another day would Jada Diamond Tanner feel guilty for living her life. She didn't owe anybody anything. Maybe she wasn't perfect, but hell, neither were they.

Sitting in the doctor's office with Wellington waiting for his test results, Jada glanced at her husband. His face was tense, jaws tight, eyes half closed.

"Everything is gonna be all right. Stop worrying. You had a checkup and they want to make sure you're fine," Jada said, gently holding her husband's hand.

Why did a woman have to be so strong for her men? Why was she the one always caring for everybody else? Who would take care of her in her time of illness or need? Jada wanted to cry but reserved her strength for Wellington.

"But what if I have to have surgery? What if I can't have sex anymore after the surgery? Or if making love to me isn't the same?"

Wellington had an epiphany when Melanie inexplicably stopped calling and visiting him. He'd thought that Jada had something to do with Melanie's disappearance but Melanie wasn't worth Jada's effort.

"I can love you ways you haven't imagined," Jada said, kissing Wellington's lips. If she'd kissed his cheek, he wouldn't have believed her. "Lots of men have prostrate cancer and recover just fine. You'll be all right. But I have to ask you, did you ask me not to divorce you because you thought your test might confirm that the doctors found cancer?"

After Wellington was told he might have cancer, living alone and dating strange women after working twelve to eighteen-hour days, Wellington wanted to come home to someone he knew cared about him. Melanie obviously thrived on the chase and once she had him, she disappeared. Or did Melanie know something that Jada did not?

Staring at the gray carpet underneath his feet, Wellington avoided looking in Jada's direction. "I've asked myself the same question and the answer is no. I love you. We've been through so much together. No woman can replace you."

"Then why the affair, Wellington? Why did you have to do this to us?" This time Jada was unable to hold back her tears.

Wellington had begged Jada not to sign the divorce papers, and he'd readily given Darius his thirty-three-and-a-third interest in Somebody's Gotta Be on Top. The emptiness of memories floating through every room they'd made love in, the loneliness of their bed, the still silence of their home filled only with the sounds of televisions or CDs or the radio, wasn't a routine Jada wanted to become accustomed to.

"Ba, I'm so sorry. I didn't mean to hurt you."

That was a lie. Wellington wouldn't have sided with Melanie every time they had an argument. "Yes, you did. I was the one who didn't mean to hurt you."

"You're right," Wellington conceded. "You're always right."

"Do not pacify me, Wellington Jones." Jada said, "Damn, I wish you had a middle name." Jada laughed, but not really. She wanted to continue their discussion but Wellington was already stressed.

"You're beautiful when you get upset, you know—"

The nurse interrupted, "The doctor will see you now, Mr. Jones."

Slowly Wellington stood. His heart sunk deeper into the carpet than his shoes. Jada walked side by side with her husband and sat next to him in the doctor's office.

"Hello, Mrs. Tanner. Mr. Jones," the doctor said, opening

Wellington's chart. "Mr. Jones, I'll get straight to my diagnosis. Your prostate cancer is no longer localized. You now have advanced prostate cancer in your lymph nodes in the groin area and your rectum, and if untreated the cancer could spread to your bones and become very painful. If you had had the surgery when I recommended it two years ago, we could've removed your prostate and you wouldn't be in this condi—"

"Excuse me, Doctor. Wellington, you've known about this for two years and didn't tell me? Honey, why?" That's why Wellington had such difficulty maintaining an erection.

"Scared. Still scared to go under a knife."

"Mr. Jones, if you don't have the surgery, you could die. We have a team of fantastic urologists and radiation and medical oncologists for you to consult with to determine the best approach. I can't make the decision for you but—"

"But I can," Jada interrupted. "And I will. You're not going to leave me here, Wellington. I love you. And I need you." Jada thought back to when Wellington began having his affair with Melanie two years ago. Did Melanie know Wellington had cancer?

The doctor continued, "But we'd like to admit you today. Right now. And begin preparing you for surgery in the morning."

Leaning his bald head into his palms, Wellington wept like a baby. "Why me? I watch what I eat. I exercise." Wellington yelled, "Why in the fuck did this have to happen to me?" Wellington pushed back his chair, stood, and said, "Sorry, Doc. I can't let you cut on me down there." Looking at his dick, he continued, "I'm not having the surgery."

The doctor remained seated and said, "It's perfectly normal to be afraid. I had prostate surgery last year. I can't promise you a successful outcome. But let me make myself clear. If you don't have the surgery, the cancer will continue to spread and you are going to die."

Wellington responded to the doctor as if Jada weren't in the room. "We're all going to die, Doc. Good-bye."

Following Wellington out of the hospital and into the parking lot, Jada pleaded, "Baby, have the surgery. Choose life, not death. I need you. And you know I'll be with you the entire time."

"Unlock the car. Let me in. Or I'll call my driver," Wellington said, retrieving his cell phone.

Driving along Interstate 5, tears streamed down Jada's and Wellington's faces. Why were men so stubborn, bullheaded, and selfish? Was she supposed to take care of Wellington? Watching him deteriorate and decompose. Waste to nothing. Die slowly in her presence. Jada refused to give up on convincing her husband to have surgery. There was so much more to their lives than sex. They had love. What did love have to do with anything? Everything. Life without her soul mate, Jada did not want to imagine.

CHAPTER 33

D ressed in his tuxedo, Darius roamed throughout his house searching for the keys to his L.A. home. Peeping out the window, the limousine driver was parked in his circular driveway.

"Where are my damn keys?" Darius grunted, lifting the newspaper on his breakfast table. "This is bullshit!" Marrying Fancy was what Darius wanted but Ciara hadn't signed the divorce papers. And there was no way he was going back to jail.

Darius had no male friends so a few of his NBA teammates had agreed on short notice to stand in his wedding. All the guests his mother invited—her clients, her staff, her former staff, Ginger, Heather, and a few other women Darius had fucked—were probably seated in the first, second, and third pews. Certain Ciara would agree to his divorce terms after he'd promised to help her raise her son, Darius had encouraged Darryl to invite all of the guys Darryl played with in the NBA, their wives, and a few head coaches. Mom had said Wellington probably wouldn't be at the wedding, but didn't say why. Wasn't that some shit? Darius knew exactly why. Now that Wellington was terminally ill, he wanted Darius's mom to take care of him.

If Darius married Ladycat before divorcing Ciara, his acting as though he was divorced would hit the paper before he signed the marriage license. Darius Jones arrested for bigamy. No way. Fancy would have to wait. If she loved him today, she'd still love him to-morrow.

Exiting into his garage, Darius sat in his car pondering a desti-nation. With so much on his mind, this wasn't a good time for Darius to drive. Walking back into his home, Darius tossed his car keys on the kitchen table, leaving his home keys and cellular in his pockets, and exited the front door.

Hurrying to open the back door, the driver smiled. "Good morning, sir. It's a beautiful day to get married. She sure is a lucky woman."

Quietly Darius settled into the backseat and instructed the driver, "Take me to Oakland."

"But sir, the wedding is here in Los Angeles."

"I'm not getting married today. Take me to Oakland."

"Certainly, sir." The driver merged onto Interstate 5 North. "Do you want to talk about it?"

"Man, talking isn't going to resolve my problems. I need to think." Darius loosened his black wingtip collar trimmed in gold, stretched his long legs across the backseat, and lay his head on the black leather cushion.

Two stops for gas and six hours later, Darius stood in front of Skates Restaurant in Berkeley. Bypassing the entrance, he contin-ued his journey. Momentarily he stopped watching the ocean water splash upon the huge slime-covered boulders. The pier adja-cent to Skates was sparsely scattered with fishermen.

"This is bullshit," Darius mumbled. Clump. Clump. Clump. Slowly Darius strolled, his heels banging every other wooden plank until he reached the end of the pier. Why was his life so bitter-sweet? A year and six months had passed since he'd met Fancy. Darius laughed internally. What a rollercoaster adventure. That woman was truly amazing. Beautiful inside and out. They had so much in common. Their loneliness, desires, need to be loved by someone who truly cared.

Darius looked out over the ocean. Yachts. Sailboats. Sunshine. The eighty degrees of sunshine convinced Darius to remove his tuxedo coat and hang it over the rail.

"Fuck!" Darius yelled over the waves splashing underneath the pier. "Man, you had to leave Los Angeles. Otherwise, you know you would've taken the vows." Darius whispered, "I love you, Fancy." For the first time, Darius was deeply in love. And it hurt not to be at that church taking vows he had every intention to keep. It felt like someone had stabbed him in his heart with disappointment continuously turning the pain over and over. Tears welled in his eyes.

When his cellular rang, Darius inhaled deeply, debating on whether to answer Fancy's call. The last one hundred and twenty-two calls all went to voice mail. His mom. Dad. Teammates. Darius wanted to press the TALK button and tell Fancy where he was but his fingers wouldn't follow his brain's command. Fancy's name disappeared, adding one more missed call to his screen. One twenty-three. Twenty-three. His new NBA jersey number. The number of days his son had lived. "God, why me?" Darius softly cried.

After Fancy's call went to voice mail, Darius recorded an outgoing message. "This is Darius. Due to an unexpected emergency, I won't be getting married today. If someone could give my mother, my family, and everyone else at the wedding this message or have them call and listen to this message, I'd appreciate it. I apologize for the inconvenience." Darius hung up right before a wave of tears poured down his cheeks. Hopefully Fancy would forgive him.

Spreading his arms wide, Darius yelled across the Pacific Ocean, "I love you, Fancy Taylor."

"I love you, too, Darius Jones," sounded from behind him.

Darius's legs froze. Had he lost his mind? He must've been hearing things. Turning his upper torso, his feet remained planted. There she stood. His beautiful bride was dressed in the most elaborate gold gown. Fancy was more beautiful than he'd envisioned her walking down that aisle into his arms.

"Ladycat, what are you doing here? You're supposed to be in Los Angeles."

"I wasn't surprised to see you here, Darius. We're two of a kind. I realized I'm not ready for marriage. And I can't give myself to you until I can give you all of me. I have to work on myself. My guilt about Thaddeus. My relationship with my mother is better but we still have a lot of healing to do. Both of us. And her baby, which you know I promised to take care of. I never thought about my mother's childhood. She's trying to overcome some horrible things that happened to her. And her parents never told her they loved her so she didn't know how to love me. Just like I'm not sure if I know how to love me. Or you. But my mom and I are healing togeth—"

Darius's eyebrows grew closer as he interrupted, "But I need you, Ladycat. I don't want to deal with these groupies jocking me all the time. I want you to be my wife. The real reason I didn't show up at the church was . . ." Darius hesitated then continued, "I didn't know how to tell you, Ciara didn't sign the divorce papers. I can't afford to become a bigamist. Don't need the bad press. And damn sure 'nuff don't need to get locked up again."

"Divorce papers? You're already married and you never told me? I love you. The funny thing is, part of the reason I didn't show up was because I wasn't sure that you were ready for a wife. And I'm not going to settle for less than all of you. Darius, I don't care about a piece of paper. I don't need a license to show you how much I love you. For the first time in my life, I'm in love. And Darius Jones, I'm in love with you."

"I'm sorry, Ladycat. I didn't think I had to tell you. I just knew Ciara would sign the papers. Especially after the paternity test showed I wasn't the father of her child."

"Darius, I don't believe you." Fancy threw her veil into the ocean. "Ciara's baby could've been yours. Desire's baby could've been yours. And Ashlee's baby was yours."

"I told you my life was complicated. But I've learned my lesson."

"No, you haven't, Darius. I'm pregnant. And there's no question that this baby I'm carrying inside of me is yours."

Darius swooped Fancy off of her feet and into his arms. Swinging her around, Darius yelled, "Ladycat, are you sure?!"

"Yes, I'm positive."

Twirling Fancy until he became dizzy, Darius said, "Ladycat, you have made me the happiest man in the world! I love you, woman. I hope it's a boy. You know how much I've suffered every day with the loss of my son."

"I know. And you know how much I suffered with the abortion

of my child. We both need somebody to love other than ourselves. I couldn't walk down that aisle without you knowing. And now that we're pregnant, I love you even more, Darius."

"It feels good hearing you say you love me. And I'm going to do right by you."

Fancy placed her finger over Darius's lips. "Let's just take life one day at time. How's that?"

Darius smiled then kissed Fancy. "Perfect. For the first time in my life, my life is perfect."

Easing out of Darius's arms, Fancy jumped on his back. "Let's go."

Hopping all the way back to the limo, Darius gave Fancy a bouncy piggy-back ride. Arriving in front of Skates, Darius hopped then stopped. The homeless woman sat on a bench by the limousine brushing her wig.

Darius froze as he silently heard the words, "Death follows you."

"Not her again," Fancy said, sliding off of Darius's back.

Darius loved Fancy so much, but he'd rather be without her than to have her follow in his shadow of death. What about their unborn child?

"This is the beginning of the ending for both of you. A few more hurdles and you're there. Always stand in your own truth with yourselves and one another. Fancy, don't forget to continue giving your love to your mother, too. Darius, one dark shadow lingers. Your father will need you before he passes away. Your mother needs you right now. Make the right choice. Merry Christmas."

Settling in the backseat of the limousine, Darius kissed Ladycat and said, "I love you," then powered on his cellular and dialed his mother.

Crying, his mother answered, "Darius, honey, I need—"

"I already know, Mom. I'm on my way."

As Darius's finger curled toward the END button, an incoming call from Ashlee appeared. Darius looked at Fancy as she stared at his caller ID.

"Answer it," Fancy insisted.

Pressing the TALK button, Darius said, "Hello."

"Darius, this is Ashlee."

"I know who it is. What's up? Why are you calling me on my wedding day?"

"I need to tell you something and, well, I didn't want you to think I was trying to ruin your wedding but you need to know. And if you would've come to visit our son's grave, I would've told you then."

"Ashlee, stop playing games. I gotta go. 'Bye."

"Darius, wait, "Ashlee pleaded in a trembling voice. "Please don't hang up."

The more Fancy stared at him, the more frustrated Darius had become. Yelling at Ashlee, Darius screamed, "What? Ashlee! What the fuck is it?"

Crying, Ashlee softly said, "You remember how I never told you the cause of our son's death?"

Darius stopped breathing. The last thing he wanted to think about was death. "Ashlee, why? Why now? Why are you doing this to me?"

"I'm sorry. I never wanted to hurt you. And no matter what, I love you. But you need to know."

Exhaling, Darius softly said, "Then tell me."

Crying, Ashlee said, "Our son, Darius Junior, died from HIV complications."

"And you?" Darius whispered.

Sniffling, Ashlee said, "Positive."

The numbness in Darius's body caused the cellular phone to slip from between his fingers.

Picking up the phone, Fancy questioned Ashlee. "What did you tell him?" Fancy looked at the phone, then said, "Hello? Hello?" Staring at Darius, Fancy began crying along with him. She muttered, "She hung up. Please tell me. What did she say?"

Banging his face against the limo window, Darius stared at the bench where the homeless woman sat only moments ago. *Death follows you,* echoed in his mind repeatedly.

Was his HIV test, taken years ago, a false negative?

AUTHOR'S MESSAGE

There'll be no need for me to write an autobiography before I die. Death is inevitable, so periodically I'll continue to share personal experiences of my life with my readers. The main reason I feel compelled to share is I know many of you have similar encounters and I'd rather have you know the real me as opposed to imagining that my world, my life, is ideal. Throughout my struggles, I stay positive and I love myself first, knowing that I am loved by God, judged by many, accountable to few, if any. I don't shrink to let others shine but I do enjoy helping those who help themselves.

Family unity is crucial to the upbringing and development of our youth. I have to ask, "Who's loving you? Who's loving the children? Who's listening? Who's investing quality time? And who's making love as opposed to having sex?" We become so consumed with daily tasks that often we forget to live, and more importantly we neglect to let the ones we love live their lives for themselves. Love begets love.

If it weren't for my great aunt and uncle, Ella Beatrice Turner and Willie Frinkle, I'd know not the journey I've traveled. They reared my brothers Wayne and Derrick, my stepbrother Bryan, and me. Although I have four sisters, I didn't grow up in the same household with them. But we are so close that if we didn't tell anyone our story, they'd never suspect that our parents pawned us off to relatives in exchange for their . . . freedom, I suppose.

My biological father was more like a friend of the family who visited us for a few hours twice a year, usually once during the summer and again at Christmas, to say hello, give us a few dollars, and occasionally take us shopping. Sadly enough, those few hours spent made him a hero to us and we longed for next time to lay eyes upon our father, while taking for granted our aunt and uncle who provided food, clothing, and shelter, sent us to the best public schools, and loved us the best way they knew how.

When I asked my father as he lay in his hospital bed in January 1991, dying of stomach cancer, why he hadn't raised us, he simply replied, "Bea, at the time you do what you think is best and if you live long enough you'll see how you could've done better." He continued, "I should've followed my first mind and sent all of you— your sisters and brothers—to live on this farm down in Texas with this family like I started to." I thought to myself, "No way in hell would I have lived on a farm probably working like a slave for nobody."

Oh well, after I was grown and relocated from New Orleans to Oakland, Daddy visited me three times a year. I guess a few memories are better than none at all. I knew his love and attempt to love us were genuine and I cherish the memories as I often share the good ones with my son, Jesse. In spirit, my son Jesse has fond memories of his Papa Joe although he was too young to remember the transition.

My biological mother was a complete stranger; I vividly remember spending only three precious moments in her presence. I can still see the pastel pink cardigan sweater she wore over a summer dress with sandals while walking me through the Magnolia projects in New Orleans to kindergarten class at Edgar P. Hornet. I can't visualize the colors of her dress but I can see the material swaying below her knees over her thick red calves. Everyone called Mama "Red" because of her fair skin. So if you're light-complected, and you're visiting in N'awlins and someone says, "Hey, Red," they're talking to you.

Anyway, the next time I saw my mother I recall myself running away from Great Aunt's home when I was eight years old. I walked down Magnolia Street to Washington Avenue to the 'Nolia projects that the rappers rap about, up the back fire escape, and knocked on my mother's door. I don't even think she realized I was in her one-bedroom apartment. My younger sister Margie and I sat in the living room. Mom was in the bedroom the entire time. After several hours, as the sun began to set, I thought I'd better get back home before they missed me. I was scared walking through the projects but by the grace of God, He made my way safely back to the house with the pink porch on the corner of First and Magnolia.

The final time I was in my mother's presence, I'm not sure if she was in mine. The coffin sat in a chillingly cold funeral parlor on Drydes Street. My mother was separated from me by one row of folding chairs. Sitting next to my then-ten-year-old brother Derrick, I forced tears down my nine-year-old cheeks, afraid others would think I didn't love Mommy if I didn't cry. Truth was my hopes and endless dreams of experiencing motherly love were buried right along with my mother. Many years later I would accidentally find my mother's death certificate. The cause of death documented was toxic overdose. I believe, fed up with my father's chronic physical abuse, birthing eight, some say nine, children, burying my then baby sister Elizabeth, struggling in poverty, constantly relocating state to state as far north as New York to escape the madness, my mother checked out of this world like many others, simply tired of longing to belong, longing to be loved.

How can folk one day lay together making love or having sex, create in unison another life, then hate or abuse one another? I'll never forget hearing my father say he was glad my mother was dead. I said, "Daddy, I don't feel that way." Wow, some folk are unforgiving even after death.

Looking back, in many ways I believe my father killed my mother's spirit long before she stopped breathing. But perhaps my father's mother was to blame, forcing him from her bosom and sending him to be raised by her sister. The same sister who raised us. And while I am grateful not to have experienced Texas, I still grew up in a household where the words "I love you" were unspoken. Not one single time.

But now I know that my great aunt and uncle, although they never told us, loved us dearly. How many people get up every day, go to work for white folk, and come home to raise four children, none of their own? That was pure love. And I am grateful to have had them.

If you choose love today, choose love tomorrow, because you always have a choice. With love, everyone can find his or her way through this unpredictable journey of peaks and valleys, successes and tragedies, called life.

I'm not sure if most parents these days realize that loving their kids and "being present" in a child's life has a significant impact on the child's future. Don't talk at, but talk with your children. Every day, many times a day, my son and I say "I love you" to one another. We say it with feeling and each time the words are spoken they come from the heart, accompanied by hugs and/or kisses.

Remember who's the parent and who's the child. Don't expect the child to take the initiative to cultivate the relationship because children don't ask to be here. If you're separated, divorced, or living together, don't expect the other parent to facilitate a healthy bond between you and your child. Both parents are equally responsible for their child or children. Individuals who decide to have children must accept the obligation to rear the child in a healthy loving environment. Even if that environment requires two households.

Chances are you, too, have longed to be loved by your parents or a mate who invested little or no time in you. What could you have done to cultivate a loving relationship? Despite the negative things that may have happened to you, what are you thankful for?

I thank God for my guardian angels, my great aunt and uncle who made my life possible, thus allowing me to, I pray to God, fulfill my greater humanitarian purpose. To love my son and family unconditionally and share written words that will hopefully improve the way we as individuals love and respect one another. One person who cares can have a lifetime's positive impact in the life of another human being. One hug. One kiss. One love. One day at a time.

What will you do today to make someone else's life better tomorrow?

NOTHING HAS EVER FELT LIKE THIS

MARY B. MORRISON

ABOUT THIS GUIDE

The suggested questions are intended to enhance
your group's reading of this book
by Mary B. Morrison.

DISCUSSION QUESTIONS

1. How do you know when you're in love? Does Darius love Fancy? Does Fancy love Darius? Are Jada and Wellington in love? Who taught you how to love? What is your definition of love?

2. Do you feel Darius should tell Fancy he might be HIV positive before he takes a test? Why? Do you think Ashlee was HIV positive and didn't know it? Kevin? When was the last time you were tested?

3. Are some individuals incapable of loving anyone? Did Caroline ever try to love Fancy? Was Caroline jealous of Fancy? Or was Fancy jealous of her mother? Do you know any parents who are envious of their children?

4. Did Thaddeus really want to kill Fancy? Was Fancy responsible for Thaddeus's incarceration? What if Thaddeus hadn't physically abused Caroline? Was Thaddeus responsible for his own demise? Have you ever wrongfully accused anyone?

5. Should Thaddeus be angry at Caroline for agreeing to have an abortion, keeping the money he'd given her to have the abortion, but changing her mind without telling him? Should Jada have aborted her husband's child without telling Lawrence? Do you think Jada was pregnant for Lawrence? What percentage of control should a woman have when deciding to have an abortion? Why?

6. Have you ever loved someone so much that you were willing to die for him/her or commit suicide or homicide?

7. Was Wellington justified in having an affair with Melanie for years? What about when Jada had an affair with Wellington during her marriage to Lawrence? Do you believe that cer-

tain behavioral traits are unbreakable? Once a cheater, always a cheater?

8. Did Mandy's termination of Fancy's sessions help or hurt Fancy? How? Was Mandy wrong for not allowing Fancy to continue her therapy? Should Fancy have hired another therapist?

9. Will Fancy marry Darius or Desmond? Why?

10. Will Darius marry Ashlee or Fancy? Why?

11. If Darius is HIV positive, how many individuals, directly and indirectly, do you estimate he could've infected? Do you believe that Darius will be spared once more from having HIV? Or does Darius deserve to have HIV?

12. Have you ever said "I love you" to someone because you felt obligated? Do you think you've been told those three words by a person who really didn't love you? The next time you say "I love you, too," think before you speak. The response has become so automatic that the words have become meaningless. Remember, meanings are in people, not in words.

13. Did the homeless woman truly have a gift from God to forecast Darius's and Fancy's future? Do you believe in psychics? Have you ever met a stranger who accurately predicted your future?

AUTHOR'S NOTE

My answer to the last discussion question is, yes, I have been given accurate predictions of my future. Twice. Once in 2000 in Detroit, Michigan, at a book conference, and again in Oakland. I did not and do not know these women nor did I ask them to tell me anything. But the first woman volunteered, never asked me for a dime, and she was accurate. My ex-husband owed me thousands of dollars in back child support. He could've opted to pay an additional $100 a month until he was paid in full or send one lump sum. Well, at the time I needed the lump sum. This woman told me, "Someone owes you restitution. And you're worried about if you're going to get it. Don't worry. It's already taken care of." When I got home from the conference, my $7,000 check from my ex-husband was in the mail.

She said so many other things that were amazing and true but I'll share just one more thing. She said, "You've never had hard times. But you will." All of my adult life I've always financially maintained my household and helped others. In 2002, all of it, the entire year, you hear me, I was at the mercy of my family and friends. My car was repossessed, I was almost evicted, I sold my home, and I had to work at Best Buy and 24 Hour Fitness just to feed my child, and trust me, we couldn't maintain our lifestyle off of minimum wage. I didn't even know what minimum wage was. Honestly. But the Kees of Kees Realty loaned me $7,000, my play-mom Barbara Cooper $3,600, my sister Andrea $2,000, my sister Regina $2,000, Gail Fred, who could've evicted me, didn't, and so forth. My girlfriend Carmen Polk said to me, "I don't know why you're complaining. You still live in that expensive-ass apartment, your son is still in private school, you got your Lexus, y'all eat every day. Mary, you haven't lost a thing." She was right. So I interpreted my lesson from God as "people need people." Before 2002 I never knew what it felt like to truly need anybody. I wouldn't give back that year in exchange for anything. Because I now know what it feels like to need somebody; therefore, I have a *greater* appreciation for all individuals irrespective of social status or income. In the midst of adversity, never forget to give thanks and count your blessings.

The second woman asked for ten dollars and thus far some of what she said has come to pass. She said, "Before the end of the week, there will be a tragedy. Don't become consumed with the problem. If you don't do anything else I tell you, take a yoga class this week." I was like, "You sure? Everything in my life is fine." But I had nothing to lose by taking a class. I'm already a member at Club One so I went to yoga on Thursday, and on Friday the family tragedy occurred. A suicide attempt. Thanks to her advice, I was the calmest family member throughout the situation, and thereby was able to peacefully console my sibling. She also said, "You'll receive a promotion. January. February. I can't see what." Again I said, "You sure? I work for myself." Well, January and February 2005, I was, thanks to all of you, #1 on the *Essence* bestsellers list. Some of this psychic's other predictions have come to pass, as well. And although I honestly believe some individuals possess the gift of sight, I don't suggest you seek them. If it's meant for you to meet a psychic, my personal belief is they will reveal themselves to you.

The following are sample chapters from
Mary B. Morrison's eagerly anticipated upcoming novel
WHEN SOMEBODY LOVES YOU BACK.

It will be available in August 2006, wherever
hardcover books are sold.

PROLOGUE

ABlack woman did it all . . . because she had to. She did it all and she did it well, caring for others while neglecting herself. Four hundred and fifty years of birthing babies for White masters and Black slaves sold off to the highest bidder leaving her to raise her children all alone. Four hundred fifty plus years struggling for freedom, while Black men died for what they seemingly couldn't live with today, dignity.

Whose fault was that?

If only a man could teach a boy how to become a man, then the question was rhetorical. If the Black woman birthed the Black man, raised the Black man, loved the Black man she gave life to, then when did the Black man begin disrespecting the Black woman, replacing her birth name with "bitch"?

Bitch. Bastard. Incontestably the Black man could win at one thing; throwing a boomerang. The Black man's life would forever remain incomplete until he learned how to love and respect the Black woman. Good or bad—what he believed was golden—a dick didn't mean shit when the Black man chose not to give back to the Black woman what she'd freely given unto him. Unconditional love. Respect. Devotion.

Freedom came with a price, and now that the Black woman could choose her mate, her fate was the same leaving her to take on more responsibility than she should, but not more than she could, so she carried on doing all she could do, the best she knew how. It's been proven that if one tried to do everything, they'd risk doing nothing well.

After dropping off the kids, working nine-to-five and then sometimes five-to-nine, picking up the kids, cooking dinner, changing diapers, checking homework, and lying down for a four-should-be-eight-hours rest, did the Black woman have any quantitative time to invest in her children's future? If she made time, did she have any quality time for herself? If the mother was unhealthy, the children were unhealthy too.

When the alarm clock sounded, the next day was a replica of yesterday and seemed like the groundhog saw its shadow every day because each tomorrow for the next eighteen years plus brought sorrows that would make demands of the Black woman to carry on humming the same old hymn . . . "I won't complain."

Who would take care of the Black woman while she sacrificed to rear her kids, pay the bills, and all too often, slept alone at night wondering if her direct deposit would post in time to keep the lights on or to balance her checkbook the day before payday to restock the refrigerator before emptying the cabinets or feeding her children the last few slices of bread while she watched them eat?

The Black woman didn't need anybody's empathy. She was a survivor by nature. The Mother of Jesus, many denied the undeniable, but what the Black woman fell short of was an epiphany: a lesson in how to love herself first and to stop stressing about not knowing if her baby daddy—daddies—would ever show up at their children's events, parent-teacher conferences, if he'd ever pay her child support, and ultimately to stop worrying about whom he had sex with when he wasn't loving her, that was, if he'd ever loved her.

Love, or the lack thereof, based on his mother's mistakes, Darius reluctantly admitted to himself, what most men at some point in their lives experienced, that he was terrified of two things: falling in love and failure. No one had taught him how to attain one while avoiding the other. Either would render him vulnerable. Destroy his character. Ultimately strip him of his manhood.

A man in love was weak for his woman. Would do anything for

his woman. The more he would give the more control she'd want. Darius didn't want to be hard on women; he had to. The cold, callous, careless, arrogant, inconsiderate, selfish person ruling his existence, primarily with his dick, wasn't him. But if Darius didn't protect his heart, who would? Surely not the women who'd emotionally broken him down. Like the one blabbering on the other end of his cell phone, wasting his time, burning up his daytime minutes.

Sitting in the white hummer limousine, next to his fiancée, Darius regretted answering his phone. If it were up to him, he would've ignored the call, but no, Fancy had to insist, "Answer it." Translation, "Put that bitch in check so I won't have to."

Darius was stuck again between the old and the new pussies.

Ashlee cried in his ear, "I'm sorry." *No she wasn't.* "I never wanted to hurt you." *Yes, she did. Otherwise she wouldn't have phoned.* "And no matter what, I love you." *That was probably the one truth.*

No woman could resist Darius's six-foot-eleven, two-hundred-forty-pound muscular caramel frame with six percent body fat, lustrous shoulder-length locks, chiseled chin, hazel eyes, perfect white teeth, his millions of dollars, or his big eight-inch dick and the fact that he knew how to sling Slugger and eat pussy, oh so sweetly, that the strongest women submitted to him.

Ashlee continued, "But you need to know."

Exhaling, Darius conceded, "Then tell me."

Crying, like most women did when they wanted sympathy for something that was their fault, Ashlee said, "Our son, Darius Junior, died from HIV complications."

Whoa, that was some cold-blooded shit to drop on a brotha on his wedding day. Hell, any day. "And you?" Darius whispered.

Sniffling, Ashlee said, "Positive."

The numbness in Darius's body caused the phone to slip from between his fingers.

Picking up the phone, Fancy questioned Ashlee. "What did you tell him?" Fancy looked at the phone, then said, "Hello? Hello?" Staring at Darius, Fancy began crying along with him. She muttered, "She hung up. Please tell me. What did she say?"

If Fancy had kept her damn mouth shut, he wouldn't be trippin' over Ashlee's bullshit. Why in the fuck did he have to answer his phone?

"Move! From now on, don't tell me what to do."

"Don't you dare turn this on me! Fine, forget I asked. You think you can handle everything by yourself. In here," Fancy scolded, pressing her finger into Darius's temple. "Well, you can't. And I'm not marrying a man who doesn't need, trust, or value my opinions."

Softly, Darius said, "It's not like that. I do respect you." Her opinion was what he didn't care for. Darius pressed a button lowering the divider window then instructed the driver, "Man, take me straight home."

"Oakland or Los Angeles?"

That's how Darius wanted his life, clear cut. Black or white. A or B. Gray areas were like women, ambiguous and complicated. Darius answered, "Los Angeles."

Banging his face against the limo window, Darius worried, "Was his HIV test, taken years ago, a false negative?" How many women had he possibly infected? Darius could begin wondering with the one sitting next to him.

CHAPTER 1

CANDICE

Alone, Candice sat in Jada's guest bedroom by the large bay window, enjoying the second floor view. Inside the cozy space, a plush Queen-sized bed with a red satin button-hole headboard rested cattycorner facing the door. The sparkling fuchsia duvet adorned a dozen tassled pillows. A pink leather bench perched adjacent to the footboard.

The glass-top computer desk faced outside, snug beneath the redwood window frame. Candice's fingers skated along the keyboard, sixty, seventy words a minute:

> *I had a dilemma many married women shared: should I divorce my now-impotent husband or not? I'd instantly trade in a broken car I couldn't fix, or sell a run-down house that cost more to maintain than its value. But my husband wasn't a thing; he was a human being. A cheating man, who'd fucked around for over twenty years, with the same woman.*

Candice paused gazing at the rolling green hillside that resembled the peaks and valleys of her friendship with Jada. She was Candice's girl, her best friend, her right hand. They'd partied, laughed, cried together, and double-dated. They even met their

husbands on the same night at Cityscape in San Francisco at a
Will Downing–Rachelle Farrell concert.

That was BM, before marriage, those were the good old days.
Jada met Wellington. Candice met Terrell. Wellington fucked up,
Jada married Lawrence. Terrell fucked up, Candice married
Terrell. They both relocated from Oakland to L.A. but not to-
gether. Jada moved to get away from Wellington. Candice would've
moved anywhere in the world to be with Terrell who lived in Los
Angeles.

Terrell was five years younger, an international model, and she
thought wealthy until she married him and realized Terrell lived
well above his means. He owned a huge house with a waterfall;
bought her an expensive wedding ring. The first sign of financial
trouble was when Terrell purchased matching his and hers Mercedes
Benz, with her money.

Accepting Terrell's ring, Candice felt obliged to get married.
What if she didn't get another chance to meet a man like him? If
Candice had remained single, and Jada had gotten married, they
wouldn't have stayed friends. Not close friends.

Assuming their wives weren't intelligent enough to think, insecure married men objected to their spouses kickin' it with single
girlfriends. A selfish man could ruin a good friendship. Hoping
her and her girl would stay close, Candice said, "I do," shortly after
Jada called off her engagement to Wellington.

The main thing Candice tried to avoid, happened. Thanks to
Terrell's controlling ways, Candice lost touch with her best friend.
For years. Without a friend and time on her hands, Candice wrote
and sold a screenplay about Jada's life. Putting Jada's business on
the big screen got Candice a not-so-warming house visit. After Jada
got over being pissed, they were friends again. How long would
their friendship last this time considering Candice was temporarily
living in Jada's house, secretly writing Part II of Jada's life? Tapping
the keys, Candice continued:

*The twenty-count blue Viagra tablets he'd hid in his office drawer
weren't used for my womanly pleasure. He'd found the sexual stamina to stick his dick in another woman but he couldn't, or wouldn't,*

make love to me. He was eager to sign the divorce papers until the doctor told him his prostate cancer had spread and they had to operate immediately. What's my obligation, to stay with a two-timer? I'm clear. I have none. But I do have a conscious. I won't leave him while he's down but after the surgery, she can have him.

Candice signed. "This is too boring. I'ma have to throw in some cussing to sell this one. Let's see," Candice said backspacing then revising:

> *"That muthafucka emptied a twenty, you hear me a twenty-count pill bottle of Viagra on that stank ass bitch. If his sorry ass wasn't dying, I swear I'd kill that dead-dick bastard! Twice!"*

Anger was better, Candice thought memorized by the fading sunrays.

Jada always had one man on her arm and another on her charm bracelet dangling from her wrist. During the ten years she was married to Lawrence, Wellington was in the background. Once Jada married Wellington, Lawrence disappeared and Darryl bopped side-to-side do-wopping as backup waiting to sing lead in her chorus.

One man at a time was Candice's style. Terrell wasn't that bad in the beginning. They'd still be married if she'd been woman enough not to let him change her. Candice never found peace with wanting but not having a child. Terrell didn't want kids. Too late now, premenopause and a baby who'd stare at her for crying, yelling, snapping, swearing, and forgetting things would drive Candice crazy.

Not so long ago, Candice remembered her husband was her life. In many ways, having Terrell was like having a child and an overprotective father. At first marriage was kinda cute, him telling her what to do. That chauvinistic shit got real old, really quick but she hung in there 'til they damn near hung one another with misery. Candice thought when he left her, she'd fall apart. Wrong. She didn't lift him up to put herself down. Surprisingly the second his shadow walked out the door, the sun seemed brighter. So was her spirit. Like before she'd gotten married, Candice felt stress free. The days of him telling her how to dress, "Cover your breasts. Take off that skirt. You're not leaving this house looking like that," were gone.

Like what? A sexy female magnet? The way she used to dress when he met her wearing a peach mini-dress. But he could bare his masculine chest or muscular thighs whenever he desired, saying, "You know baby, it's different for a man." And he had no problem being admired by women. Because of her, he'd made a great career move after their divorce that guaranteed him access to more pussy than he could eat. Terrell went from modeling to acting; she'd bartered him a supporting role in her screenplay.

Candice was happy for her ex, happier for herself. Thankful that over the years she'd respected her body by exercising, eating healthy foods, sleeping six to eight hours a day. She'd aged gracefully. Single, available, with no intentions of remarrying, she knew she was sexy, and, thanks to her girlfriend's never-a-boring-moment life, she had an eight-figure bank account and the waterfall house to cushion her divorce. Nice landing.

Tap. Tap.

The finger mouse centered atop the dash. *Click.* The screen faded to black. Candice minimized her document, closed the laptop, picked up *The Guide to Becoming a Sensuous Black Woman* by Miss T, then answered, "Come, in."

Peeping her head through the door, Jada asked, "What are you doing?"

"Just reading this book on how to seduce a man. Nothing you'd be interested in," Candice said, parting the pages.

Smiling, Jada moved closer. Slyly, Candice propped her elbow on her laptop.

Glancing at the book, Jada said, "You right. I need one on how to unseduce your husband. Do you mind going to the store? Wellington wants some more snacks."

Candice stood. "Sit down for a while."

Massaging Jada's neck and shoulders, Candice said, "You are tense."

Jada rotated her head, neck and shoulders. "Um, that feels so good. Thanks girl."

"How's he doing?" Candice asked, not giving a damn because

Wellington's sorry ass didn't want Jada to leave his side for more than five minutes at a time.

Candice had given up on investing her energy into finding a faithful man who was honest, considerate, loving, good-looking, and wealthy. If a man had three good qualities, she'd take him for what he was worth. How long he stayed with her depended upon when he became useless. Candice pressed her thumbs into Jada's muscles.

Jada sighed, "Not good. He's in a lot of pain. I'm glad he's checking into the hospital tomorrow, because he's wearing me out and not the way I'd like. All he wants to do is watch television, kiss me to death, and rub on my titties like he's doing something."

"Like this," Candice said groping her hands on Jada's shoulders.

Laughing, Jada said, "Exactly. He works me all up for nothing because he doesn't want to lick my pussy, and I'm tired of playing with her to entertain him. Girlfriend, I'm too young for this sexual frustration. There's nothing wrong with my pussy."

Candice thought, "First it was beer, now snacks. Couldn't he make a list?" She replied, "You know how I feel. Get some dick lined up on the side for tomorrow. You'll be well within your right, and ain't shit he can do from a hospital bed."

Standing, Jada said, "I can't be like him. I can't cheat on my husband for the sake of having sex. I have to love the man I'm with."

"You're delirious. That's why I'm here. For you." To write all this shit down so next time Jada got a man, probably Darryl, she wouldn't forget.

Jada lived a fairy-tale kind of life, suppressing reality to suit her beliefs. Jada could watch her screwed-up life on the big screen and think it was somebody else's claiming, "I could never do . . ."

Candice continued, "Whatever you need me to do, just tell me. And I want you to know, being here has helped me get over Terrell," she lied then told the truth, "and I am going to help you get over Wellington." Candice emotionally divorced Terrell years before he'd left.

Shaking her head, Jada said, "I shouldn't complain. I'm not trying to get over Wellington."

Dammit, Jada stop lying to yourself! When Candice co-signed with her, she defended Wellington every single time. "I should stop off at Darius's house and see if any wedding gifts arrived? They may be sitting outside?"

"Huh, what, oh yeah. Good idea. The keys are on the key rack in the kitchen."

"If Wellington thinks of anything else, call me girl." Candice supported Jada not Wellington, and no matter how many errands Wellington sent her on, she'd go, and she'd return. At least he couldn't accuse her of cock-blocking.

Waiting for Jada to leave, then watching her walk away in *Betty Boop* pjs with red eyes that were half closed, Candice wondered, why had her girlfriend stayed with Wellington after his affair? Closing the bedroom door, Candice input the information Jada had given her.

"Oh," Jada said re-entering the room, "I almost forgot. Darius is on his way home so you don't have to go to his house."

Shit, she didn't knock. Next time Candice had to lock the door.

"The hell I don't," Candice thought. Darius's life was ten times more exciting than Jada's, and this may be her only opportunity to have access to his dirt. Quickly saving the new chapter before removing her memory stick, Candice powered-off her laptop, slipped into a pink sweatsuit, laced her tennis shoes, then skipped out the front door jiggling Darius's keys.

One press of a button on her remote and the engine of her red-hot Benz convertible roared. Candice sped to the neighborhood grocery store, tossed chips, pretzels, peanuts, cashews, beef jerky, snickers, and red vines in the handbasket. "That'll do." Waiting in the "ten items or less" checkout line, Candice tapped her foot, sighed, shifting the basket to the opposite hip, her toes instantly froze. A *Keys Made* sign was near the entrance. Leaving the junk food on the conveyor, she darted to the counter, extended Darius's keys to the tall, ballheaded man and said, "One set please. Make that, two."

Spiraling her copies on her chain, Candice said, "Keep the change."

Speeding to a nearby shopping center, Candice stood outside the electronics store and dialed Jada's number.

Jada answered, "You still at the store?"

"What does he want now?"

"Ice cream. Strawberry."

"Girl, if I didn't love you. I'll pick it up later."

"I'm sorry, you called me," Jada said yawning.

"I have to make a stop but I'll get back ASAP," Candice said hanging up.

Entering the crowded store, Candice approached the first blue-vested, khaki pants wearing employee she saw. "Yes, I need ten, make that twenty, of those hidden clock cameras. And twenty one-gig memory cards."

"Twenty, twenty? Why so many?" he questioned.

"Is that part of your duties? To get personal with me young man?"

"Sorry, ma'am. I'll bring 'em to the register for you."

"Now, we're communicating. And bring me two sets of binoculars."

Standing in line, Candice tapped her foot, finally placing her items at the register.

The cashier said, "I know you'd like to protect your devices. I recommend purchasing our additional warranty—"

"Stop wasting my time," Candice replied, signing, then handing the white paper to the cashier. Candice snatched the bags, ran like a linebacker to her car, then broke every residential speed limit for a five block touchdown at Darius's house. Retrieving her keys Candice entered Darius's home, then secured the inside latch.

Quickly she raced upstairs hiding a camera in Darius's closet, aiming the motion detector toward his bed. "This is a sweet ass setup. What's this button for?" Candice said pressing the black dot. "Oh, shit!" Three hidden doors opened at once. A black leather sex-swing rocked, bright red lights beamed on a stage with a dance pole, white stars and a crescent moon danced on the ceiling as R. Kelly played in the background. Squinting and walking over to a cavelike opening in the headboard, Candice starred in disbelief. Adult toys: vibrators, butt plugs, pearls, lingerie, pasties.

"Edible what! Pina coloda dickalicious," she exhaled. "Let me get out of here. I see why women go crazy over his sexy ass. Hell, if he weren't my girlfriend's son, I'd wait right here to do him. Who would think of all this?"

R. Kelly was switched to Luther right before a projector screen lowered from the ceiling, playing an X-rated video entitled *Booty-licious*. "No he is not putting his big dick in her . . ." Pressing the black button, Candice said, "My pussy is puckerin'." Sure of one thing, the best was yet to come.

Squinting, Candice moved closer, then stepped back staring up at a red dot. "Oh, shit! I'm on his camera." Now she'd have to come back sooner than expected to find his recorder. Happy she had more material than she'd originally imagined, Candice was worried Darius might expose her first.

Swiftly planting cameras throughout the house, Candice noticed tiny red dots on every ceiling: the kitchen, living room, bathroom, garage, and five other rooms. The ten cameras she'd left in her car, she'd place in Jada's bedroom, living room, kitchen, bathroom, Wellington's office, and a few other places.

Soon, Candice Jordan—screenwriter, novelist, producer and director—would become a household name. Like before, in time, Jada's initial anger would subside. But if Darius found out, he'd kill her.